Love WITHOUT NUMBERS

THE BOUVIER FAMILY SAGA

Copyright © 2023 by Jade Dollston

All rights reserved.

No portion of this book may be reproduced in any form without written permission from the publisher or author, except as permitted by U.S. copyright law. Short quotes for book reviews are acceptable. For permissions, contact: jdollston@gmail.com

Cover Design by **K.B. Barrett Designs**

Editing and proofreading by **Chrisandra's Corrections**

This is a work of fiction. Names, characters, businesses and locations are either products of the writer's imagination or used in a fictitious manner. Any resemblance to actual persons, living or dead, is purely coincidental.

WARNING: THIS BOOK CONTAINS GRAPHIC SEXUAL CONTENT AND PROFANITY. READERS 18+ ONLY.

CONTENTS

Dedication	VI
About Love Without Numbers	1
1. Chapter 1	3
2. Chapter 2	8
3. Chapter 3	16
4. Chapter 4	21
5. Chapter 5	30
6. Chapter 6	37
7. Chapter 7	45
8. Chapter 8	49
9. Chapter 9	57
10. Chapter 10	66
11. Chapter 11	73
12. Chapter 12	81
13. Chapter 13	88
14. Chapter 14	98
15. Chapter 15	104
16. Chapter 16	113

17.	Chapter 17	119
18.	Chapter 18	127
19.	Chapter 19	132
20.	Chapter 20	138
21.	Chapter 21	150
22.	Chapter 22	161
23.	Chapter 23	168
24.	Chapter 24	184
25.	Chapter 25	192
26.	Chapter 26	198
27.	Chapter 27	210
28.	Chapter 28	220
29.	Chapter 29	234
30.	Chapter 30	246
31.	Chapter 31	253
32.	Chapter 32	261
33.	Chapter 33	272
34.	Chapter 34	277
35.	Chapter 35	282
36.	Chapter 36	286
37.	Chapter 37	294
38.	Chapter 38	300
39.	Chapter 39	309

40.	Chapter 40	317
41.	Chapter 41	327
42.	Chapter 42	333
43.	Chapter 43	340
44.	Chapter 44	344
45.	Chapter 45	354
46.	Chapter 46	361
	Epilogue	369
	Also by Jade	377
	Acknowledgements	379
	About the Author	381

Dedication

This book is dedicated to Thorunn and Lakshmi. This book would not be possible without you two. Thank you for falling in love with these characters and for encouraging me to make this a series. You both get badges!

Your constant bickering in the documents makes me want to write "just one more chapter" before bed, and I swear to God, if you ever stop arguing, I'm going to stop writing. I'm so happy I met you two, and I'm thrilled to call you my friends.

By the way, Daddy Auburn is flaring his nostrils and calling you a good girl right now.
Love,
　"The Vampire"

About Love Without Numbers

GIANNA

I hate my dad's boss.

I'd never actually met Auburn Bouvier, but I despised him on principle. He was a cold, demanding dictator who made his employees miserable.

When I moved to New York City, it was inevitable that I would run into the head of the *Bouvier* fashion empire while visiting my dad at his office, and when I did, the man was nothing like I expected.

He was worse.

Yet I somehow ended up on a date with the enigmatic Mister Bouvier. Sure, he was incredibly handsome, with jet black hair, a perfect jawline, and a mouth that looked like it was spun from sugar and sin, but he was also arrogant, overbearing, and a complete jerk. Not to mention he was fifteen years older than me.

Worst date ever.

Auburn

I needed a date. I recently broke up with my long-time girlfriend—again—so I was not looking for anything serious. I simply needed a pretty lady on my arm for one evening.

Then I met my assistant's daughter, Gianna, and couldn't peel my eyes away from her.

Since I was accustomed to getting exactly what I wanted, I demanded that she accompany me to the gala. No one dared to say no to me, so here we were.

Our age difference seemed to fade away the more I talked to Gianna. She was witty, intelligent, and the most gorgeous woman I'd ever seen.

Best date ever.

Chapter 1

I stood staring at the baggage carousel at New York's JFK Airport, hoping and praying that my suitcases would magically appear there.

They didn't.

"Shit," I muttered as the conveyor came to a complete halt, signifying that no more bags were forthcoming. "What a fabulous fucking start to my new life."

Hefting my backpack up onto my shoulder, I turned and trudged away, my eyes darting around for the lost baggage office. After twenty minutes of wandering around following two sets of conflicting directions, I finally found it.

There was a mile-long line because *of course* there was. Taking my place at the back of the queue, I dug my portable battery pack from the side pocket of my red backpack and plugged my dead cell phone into it. Waiting for the little icon to appear on my phone to indicate that it was charging, I was sorely disappointed when the screen remained black.

Probably depleted the eight-hour limit of the portable battery during the long-ass trip, I thought. Forty minutes later, I finally reached the counter, and a lady with a ratty blonde beehive hairdo stared flatly at me.

"Help you?" she asked curtly, digging a pencil from her hair. I wouldn't have been surprised if she'd pulled out a stapler or a laser printer from that hot mess on top of her head.

"Hi. Yes, Velma," I said politely, putting on a bright smile that I wasn't remotely feeling as I read her nametag. "My bags are lost."

She dug in her ear with the tip of the pencil and inspected the results before turning her bored eyes back to me. "Claim ticket?"

Pulling it from my pocket, I handed it over. She scooted the pencil with a large glob of orangish gunk on the tip toward me and nodded to a stack of forms on the counter. "Fill that out."

Ignoring the earwax-infested writing implement Velma had so kindly offered, I rooted around in my bag until I found a pen. One with precisely zero bodily excretions on it. I filled in my name, phone number, and the address where I'd be staying while the woman tapped on a keyboard with her three-inch, red-painted talons.

How does she wipe her butt with those things?

"Bags are in Miami," she said, not even gracing me with a glance. "Someone will deliver them to the address on the form." She snatched up my paperwork and yelled, "Next!"

"Wait! When will my bags arrive?"

"Dunno," she uttered before turning to the next unlucky soul in line. "Help you?"

Resigned to the fact that I wasn't leaving here with my suitcases, or any idea of when I may get them, I left the small office.

After spending twenty freaking dollars on a cappuccino and a muffin, I found a seat in the coffee shop with a USB charging port. Plugging in my phone, I sipped my coffee until the screen lit up. Thank God. I couldn't even order an Uber without my phone.

My finger tapped on a name, and I brought my cell to my ear, smiling when I heard my father's voice. "Gianna, honey. You were supposed to call me as soon as your plane landed."

"Hey, Dad. Sorry about that. My phone died. Then the airline lost my suitcases. They're apparently on vacation in Miami."

His deep chuckle made me smile, despite my weariness. "Your bags are living a better life than me."

"Tell me about it. You would think since this is all the airline's fault, they could have at least sent me to Miami with my luggage."

I was pretty sure being subjected to the fiery pits of hell would have been more enjoyable than this trip that began twenty-three hours ago. After arriving at my departure gate at the Dallas airport yesterday morning, I was told that I was being bumped and would have to take a later flight. A much later flight.

And instead of a non-stop, I was subjected to a six-hour layover in Cleveland.

"Did you at least get some rest?"

"Not a bit. I got to Cleveland late last night and went in search of caffeine. I knew that once I passed the checkpoint, I would have to go back through security to get to my gate. What I didn't know was that the TSA doesn't work through the night, so I had to roost in the baggage claim area until they opened back up at four this morning."

"Oh, shit."

"My thoughts exactly, Dad. My flight left Cleveland at five, so once I got through security, I was sprinting to get to my gate on time. By the time I got there, they were about to close the doors. Some asshole had taken my seat in the exit row—which I paid thirty dollars extra for, by the way, to accommodate my long legs—and the grumpy flight attendant told me I had to take the only open seat left."

"Let me guess? Middle seat?"

"Yep. Between a drooling snorer and a mom with an unhappy baby, so I haven't slept since I got up at five yesterday morning. And I feel gross because I'm wearing the same clothes."

"I'm sorry, honeybunch. Just drop by my office, and I'll give you the key to Nana's apartment. Then you can sleep for the rest of the day."

"Okay, I'm just going to eat this muffin and let my phone charge for a bit. I gave away all my snacks, so I'm starving."

My dad puffed out a deep sigh. "Why did you give away all your snacks, Gianna? You know you have to be careful of your blood sugar."

"I know, but a lot of homeless people sleep in the baggage claim area of the Cleveland airport. They kept coming up to me all night asking for food or money. I didn't have much cash, so I gave them my snacks so they'd leave me alone."

"Christ," came his muffled reply, and I knew he was rubbing his fingertips over his mouth like he always did when he got upset. "I should have gone to Texas and flown back with you."

"I'm twenty-three, Dad. I don't need an escort. Besides, you know the BB wouldn't let you have time off for that. You just took off a day when Nana died and then again for my graduation." BB stood for Bastard Boss, the CEO of the fashion company where my dad worked as his personal assistant.

"All right, Gia. Eat your muffin, and I'll have something delivered to my office by the time you get here." He hesitated. "I don't know... um, what kind of sandwich do you like?"

"I'm not picky. A turkey club will do."

"Gotcha," he said. "I love you, honey, and I'm really glad you're here."

"Me too," I lied.

My mom and dad had split up when I was seven, and then Dad moved back to New York to take care of his ailing father. So we didn't really know each other well. Mom wouldn't allow me to fly by myself, so Dad usually came to visit me in Dallas a few times a year.

Don't get me wrong. I was happy to be able to get to know my father better, but I wasn't thrilled about moving to New York City.

"Shit," he hissed into the phone. "BB is coming up the elevator. See you in a little bit, Gia." And then he abruptly hung up.

My dad hated his boss. *Hated*. But the pay was excellent, so he stuck it out and just bitched and moaned about Auburn Bouvier every chance he got. Behind his back, of course.

Auburn Bouvier. Even his name sounded pretentious. In my head I pictured an old curmudgeon with a crooked nose and white hair, a little stooped, and sporting fanged teeth and horns. Sometimes, when I was feeling really creative, I gave him a devil tail to complete the look.

I'd never met the man, but I despised him on my dad's behalf. I was loyal like that.

Bouvier's father, my dad's previous boss, had retired a few years ago, and Auburn had "inherited" his personal assistant.

Polishing off my muffin, I pulled up my Uber app, and my eyes did a kind of jack-in-the-box move, attempting to pop right out of my head. *That can't be right.* A hundred and twenty dollars for a ride into Manhattan? And pick up wasn't for another thirty minutes.

I sighed and leaned back in my seat, tempted to go for another muffin, but Dad said he was going to have a sandwich for me when I got there.

So, I people-watched, smiling at everyone who passed me. No one smiled back.

I wonder if they make shirts that read, "I Hate New York?"

Chapter 2

As I stepped out of the Uber and secured my backpack over my tired shoulders, my eyes went up. And up. And up some more.

The imposing, black stone building managed to look both modern and classic at the same time. The name *BOUVIER* was stamped in bold, blood-red letters above a set of dark-tinted glass doors.

"Oh, excuse me," I said, putting cheeriness in my voice when someone jostled me as I stood gawking. They didn't answer back. *Is everyone an asshole here?*

I pushed through the doors and was instantly engulfed by a blast of cool fresh-smelling air. My left tennis shoe squeaked with each step across the black marble floor, which was somehow perfectly glossy, despite the dozens of people bustling around the first level.

Approaching the steel-gray reception counter, I tried again with the smiling, and surprisingly, I was rewarded with a return curve of dark red lips. "Hello, how may I help you?"

The woman, whose name tag read *Lehra*, was stunning, her blonde hair pulled up into a pretty updo that allowed tiny curls to drape down and frame her perfectly made-up face.

"Hi, Lehra. I'm here to see Tony Moschella."

A look of concern pinched around the corners of her eyes. "Do you have an appointment?"

"No, but he's my father."

The pinching smoothed out, and her grin turned brilliant. "Oh, Tony's your dad? Everyone loves Tony!" she literally gushed. "You must be Gia."

Taken aback that she knew my name, I nodded. "Guilty as charged," I told her, lifting one hand near my shoulder in a tiny wave.

She laughed, a high tinkling sound that made me instantly like her. "I hear you just graduated from college. A Master's degree in Accounting, right?"

I was again surprised by this random woman's knowledge of me. "Yes, and I'm moving here. My grandma passed away a few months ago, and she left me her apartment. I just got in after an overnight flight through the seventh circle of Hell. That's why I look like a bag lady," I told her, indicating my wrinkled white shirt, oversized hoodie, black leggings and Converse sneakers.

My brain instantly compared my dumpy attire to her sleek, black dress that hit just above her knees and fit her like a glove. Large buttons that matched her red lipstick dotted down the garment at an angle. I suddenly felt completely out of place, but Lehra waved a dismissive hand.

"You're fine. You should see how some of the models show up when they come for fittings. I have to check IDs to make sure they're really supposed to be here and that they're not some homeless people that wandered in off the streets." She giggled. "Of course, once they're all fixed up, they look like... well, supermodels."

"Of course they do."

"Come on; I'll take you up." She turned to another woman behind the counter. "Anita, I'm taking Miss Moschella to fifty." Anita gave a bored nod. She looked like she wanted to roll her eyes if only it didn't take entirely too much effort.

"So you had a hellacious trip?" Lehra asked. "Let me guess. Layover in D.C.?"

"Cleveland," I corrected. "Throw in some lost luggage, and I'm officially done with this Monday."

"As if they weren't bad enough," she commiserated as we walked to the elevator bank.

I noticed her impossibly high heels made an elegant *tap-tap* sound as she walked, while my left shoe was squawking like a choked chicken. I attempted to lean onto my right foot a bit more, but that only succeeded in making me appear to be pimp walking. *Squeaky shoe, it is,* I thought, normalizing my gait.

She waved a card in front of the reader inside the elevator, and in less than a minute, we exited onto the fiftieth floor. The atmosphere was different up here, all creamy ivories and cozy woods.

And my dad.

"Gia!" he exclaimed, standing up and rounding an enormous oak desk to wrap me in his warm embrace. It felt so good, I wanted to cry.

"Hey, Dad."

He held me for a long while before taking my shoulders and pushing me back a little so he could take me in. Kissing me on the forehead, he said, "You look lovely, sweetheart."

I rolled my bottle-green eyes, a trait I inherited from my late mother. "I look like I've been through a battle and came out the losing side."

"You still look beautiful to me." He turned and greeted Lehra before walking back to his desk. "I've got your sandwich right here, Gia. Let me go warm it up for you."

There were three doors off this main room, one on each side and one directly behind Dad's desk, which I assumed was his boss's office. My father headed for the door on the right, and I caught a glimpse of a small, neat kitchen before the door closed behind him.

"I'm going to head back down," Lehra said. "Hey, you want to exchange numbers since you're new in town? I've only been here for five years, but I remember how hard it was at first."

My chest swelled. I'd only been in town a few hours, and I'd already made a friend. Maybe this move wasn't such a bad idea after all. Sending me a text after I told her my phone number, she did an excited little shoulder shimmy.

"Okay, I'll text you later to see how you're doing." Pressing the button for the elevator, Lehra turned back to me. "You're lucky Sexy Shrek is out of the building right now. He left about thirty minutes ago for a meeting."

My forehead creased in confusion. "Sexy Shrek?"

"The boss man. He's a total ogre, but at least he's nice to look at." She waggled her eyebrows before stepping into the elevator. Before I could ask questions, the doors closed behind her, and Dad returned from the kitchen.

"Lehra's a sweet girl," he advised, setting the container holding my sandwich on an elegant coffee table in front of an ivory couch and gesturing for me to sit. I did and opened the container, almost swooning dramatically against the back of the couch when the smell of food hit my nose.

"This is so good," I said around a mouthful after I'd taken my first bite. I was hungrier than I'd thought and devoured half the sandwich in less than a minute. My father leaned his butt against his desk and crossed his arms over his chest. "You look great, Dad."

He tugged at a charcoal lapel and grinned. "One of the perks of working here. BB insists that we wear Bouvier designs while at work."

"And he provides them?" I asked skeptically.

"Yep. The men receive two full suits when they sign a one-year contract. After that, we're given another suit every year. Same with the women, except with dresses, blouses, skirts, and pants."

I took another bite. "Huh. Tell me more about Lehra."

"Oh, she's one of the nicest people who works here. A little older than you, I think," he ruminated. "She moved to New York from Missouri a few years ago to pursue a modeling career. She applied here but was told she was too short for runway work, but she was so charming, they offered her a job in reception."

"I guess that was nice of them."

The phone on his desk trilled, and he twisted to answer it. "Auburn Bouvier's office... What?... But... Shit, okay. Thank you, Lehra."

He circled behind his desk and sat in the high-backed leather chair, a look of slight panic on his face as he shuffled and straightened stacks of paper. "Bouvier is on his way up here, and he's in a mood," he said breathlessly. "He usually breezes in, barely says hello, and then locks himself in his office. Just sit over there, and he probably won't even notice you."

"Will you get in trouble for me being here? I could hide in the bathroom or something," I said, jumping up and jerking my thumb toward the door behind me that was marked with a restroom sign.

Dad chuckled. "No, it will be fine." But he didn't look altogether convinced.

Before I could reply, the elevator doors opened.

You know how people say all the air was sucked from a room? Well, this was the exact opposite. When Auburn Bouvier entered, it felt like there was *too much* air in the room, as if you exhaled too hard in his presence, the entire space would spontaneously explode outward.

The man exuded power, walking with a grace that belied his over-six-foot tall frame. And his face? *Jesus.* His face featured eyes so blue and sharp, they could cut diamonds, as well as designer scruff that shadowed a firm, square jaw. His mouth was full and looked like it had been sculpted by an artist with nothing but time on his hands. Like he'd spent years perfecting those lips.

To put it bluntly, Auburn Bouvier was devastatingly handsome.

Oh, and did I mention that he wasn't an old curmudgeon? Sure, he was older than me by a lot, but he was nothing like I'd pictured. I'd say he was in his mid to late thirties with a few strands of gray at his temples that only made his dark hair more appealing.

My dad stood respectfully. "Mr. Bouvier, I thought you were meeting with the new textile manufacturer."

I was hoping at least Auburn's voice would be unattractive, but my wish went unfulfilled. It sounded like bourbon drizzled with butter—deep, rich, and smooth.

"The bastards tried the old bait-and-switch with me. They assured me they had the highest quality fabrics. When I got there, all of a sudden, the shipment had been delayed. Oh, but they had these *other* fabrics that were *almost* as good as the ones they'd promised."

"I'll delete them from the potential vendors' list," Dad said, picking up a black leather notebook and scratching something down.

He gave my father a curt nod before turning to his office, and I thought we were home free. Dad was right. The man hadn't noticed me at all. Thank goodness, because I looked like the wrath of God.

Glancing down my body, I quietly sighed. There was a blob of mayonnaise on the front of my T-shirt. Every damn time I ate, I managed to drip something on my boobs. Trying not to make any sudden movements, I slyly reached for a napkin on the coffee table and swiped the offending condiment away, leaving a streaky stain behind. *Perfect!*

Bouvier stopped with his hand on the doorknob and turned back around. I resisted the urge to dive behind the couch, but he still didn't seem to notice me. His middle finger and thumb massaged his temples for a moment before he lifted weary eyes to my dad's face.

"Also, Tony, can you get me a date for the hospital gala this weekend?"

"On the outs with Magdalena again?"

The man nodded. "For good this time. My mother is devastated, of course, so I'll need someone on my arm to keep her from hounding me. If I go alone, she'll be pushing Mag in my face all night. Just get one of the models to go with me."

His blue eyes flashed to me, and they were even more startling when locked directly with my own. Auburn's lips parted as his gaze dropped slowly, appraisingly, down my body. I wouldn't have been surprised if my clothing had been lasered to shreds and fallen completely off my body.

Turning back to my father, he tipped his head in my direction. "She'll do."

Wow. Okay. I felt flattered and insulted all at the same time. On one hand, he'd mistaken me for a model, but on the other, the "she'll do" line was less than complimentary.

My dad's mouth dropped open, and he started to splutter a response when Bastard Boss pivoted away, went into his office, and closed the door.

Dad's eyes turned on me, wide and filled with dread, and I'm sure my own reflected the same sentiments. He held up one finger as if to interrupt me, but it was unnecessary. I currently had no words.

"Let me just... hold on," he said, turning to the door and taking a deep breath before knocking twice.

"Yes," came the curt reply, and my father pushed open the door. I flopped down on the couch and listened to the conversation through the open door.

"Mr. Bouvier, I had an excellent idea. You haven't been out with Carmella in a while. Why don't I call her for you?"

"No. She's too loud."

"Ah, yes. Well, what about Penny?"

"Too quiet."

"Annalise?"

"Too clingy."

My dad named several other women who were dismissed by Auburn as too snobby, aloof, and obnoxious.

A long, annoyed sigh floated from the interior office. "Tony, is there a reason why you're trying to keep me from going to the gala with..." He paused, not even knowing my damn name.

"Gianna. She's my daughter." There was a long pause, and I pictured Auburn staring a hole through Dad's head until he spoke again. "She just moved here, sir. Arrived a few minutes ago, actually, and the airline lost her luggage. So you see, she doesn't have any of her things."

"Hmmm." The man's deep hum was like fine silk stroking down my body. "New in town? The gala will be an excellent place for Gianna to meet some people. Send her down to Devereaux for a gown, and book her a stylist." Then he dismissed him with a clipped, "That will be all."

My dad backed out, closed the door, and stood staring at it for a full minute. I could feel the desperation radiating from him, and I squished my eyelids closed. My heart couldn't stand to see someone struggle, especially someone I cared about. It was my greatest weakness.

Don't do it, Gianna. Do. Not. Do. It.

Despite my internal warning system, my mouth opened, and something foolhardy came out. "It's okay, Dad. I'll go."

Chapter 3

TEN MINUTES EARLIER

"I don't care, Charles," I barked into my phone. My head bobbed in acknowledgement to Lehra and Anita as I passed the reception desk. They both sat a little straighter and put on their brightest smiles until I was gone. I was accustomed to that—everyone on their best behavior when I was in their presence.

"Now, now, Auburn."

"Don't you *now, now* me. That was an utter waste of my time. I thought you said the manufacturer was reputable. I wouldn't recommend that crap they were pushing to Wal-Mart."

Done with the conversation, I hung up as Charles was attempting to apologize. I didn't have time for fucking apologies. Entering an open elevator, I placed my card in front of the scanner. No one got to the fiftieth floor without one of these cards. That was *my* floor. Actually, the entire building was mine, but the top was where my personal office was located. My sanctuary.

Stepping off the elevator, I was greeted by Tony, my PA. I immediately sensed someone else in the room—a woman. *Great.* Probably one of the models who talked her way up here to discuss some issue with Tony in the hopes that I would notice her. It happened quite often. A woman was the very last thing I needed to be thinking about right now.

Ignoring her presence, I briefly told Tony about today's meeting. I was ready to get into my office and pour myself a generous glassful of bourbon. But something niggled at the back of my mind.

My hand went to my face, and I massaged my temples when I remembered that I needed a date for the hospital charity function this weekend. Magdalena was supposed to be my date, but we'd broken up—again—on Saturday. I wasn't taking her back this time. She was entirely too high-maintenance.

Don't get me wrong. I didn't mind showering my girlfriend with expensive gifts, except the more I gave, the more she wanted. When she told me on Saturday that she wanted me to finance her latest plastic surgery, I was done. The woman had had everything on her body lifted, tucked, enhanced, and stretched, all paid for by yours truly. Seriously, what beautiful thirty-year old woman needed that much surgery?

Not a single one of these procedures was my idea; I thought Mag was stunning just the way she was when I met her five years ago. But she always said it made her "feel better about herself."

When I told her I would no longer be financing her surgery addiction, she'd lost her shit. Another reason I was out for good. Magdalena had a nasty temper, as evidenced by the destruction she'd caused in my penthouse apartment that night.

Once in a while, if I was on a break from Magdalena and not dating anyone else at the time, I would ask one of our models to accompany me to an event. They were beautiful and looked good in my clothes. Plus, I loved rewarding the hard-working ladies with a night on the town. That would probably be the best solution for this weekend, so I asked Tony to set that up for me.

For the record, I never fucked my models, or anyone that worked for me, for that matter. Business and pleasure did not mix. I'd learned that all too well by watching the rise and rapid fall of some of my business associates.

A few of the new girls still attempted to get between the sheets with me, but the majority of them knew not to even fucking try that shit. Tony would know who to choose to ensure that I had an uneventful night. He was a smart guy and an excellent employee, and he was well aware of my no fraternization rule. I made a mental note to give him a raise during the next evaluation period.

All I needed was a pretty lady on my arm Saturday night. I would pay for her ten-thousand dollar meal, mingle a bit, and then take her home. Absolutely no funny business, and everyone would be happy. Except my mother. She had her heart set on Magdalena for her oldest son.

Out of curiosity, I glanced at the woman standing beside the couch in the ante-room of my office. And I froze. My mind and other key parts of my anatomy instantly forgot why I didn't sleep with employees.

She appeared a bit disheveled, her clothes stained and wrinkled, and her face devoid of makeup, but I had a knack for seeing beyond those things. She was fucking stunning. Long, dark hair pulled up into a messy ponytail. Green eyes the shape of almonds. Flawless olive skin. A tall, slender body. The whole package.

Before I could retreat to my office, my stupid damn mouth formed the words, "She'll do." I was as surprised as the beauty before me when those two words were actually vocalized.

Shit.

Pushing through my door, I closed it behind me and adjusted my growing dick before heading directly to the bar in the corner. What the hell was I thinking? That woman was gorgeous but entirely too young for me. Eight years' age difference was my limit for dating, and she was certainly younger than thirty.

It will be fine, Bouvier. It's one night and not even a real date. You've escorted young models before. Just let her know there will be no "after-party," and everything will be okay. As soon as I sat down in my burgundy leather chair with my drink, a knock sounded at my door.

Shifting to try and relieve the tightness in my groin, I called for Tony to come in. The man looked nervous as hell. As he started spouting off names of other women I'd dated when Magdalena and I were separated—which happened a few times a year—I shot each suggestion down.

And I grew angry for some unknown reason. Despite knowing this was probably an awful idea, I couldn't help myself. I wanted *her*. She would look stunning on my arm, and her presence would keep my mother from shoving Mag at me every time I turned around. As overbearing as she was, Chloe Bouvier would rather die than make a scene at a fancy event.

"Tony, is there a reason why you're trying to keep me from going to the gala with…"

Damn, I didn't even know the woman's name. She must be new here.

"Gianna. She's my daughter."

What the fuck? That lovely lady is the offspring of my personal assistant?

When I pictured them side by side in my mind's eye, I could kind of see it. They both had dark hair and olive skin, but other than that, she looked nothing like Tony. Whereas my assistant had brown eyes and larger facial features, his daughter's face was delicate, featuring a slim, straight nose and arresting green eyes.

He was prattling on about lost luggage and Gianna being new in town as my mind whirled.

She doesn't have anything to wear? I can fix that; I'm the CEO of a fucking fashion company, after all.

"Hmmm. New in town? The gala will be an excellent place for Gianna to meet some people. Send her down to Devereaux for a gown, and book her a stylist." The look on Tony's face was one of dejected acceptance as I dismissed him.

What the hell are you doing, Auburn? You're obviously attracted to Gianna, so shut this down right now.

Yeah, but she would look fantastic in a Bouvier original. That must be the reason my unbidden demands kept popping from my mouth. I wanted to show off one of our new designs on the most breathtaking woman I'd ever seen.

That was the only reason. The design.

Yeah. Right.

Chapter 4

My dad turned to face me, his head swiveling back and forth in denial. "No, honey. You don't have to. I'll... I'll come up with something. Someone."

"Are you sure?"

He sat in his big chair and smashed his face against his hands. "No," he groaned as he let his hands slide down over his cheeks. "For some reason, he seems adamant that you go with him."

That both excited and scared me, and a little *oh* squeaked from my lips.

Dad rushed to assure me. "But he never... well, he... Auburn keeps things very *professional* when he escorts one of the models, if you know what I'm saying." He lifted one sardonic eyebrow.

"Ahh, so no bow-chicka-wow-wow?"

My dad chuckled and shook his head. "Absolutely not. In fact, if he takes one of our models to a charity event, and they are inappropriate in any way, they're deleted from the list of potential dates permanently."

"All the women you listed... Carmella and all of them... do they work here?"

"No, those are women he's actually dated in the past. I thought maybe I could tempt him with one of them since he's broken up with Magdalena—again." His last words were accompanied by a roll of his brown eyes.

"You don't like her." It was a statement rather than a question.

"No one likes her. She's a real piece of work. They break up every few months, and then he'll date someone else until she gets jealous and promises to change her ways. He'll take her back, and a few months later, it starts all over again. It's a vicious cycle, but hopefully, this time the breakup will stick."

Wrapping my arms around my waist, I quietly noted, "Sounds like Magdalena and BB were made for each other. Both assholes."

Dad grinned, but his eyes flashed to the door behind him to make sure Auburn Bouvier hadn't materialized there. "She's actually much worse than him, if you can believe it." His eyebrows lowered over his hooded eyes. "If you do decide to go—and that's totally up to you—I can promise you that he will be the utmost gentleman. He just likes to show off his designs on beautiful women. And let's be honest, honey, you would be the most gorgeous woman in the room. That's probably why he's insisting on taking you."

"I think you're a little biased, Dad," I said flatly.

His face softened. "Not a bit, Gia. You have your mother's beautiful facial features."

The mention of my mother made me sad, but I swept my emotions under the metaphorical rug. "What would I have to do?"

Dad tapped his chin with one finger. "Well, basically, you just have to stand around, smile, and mingle. Have dinner. I think there's usually dancing, but you can opt out of that particular activity."

"Thank God," I said with a giggle. I was notoriously clumsy.

Dad continued, ramping up his gentle coercion as he warmed to the idea. "And the food at this event is always superb. That's why tickets sell out months in advance. It's very exclusive."

Fiddling with the zipper on my hoodie, I dipped my head before looking back at my dad. "I'm not sure I would fit in there."

"Of course you would, Gia. You have excellent manners, thanks to your mom raising you right. You'd be fine."

The confidence I had recently lacked seeped in around the edges, and I nodded. He was right. I took a deep breath and sighed resignedly. "Okay, I'll go."

My dad's shoulders slumped in relief even as he asked, "Are you sure, Gianna?"

I lifted my chin and nodded. "I'm sure. I don't want your boss to be mad at you."

He stood and crossed the room, wrapping his arms around me. "That's for me to worry about, hon, not you. So don't go on my account. I do think you would have fun, and it would be a nice way to meet some people."

Kissing my father's cheek, I said, "You're right. It will be fun."

Thirty minutes later, I was regretting my decision. All I wanted to do was sleep, but now I apparently had to go meet with someone named Deveraux for a dress fitting. Dad had given me the key to my new apartment, and I'd walked the few blocks there since I didn't have any luggage to drag around.

As soon as I stepped into the apartment, I was hit with a wave of nostalgia and sadness. Nana, my dad's mother, had died a few months ago and left me her apartment in her will. My first inclination was to sell it and use the money to start my adult life in Texas, but then, well, some other shit happened.

And here I am.

The place smelled like her, roses and vanilla, and I inhaled a deep breath. I missed Nana so damn much. For years, she'd accompanied Dad every time he came to Texas to see me, but as she aged, the travel became too much for her. But I taught her to Facetime, so we talked face to face at least twice a week.

When she died was the first time I'd ever been to New York, but that trip was filled with funeral arrangements and greeting people who came to Dad's apartment to pay their respects. I never even had time to visit this apartment.

It was nice but a little stuffy, so I walked to the three large windows on the left wall. Two of them opened easily, but I had to put some force behind getting the third one open. The view wasn't anything special. Just another apartment building across the street. No trees or grass in sight.

As the place aired out, I gave myself a tour. A small living room, two bedrooms, one bath, a cramped kitchen, and—*aha!*—a laundry room... well, more like a laundry closet. Setting my backpack on the washing machine, I pulled out the change of clothes I'd thankfully thought to put in there. Tossing my red button-down and jeans in the dryer to hopefully release some of the wrinkles, I strolled back to the bathroom.

Dad had arranged for someone to clean out most of Nana's personal effects, but I prayed there would at least be towels and soap remaining. I was pleasantly surprised when I rummaged through the cabinets, finding those things as well as shampoo, conditioner, and—*halle-freaking-lujah*—a hair dryer.

There were also cleaning supplies, so I cleaned out the bathtub before stripping down and turning on the hot water. I waited. And waited. And waited some more. *Jesus, please let this apartment have hot water.*

Finally, the room began to fill with steam, and I climbed into the tub and shut the shower curtain. I turned beneath the spray, washing off what my mother always called "the travel dust" from my body. I'd felt disgusting for at least the past ten hours, and I wasn't sure I'd ever enjoyed a shower more. After cleaning myself and washing my hair, I coated my dark locks with conditioner.

And that's when the hot water ran out.

"Shit!" I screeched and then instantly quieted my voice for the remainder of my cursing outburst when I remembered that I was in an apartment and had close neighbors. "Dammit to hell! That's fucking freezing!" I hissed as I stuck my head beneath the icy spray, trying to keep the majority of it from dripping down my body.

I was shivering from head to toe by the time I got out and dried off. Plugging in the hair dryer, I ran the warm air over my body until my skin no longer had a blue tinge. Then I dried my hair before grabbing my last pair of clean underwear and socks from my backpack. Finding my clothes reasonably wrinkle-free from the dryer, I dressed.

Luckily the weather was cool, and I didn't sweat before finding a small pharmacy on my way back to the Bouvier building. I purchased deodorant, a toothbrush, toothpaste, and a soft pink lipstick and used all of them in the cramped bathroom.

"Thank you," I called to the gentleman working the register on my way out of the store. He didn't reply. "Hasn't anyone here ever heard of customer service?" I mumbled as I got my bearings and headed to my dress fitting.

As soon as I re-entered the Bouvier building, I was again greeted by a smiling Lehra. Anita still looked bored.

"Hey!" Lehra said, her blonde curls bouncing as she tilted her head. "I thought you were going to get some rest."

I managed to refrain from rolling my eyes. "I did too, but I had to come back for a dress fitting."

"Oooh, let me guess. Sexy Shrek took one look at your long legs and gorgeous face and decided to hire you as a model."

A little giggle escaped as I shook my head. "Not exactly," I said, lowering my voice. "He wants me to go to some hospital charity event this weekend, and since I have no clothing besides this..." I waved my hand up and down my body, "Devereaux is supposed to fit me with something appropriate." *Not that I would have anything appropriate for a fancy gala even if I did have my luggage.*

"Oh my God! Dev is the head designer, and he's a genius! I would literally die to wear one of his dresses."

Remembering that Dad said everyone here dressed in Bouvier, I asked, "Didn't he design what you're wearing?"

"He approves all designs, but the couture stuff that he designs *personally* takes ages. Like *years*."

I was a little stunned. "I'm sure he'll just put me in something they have lying around. I'm no one important, and this is just a one-time thing."

She nodded. "Maybe, but if Shrek requested that you see Dev personally... well, that's a big fucking deal."

"Okay, so now I'm nervous. Thanks for that," I said, pressing my hand over my stomach.

Lehra giggled. "Don't be. Devereaux is brilliant, and he's very kind. His assistant is a bit high-strung, but you'll love him."

She gave me directions to find the brilliant genius, and I took the elevator to the second floor, finding the door at the end of the hallway. I knew it was the correct door because the gold plate on it read, "The Lair of Devereaux."

I laughed at that and knocked. A few seconds later, the door cracked open an inch, and a big brown eye peeped out at me. "Password?"

My eyes widened and I shook my head. "Th-they didn't tell me a password." *Dammit, Lehra!*

A high-pitched laugh reached my ears as the door swung open to reveal a man in his thirties, impossibly thin with chocolate eyes that were too large for his face. He was dressed in an impeccable navy suit with a white shirt and bright purple tie.

"Kidding!" he trilled. "You must be Gianna."

"Yes," I breathed in relief. "Are you Devereaux?"

His hand went to his heart and he fake-swooned. "From your lips to God's ears!" Grabbing my wrist and dragging me into the room, he said, "If only I could have a pinkie's worth of that man's talent. I'm Tora, his lowly assistant."

An older man, probably in his fifties, judging from the generous amount of gray in his brown hair, strode confidently across the room and swatted Tora on the shoulder. "Stop being dramatic, Tor. We have a guest." His hazel eyes turned on me. "Hmmm, a very lovely guest."

His eyes swept up and down my figure, appraising me like I was a steak in a butcher's glass case. Then he stared at my face for an uncomfortable amount of time, a piercing gaze that felt like he was learning all my secrets.

"What's wrong?" I uttered, my voice a nervous whisper.

He grinned at me then, with teeth so white and shiny, they had to be veneers. "Absolutely nothing. May I touch you?"

"Ummm." My eyes darted around, taking in a room that was bursting with activity. Fabrics in a multitude of colors were draped over every solid surface, and about fifteen people were inspecting, sewing, and chatting. An occasional curious glance drifted our way. "Okay?"

The toothy man grabbed the sides of my head in his delicate hands and kissed each of my cheeks. "The lovely Gianna, my new project. I am Devereaux, your humble servant."

"Now who's being dramatic?" Tora quipped.

Shooting him a look, Devereaux took my hand and dragged me to a raised platform in front of a set of full-length mirrors. Checking my reflection, I tried not to cringe at my attire and my makeupless face. I didn't look like I belonged in this room filled with these luxurious fabrics and obviously talented people.

"The bossy man upstairs has sent down his directive," Dev said with a cheeky smile before turning to Tora and handing him a small set of keys. "He wants her in the ivory."

Tora's eyes widened in delight. "Oooh, yes!" he exclaimed before heading to a door on the left side of the room. He used the keys to unlock three deadbolts. Whatever was in there was obviously very important, and my nerves ratcheted up a notch.

The older man walked around and around me, taking my permission to touch me to the next level. He squeezed my thin waist. Prodded my behind. Pulled a tape measure from thin air and measured every inch of my body. He occasionally muttered words under his breath that I couldn't quite hear.

Tora returned, reverently holding the garment version of a wedding cake. The layers of creamy material draped perfectly as he hung it on a heavy free-standing rack near the mirror. Devereaux sighed, the sound akin to exultation as he took in his creation.

"Yes. Perfection," he murmured before turning back to me and fingering my red shirt. "Though she does look lovely in red. But what Auburn Bouvier wants, Auburn Bouvier gets."

Tell me about it. That's how I got in this situation.

"Red is my favorite color," I blurted out.

"Is it?" he asked, his gaze sharpening on mine. Then he clapped his hands. "Okay, you can undress now. Down to your panties. No need for a bra. There's plenty of support built into *The Dress*." The way he said those last two words were like he was speaking of Jesus Christ himself.

"Undress?"

"Yes, dear. We can't fit you if you're wearing your clothes under the dress." His soft smile was understanding and patient. "Trust me, everyone here has seen everything before."

Lord have mercy! I was about to take my clothes off in front of a room full of strangers.

Keeping my eyes on the floor, I quickly stripped down to my plain, white underwear. When I risked a look around, no one was casting even a glance at me. Tora and Devereaux were occupied with unfastening the dress. Everyone else was still working, and I felt slightly less awkward.

The two men carried the dress toward me like it was the lost ark of the covenant and directed me to step into it. Once they pulled it up and buttoned me into it, they circled me, tugging gently at the fabric and running hands up and down my hips and legs.

This was absolutely the most stunning dress I'd ever seen. The fabric was the palest ivory, lustrous without being shiny, and the way it fit on my frame made me feel almost celestial. Like an angel. I had to bite my tongue not to say that out loud because it sounded cheesy as hell.

"We'll let it out a smidge in the chest so you can breathe. Your breasts are slightly larger than our usual models, and I couldn't get the top two buttons done," Dev informed me. "And the waist will need to be taken in." He pinched about a half inch of fabric between his fingers before meeting my eyes in the mirror. "You have quite a figure, Miss Gianna."

"Thank you," I said. "I don't usually wear strapless because I don't like this to show." With my index finger, I indicated the small white disc on my upper arm. "It's a continuous glucose monitor."

"She could wear a wrap," Tora suggested, but his boss shook his head.

"Nooooo, but I have another idea." A wicked grin crossed his face, and he tapped his chin, staring into the distance before snapping out of some kind of daze. He bent forward at the waist staring in the direction of my upper legs. "Do you wax?"

"D-do I... you mean..." I pointed at my crotch.

"Like a Brazilian, honey. This dress shows ev-er-y-thing, and we don't want any little crinklies to be visible."

I absolutely could not believe I was discussing my pubic hair with someone I'd met less than an hour ago. Devereaux was looking at me unapologetically, and then he waved a hand at me.

"Don't worry about it; I'll set it up with the stylist. And we'll provide you with a seamless thong. The material is so thin, it will be undetectable. Now, let's get this treasure off of you so I can get to work on it."

An hour later, I re-entered Nana's apartment, flopped onto the bed, and fell into a deep sleep.

Chapter 5

Auburn

"Very debonair, sir," my chauffeur, Cruz, said as he held the door to my limousine open.

I unbuttoned the jacket of my black tuxedo and thanked him before sliding into the back. "You can retrieve Miss Moschella when we get there," I informed him though he knew the drill. I never went to the door to pick up my dates.

Dev had outdone himself with my attire. Of course the pants and jacket fit perfectly, but the man was a master with collars. Nothing irked me more than an ill-fitting collar that gapped with the slightest movement of the arms. He'd insisted that I wear an ivory shirt, probably to match Gianna's dress, but for some reason, he also included a dark-red pocket square instead of my usual white or cream one.

Gianna. Even her name evoked a response from my body. A tightening in my chest and a clenching of my jaw. I still wasn't sure this was a good idea, but what was done was done. I could make it through one evening, and then I never had to see the woman again. Annoyance seeped into my bones when I realized that idea bothered me.

A few minutes later, we pulled up in front of a prewar brick building, and Cruz exited the vehicle, jogged up the three steps, and opened the front door. No security? I didn't like that at all.

It's not any of your damn business, Bouvier.

I scrolled through my emails before movement caught my eye, and I shifted my gaze toward the front door.

God. Damn.

Gianna Moschella was descending the steps, her arm hooked in Cruz's. She looked absolutely magnificent. Most of her shiny, dark hair hung straight down her back, but part of it was swept up in an elegant knot on top of her head to show off her face.

That fucking face...

She was wearing exactly the right amount of makeup to enhance, rather than detract from, her delicate features. It was understated and sexy. Except for her lips. They were a bold red color that had my cock twitching in my pants.

The twitching intensified as my eyes dropped down her body. The reason for my red pocket square immediately became apparent. Dev had made some enhancements to the dress, which I'd already thought was perfect. I was wrong.

A piece of dark red fabric draped dramatically from one shoulder and halfway down her arm. Tiny, matching rosettes dotted the bodice, and if I knew Devereaux, they were each hand-sewn. The silhouette was a trumpet style, fitting Gianna's perfect body like a glove—like I'd known it would—before flaring out at the knee.

My intense perusal was interrupted by the ringing of my phone, and I swept my thumb over the screen and brought it to my ear without even looking at the display. "Bouvier."

"Auburn, it's Finn. I have those numbers you asked for on the Wilhelm property."

"Good. Can you email them to me? I'm on the way to a gala right now."

"Already done. Anything else I can help you with?"

Glancing at the building Cruz and Gianna had just come from, I rattled off the address to my real estate broker. "What can you tell me about this residential property?"

I heard tapping on a keyboard and then, "Got it. It's eight floors with four apartments on each, all two bedrooms. One elevator."

"Who owns it?" I asked as a spike of jealousy slid down my spine. Gianna was looking up at Cruz, and my normally stoic driver was laughing at something she said. She was laughing too, showing off a set of perfect teeth that I wanted to run my tongue over.

No, Auburn. That's not what this is. It's not a date or even a one-night fuck. It's an... accompaniment.

"It's managed by Marsh Holdings. Each apartment is individually owned, but Marsh maintains the outside, lobby, hallways, and elevator. They also provide in-apartment maintenance for a fee."

As Gianna approached the car, I literally couldn't look at her for another second. She was entirely too beautiful, and desire bubbled low in my belly. I swiveled my body toward the opposite door, and my eyes screamed in protest.

"Is there any kind of security?"

Finn's answer faded away as the door opened, and Gianna's high, sweet giggle filled the inside of the vehicle. Keeping my back to her as she slipped into the seat beside me, I attempted to focus on the words coming from my phone.

"...security desk in the lobby, but it's not manned."

As Cruz closed the door, an intoxicating aroma infused the space around me. I instantly recognized it as one of our perfumes, but it had never smelled so divine.

"Bouvier? You still there?"

What the fuck is wrong with me? I wasn't acting like myself at all. I was always in control, always had a purpose for every action. I didn't space out or randomly inquire about apartment buildings I had no use for.

"Yeah. I'm here. Thanks for the information, Finn."

"Anytime. And let me know if you have questions about Wilhelm."

"Will do," I said before ending the call.

Cruz took his place in the driver's seat, and I immediately pressed the button to engage the privacy panel. I was pissed at him for flirting with Gianna, even though I had no right to be.

Heat rose up my cheeks, and I couldn't seem to understand why I was so angry. *Maybe because you want what you can't have? Or maybe because this woman is fucking with your head without even trying.*

It seemed awkward as hell to keep my back to my guest, so I reluctantly straightened, keeping my eyes forward. That didn't help matters because I could see her reflection in the tinted partition glass. Her eyes flashed to my face every few seconds, so I looked down at my phone, scrolling through emails I wasn't even reading.

The tension became so oppressive, I felt like I needed to say something. Anything.

"I'm not going to fuck you, so don't even ask."

Okay, not that, you stupid prick.

I wasn't sure why words spewed involuntarily from my mouth when I was around this woman. She disarmed me like no one else ever had.

There was a moment of silence and stillness, like the world had stopped turning. Then her hand reached forward to tap on the glass. Before it made contact, I gently grabbed her thin wrist, finally turning my head to look at her full-on.

She was even more breathtaking up close. "What are you doing?" I asked.

"I'm going to ask Cruz to take me home," she replied in a shaky voice. Her almond-shaped eyes were filled with moisture, and I felt like the biggest dickhead in the world. "That was the rudest, most presumptuous thing anyone has ever said to me."

I couldn't explain why, but I knew I didn't want to take her back home. *Fix this. Now.*

I opened my mouth and said two words that I didn't say often. "I'm sorry."

Those green eyes narrowed, snapping with anger and hurt. "Do you realize the first words you've ever spoken to me were, 'I'm not going to fuck you?'"

She was correct. I hadn't even spoken to her to ask her on this date. Accompaniment. *Whatever.*

"You're right. I've been incredibly rude." I wet my dry lips with the tip of my tongue. "It's just...I'm very attracted to you, and I'm trying hard not to be. It wouldn't be a good idea, but you... beguile me."

Her face softened just a bit as one perfect eyebrow lifted. "You have a strange way of showing it."

"I know," I groaned. "I've never been thrown off by a woman before. Stuff just keeps flying out of my mouth."

Two little creases appeared between her eyebrows. "Why are you thrown off by me?"

I didn't answer. Instead, I asked her a question. "Can I have a do-over? Start from scratch?"

Her red lips quirked up on one side. "I think that would be best since you've made a fucking mess of things so far."

Laughter burst from my mouth at her brutal honesty. Bringing her hand to my lips, I kissed the back of it. "Hello, Gianna. I'm so happy you decided to come with me tonight. You look absolutely exquisite."

She dipped her chin and smiled shyly. "That was much better."

I found myself unable to look away from her. Unable to keep myself from getting to know her better. In fact, it was almost a burning need.

"Tell me something interesting about you."

Gianna bit into her bottom lip and tilted her head in thought. "My last name means housefly."

It was so unexpected, I snorted out another laugh. "Well, my last name means cowherd."

Her perfectly straight nose scrunched up. "That's horrible. I think I will go home. No way am I going out with Mr. Cowherd."

"Like you have room to criticize, Miss Housefly."

Her giggle warmed me from the inside. "How old are you, Cowherd?"

"Thirty-eight." I was relieved when she simply nodded, rather than scrunching up her nose at my age.

"Aren't you going to ask how old I am?"

"Nope. I know better than to ask a lady her age."

She rolled her eyes. "I don't know why women are so sensitive about telling their age, and men don't care a bit. The double standard is ridiculous."

"Okay, I'll bite. How old are you?"

"I'm twenty-three."

I nodded. "Let me start by saying I mean this in a very complimentary way, but you don't seem like it, Gianna. You're very confident for such a young woman."

"Well, thank you, Mister Bouvier."

"Please, call me Auburn."

We bandied questions back and forth for the remainder of the ride, and we discovered that we both liked cold pizza for breakfast. Gianna told me she lost her Nana, Tony's mother, a few months back, and that she inherited her apartment. My lips turned down into a frown when I found out she'd recently graduated with her Master's degree after taking care of her dying mother during the final year of her Bachelor's.

So much sadness in her young life, and yet she still keeps a smile on her face.

"What did you get your degree in?" Gianna asked me.

"I got a dual Bachelor's degree in Business Administration and Fashion Merchandising. Then I got my Master's in Business Admin."

She nodded. "Seems totally appropriate."

"What are you going to do with your accounting degree?"

"Well, I have an interview with Deloitte a week from Tuesday, but if my bags don't arrive, I'm going to have to postpone it, which I really don't want to do. I'm still waiting to hear back from EY and KPMG about interviews."

"Ahhh, going for the big firms, huh?" I asked, and she nodded.

"Yes, for the experience to start out, but that's not what I want to do long-term. I want to do something more... meaningful. I just don't know what yet." She tipped her head to the side, and her long hair brushed a tan shoulder. "I love working with numbers, spreadsheets, that kind of thing, but I also want to have a purpose."

Twisting my lips to the side, I hesitated only briefly before saying, "We have an opening in the accounting department at Bouvier. You should apply with us. We offer excellent benefit packages."

"Really?"

"Of course," I said, warming to the idea of having her in my building every day.

She did that cute little head tilt again. "Okay, I'll think about it."

That made me happier than I had any right to be.

Chapter 6

Well, this night was certainly looking up. Auburn had completely ignored me when I first got into the limo, and then he'd made the "fucking" comment, which pissed me the hell off.

When I'd threatened to end the date immediately, his face took on a stricken look before he'd transformed into an entirely different person. A person I actually kinda liked. The stick had disappeared from his ass, and he became warm and genuine. And when he told me I looked exquisite—actually, he'd said *absolutely exquisite*—it did very bubbly things to my insides.

"My turn," I piped up as the vehicle pulled up to the curb. "Why did you choose this dress for me?"

"I thought the ivory would look beautiful with your skin." His finger slid softly across my one bare shoulder, and I suppressed a shiver. "And I was correct."

Shifting my gaze down to the gorgeous frock, I shook my head. "I've never worn anything this fantastic. Or expensive. This dress has to cost thousands."

Auburn chuckled softly. "Try a hundred of them."

"A hundred of what?"

"Thousands."

My mouth dropped open in disbelief. "A hundred thousand dollars? That's how much this dress costs?"

"Yep," he said casually, as if it was no big deal. As Cruz opened the door, Auburn squeezed my hand. "There will be lots of cameras, so just smile and stick close to me."

I was still trying to process the fact that I was actually wearing something that cost a hundred grand, but suddenly I was distracted by all the yells and flashes of cameras from outside. My date stepped from the car, buttoned his jacket, and leaned back in to help me out. The voices became even louder once we were standing at the end of the red carpet.

Auburn's hand went to my lower back, and I immediately felt comforted and a little more relaxed, despite all the voices screaming questions our way. One reporter caught my attention.

"Miss? Can I get your name?"

Unsure of red carpet etiquette, I lifted my eyes to Auburn, and he gave me an encouraging nod.

"Gianna Moschella."

"Miss Moschella, who are you wearing?"

I fluttered my eyelashes at the reporter. "Bouvier, of course. Why would I wear anything else?"

Goosebumps erupted down my neck when my date bent to growl in my ear. "Excellent answer, sweetheart." His breath smelled like cinnamon, and I had the overwhelming urge to have a taste directly from the source.

Stop it, Gia. Not gonna happen.

But seriously, who could blame me? The man looked like sex on a big, fat stick in that tuxedo. His shoulders were approximately a mile wide, and he was pure elegance mixed with an equal amount of strength.

Auburn Bouvier knew exactly how to work a red carpet. He kept a cocky smirk on his face, looking like he had a secret no one else knew. I couldn't pull that off without looking constipated, so I turned on my full wattage smile, my fingers holding tightly onto the red clutch that Dev had stuffed into my hand before leaving my apartment today with the team of stylists.

I'd been poked, brushed, moisturized, and yes, even waxed, which wasn't nearly as bad as I'd imagined. By the time they'd all left, I didn't even have time to eat before Cruz was knocking at my door.

And now I wouldn't be able to eat tonight either. Not in this expensive-ass dress with my penchant for spilling food on my boobs.

Auburn kept his hand firmly on my lower back as he guided me through the horde of reporters, and within a few minutes, we were inside the hotel lobby.

"Good job, Gianna. You handled that well," he said, looking pleased as he removed his hand from my back and wrapped it around mine.

I loved the way my name sounded when it slid from his mouth. He practically purred every elongated syllable, and it made me want to purr as well. While he...

Jesus, Gia. Cut it out. You hate this man.

Yeah, well. I didn't hate how he looked in that damn tuxedo. Or how his big, warm hand engulfed my smaller one. Sure, he'd started the evening out by being a prick, but since I'd called him out on it, he'd become attentive and—dare I say—sweet.

Certainly not the Bastard Boss, Sexy Shrek hybrid I'd imagined.

Not letting go of his grip on me, he snagged two glasses of champagne from a passing waiter with his free hand and passed one to me.

Okay, girl. You can do this. Drink carefully and do not spill a drop. I briefly wondered if it would be gauche to ask for a straw, but I quickly dismissed that and took a tentative sip. I'd had champagne before, but by God, it was nothing like this. Heavenly little bubbles tingled against my tongue, and I bit back a groan.

Or maybe it was louder than I thought because Auburn looked down at me with an amused grin. "You like?"

I swallowed the mouthful I'd been savoring and inspected the glass. "This is better than sex."

He dipped his head to my ear. "Then the men you've been with haven't been doing their job."

Whew! Lord have mercy. Did someone turn on the heater in here?

When he pulled back, his lids were hooded, and his smug smirk was coated with a ton of BDE. The man looked like he could give a master class on bedroom activities.

Before I could say something extremely stupid, a couple approached us. They both appeared to be in their forties, and Auburn released my hand to shake with the gentleman and kiss the woman's cheek. They were an absolutely stunning couple.

I assumed I would just stand here, smiling and nodding, while Auburn talked business, but he placed a hand between my shoulder blades and introduced me.

"Darian, Jackson, this lovely lady is Gianna Moschella. Gianna, this is Darian and Jackson Knight."

"I'm so pleased to meet you both, Mr. and Mrs. Knight." I shook each of their hands.

"Oh, heavens. Please call us Jackson and Darian," the lady said with a brilliant smile.

Auburn's hand dropped to my lower back, and it seemed like he inched slightly closer to me because his body heat seeped into my skin. "I'll give you fair warning, Gianna, these two rascals are sure to do something inappropriate by the end of the evening." He lifted an amused eyebrow at the couple. "Remember that janitor's closet last year?"

Darian blushed slightly. "I ruined a very expensive pair of shoes when we knocked over that gallon of bleach, thank you very much. Not to mention that I almost died from asphyxiation from the smell and ran out of the closet with my dress around my waist."

My date chuckled. "Luckily, I was the only one in the corridor at that moment."

Jackson's hand dropped to his wife's butt as he gazed down at her with heat in his eyes. "It was entirely worth it."

She looked up at him with adoration and kissed his lips softly. "It certainly was. *Four times*," she said significantly, and I felt my own face blushing. Was she saying he made her come four freaking times in a broom closet? I was lucky to get one orgasm in a comfortable bed.

"And I bought you new shoes." Jackson was turned toward Darian now, their fronts pressed together as his hands roamed up and down her body. They were staring at each other like they were the only people in the room.

Auburn cleared his throat. "Save it for the closet, you two."

They broke apart, not seeming the least bit ashamed of their public displays of affection. Jackson whispered something in her ear and then swatted her on the butt as she giggled. He seemed to be obsessed with his wife's tush, and I didn't blame him. She had a fantastic figure.

"Bouvier, you want to head to the bar with me? I wanted to talk to you about an investment opportunity here in New York. I think you've dealt with some of the same people."

Auburn's brow creased, and he leaned close to me, his blue eyes piercing. "I hate to leave you alone."

"That's very considerate of you, but I'm not the kind of girl who needs to be babysat."

He seemed pleased with that answer, his smile broadening as he reached down and squeezed my hand. "I won't be long. Would you like something else to drink?"

My head shook side to side. Maybe Sexy Shrek wasn't such an ogre after all; he was being awfully nice. "No, I'll stick with the champagne, thank you."

"The *better than sex* champagne?"

The way he said "sex" had things fluttering in my belly, and I couldn't even seem to form a response. He winked before turning toward the bar with Jackson Knight. They looked dashing in their tuxedos, and Darian and I both stared after them. It was almost impossible not to.

When the crowd swallowed them up, the other woman linked her arm with mine and led me to a high table with tall bar chairs. "Here we are. Just us girls who are with the hottest men in the room tonight."

I giggled. "You're not lying." Perching on the chair, I was amazed by how comfortable the dress I was wearing was. The fabric moved with me like a second skin without binding or bunching.

Darian's eyes swept down and then back up my body. "That dress is absolutely incredible. Bouvier, I assume?" When I nodded, she asked, "It's couture, isn't it? I've never seen another like it."

I took a careful sip of my champagne. "It is, and I'm scared to death to be wearing it. Do you know how much this thing costs?"

She laughed. "I can only imagine." One of her perfectly plucked eyebrows lifted. "I've never seen Auburn's ex, Magdalena, in one of Bouvier's original designs. She's always fitted in one of their ready-to-wear dresses. You must be special."

My eyes turned into dinner plates as I almost choked on my beverage. "Oh, no. I'm no one special. We only met a few days ago, and he needed someone to go with him to this shindig, so I was a convenient choice. He just chose this dress because he thought it would look good on me."

Her widened eyes matched my own. "He chose your dress himself? Honey, that's... wow."

"I can promise you, it's no big deal." Needing a change of subject, I asked, "So, how long have you and Jackson been married?"

She surprised me when she told me they'd only been married for three years. They seemed like they'd been together forever. I was further shocked when she informed me they were in their early fifties, not their forties. They were both so... hot.

Over another glass of bubbly, I told her about my trip from hell, and she told me all about her daughters and the antics of her best friend, Cassandra. By the time the guys returned, we were laughing uncontrollably and dabbing at our eyes with cocktail napkins.

Feeling a hand on my shoulder, I looked up to find eyes the color of moonlight on a cloudy night. "Seems like you ladies are getting along well," Auburn said with a soft smile directed at me. I liked when he smiled like that. Very much.

After saying goodbye to Jackson and Darian, we mingled through the crowd. Auburn was never less than attentive, introducing me to everyone he spoke to. I met at least thirty different people and drank another glass of champagne.

"Uh-oh," he said, nodding his head toward a woman who was working her way through the crowd toward us. "That's my mother." He wrapped an arm tightly around my waist and looked nervously down at me. "Could... would you mind acting enamored of me while we talk to her?"

A couple of hours ago, my answer would have been, "Hell no. Even Meryl Streep isn't that good of an actress." But now? Well, Auburn Bouvier was growing on me, and maybe I *was* just a tiny bit enamored.

"Of course," I assured him, and he squeezed my waist.

"Mother," he said, keeping his hold on me even as he leaned forward and kissed her cheek. "You look lovely."

She ran a hand over his lapel. "How is my son tonight?" The woman had dark hair, and her face was... well-preserved, for lack of a better term. "Magdalena is here," she cooed.

"Good for her," he said coolly. "I'd like to introduce you to someone I'm seeing. This is Gianna Moschella. Gianna, this is Chloe Bouvier, my mother."

"So happy to meet you, Mrs. Bouvier," I said, shaking her hand briefly before wrapping my arm around Auburn's back. I glanced adoringly up at him, and he returned the look with an amused tilt of his lips. "So you're the woman responsible for this incredibly handsome man?" Returning my gaze to hers, I noticed her nostrils flare in annoyance. "I should probably thank you."

"Well..." she said with a simpering fake smile before dropping her eyes to my dress, perusing me slowly. A small muscle ticced in her jaw. "Maybe you should bring Gina to the house for dinner tomorrow. If it's serious." She said that last line with a slight sneer.

"Her name is Gianna," he said through gritted teeth. "And we'll see. She's new in town, so we've been very busy."

"How nice," Chloe said in a catty way that indicated she didn't think it was nice at all. "I'm concerned that you've moved on awfully quickly from the love of your life, son." She flashed the fakest smile I had ever seen. "But I'm happy for you. Oh, look! There's the mayor. I do hope to see you again soon, Gina." She bared her teeth in a grimace of a smile before sauntering away with a haughty lift of her chin.

"Christ," he muttered. "I'm sorry, Gianna. She's just..." He massaged his temples with his thumb and middle finger like I'd seen him do in his office on Monday.

"It's okay," I assured him, "but can I ask you a question?"

His jaw relaxed slightly. "Certainly."

"When we go to your mother's house, should I bring a cake, or does she prefer pie?"

Chapter 7

A frown creased Auburn's brow for a few seconds, and then his lips curled up at the edges when he figured out I was joking. "God, you're refreshing," he said with a low chuckle as he stroked a fingertip over my cheek and down to my jaw. "And a bit of a smartass."

"Guilty as charged," I conceded, trying not to swoon at the soft, intimate touch. Instead, I grabbed another glass from a passing waiter and took a swig.

By the time Auburn led me to our table for dinner, I was feeling a little woozy. *Okay, girl. No more champagne for you. Stick to water.*

Once I was seated, he filled the chair beside me, draping his arm around the back of mine. Chloe was seated across the table from us, but I did my best to ignore her watchful eyes.

"So, is your dad here tonight?" My father always liked Paul Bouvier, and I was curious to meet him.

"No, he's in Maryland visiting his sister."

Auburn was angled toward me, so he didn't see when a platinum blonde woman sat on the other side of him. It was difficult to determine her age because she'd had so much work done to her face. She barely had a nose left at all, and her skin was stretched so tightly, it looked almost painful. The look she was shooting at me was so sharp, I had no doubt the woman had a fierce stinger. Metaphorically speaking.

"Hello, Auburn." Her voice was throaty and sexy, but Auburn didn't seem impressed. In fact, his teeth grinded together almost audibly as he turned.

"Hello, Magdalena."

Oh. This is his ex. His recent ex.

Despite her extensive facial work, she was attractive. Her hair was perfectly coiffed into a stylish updo, and her ample breasts were jacked up almost to her chin.

Her eyes dropped to my dress, and if she'd been able to move her forehead, I think she would have frowned. "And who is this?"

"This is my date, Gianna." He swiveled his head back to me, giving me a gentle smile and effectively snubbing his ex-girlfriend. My eyes stayed on his, but from my peripheral vision, I could tell the woman wasn't happy.

As dinner was served, Auburn attempted to talk to me, but Magdalena interrupted every few seconds with some inane question or comment. My eyes dropped to my plate. A delicious looking steak with a dark red sauce was the star of the meal.

Nope. Absolutely no sauces of any kind while wearing a 100K dress. The only problem was that everything on the plate was messy. The potatoes were drenched in butter, and the asparagus was drizzled with hollandaise sauce. The roll looked relatively safe, so I pinched off a bite and stuck it into my mouth, sighing at the warm softness on my tongue. I really was hungry.

By the end of the meal, Auburn and I had hardly said two words to each other because Magdalena was monopolizing him so effectively. And she kept touching him, which pissed me the fuck off. I knew he didn't belong to me, and this wasn't even a real date, but still. The silver lining was, since his attention was diverted the majority of the time, he didn't even notice that my plate was still full as the server whisked it away.

When he twisted his head back to me and mouthed, *"Help me,"* I decided to have mercy on him. His blue eyes looked so desperate.

"Auburn," the witch was saying, tugging at his sleeve, "let's get together tomorrow."

My inner possessive bitch took over, and I grabbed his hand, linking our fingers together. "Oh sugar, you can't tomorrow. Remember Chloe invited us over?" I shifted my gaze toward Magdalena and smiled sweetly. "I'm bringing a pie."

Auburn barely contained a snort before he schooled his features into something more neutral, and I could tell he was happy with me. The other woman looked peeved, shooting a look of betrayal across the table at Auburn's mother.

When Magdalena straightened in her seat and crossed her arms like a petulant child, Auburn lifted our joined hands to his lips and kissed my knuckles. "You're a fucking savage, sweetheart," he whispered so that only I could hear it.

I would have been happy to sit there all night, holding hands, reveling in the tingling sensation where he had kissed me, but nature was calling. Loudly.

"I need to powder my nose," I said quietly.

Auburn stood immediately and pulled out my chair, stroking a hand down my arm. "Would you like for me to walk with you?"

As soon as I was standing, a wave of dizziness hit me, and sweat began beading on my top lip. Needing to get away ASAP, I shook my head. "No, I remember where it's at." I had used the facilities earlier in the evening while we were mingling.

Walking away as quickly as I could without staggering, I made my way to the restrooms at the back of the room. I breathed a sigh of relief when I spotted the sign a few steps down the wide hallway. Twisting the doorknob, I almost cried when I found it locked. My eyes lit on the men's room, but two gentlemen entered just then.

Shit! I need to sit for a few minutes. Blot my neck with a cool cloth. Take my glucose.

I suddenly remembered that the doorknob was loose when I came in here earlier because I had jokingly thought, *I wish I had my Swiss Army knife in this delicate little bag. I would tighten those screws right up.*

Desperation took over me, and I put all the strength I had left into shoving at the door, grateful when it popped open. I scooted inside and pushed the door closed before sinking onto a fancy, silk-covered couch in the lounge.

Almost immediately, I understood why the door had been locked as I heard noises from one of the stalls.

Low grunts met my ears, and then "God, fuck me harder, Jackson." Even in my weakened state, I smiled when I recognized Darian's voice.

"Baby, if I go any harder, I'm going to fuck you right through this wall."

"Yes! Fuck me through the damn wall," she groaned.

My fingers were shaking as I tried to open my purse to get my phone and my glucose. My fumbling hands dropped my purse, and I cursed quietly. As I bent to retrieve it, my dizziness intensified, and I fell face-first onto the floor.

Just before the world went black, I heard, "I'm coming, Jackson."

My last thought was, *You go, Darian!*

Chapter 8

As soon as Gianna left the table, Magdalena started up again. I was trying really hard not to be a dick in front of the entire table, but *Jesus fucking Christ*. The woman just didn't take a hint.

"Excuse me. I need a drink," I said, cutting off whatever the hell she was prattling on about. Tossing my napkin onto my chair, I nodded politely at the rest of the table before high-tailing it to the closest bar and ordering a bourbon.

I needed a moment of peace and quiet to sort through my feelings. And I was having feelings. For Gianna. She had taken me by storm, a totally unexpected breath of fresh air.

Her wit and humor were undeniable, but she was also incredibly sweet and intelligent. She remembered people's names and used those names while conversing. It might seem like a small thing, but it was a very important thing. I'd introduced her to a ton of people tonight—some high-profile ones—and she didn't bat an eye. She chatted in her easy way, and everyone was utterly charmed by her.

Including me. I just felt so… comfortable with her, and our large age gap seemed to shrink by the minute.

Not to mention that she was a total fucking knockout.

Lifting the glass to my lips, I let the bourbon slide smoothly down my throat. *Maybe there could be something between us.* I ruminated on that a while and found I really liked the idea. A lot.

My eyes searched the room for her; they seemed to be doing that quite often tonight. Even when I was talking with someone else, I still sought her out. A simple glimpse to make sure she was okay. I'd never been like that with a woman before, not even Magdalena. Probably because Mag constantly hung on my arm like a leech, so I didn't have to look for her.

But not Gianna. She was a social butterfly.

What the hell is taking her so long? My eyes drifted to the back of the room in search of my date. My *real* date. That's what this had morphed into in my opinion. No longer an "accompaniment."

I didn't see Gianna, but I did notice Jackson Knight jogging from the direction of the restrooms. Why was he in such a hurry? *Probably rushing to get back to Darian.* Chuckling into my glass, I took another drink. I'd never seen a couple so in love; they were obsessed with each other.

But Knight didn't go to his table. He seemed to be looking for something, his eyes a bit frantic, and when they found mine, he took off at a fast clip toward me.

"Knight, what's got you looking so frazzled? Did they lock all the closets this year?" I asked as he approached.

He shook his head, speaking in a low voice. "Auburn, Darian and I were in the, um, the ladies' restroom…"

I burst into laughter. "Good Lord, man. Can't you keep your zipper up for more than an hour around her?"

The man didn't even crack a grin. In fact, his face was more serious than I had ever seen it. "It's Gianna."

An ominous pit took root in my stomach, and my airway seemed to stop working. "What?" I croaked out.

"I don't know. Darian and I came out of the stall when we were… finished, and she was just lying on the floor. Unconscious."

I threw my drink on the bar, not giving a shit that it spilled everywhere, and took off at a sprint with Jackson right on my heels. "Did you call an ambulance?"

"No, we... how well do you know this girl, Auburn?"

I slowed slightly so I could look back at him. "It's new. Why?"

"Does she take drugs?" he hissed, and I almost tripped over my custom-made shoes as I ground to a halt at the opening of the hallway.

My mind was racing. *No, surely not. Not that beautiful, vibrant woman.* "I can't imagine that she would. Do you know Dr. Betty Bourne?" He nodded, and I snapped, "Find her. Please."

Betty was a friend. I didn't have many, but I counted her among the few. She was also a brilliant internist and would know what to do. Discreetly. Knight and I separated, and I skidded into the women's restroom to find Gianna on the floor in front of a couch with Darian kneeling beside her. She was lightly tapping her face and speaking softly to her.

Darian glanced up when I busted through the door, concern written all over her face. "She's still unconscious, but she's starting to mumble a little," she reported, scooting down to hold Gianna's hand and give me room.

I dropped to my knees beside her, cupping her delicate cheek. "Gianna, honey. Can you hear me? Did you take something?"

Her glazed eyes flickered slightly open and then closed again as her lips parted. I leaned in close to hear her slurred words. "Bub slutter."

Darian and I shared a confused look. "Bub slutter?" I asked. She shrugged.

A frown crossed Gianna's face, and she tried again. "Bum. Shutter." She seemed to be trying so hard to get the words out, but I didn't know what the fuck they meant. My heart fractured when a tear slipped down her face. I dashed it away with my thumb.

"It's all right, sweetheart, don't try to talk anymore. The doctor is on the way. She'll help you, okay?"

"Obbun?" she breathed, her voice a weak wisp.

That one I understood. Brushing a damp piece of hair from her neck, I replied. "Yes, sweetheart. It's Auburn."

Her breathing slowed, and I didn't know if that was a good thing or not. *Where the fuck is Betty?*

As if on cue, she appeared, shoving me away and taking my place beside Gianna. "What do we know?" she asked, her thick fingers measuring the pulse in her patient's wrist.

I kneeled at the top of her head and rattled off the small amount of information I had. "Her name's Gianna Moschella, and she's twenty-three years old. The Knights found her on the floor about..." I looked up at Jackson, and he answered.

"Six minutes ago."

"She's been mumbling but we can't understand what she's saying," Darian supplied.

The doctor pulled out her phone, turning on the flashlight and shining it into Gianna's eyes. The patient made a noise of disapproval at that, and I stroked her hair softly.

"Any significant medical history or history of drug or alcohol abuse?"

Jesus, I had never felt more fucking helpless. "I don't know, Betty. This is our first date. She doesn't seem the type to do drugs, and she had three glasses of champagne over the course of a few hours. But she just sipped." I sounded defensive even to my own ears.

"Don't get your panties in a bunch, Bouvier. I'm just asking the questions I need answers to." She started running her hands up and down Gianna's arms and inspecting the crooks of her elbows. Probably searching for track marks. *Please don't let her find any—*

"Aha," my friend said, and I froze. She'd found something. *Fuck!* Lifting the draping red sleeve, she pointed to a small, white disc on Gianna's upper arm. "Continuous glucose monitor," she explained. "Where is her purse?"

I had seen advertisements on TV for those monitors, and things started to make sense now. Gianna had been trying to say "blood sugar."

Darian handed over the red clutch from where it was lying on the floor, and Betty dug out a cell phone, punching something on the screen and then holding it over the disc. "Shit," she muttered. "Fifty-two."

"Is that bad?"

"Well, it's not good," she retorted before turning to Jackson and snapping out her orders. "Go to the kitchen and get me a large glass of orange juice. Also, see if they have one of those small tubes of icing like they use to write on cakes. And move your ass, please."

Jackson was gone before I knew it.

"Icing?" I asked, my eyes flicking toward my friend.

She nodded. "The major ingredient in most of them is glucose, which is what she desperately needs right now."

Betty rummaged in the purse some more and murmured, "Ah, good girl," when she pulled out a small white tube with red writing. As she took the lid off, she asked, "Darian, can you catch Jackson and tell him not to waste time getting the icing? Just the juice is fine."

"Of course," she said, rising and heading for the door.

"Sit her up for me," Betty ordered, and I lifted Gianna in my arms and rested her back against my chest with one arm around her waist.

My lips moved of their own accord, pressing softly against her damp cheek before whispering, "You're going to be okay, baby." *You have to be okay.*

Betty flashed me a lifted eyebrow before opening her patient's mouth and squirting some of the contents of the tube on the inside of her cheek.

"What is that?" I asked.

"It's called Glutose 15. It's a glucose gel. Very smart of her to carry it. I'm guessing she came to the restroom to take some, but she was probably too weak by that point."

Regret filled my chest. "I should have walked with her. I didn't know."

"Of course you didn't. She was probably embarrassed to tell you since this is your first date." Gianna began moving her mouth, and I saw her swallow. Betty added a little more of the gel substance to her mouth. "You like her."

Glancing down at the woman in my arms, I nodded. "I didn't know how much until I saw her lying on the floor. I felt panic like I've never felt before." My eyes met Betty's and searched for judgment there at my next words. "She's a lot younger than I am."

My friend rolled her eyes. I should have known I wouldn't receive any criticism from her since her own husband was twenty years her junior. "It may sound cliché, but age really is just a number, Auburn. It doesn't dictate how two people connect on a deeper level. Look at me and Ferdinand."

"How is he anyway?" I asked.

"He's fine. When Jackson told me there was a medical emergency, I put him on guard duty in the hallway. He's rerouting people to the restrooms up front. I didn't want any looky-loos."

My lips curved into a grateful smile. "I appreciate that. No one will get around Ferdinand the Bull," I said, referring to her giant of a husband.

Gianna let out a little moan, and my arm tightened around her waist as her eyes fluttered open.

"Well, good morning, sunshine," Betty said kindly. "Nice of you to join us. Can you take the rest of your gel now?"

Her eyes closed again, as if they weighed a hundred pounds, but she nodded. A few minutes after swallowing the rest of the glucose, her eyes opened fully as she blinked slowly.

"I'm Dr. Bourne. Can you tell me if you're diabetic, Gianna?"

Shaking her head a little, she said, "No. Hypo—" Her brow creased in concentration as she seemed to forget the word.

"Hypoglycemic," Betty filled in, patting her hand. "You're coming around, but it will take a few minutes."

"Do you hurt anywhere?" I asked, and she tilted her head back to look at me, her eyes widening when she recognized me.

Tears formed on her lash line. "Auburn, I'm so s-sorry."

"Shhh, you have nothing to be sorry about," I assured her, swiping an escaped tear from her soft cheek. "I'm just glad you're okay."

"I didn't eat enough."

"Yes, I noticed you didn't eat much of your dinner. I thought maybe you didn't like it or that you were a vegetarian or something." I pursed my lips. "Do they have vegetarians in Texas?"

That brought a genuine smile to her face. "Yes, we have vegetarians. We even have... *vegans*." She whispered that last word like it was scandalous, and I grinned for the first time since this all started. My smartass girl was back.

"I should have had them bring you something you liked. I apologize, Gianna. I'll be more conscientious next time."

"For the record, I do like steak. I was just scared I would drip something on my dress."

My mouth dropped open in shock, but before I could reprimand her, Jackson and Darian returned. "Sorry it took so long," Jackson huffed in annoyance. "Two of the chefs began arguing over whether to send OJ with pulp or no pulp. I finally just grabbed a carton and poured it my damn self while they were screaming at each other." He knelt beside our little party and handed the glass to Betty. "Hey, Gianna. You're back."

"Sorry to be so much trouble."

"Would you please stop apologizing?" I requested, but she didn't reply because Betty was holding the glass to her lips. After a few swallows, Betty checked her blood sugar again with what I assumed was an app on Gianna's phone.

"Sixty-six," she reported. "Much better. The glucose is helping."

"What was it before?"

"Fifty-two."

"Shit," Gianna muttered.

"Indeed," Betty agreed. "Auburn, can I speak with you in the hall for a moment?"

Fuck no, my harsh glare told her. *I'm not leaving Gianna.*

Darian patted me on the shoulder, obviously reading the vibes I was putting off. "Go ahead. I'll stay with her."

"I'll be brief," Betty promised, and I reluctantly stood before lifting Gianna in my arms and setting her gently on the couch.

"I'll be right back," I told her firmly, pressing a kiss against the back of her hand, and she nodded, a pinkish hue coloring her previously pale cheeks.

"What should we do now? Does she need to go to the hospital?" I demanded immediately when we got outside.

"Let's get the rest of the juice in her, and if her sugar is above seventy-five, I don't think it will be necessary. Though I really don't want her to be alone tonight. She needs her reading checked every five hours."

"She won't be alone."

"And you'll call me if it drops below seventy?"

"I will." I pulled my old friend into a hug and thanked her.

"Hey, hands off my wife," I heard a deep voice say, and I turned around to find Ferdinand striding toward us, a grin on his furry face. He pulled Betty's back against his massive chest and gave her a loud kiss on the neck. "Mine," he growled.

She looked lovingly up at him and patted his cheek. "He doesn't want me, you big caveman." Her eyes returned to me, and a knowing smirk slipped across her lips. "I think Auburn already has a lady of his own."

Chapter 9

I woke reluctantly, but my eyes refused to open because I was so content. My body was very warm and extremely cozy, and I realized I was definitely not in my bed. This was some kind of cloud bed. Had I died and gone to Heaven?

And this pillow... Good God, was it made of marshmallows and baby bunny fur? I nuzzled my nose down into it and froze. The pillow smelled like... *him*.

Fucking hell.

My eyes peeled open, taking in a soft gray wall with tall, arched windows, and I turned over slowly to confirm what I already knew.

Auburn Bouvier was propped up on one elbow, looking like sin personified as he gazed down at me.

"How are you feeling?" His voice was deep and rumbly with just the right amount of grit to make me *almost* not regret whatever happened last night.

After clearing my throat and licking my dry lips, I said, "Well, I apparently slept with a man I barely know, so I'm not doing all that great right now."

He laughed, and I had the crazy urge to roll on top of him and bite his beautiful lips. Hell, maybe I already did that. *Wish I could remember it.*

"We just slept, sweetheart. I promise. I wouldn't take advantage of you while you're sick." His hand smoothed my hair away from my face, and flashes of last night began to flicker through my mind like a bad movie.

"Shit. I bottomed out, didn't I? What time is it? I need to check my blood sugar." My heart was beating a frantic rhythm, and I tried to sit up, but Auburn pushed me back down gently.

"It's okay. I checked it five minutes ago, and you were at eighty-seven."

"Oh. Well, that's good." The memories were filtering in slowly, just bits and pieces. "Wait. How did you know how to do that?"

"Do you remember my friend Betty from last night? She taught me to do it. She said to check it every five hours, but I've been doing it every two to be safe."

"Betty. She's the doctor, right?" He nodded. "She gave me orange juice."

"And your glucose. I had Cruz go to the pharmacy and get you some more last night after he dropped us off. They didn't have the grape flavor, so he got lemon. I hope that's okay."

There was a lot to unpack there, so I started with the easiest. "It's fine. I don't really care about the flavor." My mind worked through his previous statement. "Why would you make Cruz go buy glucose in the middle of the night?"

"I wanted to make sure to replace the one in your purse in case you needed it. He also bought extras to keep here in case of emergencies. They're in the drawer," he said, nodding his head toward a dark wood nightstand.

To keep here? Why in the hell would he think he needed to keep glucose here?

My eyes flitted around the room. "Where is here?"

He smiled gently. "My apartment."

This was just too much. "Why am I in your apartment?"

"Betty said you shouldn't be left alone for the night, so I brought you back here. I carried you out the back door of the hotel, and no one at the gala saw, so don't worry about that."

"You carried me?" I groaned, and mortification simmered deep in my belly. "If you need to see a chiropractor, just send me the bill."

He laughed and tapped the end of my nose. "I think I can handle it."

That's when I noticed he wasn't wearing a shirt, and *holy fuck!* This is what he's been hiding beneath those fancy suits? Well-cut arms, a chiseled chest, and shoulders that looked like they could tote a small Chevy? As fine as his suits were, it was a damn shame the man didn't walk around naked all the time.

Moisture pooled between my legs, and I knew I was getting into dangerous territory. I needed to get the hell outta here as soon as humanly possible. *But, wait.* If he was shirtless, what was I wearing?

My eyeballs felt like they were moving in slow motion as they edged downward to find I was wearing a light-blue T-shirt that definitely wasn't mine.

"Whose shirt is this?" I whispered, afraid of making eye contact. And of the answer.

"It's mine."

Ohfuckohfuckohfuck!

I cleared my throat, which suddenly seemed to be filled with sand. "And how did *your* shirt get on *my* body?"

Placing a finger beneath my chin, he lifted my face until we were eye to eye. Except my eyes were squished shut. "Look at me, Gianna." His voice was gentle but so commanding, I lifted my lids immediately and found myself staring into gorgeous blue pools. "You fell asleep in the car. I tried to wake you up, but you kept falling back asleep. When we got back here, I put my shirt on you. But it wasn't like that, okay? I was just taking care of you. I promise I would never take advantage of you."

I pulled away and rolled onto my stomach, my voice muffled by the fluffiest pillow in existence. "You saw me naked! Please kill me now, and make it quick so I don't suffer."

His hand stroked soothingly up and down my back. "You have absolutely nothing to be ashamed of, Gianna."

Turning my head slightly, I peeked at him with one eye. "I thought you said it wasn't like that."

His hand stilled before resuming that delicious rubbing. "I wasn't perving out on you or anything. You were sick and vulnerable, so I wanted to get you comfortable as quickly as possible. But there were some, ah, visuals I couldn't help noticing."

"Visuals..."

He patted my back and sat up. "Don't make it weird, Gianna. You're a beautiful woman, and I'm a healthy red-blooded man. It would be unnatural if I didn't notice." He stood, and I saw exactly how "healthy" he was. I rolled over onto my side and tried unsuccessfully not to stare.

Cheese and crackers! Stop gawking, Gia!

Auburn was *very* "healthy" beneath those soft pajama pants he was wearing. Like, the "healthiest" man I'd ever seen in person.

"I'm going to start breakfast. There are clothes on top of the dresser for you. You're welcome to use my shower or anything in the bathroom that you need." Both of his fists and one knee dented the mattress as he leaned toward me, his face stern. "Call for me if you feel dizzy or sick at all. Understand?" His bossy tone left no room for argument.

"I understand," I said, hating myself for sounding so breathless.

"Good girl," he said, stroking his knuckles down my cheek, and I hated myself even more for the gush of wetness from my pussy. I loved being called a good girl. My ex-boyfriend hadn't understood it and accused me of having "daddy issues." *Asshole.*

When I was alone in Auburn Bouvier's bedroom, I flopped onto my back and groaned. What the hell was this, and why was he being so nice to me?

He's just being polite so you'll get the hell out of his house and he'll never have to see you again. And no wonder. He'd taken me to a fancy event, and

I'd totally fucked things up to the point that I had to be *carried* out the back door.

Sliding to the edge of the bed, I sat up and opened the drawer to see if he'd really bought extra Glutose 15 tubes for me. I spotted them as well as... *sweet Jesus!* I swiftly slammed the drawer shut to block out the image of the box of Magnums that had been taunting me from inside. I'd never been with a man "healthy" enough to require extra-large condoms.

It was seriously time to go, but if he thought I was going to wear Magdalena's or some other random woman's clothes, he had another damn thing coming. Though the thought of traipsing home butt naked didn't sound any more appealing.

Finally gathering myself enough to check out the clothes on the dresser, I was surprised to see that they all had tags on them.

I held up each item. A gorgeous, sheer, ivory peasant shirt with a matching tank to go beneath it. Designer jeans. Nude panties and bra. A pair of gold Kate Spade sandals with a cute bow. All in my sizes.

What the actual fuck? Did he just have women's clothing of all sizes lying around his apartment? And what did that say about him?

Whatever. I needed to get home. I'd humiliated myself in front of this man enough for ten lifetimes.

Scooping the clothes into my arms, I headed to the bathroom, my mouth dropping in awe at the luxury of this space. After setting the clothes on the black marble vanity, I looked at myself in the mirror. I'd expected to see smudged lipstick and racoon eyes, but my face was completely devoid of the makeup I'd worn last night. *What the eff? Did he remove my makeup too?*

Beside one of the sinks, there was a pink toothbrush still in the wrapper, so, assuming it was meant for me, I used it. Then I tied my hair into a knot on top of my head.

I quickly stripped and padded across the wide tiles to the school-bus-sized shower, taking a moment to figure out all the buttons and knobs. Finally finding the one to turn on the side jets lining the back wall, I stepped in and let the hot water stream over my body as I turned. I'd become a master at speed-showering in my new apartment, so it was lovely to be able to take my time.

When I was done, I dressed and opened the bedroom door. Hearing music, I headed in that direction. What I found had my mouth dropping open in shock.

Auburn Bouvier, the always perfectly put-together Bastard Boss, was standing in front of his stove, shaking his ass to "U Can't Touch This." His shoulder muscles bunched as he flipped the bacon with a fork, and then he picked up the spatula, pointing it at imaginary audience members as he sang the lyrics to them.

"I swear, if you do the typewriter move, I'm joining in," I said loudly.

He whirled around, bobbling the spatula before catching it deftly as a chagrined smirk slid across his face. "Dammit, you scared me," he said, turning off the music. "Sneaky ass woman."

He walked toward me—no, scratch that. Shirtless Auburn Bouvier didn't walk; he prowled. Fingering the sleeve of my shirt, he said, "This looks nice on you."

A frown creased my brow. "Auburn, where did these clothes come from?"

He went back to cooking and turned the eggs. "I had Cruz pick them up for you this morning."

I was so damn confused. "What store was open before eight on a Sunday morning? These obviously didn't come from Target."

Auburn glanced back at me and shook his head. "No. They're from a boutique that carries Bouvier clothing. The owner, Athena, lives above the store, so I called her this morning and asked her to have something ready for my driver to pick up."

"That was... very thoughtful. Thank her for me, but how did she know my sizes?"

He shrugged as he turned off the stove and plated the eggs and bacon. "She's good at that. All she needs is a picture, and she can determine your sizes pretty accurately." He turned toward me, his eyes sweeping up and down my frame. "Everything fit okay?"

"Perfect. I'll launder everything and send it back to you."

He set the plates in front of two cushy stools at the center island and pulled out one seat for me. "Sit. And you're not sending the clothes back. I bought them for you." He gestured impatiently at the stool, but I stood firm.

"Auburn, I wouldn't feel right keeping them."

"Stop being stubborn, Gianna. What am I going to do with them? Wear them myself?" He held both hands out wide, as if to demonstrate what a silly idea that was.

I couldn't help my giggle at the mental picture. "These jeans would make nice capri pants for you."

He rolled his eyes good-naturedly before grabbing a plate piled with fresh fruit from the Viking refrigerator. With a set of silver tongs, he placed pineapple slices and chubby purple grapes onto each plate.

"Would you please sit and eat? Betty told me to feed you some protein and high-sugar fruits this morning, and I'm a little bit scared of what she'll do to me if I don't comply."

I hesitated for only a second before climbing onto the stool. I did need to eat, and everything looked and smelled wonderful. Auburn sat and ate beside me, appearing satisfied with my ravenous appetite.

Something occurred to me. "Where did Athena see a picture of me?"

His lips quirked up on one side as he turned over a newspaper and slid it toward me. "Everyone in New York knows what you look like now."

The paper was folded to the society page, and my eyes almost fell out of my head when they landed on a picture of me and Auburn on the red carpet last night. We were side by side, and he was smiling down as I laughed at something he said. We looked like an actual couple. A happy one.

The caption read:

NYC'S AUBURN BOUVIER - ELIGIBLE BACHELOR NO MORE? Auburn Bouvier, one of New York's fashion giants, was spotted last night with a new lady on his arm. The lovely and charming Gianna Moschella accompanied Mr. Bouvier to the exclusive NYH Gala, and the two seemed quite cozy, leading every single—and some not-so-single—woman in the city to mourn the potential loss of Bouvier's "eligible" status. We don't know who Miss Moschella is, but we're keeping an eye on this one, folks.

Closing my eyes, I flipped the paper over as my appetite faded into nothing. "I'm sorry, Auburn."

He gripped my shoulder and squeezed before turning the article faceup again. "What are you sorry for? It's a great picture." My eyes opened and shifted to his. "Of both of us," he added with a cocky grin.

God, why does he have to be so damn good-looking. And nice. Why can't he just be Sexy Shrek? Or Ugly Shrek for that matter?

"I'm going to go and get out of your hair." *Your sexy, dark, perfectly mussed hair.*

His smile faded, and he dropped his hand to my wrist, wrapping his long fingers around it. "You don't want to stay for a while?"

"I don't think so. I've done enough to inconvenience you."

"Why do you keep saying things like that, Gianna? You're not an inconvenience."

I widened my eyes at him. "Seriously? First of all, I passed out in the bathroom at a fancy hotel so you and your friends had to take care of me. You brought me to your apartment, bought me glucose and clothes, and had your sleep interrupted because you checked my blood sugar every two hours. And then you made me breakfast." I lifted my hands and let them fall. "Not to mention, you had to undress me and put me to bed like I was a child."

"I honestly didn't mind that last part at all." His grin was pure cheekiness.

"Stop it," I said, unable to hold back a laugh. "I've been nothing but a pain in your ass since you picked me up."

His face turned serious. "You let me worry about my ass, which is completely pain free, by the way." The way he was looking at me was just so...

"I'm going to call a cab."

"No, Gianna. You're not."

Stuffing my hands on my hips, I narrowed my eyes at him. "Excuse me? Are you planning to tie me up in your apartment to keep me here or something?"

"Don't fucking tempt me," he said, his voice low and filled with gravel.

Oh, holy hell. Now my brand new panties are saturated.

Chapter 10

Gianna Moschella had to be the most stubborn woman on the planet. Unfortunately for her, I currently held the title of "Most Stubborn Human on the Planet," so I was driving her home despite her complaints.

Maneuvering my black Jaguar F-Type around a cab stopped in the middle of the street, I tried to keep my eyes on the road, but I couldn't help but notice that her hands were fidgeting in her lap.

"Something wrong, Gianna?"

She took a deep breath, and then I could feel her eyes shift to the side of my face. "Is there any way you could *not* tell my dad about my episode last night?"

"Of course," I replied easily. "You're a grown woman, and your business is your own."

I relaxed when I sensed her relax. It was strange how my moods ran parallel to hers, even though we barely knew each other.

"So, what do you like to eat besides cold pizza?" I asked, fishing for information about anything and everything related to Gianna.

"Hot pizza," she answered, her lips curling up at the edges.

I laughed and nodded. "Me too. Have you had New York pizza before?"

"No, but I've heard it's great."

"It's the best. I know a little place that doesn't look like much, but it's my favorite. I'll take you later, if you want. We can each get two slices so we can eat some cold for breakfast."

"I'm not sure that's a good idea."

"Okay then. Only one slice each."

"You know that's not what I mean, Auburn," she said sternly. "This was just a one-time thing."

My teeth sunk into the inside of my cheek. "What if I don't want it to be?"

"Look, I really appreciate you being so kind to me and for everything you've done. I know last night was probably a bit... disconcerting for you. But I'm fine now, and you're absolved of all responsibility, okay? So you can stop pretending."

I wanted to slam my fist against the steering wheel and curse, but I just tightened my hands around it instead. "I'm not pretending, Gianna. I had a really good time with you last night. Well, up until you got sick. That scared the shit out of me."

Her head drooped. "I'm sorry."

"Would you please stop apologizing?" I gritted out. "The point I'm trying to make is that I like you, and I want to see you again." *Jesus, is this how most guys feel when they ask a girl out? It's fucking terrifying.*

A glance at her face showed that she was dumbfounded. "Why? I ruined your entire night."

She was really starting to piss me off with that shit. "You did not ruin my entire night, and if you say anything like that again, I'm going to take you over my knee."

Her tiny gasp, combined with a subtle shifting in her seat, made my dick hard instantly, and I did a little shifting of my own. I hadn't meant to blurt that out, but I was learning that my involuntary word vomit was going to be a common occurrence around this gorgeous woman, so I fucking rolled with it.

"Have you ever been spanked before?"

Her breathing hitched, and then she bit that bottom lip. I'd gently removed her makeup last night to reveal that she didn't need a single bit of it, and the color of her bare lips had fascinated me. They were a deep pink color, the same color as the nipples I'd heroically not stared at for longer than absolutely necessary.

"Not since I was a child and my mom spanked me for trying to stick a screwdriver in the light socket."

My chuckle was low and deep. "Trust me. This would be nothing like that." Stopping the car at a red light, I looked over at her. "You would enjoy it much more."

Her pretty lips rolled inward as her pupils dilated with interest. "And after you spanked me?"

My lips twitched. "Then I would fuck you until your throat was raw from screaming my name."

"Oh." She swallowed audibly, and I had the urge to push my cock down into the tight channel of her throat. "So, you want to... what? Have a sexual relationship with me, or would it be a one-time thing? Like a spank-and-go type situation."

God, she made me smile. Liberating one of her fidgeting hands from her lap, I linked our fingers together and kissed her knuckles. "I would very much like to have a sexual relationship with you, Gianna. And..." A honk behind me forced me to turn my attention back to the road, my foot pressing on the accelerator as I held the back of her hand captive against my lips.

She had used my body wash, and the smell of *me* on her skin didn't help the situation with my throbbing cock. I wanted to smell *all* of me all over her. I wanted to jack off onto her flat stomach and rub my cum into her until her flesh absorbed me so that I could run my nose over it and smell where I marked her.

Christ.

"And?" she prompted, and I had to gather my thoughts to remember what I'd been saying.

"And... I just don't know, Gianna. I haven't had the best of luck selecting women for myself." I was going for total honesty here and hoping it didn't bite me in the ass.

Speaking of biting asses, my dick shouted, *Gianna's would look lovely with your teeth marks imprinted there.* I resisted the urge to reach down and strangle him into silence.

"So I'll probably just end up as another bad choice? Someone too loud, snobby, or obnoxious?" she asked, rattling off some of my own excuses from that first day back in my office.

I wheeled into the parking garage beside her apartment, finding a spot and putting the car in park before turning to face her. "No, you're none of those things. You're... perfect."

The snap of anger in her green eyes softened, and her lips twisted into a wry grin. "Except the part where I crash on the floor at fancy events."

A noise rumbled from somewhere deep inside my chest, and my nostrils flared with annoyance. "You're pushing your luck, Gianna."

Her face creased with concern. "I've never been spanked, but the idea of it..." She cut herself off, and I was curious about what she was going to say. "Do you like doing that to women?"

I cupped her chin tenderly in my palm, letting my thumb graze the smooth skin of her jaw. "Honey, I would never hit you in an abusive way. I enjoy some rough play during sex, that's all. And I never give pain without also providing pleasure. Immense pleasure."

Flecks of gold came to life in her green eyes. "Can I think about it?"

I wasn't known for being a patient man, but I had a feeling Gianna Moschella would be worth any wait. "Of course. Now, come on, and I'll walk you in."

"You really don't have to—"

I quieted that statement with a glare, and she rolled her fucking eyes at me. My hand itched.

Exiting the parking garage, we entered the front door of her building, and I was struck again by the lack of security. There wasn't even a lock on the outside door.

"The elevator has been out this week," she informed me, pushing open the door to the stairwell. It was dim and narrow, and I clenched my teeth, my only comfort coming from looking at her ass in those tight jeans as I followed her up to the third floor.

There were two suitcases beside her door, and I laughed when I saw them. "Looks like your luggage arrived."

Gianna planted her hands on her hips and stomped her foot. *Jesus, she's fucking adorable.*

"These," she fumed, waving a hand at the ridiculous suitcases covered with brightly-colored Star Wars images, "are not my bags."

"Are you sure?" I teased, drawing out the last word.

"Damn airline! Can't get shit right. My only suit is in one of my suitcases, and now I'm worried it won't be here in time for my interview next week. Fucking ridiculous."

I'll be honest. Seeing her riled up was not helping my erection at all. In fact, I was more turned on than I'd ever been.

"Are you forgetting I own a clothing company?"

She whirled on me, her eyes looking like green fire as a few tendrils of hair slipped from her topknot. Yep, at some point, I definitely needed to fuck her while she was angry.

"Are you forgetting I don't have a job yet?"

I clasped my hand around hers and squeezed, and a little of the fire went out of her. "Go inside and call them. If you need a ride to the airport, I can take you," I told her soothingly.

"You don't have to do that, Auburn. It's their screwup. They can come and pick them up themselves."

"Okay, but if you change your mind, let me know. Should we go through the bags and see if they have anything interesting in there?"

Her eyes widened, and a tiny smile etched across her mouth. "I'm a little scared to."

"Yeah, me too." Using her hand, I tugged her closer until our bodies were an inch apart. "You'll think about what we talked about?"

"I will."

"Can I kiss you goodbye?"

Her eyes dipped to my lips, and she whispered, "Yes."

I stepped into her, sliding my hand up her arm to grip the back of her neck. My nose nuzzled against hers for a second before I tilted her head and pressed my mouth to hers. I kept it soft... smooth... a gentle brush of warm lips before pulling back and looking down into her eyes. When desire flared there, I fisted the hair at her nape and pulled her closer, closing my mouth over hers and sucking at those sweet fucking lips.

My erection rested against her belly, and she arched into it as her lips parted and the prettiest little moan escaped into my mouth. My tongue sought hers, found it, and made one bold swirl before I forced myself to back away.

Her eyelids drifted open, but I was already a foot away. Otherwise, I was going to take her against the goddamn wall. Because I was fucking hooked. One brief taste, and Gianna Moschella had me under her spell.

Pulling a card from my wallet, I pressed it into her hand. "If you want more, call me. My cell number is on there." Then I turned and walked back toward the stairwell.

"My mother always told me that good girls don't call boys."

I froze, paused, and then turned around, stalking back to the enchantress who was smirking at me. "And what did your mother tell you about bad boys?"

"Only that I was to avoid them at all costs."

Leaning down, I put my lips against the shell of her ear and was pleased when my hot breath gave her a little shiver. "If I were you, I would reject that advice. Bad boys are a lot more fun,"

Flicking the lobe of her ear with my tongue, I once again retreated, grinning to myself as I heard her breathe, "Holy shit," behind me.

Once I was back in the car, I pulled out my phone and hit a number. "Albert Finneous's office," the voice who answered said.

"Finn, it's Auburn. You know that apartment building I was inquiring about last night?"

"Yes. What about it?"

"I want it."

I heard him laugh, and it pissed me off. "It's not for sale, Bouvier. Now, the building next to it is. It's slightly newer and would be an excellent investment."

"No," I snapped. "It has to be that one. Get it for me."

"Oh. Okay, I'll see what I can do. Uh, do we have a budget?"

"No budget," I huffed out.

"Well, that will certainly help to grease the wheels."

"Let me know when it's done," I said before hanging up and hitting another phone number.

"Hello, Mister sir," came a sassy purr.

My lips curved up as I shook my head. "Tora, I hate to bother you on your day off, but I need some help with something."

"Oh, you know Dev is a slave driver, Mr. Bouvier. I'm in the lair working on the newest samples right now."

"I'm on my way."

Chapter 11

"Look, I'm getting tired of this. I need my bags," I told the woman on the phone. I'd called the airline when I found the bags on my doorstep on Sunday, and they'd sent someone to pick them up on Monday morning but hadn't brought my bags in exchange. Today was Friday, and, so far, I'd talked to customer service six times since then.

"Your bags are at DFW," the most unhelpful person on the planet said in her nasally voice.

"Well, that doesn't help me at all since I'm in New York, Jenna," I said through gritted teeth.

"Well, when you didn't pick up your bags in Miami, they were sent back."

Massaging my forehead with my fingers, I explained it for the fiftieth time. "I never went to Miami."

"Did you miss your flight? Because that's not the airline's fault."

Jesus, Mary, and Joseph.

"I. Did. Not. Miss. My. Flight. I was never scheduled to go to Miami. I was scheduled for New York, and for some ungodly reason, your airline sent my luggage to Miami."

"Hmmm," the wench said, "there's really nothing I can do to help you then."

"You can help me by sending my bags to New York. I'll even go to the airport and pick them up."

"We're not allowed to put bags on a plane unless the owner of the bags is a passenger."

"So, let me get this straight. You're telling me I have to fly to Dallas from New York to accompany my bags—which your airline lost, just to be clear—back to JFK."

"Or LaGuardia," she supplied.

"Oh, well that helps a lot, Jenna. Thank you."

"You're welcome," she said, missing my sarcasm. "Would you like me to transfer you so you can book a flight?"

"Are you going to pay for it?"

"Unfortunately, we're not allowed to do that." I pinched my lips together and quiet-screamed. "We do have a flight leaving from Miami this afternoon, if that helps."

A knock at my door saved Jenna from being strangled through the phone, and I hung up without dignifying her last comment with a response.

Peeking through the peephole in the door, I was confused to see Tora standing there. I swung open the door and was engulfed by gangly arms.

"Oh, honey! I saw your picture in the paper. You were stunning, baby doll. Simply *stunning*. That dress..." He fanned himself with one dainty hand.

I laughed, my mood instantly lifted by this sweet, funny man. "Thank you, Tora, but what are you doing here? And what is all this stuff?" I asked, gesturing to the dozens of boxes that were piled high in the arms of four burly men.

"From Bossy Man," he chirped before turning to the other guys and clapping. "Let's go." They all piled into my apartment as I stood there dumbfounded.

From Auburn? I hadn't called him this week, and he hadn't called me either, so we were at a bit of an impasse. And now this? Whatever "this" was.

"Take me to your closet," Tora said in a funny alien voice, and I giggled through my shock.

"I have no idea what's going on here."

"Mr. Bouvier said that your bags were lost, so we chose a few things to get you by until they arrived."

"A few things?"

"Uh-huh," he said, unfazed by my dry tone. "Is this your room back here?" He strutted down the hallway to my bedroom with me and the muscle crew on his heels and flung open the closet door. "Well. This is just abysmal," he said, taking in the few jeans and shirts I'd purchased at a discount store this week.

"Lost bags, remember?"

Tora patted my cheek. "Oh, you are a sassy one, aren't you?" He snapped his fingers, pointing to my unmade bed, and the men arranged the boxes in stacks on the mattress. My gaze fell on my purple vibrator sitting on my nightstand, and I quickly stuffed it into a drawer and slammed it shut, praying no one saw.

I usually kept my toy in the drawer, but since I'd used it *several* times this week, I finally decided to keep it within arms reach for "emergencies." I'd been especially needy since Auburn had kissed me with those slow, sultry lips on Sunday, and every time I thought about his filthy words, I found myself reaching for my purple friend.

Surveying the piles on the bed, Tora cocked one hip and pursed his lips. "Okay, sweetie. Shirts and blouses are in the boxes with red ribbons, pants and skirts in blue, dresses in pink, and miscellaneous in purple. Where would you like to start?"

"Actually, can you give me a minute? I need to make a phone call."

"Of course," he said before turning to the other men in the room. "Guys, bring the shoe boxes up and then you can go. I'll be here for a while."

Shoe boxes?

Slipping out of the room, I retrieved my cell phone and the card Auburn had given me before closing myself in the laundry room. I took a deep breath and dialed.

"Ah, I see you've chosen the naughty girl route," a deep voice purred upon answering, and I wished I'd brought my vibrator in here with me. I could easily rub one out in a matter of seconds with Auburn Bouvier's seductive voice in my ear.

No, Gia. You're supposed to be angry.

"Auburn, what the hell is going on?"

"I'm assuming Tora has arrived?" Without waiting for me to answer, he continued. "You needed clothing, so I sent you a few things."

"A few? I could open my own boutique with all this stuff."

"It's always good to have choices."

Bending at the waist, I rested my forehead against the cool lid of the washing machine. "You know I can't accept this, Auburn."

His voice was stern, yet quiet. "I don't know any such thing, Gianna. Just take a look at what I sent. I only chose things I thought you would like."

I stood, wrapping my free arm around my waist. "You chose everything in those boxes?"

"Every single piece, sweetheart."

I wasn't sure why that made a difference, but it did, and my posture and attitude softened.

"Thank you."

"I know this sounds crazy because we've only been on one date, but I can't seem to get you off my mind, Gianna Moschella."

"Because you want to sleep with me," I stated.

"I do," he replied without apology, and then his voice sank into a deep rumble. "Have you thought about me inside your body? Giving you exactly what you need? Have you touched yourself and wished it was my hands and my mouth on your body?" My breath hitched in my throat but I didn't answer. "I didn't hear a no, Gianna. Answer me."

The raw dominance in those last two words had me clenching my thighs to gain a hint of the friction I needed. "Yes," I whispered, and a low rumble sounded through the phone.

"Good. The same goes for me."

Dear God! The thought of him doing... *that* to himself while he thought about me? *Holy hot pants!*

"Is that why you sent all these clothes and things? So I would sleep with you?" There was a long silence, and I thought the call had dropped. "Auburn?"

The tight anger in his voice had my spine stiffening. "If that's what you think, we have nothing left to discuss. You can keep the clothes, but don't contact me again."

And he hung up.

Shit.

I immediately rang him back, but it went to voicemail. Same with the next two times. Tossing my cell on the washing machine, I paced the tiny space. *Dammit, Gia. You insulted him.*

After crossing the room ten or fifteen times, I paused and stared at the phone before tentatively picking it up. Desperate to get him to answer, I pressed the Facetime button.

One ring.

Two rings.

"Come on. Pick up," I mumbled a second before his face appeared on my screen. His very livid face. If I'd thought Auburn Bouvier was hot before, I had underestimated what angry Auburn would do to my insides. Lowered eyebrows, clenched jaw, flared nostrils.

Even though he looked like he wanted to commit homicide, a sense of relief skittered down my neck because he answered. "Auburn, I'm sorry. That was completely uncalled for, and I apologize." A muscle flinched in that square jaw, but he didn't comment. Massaging my eyebrow with two fingers, I attempted to explain. "I'm not accustomed to all of this. Gifts and limousines and fancy galas. Please forgive me." I wasn't sure what else I could say.

The tension in his handsome face relaxed slightly as his lips parted. "No one's ever spoiled you before?"

I shook my head, and my voice was barely audible. "No."

Those scowly eyebrows lifted slightly. "That's a damn shame because you deserve to be spoiled, Gianna. You're honestly the most beautiful and genuine person I've ever met. You make me smile. You make me laugh. You make me want to spend every spare moment of my days with you. *That's why I want to do nice things for you, not because I want in your panties.*"

My mind reeled in shock at his words.

"Gianna, let me see if I can make this clear to you. I won't deny that I want you sexually. I want you more than I've ever wanted another woman. But my sexual desire for you is completely separate from my desire to not see you struggle. Even if things never progress beyond that kiss we shared, I would still want to do anything I could to help you. I know you're a perfectly capable woman who can take care of herself, but I have the means to help you through your missing luggage predicament. That's all I was trying to do."

A smile crept across my lips at his visceral candidness. "Thank you, Auburn. Though I still think you may have gone a little overboard."

"I always say, 'Go big or go home.'" His mouth tipped up on one side. "I may have gotten a tad carried away, but I was having fun picking out beautiful things for you. Things I thought would look good with your incredible eyes or that would make you happy."

Okay, full disclosure: I may be swooning a teeny bit.

"Auburn?" He lifted one brow in response. "I'm sorry I implied that you were trying to turn me into a ho."

He burst into laughter, a deep sound that resonated through my bones. "God, you're a breath of fresh air I didn't even know I needed in my life."

I hesitated before speaking again. "Can I see you tonight?"

His bright blue eyes flared. "Yes, of course." Then his brow wrinkled, and I wondered if he was having second thoughts.

"If you have plans, it's okay…"

"No, no. I'm just wrapping up some things, but I can come pick you up in a few hours."

"Okay, I look forward to seeing you."

"Me too. Goodbye, Gianna."

"Bye."

Tora and I spent the next two hours going through boxes and boxes of clothing, and I was a bit in awe. I loved *everything*. From the simplest of T-shirts to the prettiest of dresses, every piece of clothing was something I would have chosen for myself… if I'd had a shit-ton of money.

"And now, for the pièce de résistance," my new friend said, handing me a box that he had set aside earlier and wouldn't let me open. I gave him the old side eye before sliding the ribbon off and lifting the lid.

"Oh," I breathed as I peeled back the tissue paper and lifted out the pine-green suit jacket and skirt.

"Do you like it?" Tora asked anxiously. "Bossy Man said you have an interview coming up and needed a suit."

"It's… incredible." My fingers traced over the matte-green buttons, each with a subtle, raised *B* in a pretty script.

"Those are Bouvier's signature buttons for our women's suits. They're very distinctive and tell the world, 'I am a Bouvier woman.'" He lifted his chin haughtily, and I giggled at his antics.

"I absolutely love it."

Tora looked incredibly pleased as he winked at me. "He insisted on this particular shade of green to match your eyes. We didn't have anything in stock in this exact color, so he had Devereaux make it especially for you."

To say I was blown away would be an understatement.

"Well, sweetie-pie. I'm going to skedaddle. I've gotten your closet organized by style and color, so you should be able to find anything you need in there."

"What about those?" I asked, pointing to two boxes with black ribbons on the dresser.

"Oh, honey. Mr. Bouvier insisted on packaging those himself. I was told not to look inside them." He waggled his perfectly arched eyebrows at me. "I can guess what's inside, but I'll leave that for you to find out."

Chapter 12

"I think that's it, Auburn," Finn said, packing up the mounds of paperwork I'd just signed. "You're now the proud owner of the West Town Apartment Building." At my frown, he corrected himself. "Excuse me. The G West Apartments. The new signage should be up by Monday."

Shaking his hand, I thanked him. "I've emailed George, and he said they'll get to work on the changes I want implemented immediately." I owned the apartment building I lived in and had contracted with the company that managed it to also take charge of Gianna's building.

"You work fast, Bouvier."

"Yes, I do," I said as I showed him to the door.

When he was gone, I checked the time and sent a text message to Gianna, letting her know I would be there shortly and she was welcome to pack a bag if she wanted to spend the night. She replied that she would be ready but didn't mention whether she would be staying over.

Thirty minutes later, I was showered and dressed casually in khakis, loafers, and a fitted three-button blue henley. As Cruz pulled up in front of Gianna's residence, he started to get out to go retrieve her, but I stopped him.

"It's okay, Cruz. I've got it."

He turned slowly and stared at me like I'd sprouted an extra head, and then he swiveled back around. But not before I caught the grin he was attempting to smother. "Very good, sir."

I made it to the third floor via the stairs and knocked on the door of 3B. Realizing I was holding my breath, I pursed my lips and blew it out in a slow stream as I heard footsteps from inside the apartment.

When the door swung open, my lungs completely forgot how to function. Gianna was wearing one of the dresses I'd sent her, a casual little sleeveless number with a flirty hemline and a soft pink floral pattern. Her baby pink wedge sandals made her tanned legs look a mile long.

My eyes dragged slowly back up her body, eating up every perfect inch before landing on her face. "Damn, I have good taste."

She laughed at my cockiness and smoothed her hands over the fabric covering the curves of her hips. "Thank you. I really like this one."

Stepping into the apartment, I kicked the door shut behind me and wrapped her in my arms. "I wasn't talking about the dress, sweetheart."

Her smile lit up her entire face, and my heart thumped mightily in my chest. The rate quickened when she took my cheeks in both of her hands and stretched up to press her pink, pillowy lips to mine. Tightening my arms, I lifted her off the ground to even our height difference as our lips parted at the same time.

The kiss intensified when our tongues got in on the action. Though it was against my nature, I let Gianna set the pace, and goddamn, she blew my mind. Her sweet tongue snaked seductively around mine, and I slid one hand up her back to fist her high, sleek ponytail.

She tasted like mint and sugar, and the sensuality of the kiss had me hardening behind my zipper. A small moan broke from her chest, and I swallowed the sound as we continued to devour each other.

When I finally ended the kiss and rested my forehead against hers, we were both a little breathless. "You sure know how to greet a lady," she murmured, and I smiled, pecking her lips one more time.

"Are you ready to go?" I asked, lowering her back to her feet, and she nodded.

"Let me grab my bag," she said, and my heart flip-flopped in my chest. *She wants to stay with me.*

"I've got it," I told her, picking up the red backpack while she hung her purse over her shoulder.

As soon as we got into the car, Cruz flashed a smile in the rearview mirror. "Good evening, Miss Moschella," he said, his voice friendly, but it annoyed me nonetheless.

"Hello, Cruz," she called as I raised the privacy partition between them.

Linking our fingers together, I rested our joined hands on my thigh. Her expression turned contemplative as we drove through the crowded streets, her gaze on the people and buildings we passed. My thumb sought out the pulse in her wrist, finding it thrumming beneath the thin skin.

"Anything you want to talk about, Gianna?" Her eyes met mine, and she nodded.

"A few things." But she remained silent, gnawing on that fleshy bottom lip.

Pulling her across my lap, I cuddled her close to me with one arm, letting my other hand rest between her knees. "You can ask me anything. What are your concerns?"

She released her lip from between her teeth, and I resisted the urge to soothe the swollen area with my tongue. "First of all," she started, "I'm not sure if I'm going to stay the night. I brought clothes just in case."

I didn't like that, but she was being open and honest with me, so I nodded. "Okay, whatever you want, sweetheart. I can take you home at any time."

She seemed to relax marginally as she continued. "If you haven't noticed, there's a bit of an age gap between us."

A smug grin made its way across my lips. "I think I can keep up."

She returned my smile with a sly one of her own as her hand slid up my chest and over my shoulder to squeeze my bicep. "I'm sure you can."

Fuck. "Does our age difference bother you?"

Her lips pressed together as she shook her head. "No. Guys my age are too... immature. Does it bother you?"

"At first I was apprehensive," I told her candidly, "but after spending time with you, I don't even notice it anymore." That seemed to relieve her. "What else?"

Her green eyes pierced into mine. "My dad can't know about this."

Though I didn't like the idea of sneaking around, I couldn't really argue with that. "Agreed." Then I added, "For now." If things progressed and became serious, there was no way I was going to keep this a secret. I would be shouting it from the rooftops.

I couldn't be sure how things would go. For some reason, I didn't seem capable of being a one-woman man. Hell, Magdalena and I had been together for five years, and we'd been broken up on and off for about half that time. Though I was completely faithful while we were together, when we broke up, I fucked whoever I wanted. Casually. No one else had held my interest for more than a few weeks.

But I sensed—no, I *knew*—that Gianna was different. I'd never been so excited about the prospect of dating a woman before.

"I think that's all. I just needed to get all that off my chest."

Lifting her chin, I brushed my lips tenderly over her jaw. "Anytime, sweetheart. You can ask or tell me anything."

As I led her into my living room, Gianna looked around as if seeing everything anew. And I guess she was since the first time she was here, she was barely conscious, and then she left in a rush.

"Have you eaten dinner?" I tried not to show my frustration when she shook her head. "Come on. I made a pasta salad last night, and it's always better the second day," I said, settling her at the kitchen island and pulling out the food from the refrigerator. I spooned us both a generous helping into crystal salad bowls and then added the crushed croutons that I'd made fresh yesterday.

As we sat together and ate, I was once again fascinated by how easy this woman was to talk to. *Age gap, my ass.* When we were done, she rinsed the dishes, and I loaded them into the dishwasher.

"Would you like a tour of the apartment?"

"Sure. I don't remember much of it from last time I was here."

After I'd shown her around the right side of my home, including the home gym, my office, and the spare bedrooms, we headed down the other hallway to the master suite.

"I can't believe you have three guest rooms. Do you have company often?"

"Hmm, not really. My cousin Blaire and her husband Axel came to visit me last year, along with their five kids. They're from Texas too."

Gianna stopped before we reached my room, her eyes wide. "You're not talking about Axel Broxton, are you?"

"Yeah, the football player for the Fort Worth Wranglers."

"I can't believe you're related to him!" she exclaimed. "He's a legend."

My lips curved up at her enthusiasm. "I'm not a Wranglers fan, but I do cheer for Ax because he's family now."

"I read an article on them. Blaire is brilliant. An orthopedic surgeon, right?" I nodded as she continued gushing about my cousin. "And she looks amazing, especially after having five kids, three of them triplets."

"Brains and good looks run in our family," I said with a wink. "And those triplets are naughty as hell. Completely adorable, but shit, they have a lot of energy."

She shook her head, looking awestruck. "I can't believe you know them."

"Blaire's older brother, Beau, and his wife are coming from Dallas to visit me in a few weeks, and they're bringing their son. I know it's not as exciting as meeting a football god," I teased, "but I'd love to introduce you to them."

Her sweet smile melted my heart. "You really want me to meet them?"

"Yeah, I think I would like that," I told her honestly. My cousin had been a total playboy until he'd met a cute little nanny named Charli, and I would love to get his take on Gianna. He and Charli had a bit of an age gap as well—not as large as ours—but it would be nice to get his perspective.

I could practically hear her mind whirling as we entered my bedroom, and I turned to face her. "What's going on in that pretty head of yours?"

She huffed out a breath. "I talked to the airline again today, and they said if I want my bags, I have to fly to Dallas and get them because bags can't fly without a passenger. If I sent your cousin some money for the baggage fee... I know it's a lot to ask—"

I frowned and cupped her cheek. "Why didn't you tell me, Gianna? I could have sent my plane to pick up your bags."

Her mouth gaped open. "You have a plane?"

"Yes, and I'm sending it to pick up Beau, Charli, and little L.J. Since it's the baby's first flight, I didn't want to make them fly commercial. I'll just have your bags loaded onto my jet. Unless you want me to send it this weekend."

She looked stunned. "No, it's fine since I'm obviously set for clothing now." Her head tilted, allowing that dark ponytail to brush one bare shoulder. "Thank you, Auburn."

Dragging my knuckles down her cheek, I grazed her lips with mine. "Anything you need, all you have to do is ask."

I wasn't sure what it was about this woman, but I meant every word, and that wasn't like me, especially when it came to my jet. I was a tad possessive of it because it was a goddamn airplane, for fuck's sake. Magdalena had asked to borrow it for a girls' trip to Fiji recently, and I'd declined her request without a second thought.

But for Gianna? I would have eagerly flown to Dallas and picked up her luggage myself.

Kicking off my shoes and lining them up against the wall, I gestured for her to do the same. "Make yourself comfortable. I'm just going to use the restroom real quick."

I did my business, and when I opened the door to my bedroom, I had to grasp onto the door frame with both hands to keep my legs from buckling beneath me at the sight of her.

Each syllable dripped like honey from my tongue as I uttered her name.

"*Gianna...*"

Chapter 13

Auburn

The black-ribboned boxes I had sent to Gianna contained a selection of bras and panties, most of it being from the Fox and Rose brand. It was an outstanding company with two distinctive collections to show off the contrasting, but equally intriguing, sides of a woman, the beautiful and sophisticated Rose and the more seductive Fox.

Begging my knees to hold up so that I could close the distance between us—only a few feet, but it felt like a mile—I unpeeled my clenching fingers from the door frame. My legs seemed to be as eager as the rest of me because they managed to carry me slowly toward her as my eyes raked up and down her perfect form.

Gianna had removed her dress and was standing before me in only a black lace bra and the tiniest matching panties I had ever seen. They barely covered what I yearned for most.

Swallowing the desire that seemed to be clogging my throat, I was surprisingly able to form words. "I see you went with the Fox collection," I murmured, stroking the dainty strap over one tanned shoulder with a single finger.

"I thought it would please you," she said, and I can't even describe how quickly every bit of my blood migrated to my cock at those words. Then her chin lifted with a boldness that I hadn't expected of her. "Someone recently told me to 'go big or go home.'"

"That guy sounds like a fucking genius," I told her, meeting her eyes.

"He likes to think so," she retorted mildly.

I fought a smile. *This woman...*

"For the record, you're not *going home* anytime soon."

"So you like?" Her teeth sunk into the corner of her bottom lip, making her appear a bit insecure. *How can she not know how goddamn stunning she is?* Perhaps she needed someone to make it perfectly fucking clear.

Strolling a half-revolution around the woman that was currently the center of my own personal solar system, I stopped behind her and subtly adjusted my rock-hard dick.

"If I could dream up the perfect woman, Gianna," I whispered as my lips barely brushed her ear, "she would look exactly like you."

I reveled in the fact that she shivered, even more so when goosebumps followed my fingertips as I trailed them slowly over her shoulders and down her arms. Dropping my lips to the side of her slender neck, I let out a little groan when she tilted her head to allow me better access.

My hands rested on her waist, and I showered her with sweet words punctuated with slow, tender kisses down her neck and across her shoulder. "You are so stunning, baby." *Kiss.* "Exquisitely beautiful." *Kiss.* "You take my breath away." *Kiss.*

I watched Gianna in profile as a blush stained her cheeks, and her eyes fluttered closed. Pulling her back a half step, I plastered our bodies together, allowing her to feel my hardness against her ass. Sliding my arms around her, I cupped her lace-covered breasts, measuring their heavy weight in my palms.

A needy whimper escaped her parted lips when I scraped my thumbnails against her nipples, drawing them into hard pills beneath her lingerie. "Auburn. Please."

Continuing my ministrations against her stiff peak with one hand, I slid the other up to wrap around her delicate neck, holding her body snugly against my own.

Her vocal cords vibrated against my palm as she hummed softly, and I smiled. *I think my girl likes having a hand necklace.*

"Until I'm done exploring this luscious body of yours, I don't want you to speak unless I ask you a question," I growled into her ear. "Or if you need me to stop at any point. Do you understand?"

"Yes, Auburn."

Jesus fucking hell. Her quiet acquiescence had my cock throbbing painfully in my pants, and I tightened my fingers around the sides of her throat.

"Mmmm, what a good girl." Those words elicited a full-body tremble which shook through her body and straight into my own. "Are you my good fucking girl, Gianna?" I asked, closing my mouth over the curve of her shoulder and sucking.

"I want to be, but I thought you said I chose the naughty girl route."

My lips curved into a smile against her shoulder. "Good and naughty are two sides of the same coin, my sweet pet. There's a very fine line between a proper lady in public, and a filthy little slut when I'm fucking your pussy until it's raw behind closed doors."

Gianna let out a short squeaking noise and squeezed her legs together, searching for the friction that I wasn't ready for her to have yet. Sliding both hands languorously down the outsides of her shapely thighs, I squeezed before shifting my grip to her inner thigh muscles, parting her legs for me.

With one hand, I cupped her hot cunt possessively while the other roamed her body, touching, exploring, learning. Her stomach was flat and smooth, her ab muscles clenching beneath my fingers. The area between her legs was practically scorching my fingers with her wet heat. Those tiny panties were fucking soaked, and I could feel my dick dripping in response.

My free hand skimmed up her body to that perfect face, memorizing every inch of it with my fingertips before reaching for her long ponytail.

"Can I let your hair down, pet?"

"Yes," she panted.

"Very soon, I'm going to wrap my fist around your ponytail and take you from behind," I informed her as I removed the band from her hair, allowing her silken strands to drape across my shoulder and arm. "But for tonight, I want to see it free against my pillow while I fill you up."

She tried to grind against my hand, but I tightened my fingers roughly against her sex. "Be still, Gianna," I commanded, and she froze, but not without a whimpering protest. "This pussy belongs to me until I decide you can have it back. Do you understand?"

"Y-yes, Auburn." I loved the way she said my name, her sexy little drawl stretching out the vowels.

When I rewarded her with a drag of my middle finger against her clit, her legs gave out, and I took all her weight. Turning her in my arms until she was facing me, I lifted her so she could wrap her long legs around my waist.

As I carried her toward my huge four-poster bed, I was eye-to-nipple with her fantastic tits. "This black, lacy bra is sexy as fuck, but it will look even better on the floor," I told her, reaching around her and unsnapping it with one practiced hand before tugging it off. My mouth literally watered at the sight of her, and I traced my tongue around one pebbled nipple as I held her churning hips with both hands.

Gianna's small hands tangled in my hair, twisting when I sucked until her breast filled my mouth. The scent of her arousal and the feel of her wet cunt soaking my pants was driving me fucking crazy. After giving her other breast equal attention, I released it with a soft pop and then reached behind me and ripped off my shirt, tossing it aside as she pressed her chest to mine.

"Au—" she started before clamping her lips shut like the obedient little doll that she was.

Stroking my hand through the hair hanging down her back, I told her, "It's okay, sweet pet. You can talk now. I want to hear everything."

"I want you to kiss me," she requested, and I willingly obliged, crashing my mouth to hers in a messy, passionate mingling of tongues and lips.

Brushing soft kisses across her cheek, I whispered, "I want to spank you, pet. Will you let me?"

She lifted her head to look at me, apprehension filling her eyes, but she nodded. "Yes."

"Trust me, Gianna," I implored her. "You'll enjoy it, and if you don't, just say the word, and I'll stop."

"I trust you, Auburn."

Those four little words made my dick ache painfully, so after I positioned her on her hands and knees on the end of my bed, I quickly stripped off my khakis, giving marginal relief to my erection.

"I've never seen anything more beautiful," I told her, rubbing my hands over the rounded globes of her ass. I gripped her hip with my left hand before delivering a soft spank to her right butt cheek. She jolted at first, and then her spine softened as I soothed the area with my palm.

"No pain without pleasure," I reminded her, dipping my head and dragging my tongue across the soft, textured fabric covering her crotch.

"God. Yes," she panted as I stood.

The next smack against her left cheek was a little harder, but she took it without even a flinch. My cock leaked like a faucet when my red handprint bloomed prettily on her skin. This time, I pulled her panties to the side and rewarded her with a long lick, from her clit to her tight asshole. The sweet, seductive taste of her on my tongue almost had me blowing in my boxer briefs.

"You okay, baby?" I asked her as I straightened.

I watched in fascination as she nodded, and her fingers cinched one by one into my crisp gray sheets. Then she lowered her chest to the mattress in a gesture so submissive, it took every ounce of strength I had not to bury my cock so far inside her, we both forgot our own names.

I spanked her four more times, following each strike with my mouth devouring her pussy for longer and longer amounts of time. Gianna writhed with need, and I finally flipped her over, fisting the tiny string at her hip and ripping her new panties right the fuck off. Then I groaned as I buried my tongue inside her sweetness, and her hips lifted from the bed to grind against my face.

Sliding one finger inside her, I let my tongue work her swollen clit with quick, firm licks. "Fuck, you're tight," I mumbled against her moist flesh as her pussy clenched and released around my finger. I added another, and she went fucking wild when I curled them forward to caress her G-spot.

"Auburn, I'm coming," she called out, her voice raspy with need as I finger-fucked her and sucked hard on her little pearl.

Gianna's back arched sharply off the bed, and a stream of her sweet cum flooded my fingers and coated the lower half of my face. Reaching between my legs, I clamped my hand around the head of my cock to stave off my own impending release.

Doing my best to be patient, I let her come down slowly before lifting my head to take in her disheveled appearance. Her chest and face were damp with sweat, and tendrils of hair stuck to her skin.

Swiping my mouth with the back of my hand, I couldn't peel my eyes from her for even a second.

She is fucking magnificent, I thought, lifting and scooting her up the bed until her pretty head rested on my pillow. Crawling up her body, I straddled her hips as my hands roved over every inch of her from the waist up.

Gianna's lids fluttered open, and the usually bright green of her eyes was muted by the haze of satisfaction. As her hands smoothed up my thighs, a smug little smirk curled her lips, and she gripped my cock through my underwear.

"Auburn?" she inquired, giving me a squeeze that almost had me coming in her hand. "Why isn't this inside me right now?"

Fuck me. This woman...

"That's a damn good question, pet," I told her, reaching for the bedside drawer and opening it. My gaze fell on the glucose tubes beside the condoms and I froze before removing one condom from the box and turning back to the beauty in my bed. "Do we need to check your sugar, baby?"

Her face creased into the cutest little pout. "I don't want you treating me any differently because I have a... condition."

I leaned down and kissed her tenderly. "That's not what I was trying to do, Gianna. I just want to make sure you're okay before we get started." I kissed her again, this time deeper. "Because you're going to need every bit of your strength for the rest of the night."

Her teeth sunk seductively into that full bottom lip of hers, and her mouth curled up at the edges. "Bring it on, Bouvier."

"Consider it brung, baby," I told her with a chuckle as I removed my underwear and freed my straining cock. I let out a deep groan of relief and gave myself a tight stroke before rolling on the rubber.

Gianna's eyes widened as her eyes laser-focused on my thick length, and she rolled over, attempting to scramble off the bed. "Nope. Not gonna happen. That thing is not going to fit."

I laughed and grabbed her ankle, pulling her to me. "Get over here, woman. We'll make it fit."

"That's easy for you to say. You're not going to be the one with the shredded vagina," she retorted.

Resting on my knees, I scooped her up and pulled her against my body with her knees straddling my hips as I rubbed her hair gently. My lips pressed soft, coaxing kisses against hers. "I thought you were going to be my good girl, Gianna."

She melted at my words, rocking her slick sex over mine. "I want to be."

"Mmm, well, good girls take fat cocks in their tight little pussies when they're told to."

Gianna let out a little moan, and then she lifted, notching the entrance of her pussy right over the tip of my anxious dick. Her hips swiveled around and around, saturating my crown as her thick juices trickled down my shaft. It was fucking incredible.

"You feel that, sweet girl? You feel how wet you are for me? How hard I am for you?"

Her pussy swallowed a couple inches of me, and she threw back her head and sighed, giving me access to that swan-like throat. Swirling my tongue in the hollow, I murmured against her silky skin. Sweet things. Dirty things. Whatever would get her to take more of my cock inside her heaven.

And she did. It was slow, but that only made it hotter as our bodies acclimated to each other. Taking one of her dark pink nipples between my teeth, I bit down, and Gianna rewarded me by sinking down the last two inches. Soothing her nipple with my tongue, I groaned around her swollen tit.

My mouth trailed up her neck, licking a wet stripe up the side and to her ear. "You take me so beautifully, my pet."

She clung to me, her arms wrapped around my neck until I placed one hand between her breasts and gently pushed her back a couple inches. "Look down, Gianna. Look at your pink cunt stretched around my cock."

Her eyes glided down, and her lips parted when she saw where we were joined. "That's so fucking hot." Then her eyes raised to mine, and she smiled coyly. "So, am I your good girl?"

My dick twitched inside her, and she lifted a dark brow as she swiveled her hips, dragging her tight walls against my cock. The little vixen was seducing me.

Cupping her cheek, I stroked her bottom lip with my thumb. "You *are* my good girl, Gianna. You're my perfect girl for taking all of me."

Her cheeks flushed with pleasure, and she leaned back, pressing her hands into the mattress behind her. Then she started fucking me. It was slow and sensual, her eyes closed and her long hair dragging the sheet as she slid up and down my shaft, adding unexpected little twists and grinds that had me panting for more.

"Goddamn. Where did you learn to fuck like this, Gianna?" I groaned, not sure if I wanted to know the answer. Because I had the urge to find anyone who had ever touched her and set the motherfuckers on fire.

"I'm just doing what feels good." She let out a moan that was so deep and sultry, it almost snapped the thin thread of control I was holding onto. "And you feel soooo good inside me, Auburn." My thumb was still on her bottom lip, and my cock grew impossibly thicker when she sucked my digit into her warm mouth as she continued her sexy ride.

Gianna hollowed her cheeks, rubbing her velvety tongue against the pad of my thumb until I couldn't take it anymore. Pulling from her mouth, I lowered my hand and coated her clit with her own saliva, drawing circles around the button until she clenched hard around me.

"Auburn... oh my God!" she screamed to the ceiling as she came. Her hips were churning, grinding down onto my erection as she called my name over and over. My gaze alternated between her erotic grimace and her cunt sliding up and down my shaft. Both were equally as beautiful.

When her arms collapsed under the weight of her ecstasy, I followed her down to the bed, straightening my legs so that I was lying on top of her.

"Hold on, baby girl. This is about to get rough." Drawing back my hips, I slammed into her and roared my approval. "Fuck. Yes."

Even through her post-orgasmic fog, Gianna responded, opening her thighs wide for me. "Fuck your pussy, Auburn," she groaned, her eyes finding mine hovering above her.

Straightening my arms, I gave her what she asked for, widening my knees and fucking her like a jackhammer. In and out. Over and over. She met me with lifted hips, taking every one of my hard thrusts—each of them punctuated with an animalistic grunt from the back of my throat.

Gianna grabbed hold of the wooden headboard behind her, closing her eyes and crying out as I picked up the pace. I needed her pleasure even more than I needed my own. A sense of urgency took over my body, insisting that I make her come again. My hips tilted, finding that spot inside her and nudging it with the crown of my dick with every movement.

I wanted to fucking ruin her for other men because she sure as hell was ruining me for other women.

I'd had good sex before. I'd even had great sex. But I'd never had perfect sex. This woman though... seeing her writhing on the bed, enjoying the pounding I was giving her as much as I was... utter perfection.

Lowering myself to my forearms, I gave her some of my weight as our sweat mixed and lubricated the slide of our bodies. "Open your eyes for me, pet." She did, and I got fucking lost in the green depths. "Give me another one. I want us to come together," I said through gritted teeth.

Strange as it may seem, I'd never come simultaneously with a woman before. I'd always gotten her off and then found my own climax a minute or two later. But there was a burning need inside me to watch Gianna come—*feel* her come—as I released myself inside her. To share that moment with her.

As my orgasm built to the point that I couldn't hold back another second, my lips hovered over hers, and I lowered my voice. "Now, Gianna."

My soft command pitched us both into the stratosphere, our faces a mere inch apart as our eyes locked. And in that moment, something changed. Built. Grew.

And I knew...

I'll never be the same after this.

Chapter 14

For the second time in a week, I felt like I was floating on a cloud. But this time, it had nothing to do with the softest bed in the known universe.

This time, I was floating on a cloud of pure ecstasy.

Auburn Bouvier was on top of me, his lips barely touching mine as his extremely large cock coaxed my orgasm to continue. A full thirty seconds after I'd come, I was still trembling in his arms.

His sculpted lips covered mine, his tongue teasing gently until I opened for him. Then we were kissing, and it was *everything*. Soft and demanding and deep. I peeled my hands from the headboard and cradled his cheeks as he continued to slowly move in and out of me.

As rough as he'd been with me, this felt special.

Jesus, slow down, Gianna. You're just a hot, young fuck to him. He only wants a "sexual relationship," remember?

I let my hands roam down, over his broad shoulders and around to his back. The muscles there bunched beneath my fingers as he continued fucking lazily into me. Pulling from the kiss, his lips curved into a sweet smile before he nestled his face into my neck.

"Did you enjoy it, Gianna?"

Seriously? "Read the room, Bouvier. Even if you couldn't tell from my body's response, the screaming should have given it away."

His body shook with laughter, and he wrapped both arms beneath me, binding our bodies even closer together as he pushed that magnificent dick deeply inside me and held it there. A vibration traveled up my throat, and I released the moan against his shoulder.

"Fuck, it turns me on when you get sassy. I think I could go again right now," he said into my ear.

Gulp

"Sh-shouldn't you change the condom?" I stammered. Hell, I'd never had a man go more than once in a night, but I remembered from health class that you should never reuse one.

"Yeah," he said, sounding reluctant as he unfolded his arms and pushed away from me. "We could probably both use a break after that."

No fucking shit. I'd never had a man own me like Auburn Bouvier had. The man took complete possession of my mind and body when he touched me, and I could use a few minutes to process all that.

Gripping one of my hips, he pulled out of me with a groan, and I noticed that he was still semi-hard when he stood. "Be right back," he said, tucking a tendril of my hair behind one ear.

I stared without an ounce of shame when he walked to the bathroom, admiring the buff form of Auburn Bouvier. The man had an ass like a ripe apple, and his back muscles made my pussy clench around the void he'd left when he pulled out. There was just something about a man with a strong back...

When he returned a few minutes later, the front was just as appealing as the back, his six-pack abs being the star of the show. Correction: As fine as they were, they played second fiddle to what was hanging between his legs. *Good God!* I still couldn't believe I'd taken all of that inside me and lived to tell about it.

Catching me looking, he grinned, the cocky bastard. Crawling onto the bed, he gave me an up close and personal view when he kneeled beside me. "Spread your legs for me, pet."

Excuse me. What? "Uh, I thought we were taking a break."

I giggled when he held up a cloth, popping a sardonic eyebrow up to his hairline. "I'm going to clean you up."

"Oh, I can do it," I said, reaching for the cloth, my face flushing with embarrassment. He stopped me with a hand around my wrist before bringing my palm to his lips for a gentle kiss.

"I want to," he said simply, and my knees spread of their own accord. *Dammit. What is this hold he has over me?*

Positioning himself between my legs, he cleaned me with a tenderness I didn't expect from a man like him. A domineering, bossy-ass man. With a final kiss against my belly, he closed my legs and flipped me over.

I didn't know what I was feeling at first, and then I realized it was his lips, feather-light across my spanked bottom. "My good girl," he whispered, and I buried my face in the pillow. *Why do I like that so much?* A soft groan escaped me when his big hands rubbed something cool over the heated flesh of my ass.

"What is that?"

"Just a lotion to soothe you, sweetheart. It has arnica and aloe in it."

Turning my head to rest my cheek on the bed, I caught a whiff of something sweet. "It smells good."

"It's peach-scented," he informed me.

"Oh, goody. I've always wanted my ass to smell like peaches."

Auburn chuckled and sat on the edge of the bed, shifting me into his lap. He kissed my forehead, and then nestled my face into his neck. I inhaled his intoxicating scent, salty sweat, a hint of cologne, and pure manliness.

"Is there anything you want to talk about, sweetheart?" When I didn't answer, he cuddled me closer to his bare chest. "About what we just did? Were you okay with the spanking?"

"Yes, I was okay with it."

"Just okay?"

"I liked it," I admitted in a small voice.

He noticed. Because *of course* he did. "That's nothing to be ashamed of, Gianna. Lots of people enjoy spanking during playtime. Whatever you like is only between you and me."

My body relaxed, releasing tension that I didn't realize I was carrying. "Thank you," I said, kissing his chest. "I *really* liked it." This time my voice sounded stronger.

"Good girl," he murmured, kissing my hair.

"I like when you call me 'good girl,'" I declared, feeling bolder now, "but I don't understand why. A previous partner made me feel weird about it."

"Give me his name, and I'll teach him a fucking lesson," he growled before lifting my chin so we were eye to eye. "You like being praised, and there's nothing wrong with that either."

My nose wrinkled as I tried to lower my chin, but he wouldn't let me. "That makes me sound like a narcissist."

"Not at all, Gianna. You like reassurance that what you're doing is pleasing to me. It's actually very selfless."

Well, when you put it like that...

Auburn's hand wrapped around the back of my head and pulled me to him for a kiss. We made out for a while, his tongue sweet and soothing against mine, before he pressed my head into his neck again. He didn't speak. He just held me, his hands stroking my hair until I was so comfortable, I almost fell asleep.

He stood and tucked me into his bed, covering my naked body with the sheet. After tossing the washcloth in the bathroom, he slipped into a pair of black plaid pajama pants.

Unsure what to do, I asked, "Should I get dressed?" as he turned to the door leading to the rest of his magnificent apartment.

Glancing back, his eyes raked up and down my covered body, as if he had X-ray vision and could see right through the sheet. He licked his lips and said, "I'd rather you didn't."

Okay. Well. Naked time it is, I guess.

While he was gone, I took the time to take in my surroundings. Auburn's bedroom was tastefully decorated. It was definitely masculine, but it was also warm and inviting, from the pale gray walls to the matching bleached floorboards. The furnishings were a dark contrast, including the massive bed with intricate carvings on each post.

My mind drifted back to everything we'd just done in this bed and his attentiveness once we were done, and I determined that Auburn Bouvier's fucking was first-rate, rivaled only by his doting aftercare.

When he strolled back in, he was carrying a small wooden tray, which he set on the nightstand before removing his pants. My mind squealed at the sight of naked Auburn.

Situating himself against the headboard, he gestured for me to sit between his spread legs. I scooted over, leaning my back against his chest, and he drew the sheet up over our laps before reaching for the tall glass on the tray. He held the straw to my lips, and I sipped the icy water.

After he took a drink, I teased, "Hey! Maybe I didn't want your spit on my straw."

He banded an arm beneath my breasts and nuzzled my ear with his nose. "Sweetheart, get used to the fact that by the end of the night, my spit is going to have touched every inch of your perfect body."

Oh. My. Fuck.

We finished off the water, and Auburn set it aside, reaching for the blue crystal bowl piled high with juicy grapes. He selected one and popped it into his mouth before lifting my chin and pushing it between my lips with his tongue. His grin was mischievous and playful as I chewed. I wasn't sure how a move so dominant could also be so sweet.

Auburn fed me the rest of the grapes, but when he picked up the last one, he slid it beneath the sheet, simultaneously wrapping his ankles around mine and spreading my legs. He dipped the cool fruit into my pussy and then raised it to his lips, boldly licking it while his eyes stayed glued to mine.

"This one is all for me," he said, sucking it into his mouth and rolling it around. "Mmmm, this is my new favorite way to eat grapes, pet."

Whoo, boy! Is it getting hot in here?

I rolled over, resting my hands on his chest and propping my chin there. "So, I'm your pet."

"You are." His lips crooked up on one side as he brushed my hair behind my shoulder. "Does it bother you that I call you my sweet pet?"

"No."

"It shouldn't. It just means..." he took a deep breath, his face pinkening as he took my face in both of his large hands. "It means that I treasure you, Gianna." His blue eyes turned vulnerable, and I marveled at the sight of Auburn Bouvier blushing.

Just... wow!

I stretched up and kissed him, meaning it only to be a peck, but it quickly turned into more. Rolling us over, his hard body pressed mine into the mattress as his tongue plunged deeply into my mouth.

He was hard again, sliding his steel rod between my legs, slickening it with our combined arousal. Dipping his mouth to my neck, he sucked the sensitive spot just below my ear, causing my back to arch completely off the mattress.

"Auburn," I breathed, "you know how you said you can keep up with a younger woman?"

"Mmhmm," he grunted, progressing from sucking to biting the tender flesh of my neck.

"Prove it," I challenged as I wrapped my legs around him and grinded my pussy against his erection.

He lifted his head and flashed me a wicked grin. "Prepare to be amazed at my prowess," he promised as he reached for another condom.

Spoiler alert: I was completely amazed. *All night long.*

Chapter 15

"Would you stop it, Gianna? You're going to make me late for work." Auburn scowled across the table at me on Monday morning.

I blinked innocently at him. "I'm just eating my breakfast."

His jaw clenched, and his eyes narrowed into thin slits. "You're eating that banana like it's your greatest fantasy."

"Maybe it is," I retorted, taking another bite and making sure to drag my lips along the surface of the phallic fruit as I moaned.

He closed his eyes and appeared to be counting to ten, his hands fisted into tight balls beside his empty plate. I waited until his lids lifted, and then I stuffed the last four inches of banana into my mouth, my gaze locked with his.

Auburn ran his tongue over his top teeth as his eyes flashed with desire. Rising slowly from his chair, he prowled around the huge table, never looking away from me for a second. He was wearing a black three-piece suit with a baby-blue tie that perfectly matched his irises, making him appear more dominant than usual.

With a loud screech, he twisted my chair until I was facing him. I swallowed the remainder of the food in my mouth and gazed up at him, doing my damnedest to fight a smile. He rested his hands on the arms of the chair and leaned down until his face was an inch from mine.

"New rule. No bananas for breakfast."

"Whatever you say, *sir*," I purred.

His breaths were harsh as he inhaled and exhaled several times. He finally stood and reached for his belt. "Goddammit, Gianna. Get on your fucking knees and open your mouth."

This time I couldn't help my triumphant smile and shimmied my shoulders with excitement as I assumed the position. I had been trying to give the man a blow job all weekend, but every time I tried, he threw me on the nearest flat surface and went down on me instead.

Not that I was complaining. The man was a wonder with that damn mouth of his.

Seeming to gain some semblance of control, he grasped my jaw, bent, and kissed me firmly on the mouth. "You know you don't have to do this, right?"

My mouth turned down into a pout. "I never should have told you I've never given head before. You think I'm going to suck at it." His responding grin was pure naughtiness, and I realized what I'd said. "You know what I mean."

"I think you're going to be absolutely fantastic at sucking my dick, Gianna. Your pretty lips are the stuff dreams are made of." His little frown was back. "I just don't want your first experience to be spoiled because I can't seem to control myself around you."

"So you'd rather me get experience elsewhere first?" I asked, blinking up at him and watching his face morph into a rage.

"Don't. Even. Say that," he growled as he unfastened his pants.

Yeah, Auburn Bouvier is a wee bit possessive.

With each downward tick of his zipper, my mouth watered even more. He lowered his pants and then picked up my hand, kissing my fingertips. "If you need me to stop at any time, tap my leg," he said, placing my hand on his strong upper thigh. "Understood?"

"Yes, Auburn." A shudder passed through him, and he wrapped that big fist around his erection and pointed it at my mouth.

"Let me see your tongue, pet." I stuck it out, and he groaned, rubbing the head of his cock against it. From the first taste of him, I was addicted. His thick precum dripped against my tongue as he began to move, pressing just the head inside the cavern of my mouth. "Fuck, Gianna. Open wider for me, baby."

I did, and he slid more of his thickness inside. Closing instinctively around him, I tightened my lips until his eyes rolled back in his head. "Yeah. That's good, my pet. So good."

Swirling my tongue around his crown, I savored the taste and smell of him. The smoothness of the mushroom head and the swollen veins of his shaft. This may have been my first time, but I'd done extensive research—in the form of articles on the art of fellatio—and the tongue-swirling thing seemed to be the go-to move for professional dick suckers worldwide.

"Gi-an-na." My name escaped from him in harsh syllables when I gripped the base in my fist and lowered my head to eat another inch. I kept my eyes cast upward, learning the things that drew the most intense responses from him, and I repeated those actions over and over.

He loved the swirl—thank you very much, *Vogue*—and when I twisted my hand around his hardness, he growled. Letting him pop from my mouth, I dug my tongue into his slit and smiled up at him.

"I love the way you taste, Auburn."

"And I love the way you look with your mouth full of my cock."

I hummed happily at his praise and licked a wide trail down to his balls, giving them each a flicker of my tongue before pulling one into my mouth. My hand had memorized exactly how much pressure he liked from this weekend's activities, and I stroked his erection, using my saliva to lubricate the slide as I worked my tongue around and around the heavy globe in my mouth.

When I switched to the other one, I let my thumb graze his slick tip on every upstroke, and Auburn's low groan filled the room. "You're such a good girl, pet. So fucking amazing."

His fingers were gripping his thighs so tightly, I was surprised he wasn't breaking the skin, and I knew he was fighting for control. But controlled was the opposite of what I wanted him to be.

Releasing him from my mouth, I took one of his hands and placed it on the back of my head.

"Pull my hair and fuck my mouth, Daddy."

We both froze.

Well. Shit. Where the hell had that come from?

As I was trying to formulate something to say... *anything to fix this*... a harsh shudder rocked through his body, and he growled like an angry bear. Plunging both hands into my hair, he twisted and pulled, arching my neck back as his fierce blue eyes filled with thunder.

All traces of his struggles to be gentle were poofed away in a cloud of smoke. I barely recognized his strained voice when he bent and bit my bottom lip. "You're going to take your daddy's cock down that tight little throat, aren't you, baby girl?"

My pussy instantly flooded, and I slid my tongue over the bite, nodding with wide eyes since my vocal cords had apparently forgotten their intended function. But that was probably a good thing since I'd blurted out... *that*.

Tugging my head until my lips were directly over his crown, his fingers massaged my scalp a split second before he shoved deeply into my mouth with an earth-shattering roar. When I gagged, he pulled out to the tip and panted out a reminder for me to breathe through my nose.

Then he slammed in again, hitting the back of my throat, and this time I took it, my eyes watering as he began to thrust roughly in and out.

"God, baby. I've never... had... my cock... sucked like this." His words were ragged and raw as he used me for his pleasure. "Fuck, I'm about to—"

Auburn's face contorted into a painful wince as he pulled from my mouth, his body shaking like a leaf in a hurricane. On my knees before him with my makeup smeared and saliva dripping from my chin, I had never felt more powerful.

"Give me... a minute," he panted. Wrinkles formed around the corners of his eyes as he squished them shut, and I was genuinely afraid that a tendon in his jaw was about to snap. Finally managing to gain some control, he bent at the waist and kissed my sore, wet lips.

"Gianna, pet, I'm about to blow the biggest load of my life. If you don't want me to come in your mouth, you can unbutton your shirt, and I'll come on your tits." He kissed me again, this one more tender. "Either way, you're still my perfect, good girl, okay?"

I loved how reassuring he was, but I knew exactly what I wanted. "In my mouth, please."

A growl of approval scraped through his voice box, and he stood, angling that angry-looking cock back between my lips. Gripping my head, he rocked hard into my mouth as he uttered every filthy curse word known to man. The first gush hit the front of my tongue, and then I sucked him deep, letting him shoot the rest down my throat.

I almost choked from the sheer volume, but he finally pulled out and collapsed into a chair, allowing me to swallow every drop of him.

"Holy shit. That was amazing," he breathed, his entire body loose and relaxed. Opening his eyes, he smiled a sleepy, sated smile before holding out a hand to help me up. He grabbed his napkin and gave himself a cursory clean-up before pulling me into his lap. Then he reached across the table to grab my white linen napkin and gently cleaned the saliva and tears from my face.

My face snuggled into the crook of his neck, and he kissed my temple. "Are you okay, pet? Did I hurt you?"

"No, did I hurt you?" I asked teasingly, and he laughed.

"That was fucking stellar, Gianna. Are you sure you're not secretly a porn star?"

"Not that I know of, but I may look into it now that I know what I'm doing."

He shook his head mirthfully and rubbed my back as silence overtook us, both of us probably thinking about the *Daddy* elephant in the room.

Finally drawing up the courage, I lifted my head, an apology on my swollen lips. "Auburn..."

"Auburn?" came an echo, this one deeper, and I was confused for a second.

"Fuck. It's Cruz," Auburn said, lifting me off his lap and tucking his dick away before attempting to straighten his clothing. "I'm in the dining room," he called out. "I'll be—"

He was interrupted mid-sentence when Cruz pushed open the door. "I was getting worried, boss. You're never late for work." He noticed me then and grinned. "Oh, hey, Gia."

"Out!" Auburn yelled, and poor Cruz startled before taking in the scene, his face turning scarlet.

"Shit!" he said, turning on his heel and running back through the door, calling out, "I'm sorry, guys!"

Auburn was fuming. "That's it. I'm fucking firing him."

Jamming my hands on my waist, I cocked one hip in indignation. "What? No you're not!"

His eyes goggled out at me as he paused his redressing. "Excuse me?"

"You're not firing Cruz. Why would you even say that?"

"He just walked in here right after we... he almost saw..."

"Did he break in, or did you give him a key?" I demanded.

"He's got a key," Auburn mumbled, zipping up his pants. "He comes in and mooches my coffee every morning."

"So, what did he do wrong?"

He stepped toward me until our bodies almost touched. "He flirted with you."

"Oh, good grief, Bouvier. He said 'hi.'"

His angry bull breaths puffed against my forehead as we stared each other down. "Are you always going to call me out on my bullshit?"

"Yes."

He worked his jaw back and forth. "And are you always going to point out when I'm acting like an overbearing jackass?"

"Also yes."

His eyes lingered on mine, losing a bit of their fire as his lips twitched. "Okay," he sighed, leaning down and kissing the tip of my nose. "Now, come on. You've already made me late for work with your wicked ways."

"I didn't hear you complaining a few minutes ago," I pointed out as he took my hand and led me from the room.

"Brat," he mumbled under his breath.

Auburn stared out the window, uncharacteristically quiet as we sat in the back of his Bentley. He wasn't even touching me, which wasn't like him, and nerves bubbled in my stomach. I reached over to lay my hand on his thigh, and he gave me a distant smile, covering my hand with his own before turning his attention back to the outside world.

Something is wrong.

"Auburn," I said, trying and failing to keep my voice steady, "I'm sorry for what I said."

Two lines appeared between his eyebrows as he swiveled his head toward me. "What did you say?"

"You know... the D-word?"

Comprehension dawned on his face after a moment, and he pursed his lips thoughtfully. "Were you under the impression that I didn't like when you called me Daddy?"

Pretty sure my face was the color of a tomato, I shrugged. "It just came out. I've never said that before to anyone; I've never even thought it. And now you're upset with me because I'm some kind of weirdo," I babbled.

His expression turned stern, and I couldn't look at him for another second. My gaze dropped to our clasped hands as I tried to stem the threatening tears of embarrassment.

"What have I told you, Gianna?"

"A lot of things," I mumbled.

Auburn lifted me easily onto his lap and dipped his head until I was forced to look at him. "What have I told you about kinks?"

"Not to be ashamed of what I like."

"No matter what it is," he reiterated. "If you haven't been paying attention, I'm a kinky fucker, Gianna. Nothing is out of bounds. If it turns you on, odds are that it will turn me on too."

A hint of a smile played across my lips as the tension left my body. "What if I have a Little Bo Peep fantasy?"

"Then give me a shepherd's crook and a bonnet, and we'll do the damn thing, little lamb."

A giggle burst from my lips. "I was talking about *me* being Bo Peep."

"Even better," he said, kissing my temple. "And for the record, I've never gotten into 'Daddy play' before, but when you said that... fuck! I've never been more turned on in my life." He nuzzled against my ear. "I'm going to be thinking about it all day long."

I wiggled against the erection that was thickening beneath my ass. "What if you're in a meeting?"

"I'll be thinking of you."

"On the phone?"

"Thinking of you."

"What about in the bathroom?"

"Probably thinking of you while I jerk off."

I laughed and kissed his smooth cheek. "Why were you so... contemplative a few minutes ago?"

Auburn brushed his fingers through my high ponytail. "I really enjoyed our weekend together, Gianna." *Here it comes. The old brushoff.* "I was just sorting through my thoughts. Trying to figure out what this is." He waved a finger between our bodies.

"I thought you said it was only a sexual relationship."

As the car pulled to the curb in front of his office building, he averted his gaze once again, and though I was still sitting on his lap, I felt the distance between us grow.

"You're right. I did say that."

Chapter 16

So lost in my thoughts about Auburn's strange behavior, I almost missed the fact that my apartment building had a brand new sign.

G West Apartments? That was strange. When I left on Friday, it was definitely called West Town.

Cruz's eyes met mine in the rearview mirror. "I'm supposed to walk you in," he said as he put the car in park.

"You sure your boss won't think you're flirting?" I said in a lilting, teasing voice.

His brow crinkled in confusion. "I don't know what the hell is going on. He's never accused me of flirting with one of his women before, but he did apologize to me earlier."

One of his women. That's all you are, Gia.

Cruz got out and came around to open my door and help me from the car. That's when I noticed that there was another new addition to the building—a black awning that covered the door and reached all the way to the street.

"Well, this is nice," I commented as Cruz let me go up the steps before him.

A tall, stoic man in an impeccable black suit stood in front of the door. "Hello. Are you residents, or are you visiting a resident?"

I was about to tell him that it was none of his business when Cruz spoke up. "Miss Moschella lives here."

The suit man's face broke into a friendly smile as he stepped back and opened the door for us. "Excellent. Welcome home, Miss Moschella."

"Oh, um, thank you..."

"Anderson, ma'am."

"Thank you, Anderson."

"Of course. You'll just need to check in at the security desk with Hanson."

Security desk?

Stepping into the lobby, I halted, my mind obviously playing tricks on me. The worn flooring had been replaced with pristine black and white checkerboard tiles, and the walls had a fresh coat of creamy white paint. The previously-unmanned security desk had been replaced with a black marble counter, complete with a man—Hanson, I assumed—standing behind it.

"Am I in the wrong building?" I muttered to Cruz, and he laughed.

"I don't think so. Go ahead and check in. I've got some errands to run."

When he left, I approached the desk. "Hi. I was told to check in here?" It came out as more a question than a statement.

Hanson smiled. "May I see your identification, please?"

I dug through my purse and pulled it out, handing it over.

"Ah, Miss Moschella. Welcome home," he said, handing my ID back after perusing it. "You're in 3B, correct?"

Nodding dumbly, I put my wallet back in my bag. "I'm a little confused," I admitted. "I've been gone for a couple of days, and..." I waved my hand around the room.

"Yes, ma'am. The new owner has made some improvements over the weekend." *I'll say.* He dug through a box and handed me a large manila envelope with my name and apartment number on it. "Here's your paperwork. Read through it, and let me know if you have any questions."

"Thank you, Hanson," I said, turning toward the door leading to the stairs.

"Miss Moschella, I'm sorry, but you can't take the stairs right now. They're updating the lighting."

I shook my head. "How am I supposed to get to my apartment?"

"The elevator," he said, gesturing with one hand. "It was repaired this weekend. The plumbing and hot water heaters were also updated on floors one through three, so you're one of the lucky ones. The rest are scheduled for next week."

I wanted to squeal with excitement. *Long, hot showers in my own apartment? Yes, please!*

After thanking him, I took the elevator up to my floor and entered my apartment. I tossed the envelope on the coffee table and collapsed onto the couch, my mind immediately going to Auburn and the time we'd spent together the past few days.

It had been the best weekend of my life, filled with laughter, great food, and sex. Lots of sex. Auburn Bouvier may fuck like a stallion, but the cuddle times when we were through were my favorites. He turned from a raging beast into a doting sweetheart, holding me close and kissing me softly. Stroking my hair. Making sure I was okay.

Knowing it was crazy to even think this, I couldn't help but feel that it seemed like... more. More than just hot, dirty sex—the kind that had been missing from my life. But I needed to put those *more* thoughts right out of my head and enjoy the ride while it lasted.

The only problem? I was pretty sure I was falling for Auburn. I could hardly believe that two weeks ago, I had hated the man on sight. And now? Well, now I didn't.

He certainly made it difficult not to be captivated by him. When I'd awoken on Saturday morning with his face between my legs, I tossed back the covers to find his wet lips smiling that wicked smile of his. I was already on the verge of coming, but when he informed me that a nice juicy pussy was the best way to start the day, it only took two more flicks of his tongue before I tipped over the edge.

Then he'd fucked me like an animal in the shower, after which he sweetly washed and conditioned my hair, his kisses slow and tender while his magical fingers massaged my scalp.

The quiet, distant Auburn from the car earlier was nothing like the indulgent, attentive man I had spent the past few days with. The man who took me to Magnolia Bakery, where we shared their World-Famous Banana Pudding. The man who held my hand as we explored the city together. The very same man who led me to his balcony and pulled me into his lap so we could watch the rain together on Sunday afternoon.

The entire weekend, I kept waiting for him to suggest that it was time for me to leave, but he never did.

And now, here I was on Monday morning with a sore vagina and more questions than answers. Was he trying to think of a nice way to brush me off? *"Thanks for the sex, pet. Don't call me; I'll call you."*

The thought of that made my insides ache, so I picked up the envelope to try and distract myself. Inside, I found a sheaf of papers that I quickly scanned.

Improvements. Doorman. Security desk.

The last page informed me that there would be security systems installed in each apartment within the week, as well as an emergency medical alert system. *Wow. These new owners move fast.*

My eyes moved down the page, taking in the information about the new system.

If you accidentally set off the alarm, you will need to give your password when the security company calls you.

My mouth dropped open when I read the last line at the bottom of the page.

Your unique password is housefly.

Hold on a damn minute. Auburn was the only one who knew the meaning behind my last name, and now that meaning was my personal password? That couldn't be a coincidence. Did he buy this building?

No. Surely not. Then again, this was Auburn fucking Bouvier we were talking about. The king of going overboard.

There was only one way to find out, so I picked up my phone and tapped his name. When a familiar voice answered, I realized my mistake. I had called the office phone instead of his cell.

"Auburn Bouvier's office," my dad said in his professional tone.

Fuck! Disguising my voice with a British accent I had learned in theater arts class in high school, I said, "Hello, dear. I'd like to speak with Mr. Bouvier."

"May I ask your name and what this is regarding?" I should have known that a random caller wouldn't be put straight through to the big boss.

"Um, yes. Please tell him it's..." I paused, mentally scrambling for a name... "Miss Fly."

"Miss Fly?" Dad asked skeptically.

"Yes. I'm sure he'll remember me. Tell him this is his friend who loves bananas and wet grapes."

I slapped my hand over my mouth. Had I really just said that? *To my Dad?*

I could hear the amusement in my father's voice as he told me to hold. Ten seconds later, a different voice—this one deeper—purred into my ear, "Well, hello, Miss Fly. Do you miss me already?"

Shaking my head, I tried to tamp down the arousal I felt at the sound of his voice. "Auburn, if I ask you a question, will you give me an honest answer?"

"Always."

"Did you buy my apartment building?"

"Yes."

That was it? Just *yes*? Anger flared inside me, heating my face.

"Why in the hell would you do that?"

"The building was being mismanaged."

"So you just decided to take it upon yourself to buy it?"

"It was a sound real estate decision."

"Dammit, Auburn. This is crazy."

His voice was soft when he spoke again. "You're angry."

"Yes, yes, I am. And confused as hell."

"I'll be right over."

"What? No, you don't—"

But he'd disconnected, leaving me staring at my phone in bewilderment.

Chapter 17

"Good morning, Anderson," I said, striding up the steps beneath the awning.

"M-Mister Bouvier. So nice to see you, sir," he replied, practically bowing at the waist as he opened the door for me.

I got an equally deferential response from Hanson at the guard desk inside, only his posture straightened, and he gave me a respectful nod. "Mister Bouvier, so happy to see you, sir."

"Hanson. Everything on track for the installation of the security systems?"

"Yes, sir. They should be completed this week."

"Excellent. Please inform me if there are any issues."

"Of course, sir. Is there anything else I can help you with today?"

"I'm here to visit with Miss Moschella."

Hanson's lips turned up. "Certainly. The lighting is being installed in the stairwells, but the new elevator is up and running."

"Thank you," I said curtly as I pushed the button and then stepped through the shiny doors.

I paused outside apartment 3B, taking a deep breath and preparing myself for the angry little wildcat on the other side of the door. As soon as I knocked, the door swung open, and there she was, eyes narrowed and full lips pursed. *Fucking magnificent.*

"What. Are. You. Doing. Here?" she bit out.

"You're upset with me," I replied calmly as I strode through the door.

"You're damn right, I am," she said, slamming the door behind me. We faced off, her cheeks and chest flushed pink with ire. She was absolutely stunning. "What could have possibly possessed you to buy this building and do all this... stuff to it?"

"Are you unhappy with some of the improvements? I can change anything you don't like. Perhaps put the shitty old hot water heaters back in?"

"No, that's actually..." Her eyebrows pressed together. "That's not the point, Auburn. You've stepped way over the line here."

"Then we'll move the line," I suggested, and her face went from pink to red as she stomped her foot in frustration. *Ah, yes, my little pet. Show me that fire.*

"God, you're infuriating." She did another of those adorable foot stomps, and that was it for me.

I removed my cufflinks and dropped them on the wooden coffee table. "Take your clothes off," I commanded as I shrugged my jacket over my shoulders and down my arms.

Her eyes widened and then dropped to mere slits. "This is not the time for *that*, Bouvier."

My tie hit the floor, and I began slowly unbuttoning my shirt. "Oh, this is exactly the time for *that*, sweetheart."

She marched toward me and swatted ineffectively at my hands, though I could see the desire blooming in her eyes as I revealed my bare torso. After removing my vest and shirt, I grasped the back of her neck and pulled her toward me.

"We're going to fuck, and it's going to be hot and filthy, pet. And it will make you feel better."

"I don't want to feel better. I want to be mad," she retorted.

"That's exactly how I want you." Sliding my hand to the back of her head, I held her still as my mouth crashed to hers, her lips stiffening as my tongue sought entrance into that sweet cavern. "Let me in, Gianna," I murmured against her lips. After another few seconds of stubbornness, she did, and it was glorious, our tongues battling hard and fast as she gripped my shoulders. My other hand grabbed her round ass and hauled her against me so she could feel exactly how turned on I was.

Trailing kisses across her flushed cheek, I worked my way down her neck, sinking my teeth softly into the juncture of neck and shoulder.

"Ever since the first time I saw anger flash in those green eyes of yours, I knew I had to fuck you while you were mad." Lifting my head, I pressed my lips hard against hers. "And since I don't plan on making you angry very often, I feel that I should take this opportunity to fulfill my fantasy."

"Screw your fantasy."

"I'd rather screw you into the back of that couch. A few orgasms will greatly relieve your tension."

"I'm not tense; I'm pissed," she said, but I noticed that desire had taken its place alongside the anger in her eyes.

"Good. Now get your clothes off." I released her and reached for my belt buckle, raising a challenging eyebrow when she didn't move. "Don't deny me, Gianna. Let me fuck some of that sass out of you, and then we'll talk."

She glared at me and then—*fuck yes*—she pulled her dress off over her head and slung it to the ground. "You better bring your A-game, Bouvier, because I've got a lot of sass right now."

My lips twitched with a restrained smile. I fucking loved this. "Better take those panties off too, unless you want me to destroy another pair."

Her teeth gritted, but she reached down and pulled them off before flinging them at my chest. I caught them and brought them to my nose, inhaling deeply and releasing a low groan. Spreading the satin in my fingers, I dragged my tongue through the crotch, tasting her essence as I held her spellbound with my eyes. "Fucking delicious," I told her, giving her panties another lick.

I tucked them into my pocket so I could enjoy them later, and after shedding my pants and underwear, I removed a condom from my wallet. My arm banded around her waist, pulling her to me and pumping my erection against her stomach. "Feel what you do to me, pet?"

She leaned forward, and I readied myself for her kiss, but she grasped my lower lip between her teeth and bit me. I was equal parts amused and turned on by her ferocity.

"Oh, you are a feisty one, aren't you?" I asked, running my tongue over the bite and tasting the metallic tang of blood.

"You have no idea," she retorted.

"I have a feeling I'm about to find out," I said, spinning her around and lowering her chest against the back of the couch. Holding her down with my forearm across her back, I slid my fingers up the inside of one thigh, reveling in her dripping arousal. "My, my, Miss Moschella. You seem to have made quite a mess down here."

"Fuck you," she snapped.

"You'll get your chance, my sweet impatient pet."

"I'm—" Whatever she was going to say was abandoned as I plunged two fingers into her pussy, immediately finding that sensitive spot inside her. I closed my eyes as I finger-fucked her, concentrating on her sweet moans and the scent of her desire. My cock grew even harder at the knowledge that her desire belonged solely to me.

Gianna began shoving back against my hand, riding my fingers and clamping those tight walls around them. "God, why does this feel so good?"

"Because you're fire, Gianna. All you need is someone to stoke the flames, and you could burn the world down with your heat." Taking my thumb to her clit, I massaged exactly how I knew she liked—small flickers followed by firm, circular pressure—while my fingertips concentrated on her G-spot.

She bucked hard as she cried out, her pussy flooding my fingers. I smoothed my hand up and down her back as she recovered. "There you go, my pet. Feel better now?"

"No," she gritted out stubbornly.

"Okay," I conceded, "more orgasms then." Stepping behind her, I rolled on the condom and kicked her legs out wide before gripping her hips and rubbing my crown through her center. "Ready to burn for me, Gianna?"

She wiggled her ass in answer, and I couldn't hold back my smile. Lining my erection up with her entrance, I pushed in to the root. "Fuck!" she cried.

"Are you sore from my cock being inside you so many times this weekend?"

"Yes, you smug bastard."

I chuckled as I rotated my hips to stretch her out. "Only one way to fix that. A nice fuck."

"There's nothing nice about the way you fuck, Bouvier."

She wasn't wrong. Pulling almost all the way out, I slapped her ass before I slammed my dick inside her. Hard. Her long, needy moan was everything I wanted. Gripping her hip with one hand and her ponytail with the other, I gave in to my basest desires. I fucked her. *Really* fucked her. Long, punishing strokes that had her dripping all over me as her hips moved in a counter-rhythm to mine.

"Jesus, Gianna," I groaned. "I love the way you fuck me back. You're so wild and beautiful." The sounds of her wetness and our skin slapping together filled the room, and I drove into her harder and faster as she came around me, screaming my name. "That's it, pet. Give me that cum."

I wrapped my hand around her throat, tugging until she was standing upright as I continued to shove my cock roughly up into her. "Feeling better?" I inquired.

One of Gianna's hands reached up and behind us, burying her fingers in my hair and twisting violently. "Still. Pissed," she panted, and I lowered my other hand to her cunt, rubbing her clit with two fingers.

"Then I guess I need to make you come again."

Her head lolled back against my shoulder, and she whimpered, "Auburn, I can't."

"Yes, pet, you can. I'll talk you through it. Just give me one more." Slowing my pace, I whispered how beautiful she was, how sexy and alluring, into her ear until I finally felt her pulsing around me. "Good girl, Gianna. Come with me."

We shared our orgasms with each other, hips rocking and grinding until every tremble had faded away. Then I pulled out, turned her around, and kissed her deeply for a long time before carrying her to the bathroom. After I cleaned us both up, we settled face to face on her bed.

"Now. You wanted to have a discussion with me?" I asked, and my wild woman gave me a smirk.

"Why did you buy this building?"

I stroked a finger down her pinkened cheek. "I'm not a man who sits around and waits for things to happen, Gianna. I'm the man who *makes* things happen."

She was silent for a long moment, her gaze dropping before lifting back to mine. "Do you do this kind of thing with all the women you fuck?" she asked quietly.

Anger bubbled up inside me at her words. "Do not say that, Gianna Moschella. You are much more than some woman I'm fucking. But no, I've never bought a building because a particular woman lived there." I rolled onto my back and covered my eyes with my forearm, struggling to come up with the words I wanted to say. "I think I'm a little obsessed with you."

She snuggled up next to me, her arm snaking around me as she rested her head on my chest. "That's okay. I think I'm a little obsessed with you too."

An hour later, I entered the elevator at my office, and Tora scurried in after me. "Morning, Mr. Bouvier. Can I ride up with you? I have to talk to Tony about a shipping delay on some thread."

"Of course," I said with a brief nod, my mind still on Gianna. We'd talked a little more, and she was much calmer when I left. Feeling Tora's eyes on me, I asked, "Why are you staring at me?"

"Just wondering what you've been up to that messed up your hair," he replied with a sly grin.

I glanced at my reflection in the mirrored wall of the elevator and saw the damage Gianna had done to the back of my hair. "Shit. Thanks," I mumbled, flattening it with my hand. When the elevator opened, I gestured for Tora to exit first and followed him out. Knocking on Tony's desk as I passed, I told him, "I need to order some flowers." Gianna's interview was tomorrow, and I wanted to send her something for good luck.

Tony couldn't keep the sigh from his voice when he asked, "Magdalena?"

"No, for..." I cut myself off with his daughter's name on the tip of my tongue. Shit! "Actually, I think I'd like to order them myself. Just get me the number. Thank you, Tony."

By the time I sat down and turned on my computer, the website for the florist was on my screen. On second thought, maybe it wasn't such a good idea to send flowers from my regular place. What if they put the recipient's name or address on the bill, and Tony saw it? I would need to order from somewhere else and have the bill sent to my apartment.

I spent the next twenty minutes searching local florists' websites, grinning like a fool when I found one that would deliver flowers with a variety of gourmet desserts. Including the one Gianna had admitted was her favorite during our talks this weekend.

Picking up the phone, I dialed the number. "Hello, this is Auburn Bouvier, and I'd like to place a very special order."

Chapter 18

My dad was leaning against the counter chatting with Lehra when I walked into the lobby at Bouvier. Sneaking up behind him, I covered his eyes with my hands.

"Guess who?" I sang.

"My favorite girl in the whole wide world. Taylor Swift."

I pulled my hands from his eyes and planted them on my waist as I cocked out a hip. "Well, that was rude."

Dad was grinning when he turned around. "I'm kidding. My lovely daughter will always be my favorite."

I pursed my lips. "Better."

"How was your interview, sweetie?"

"My nerves are completely shot," I told him, fanning myself with one hand.

He hugged me, and his embrace was warm and everything I needed to feel just then. "I'm sure you knocked 'em dead, Gia." Pulling back, his face was infused with so much pride, it made my chest ache. After only a little over two weeks, my dad and I had grown much closer. We shared a couple dinners and several lunches together each week, and we talked on the phone every day.

"You definitely knocked their socks off," Lehra said, reaching over the counter and gripping one of my hands. "You look so professional. Want to have dinner tonight and tell me all about it?"

"Sounds good. Call me," I said, giving her a little finger wave as Dad led me toward the elevator bank.

As we rode up to the fiftieth floor, he said, "You really do look fantastic today." Picking up my hand and peering at the buttons on the sleeve of my dark green jacket, he asked, "Is this a Bouvier?"

Damn, I should have known he would notice that.

I was saved from answering when the elevator doors opened, and I quickly switched the subject. "There were so many people being interviewed today, Dad. I thought it went well, but there was some pretty stiff competition."

"I'm sure you did just fine, honey. Now, sit and tell me all about it."

We chatted for a few minutes, and then I had the sense that the room was too full to hold any more air. Looking up, my eyes met the icy blue ones of Auburn Bouvier when he emerged from his office. He was wearing a black suit, ivory shirt, and patterned burgundy tie, looking every bit the powerful man that he was.

Our eyes held for what seemed like an eternity before I remembered that we weren't alone. Suppressing the urge to leap over the coffee table, I stood calmly and put on a practiced smile. He snapped out of our mutual trance at the same time and gave me a respectful nod.

"Gianna. It's so nice to see you again," he said.

"You as well, Mister Bouvier." I held out my hand, and he shook it with a bemused smile on his sculpted lips, his middle finger dragging teasingly against my palm as he released me.

"The suit looks lovely on you."

Oh my God! Shut the fuck up, Auburn.

Dad stood as well. "I noticed she was wearing one of ours." He turned questioning eyes on me, probably wondering how I bought an outfit this expensive, but I was saved again by Auburn.

"When Gianna told me of her luggage woes, I offered her a voucher for a free suit," he explained to my dad so smoothly, it was difficult to remember that it was a total fabrication. "I do like employees and their families to represent the brand. And Gianna certainly represents us well."

Dipping my head in acknowledgement, I said, "Thank you again for your kindness, Mister Bouvier. One of the female interviewers noticed. She's apparently a fan of your clothing also."

Auburn licked his bottom lip. "I'm happy it worked out for you. Nothing would please me more than for you to wear *only Bouvier*." He literally purred the last two words, and the innuendo was not lost on me. In fact, it soaked my panties.

"Excellent idea," my dad said agreeably, thankfully unaware that his boss was turning my vagina into Niagara Falls. He walked to his desk and rifled through some papers.

As soon as Dad's back was turned, Auburn's gaze strayed up and down my body, his eyes burning me up. "Gianna should do some modeling for us. She has exactly the look that Bouvier wants to portray. Classy. Elegant." He bit his bottom lip and mouthed, "Sexy."

"Stop it," I hissed quietly, doing my best not to giggle at his sly flirtations.

"Here we are," Dad said, striding back to us and handing me two slender cards. The cardstock was deep red, and the writing was in a chic white script, informing me that each was good for two-hundred dollars worth of Bouvier clothing at their store on Madison Avenue.

"Oh, no. I really couldn't," I protested, attempting to hand them back.

"Nonsense," Dad said. "Mister Bouvier kindly gives us these each quarter to share with friends or family. I should have thought of it earlier."

"Thank you. Both of you." My eyes flitted nervously between the men, both staring at me with differing expressions. Dad's with love and pride, and Auburn's with... well, there was no doubt what his eyes were conveying.

"Honey, I have a few things to wrap up, and then we can go to lunch. Did you have breakfast today?"

Two faces awaited my answer, and neither looked happy when I shook my head. "My stomach was too tied in knots to eat a thing."

Dad sighed. "It's going to be about an hour before I can get out of here, so let me grab you a snack." He turned to his boss. "Gianna has trouble with her blood sugar and has to eat regularly."

"You don't say?" the tall, enigmatic man asked, his blue eyes snapping as he traced his bottom lip with his long index finger. "That's something you need to be very cautious of, Gianna. I believe we have some grapes in the refrigerator, Tony. I understand they're a high-sugar fruit."

"I'll get them," Dad said with a smile, and I wasn't sure how he could be oblivious to the palpable passion thickening the atmosphere.

As soon as the door to the kitchen closed behind him, Auburn dropped all pretense of professionalism and lifted me over the coffee table and against his firm body, his hands cupping my face.

"Thank you for the delivery you sent this morning," I told him.

"I'm so glad you liked it, sweetheart." He pressed his lips hard to mine before pulling back with the perfect amount of suction. "God, you are so fucking beautiful. I want nothing more than to take you into my office and bend you over my desk."

Lifting an eyebrow, I asked, "And what would you do with me once you had me bent over?"

He bent and nibbled my earlobe. "I would turn your sweet little ass red for not eating breakfast."

My breathing picked up about forty notches. "And then?"

"I think we both know what would happen after that, pet. I'd use my—" He backed away suddenly as the doorknob to the kitchen turned.

Still reeling from the onslaught of lust that his words had evoked, my gaze fell on his lush mouth. Widening my eyes at Auburn, I tapped my lips twice. He looked confused for a second and then realized that he must be wearing my lipstick.

"Fuck," he mouthed, shifting toward his office and calling over his shoulder, "Tony, on second thought, why don't you take Gianna to lunch now? You can finish those invoices when you return." While my dad was distracted, I quickly swiped around my own lips to clean up any smears.

"Oh, if you're sure?"

"Yes, that's perfectly fine. Go celebrate with your daughter." Keeping his face averted, he entered his office and closed the door behind him.

Dad lifted the cup of grapes and shrugged. "Guess we can snack on these on the way to the deli."

Once in the elevator, he shook his head. "I don't know what's gotten into Bouvier the past couple of days. He's been downright pleasant. Maybe he's got a new lady friend."

I fake coughed to cover my giggle before schooling my features.

"You never know, Dad."

Chapter 19

"And then I opened the box to find *three dozen* chocolate covered strawberries," Gianna said. My cousin Beau chuckled while his wife giggled with my beautiful lady.

I smiled indulgently and put my arm around Gianna. "Okay, so maybe I went a little overboard."

She looked up at me, her eyes showing nothing but adoration, despite her teasing. "Your middle name is Overboard," she informed me, planting a soft kiss on my jaw.

It was Friday—almost six weeks since I'd first laid eyes on Gianna Moschella—and Beau and Charli had arrived in New York today. Their son, L.J., was sleeping peacefully in his portable playpen beside the couch.

"So, how did your interview go?" Charli asked. She and Gianna had hit it off instantly. They'd talked like old friends all throughout dinner, leaving me time to catch up with Beau.

"It was good," Gianna replied, tilting her head back and forth, "but there were so many applicants, and most of them were older than me, so I'm not getting my hopes up."

"Age doesn't matter," Beau piped up, sweeping Charli over onto his lap. "Not when you find the one, right Peach?" His hand was on her ass and his lips on her neck, and I was pretty sure we weren't talking about accounting anymore.

"Why do you call her Peach?" I asked, curious because I'd heard him use that nickname several times tonight.

"Because she's sweet and juicy as fuck," he said, earning him a playful swat from his wife.

My cousin was a Navy SEAL for years before opening his own private security company, and the man was the very definition of badass. I certainly never expected to see him like this over a woman. I went to their wedding last year, and of course they were all lovey-dovey at the ceremony and reception, but I figured that would die out a little as time passed. Apparently, I figured wrong. If anything, they were even more in love now. And in lust, if their wandering hands were any indication.

Drawing Gianna closer, I said, "I was just wondering since Gianna's favorite lotion is peach-scented." I winked down at her, and her eyes widened as she mouthed, "Stop it!"

Charli's eyes darted back and forth between us, and her lips turned up in amusement. "From the naughty looks on your faces, I assume you're talking about that peach aftercare lotion with the arnica and aloe?" She turned back to her husband and kissed his cheek. "We really like that one too, don't we, babe?"

He growled at her. "You remembered to pack it, didn't you?"

"Thank God you two are on the other end of the house," I quipped. "I really don't need to hear all that."

"It's not like we're not used to someone listening. When we started dating, Beau's roommate, Cam, liked listening."

"Cam Fitz?" I asked with a grin. "How is that crazy fucker doing?"

"Married," Beau informed me. "For six months, and to his high school sweetheart, though they were separated for a really long time before they found each other again."

"They are so sweet together," Charli gushed. "Cam was always so... *Cam*. I never thought I'd see him settle down, but I guess he was just waiting for the right one."

I know exactly how that feels, I thought as I kissed the side of Gianna's head.

The baby stirred in his portable playpen, and Gianna jumped to her feet, scrunching her shoulders up excitedly. "Oh, please, can I get him? He's been asleep since y'all got here, and I've been dying to hold him."

Charli nodded, and my eyes were glued to Gianna's fine ass as she bent over to pick L.J. up. When she turned around with the little one cuddled to her chest, something flip-flopped inside me. Very foreign thoughts began to slither through my brain. Gianna's belly full with *my* child. Gianna holding *our* son or daughter.

What the fuck is wrong with you, Bouvier? You've never been interested in having kids.

My dick disagreed as I became aroused watching her settle onto the couch beside me. She stroked L.J.'s hair from his face with a gentle hand as she cooed at him, and all the breath left my body at the beautiful sight.

"Well, hello there, handsome. Did you have a nice nap?" The kid nuzzled his nose against her chest before lifting his head, his eyes fully open now.

"Ma-ma?"

"Mama is right over there," Gianna said, speaking softly to the boy as she swiveled her body so he could see his mother. Charli gave him a cute little finger wave, and he smiled before snuggling back against Gianna.

When I was finally able to look away, I saw Beau staring directly at me. He tossed me a wink as if he knew the thoughts running through my head. I turned my gaze back to Gianna, who was playfully gobbling at L.J.'s chubby little hand, making him laugh hysterically.

Maybe...

"He's probably wet," Charli said, standing from their side of the sectional couch. "I need to change him and then get some food into him because the only time he really gets cranky is when he's hungry. And no one wants to witness our son throwing a hangry fit." She smiled at me.

"Out of respect for your lovely furniture, I'll feed him in the kitchen. He's a bit of a Messy Marvin."

She and Beau shared a look. The kind of intimate look that parents share when talking about their kids, and I was suddenly jealous. And confused by the direction my thoughts were going.

"I'll help," Gianna said, lifting from the couch and leading Charli down the hallway.

I stared after her. She was going to be such a wonderful mother one day, and the thought of it being with another man? I had to suppress an angry growl at the idea of it.

"Well, well, well," Beau said when the girls were out of earshot. "How the mighty have fallen."

"Shut the fuck up," I groaned, rubbing a hand up my face and over my hair. "Like you have room to talk."

He grinned without an ounce of shame. "It took me a little time to come to terms with my feelings for Charli. I was worried about her being younger, not to mention my less-than-stellar past with women. But the more time I spent with her, I realized none of that mattered. I'd found my *one*." I lifted my eyes to his piercing green gaze. "Have you?"

"I don't know, man. Gianna's a lot younger than me. She's only twenty-three."

Beau tilted his head to the side in thought. "She doesn't act like it. Charli's twenty-nine, and they get along great. If you hadn't told me, I never would have realized Gianna was that young." He picked up his beer and took a swig before resting his elbows on his knees and leaning toward me. "If you like her like I think you like her, don't fuck it up because of numbers."

"It's still early..." I couldn't even seem to articulate my thoughts because they sounded strange even in my head. "I try to tell myself that we're just having fun, but when I think of letting her go... I'm not sure I'll be able to."

Beau leaned back in his chair, crossing one ankle over his knee as a mischievous smile took over his face. He lifted his beer bottle in a toast. "Welcome to the club, cuz. Welcome to the motherfucking club."

Hours later, Gianna and I were in my bed, cuddling after a romp in the shower, where I'd fucked her against the tiles until I had to put my hand over her mouth to keep her from waking the entire house.

"I really like your family," she said, giving me a soft kiss on my chest.

"They like you too, pet." I swiped some hair that had escaped from her long braid away from her face.

"You know, it's a really small world. Charli's friend used the same neurologist that I used when I was in Texas."

"Really?" I leaned in for a kiss but froze a half inch away as her words sank in. "Wait. Why did you see a neurologist?"

"Well, you know I have issues with hypoglycemia, right?" I nodded, and she continued. "It's caused by a pituitary tumor."

Tumor? And what the fuck is a pituitary?

Swallowing the iceberg-sized lump in my throat, I croaked, "What does that mean?"

"The pituitary gland is about the size of a pea. A tumor there can cause hormonal imbalances, including messing with blood sugar levels."

She was speaking so matter-of-factly, while I was trying not to hyperventilate.

"And where is this gland?"

"It's at the base of the brain."

The words pounded through my head like waves crashing on a beach.

Brain. Tumor.

My Gianna has a brain tumor.

This couldn't be happening. My mouth refused to form the words I wanted to ask because I didn't know if I could handle the answer.

Because...

I...

I...

I love her.

Chapter 20

"Gianna..." Auburn breathed, and even in the darkness, I could make out the moisture in his eyes. "Am I going to lose you?" I'd never heard his voice tremble before. He was always in total control.

"What? No, of course not," I assured him, caressing his beautiful face with my fingertips. "It's benign and hasn't changed in six years."

His body seemed to melt as he pulled me closer, resting his forehead against mine. "Thank God. I can't... I can't lose you, Gianna." His kisses were tender brushes against my forehead, my nose, my cheeks. And finally, my lips. When I teased my tongue into his mouth, he reciprocated.

Though this kiss was the absolute sweetest we had shared, it was also the most passionate. Because something else was there too... emotion.

From Auburn Bouvier?

His tongue coaxed mine easily until nothing existed except for him. This man... *God, this man!* He occupied my mouth, my body, and if I was being honest, my heart. My fingers found moisture at the outside corner of his eye, and I brushed it away before plunging my hands into his thick, dark hair.

When he finally pulled away, he rolled onto his back and flicked the lamp on. Squinting against the sudden intrusion on my retinas, I peered at him as he sat up against the headboard.

"Gianna, come here." Strangely, it didn't sound like a command from Mister Commanding himself; instead, it was more of a plea. When I rose to my knees, he pulled me to him, lifting one of my legs to rest on the other side of his hips so I was straddling him.

We were completely naked, of course. Auburn insisted on naked sleeping; said he enjoyed the "unencumbered access" it gave him to my body. I stayed over at his apartment a few nights a week though he always asked me to stay every night.

I just couldn't. It's not that I didn't want to; I simply needed to put some distance between us for my own sanity. But this seemed like the opposite of distance, and I didn't know how to feel about it. The more space I tried to insert, the more I felt drawn to him.

He's going to absolutely crush you when he dumps you, Gia.

Was that what was going on now? He didn't want to deal with me and my complex medical issues?

His big hands cupped my face, and his brow furrowed. "I can't lose you, Gianna," he repeated. "Because..." *Oh God, here it comes.* He closed his eyes and inhaled a deep breath before blowing it out slowly. When he opened his eyelids, those blue beacons shone directly into my soul.

"Because I'm in love with you."

Well.

I didn't expect that.

My heart thumped like a bass drum. "Auburn..."

He quieted me with a soft finger against my lips. "I don't expect you to say it back. Not yet. I just had to tell you how I feel. I'm not very good at this emotional stuff, Gianna." His brow puckered again. "I don't know how..."

Seeing his struggle, I calmed him with my smile. "I think you're doing just fine, Mister Bouvier." Pulling one of his hands from my face, I placed it over my chest. "You said what you were feeling, and it made my heart race, so you're doing something right."

My handsome man wrapped his arms around me and pulled me close until my face was nestled against the side of his neck, which had quickly become my most comforting place to be.

"I don't trust easily, Gianna, but I trust you. You're the realest person I know. You're kind and smart and so fucking sassy." I smiled at that, pressing a kiss to his pulse. "I know it seems fast, but this didn't come out of the blue. I've been falling for you since the moment I laid eyes on you." He chuckled and admitted, "Of course, my initial reaction was entirely physical because, let's be honest, you're sexy as hell. But when you challenged me that first time in my limo, you made something inside me stir to life."

"I thought you were hot too but a total ass."

"I was definitely an ass."

"A total ass," I corrected and felt his chest shake with laughter.

"Total ass," he amended, kissing the top of my head. "Then you made me laugh, and it felt so fucking good. It always seemed like women were trying to put their best face on around me. They wouldn't speak their minds. But you're not like that. You're more of a true partner to me than anyone I've ever been with."

"I think you lied to me."

Auburn stiffened, and I straightened up to face him, finding worry in his eyes. "What did I say?"

Taking his face in my hands, I kissed him softly. "You said you weren't good at the emotional stuff, and here you are being all swoony." He visibly relaxed, and I swallowed the lump that had formed in my throat. I had fallen so hard for this man.

His eyes searched my face, and his hands covered mine. "I want to make love to you, Gianna. Like, *really* make love." I nodded because that sounded like the best idea I'd heard in a long time. Then he added, "Raw."

A small giggle escaped my lips. "Everytime we're together, it's raw." *And dirty. And hot.* Then it dawned on me. "Oh. You mean... *raw.*"

He nodded. "I want to feel every single inch of you." His eyes searched my face. "I'm clean. I've never gone unprotected with anyone, nor have I wanted to. But it's completely your call."

"I haven't either, and I'm on birth control." His teeth sunk into his bottom lip, awaiting my answer, and I tugged it free with my thumb and brushed my tongue over it. "Yes," I whispered against his mouth.

His moan was a low, satisfied "Mmmmm" as our lips merged and our tongues tangled. Reaching between us, I drew his big cock away from his stomach and lifted up on my knees to account for his impressive length. My hips rotated against his crown, wetting him with my desire. As I dripped down his shaft, I stroked him with my natural lubricants.

"You're so hard," I purred into his mouth. "Always so ready for me."

"Always." Circling the inside of my lips with his tongue, he ended the kiss with a soft peck before looking down between us. I did too. "We're beautiful together."

His words were raw and gritty, and my heart raced as I sank down onto the tip.

I felt so damn vulnerable. Like I was giving a part of me away. When our eyes met, and I saw so much love reflected back at me, I gave that part willingly. Spreading my knees, I took more of him and got my first real taste of the intimacy that comes with trusting someone enough to take them inside your body like this.

Tilting my head forward, I rested my forehead against his, our eyes meeting and our breaths blending between us. "You feel so good inside me, Auburn." I was extremely sensitive down there since I'd gotten a fresh wax this week, and his thick, smooth head pressing against my walls with nothing between us only intensified the hypersensation.

"I've never felt anything better, Gianna. You're so slick and warm." His hands skated up my thighs to grip my hips. His voice was commanding, yet so gentle, when he requested, "Take all of me, pet. I'm yours."

He's mine.

Both of our mouths dropped open when I slid down all the way to the hilt.

"Don't move," he whispered. "Let me just feel you like this for a while."

The overwhelming intimacy of the moment, combined with the satisfying ache of having Auburn inside me with no barriers, triggered a surprise orgasm to bloom between my legs.

"Oh..." was all I managed to say as I tightened around him, my body shaking with the force of it. Soft, unintelligible noises were making their way up my throat as Auburn held me down on him and watched me with what looked like wonder.

"That's it, Gianna. Keep your eyes on mine and give me everything." His gaze never wavered for a second as he talked me through it. Sweet, encouraging words, eschewing his usual dirty talk for the time being.

As my intense climax subsided, twin tears snaked down my face, and Auburn frowned. "What's wrong, pet. Are you hurt?"

I swallowed, fighting this strange urge to cry, and shook my head. "I'm feeling very vulnerable right now. I'm sorry. I don't know..."

He pulled my head immediately against the side of his neck, and I quieted. This man always knew exactly what I needed, even before I knew myself.

"Better?"

"Yes," I murmured into my happy place, wrapping my arms around his neck.

Auburn released the band around the bottom of my high braid and loosened it with gentle fingers, leaving me with a long, wavy ponytail. While his neck brought me comfort, my hair seemed to do the same for him. Every night I'd spent with him, I woke up with either his hand or his face buried in my hair.

Wrapping my locks around one hand, he used the other to grip my bottom and pull me closer to him. Despite just having an orgasm sent straight from heaven, fresh need blossomed inside of me, and I began to move.

"That's it, baby," he whispered, kissing my ear as his hips lifted to meet mine. "You feel amazing wrapped around me." He rested his face against my shoulder while mine remained nestled against his neck.

And we rocked. Smooth and slow, like gentle waves on a mostly calm sea. Our bodies and our souls wrapped around each other, and I sensed something shifting. Something wonderful and profound. With certainty, I knew this was special. *We* were special.

"I love you too," I told him, and he stilled before rolling us so that he was on top of me while keeping us connected.

"You mean it?" he asked, his gorgeous face hovering over mine.

I nodded. "I've never meant anything more."

He gave me a gentle smile. "I haven't been in love before. I'll probably screw something up."

"And I'll call you out on it when you do."

His smile broadened to something purely luminous. "I would expect nothing less. Now, wrap your legs around me, and I'll show you the benefits of being mine."

Mine. I liked the sound of that. Curling my legs around his waist, I pulled him deeper, and his mouth covered mine. Lips and tongues explored, as if this was our first kiss again, learning each other anew in this new chapter. Our love chapter.

Auburn's sweet lovemaking may have differed from his usual hard fucking, but it was no less intense. Maybe even more so because of all the emotions roiling between us. His thick cock was as unyielding as ever, taking the deepest parts of me, but his hips moved slowly. Sensually. With unhurried grinds that stimulated every nerve ending in my pussy.

"You're close," he murmured against my lips, and I nodded. "Wait for me."

Holding himself up on one elbow, he trailed his other hand down my side, pausing to cradle my breast and thumb my nipple before sliding beneath my bottom. His fingers dug into my soft flesh as he pulled, molding my hip to his.

"Ah! That's... that's the spot," I cried when his crown stroked over the tender area that had me squeezing around him.

"I want you coming around my cock when I fill you with my cum for the first time."

His rough demand had every muscle in my body contracting until I was curled around him, clinging to him like my life depended on it.

"You're going to take Daddy's cum inside you like a good girl, aren't you?"

Oh, holy shit! Why is that such a turn-on?

"Yes," I whispered.

"Because you love me?"

I pressed my face against his shoulder as his words triggered my orgasm. "No," I panted, "because *you* love *me*."

"Ah, fuck, Gianna," he growled, hitting me hard and deep as he buried his face in the pillow beside my head. My climax started down low but quickly spread until every cell in my body was vibrating... for him. For my love.

My teeth bit into his shoulder, and my fingernails scored his back. He grunted, sinking all the way in and holding himself there as he warmed my inner walls with his hot seed. His big body collapsed on top of mine, depleting what little air was left in my lungs.

"Can't. Breathe," I managed to eke out, and he lifted himself on his elbows, his gaze meeting mine with mutual affection.

"I do love you, my pet," he breathed. "I adore everything about you."

"I love you too," I told him, overwhelmed by the depth of my feelings for this man. He seemed to be feeling the same way because his eyes closed as he rubbed his nose against mine.

"Would you like for me to give you a bath?"

God, could he be any more perfect?

"I'd rather cuddle in this bed and bask in the afterglow until we both pass smooth out."

His lips touched mine with the softest kiss. "Okay, baby. I like the thought of you sleeping with part of me inside you."

When he pulled out, I clamped my legs together to keep from leaking all over his pristine white sheets, but Auburn had a different idea. Prying my legs apart, he knelt with his face right at crotch level.

"Auburn, I'm going to make a stain," I complained.

"So fucking beautiful," he murmured, watching his cum seep from me. Then he looked up and winked. "And you already made a wet spot because you were dripping all over for me."

"You sound awfully smug, Mister Bouvier," I teased.

Kissing my belly, he rose and slid off the bed. "Not smug. I'm just confident that I know exactly how to take care of my woman."

His woman. Sa-woon!

I admired his firm ass as he walked across the room, and he caught me when he glanced over his shoulder. "See something you like, Miss Moschella?" he asked, shaking his fine tush at me.

"Ooh, let me turn on some MC Hammer so you can dance for me again."

He strode into the bathroom, calling back, "Keep it up, pet. You're about to fuck around and find out."

A giggle escaped my lips. I loved sweet Auburn. I lived for sexy Auburn. But I absolutely adored playful Auburn. I had a feeling not many people got to see him like I did when he let his walls down.

When he returned, he cleaned me up before laying a towel across the messy wet spot on the bed. "Come here, sweetheart," he said, flicking off the lamp before pulling me close to his warm body and covering us.

I smoothed a hand over the bite mark on his shoulder and the scratches I'd left down his back. "I'm sorry I bit and scratched you."

His lips curled upward against my forehead. "Baby girl, with sex like that, I would gladly bear every single one of your marks." He paused for a moment before saying, "You little savage."

"Hush," I said on a giggle. "It's your fault for making it feel so good."

"Ah, it's my cross to bear," he said dramatically. His hand swept slowly up and down my back as I nuzzled against his hard chest. "Gianna, will you tell me what happened with your last boyfriend? I know you said you broke up about five months ago."

Sighing, I nodded my head. I didn't want there to be secrets between us, though I hated talking about my ex.

"Ryan Weston and I met sophomore year of college. He was a finance major, so we had a lot of classes together. We became friends, and then we started dating. I would say it became serious after about six months." Hearing an abrasive noise, I placed my hand on Auburn's jaw. "If you're going to grind your teeth into nubs, I'm not telling you anything else."

He softened at my touch. "Sorry. I'll try to be good."

I took a deep breath and continued. "Everything was going great. We got along well and enjoyed spending time together when we weren't studying. I didn't like studying with Ryan because he goofed off too much. Plus, I liked going to the library, and he preferred this little diner with cheap food and free coffee."

Auburn reached for my hair, sifting his fingers through it as I spoke. "One night, about a year ago, I finished up early and went to the diner to grab a quick bite. Ryan was there, but there was a girl sitting across the table from him."

"Fuck," Auburn muttered.

"I didn't really suspect anything because he seemed happy to see me and scooted over so I could sit beside him in the booth. He introduced me to Emma and said they'd been studying for a class together. That wasn't really unusual because I had a group that I studied with, and it was a mixture of guys and girls. So, no big deal, right?"

"Hmmm," he answered noncommittally.

"Ryan's hometown was about forty-five minutes from our campus, so he went home at least once a month, sometimes twice."

"He didn't ask you to go home with him?"

"No. I'd met his parents a couple times when they came to campus for parents' weekend and once for a football game. They were nice, and I got along with them fine, but Ryan never invited me home with him. His mom has lupus, so I thought he was just being a good son and wanted to spend time with her."

"But there was more to the story?"

"Oh, yeah. It turns out that Emma—the girl I saw him with in the diner—was his high school sweetheart. He was going back home to see her."

Auburn's hand squeezed my hip before resuming its trail up and down my back. "Shit, baby. I'm sorry. How did you find out?"

"A friend of mine, Maribeth, was friends with Emma on Facebook. She sent me a screenshot…" I rolled my lips in and then puffed out a long breath. "She sent me a screenshot of a post Emma made with a sonogram picture. The caption read, 'Baby Weston will be here in only four months. Ryan is going to be such a good daddy!' And she'd tagged my boyfriend in the post."

I heard Auburn's sharp intake of breath. "Are you telling me he got another girl pregnant, and was keeping you on the hook?"

"Yep," I said, popping the P. "This was in late January, right after the last semester started. I thought for a split second about just quitting, but I decided, *fuck that*. They're not going to run me off. I'm finishing my degree."

"Good for you, sweetheart. It must have been hard seeing him on campus after that."

"Yeah. When I confronted him, he tried to make up all these excuses about why he'd turned to her."

"Asshole," Auburn growled. "What the hell kind of excuse could he have for that?"

I shrugged. "You know, just gaslighting me, trying to make it seem like my fault. I wasn't as sweet as Emma. I spoke my mind while she just went along with whatever he wanted. I studied too much and wasn't available to him. Stuff like that."

Auburn lifted my chin and kissed me hard on the mouth. "That's utter bullshit, Gianna. You're a strong, gorgeous woman. Don't you ever change for any man. *Ever.* Not even me." He kissed me again, but this one was softer. "Especially not for me. I happen to like your boldness. Your beautiful, passionate spirit."

Leave it to Auburn Bouvier to take my insecurities and turn them into strengths.

"Okay, I'll keep being a smartass," I informed him and felt him chuckle when I rested my cheek on his chest again.

"Anyway, Ryan ended up moving Emma to Dallas to live with him. She came to campus with him every day, and she'd sit in the library or coffee shop while he was in class, flashing her sparkly new engagement ring around. So I couldn't go to either of those places anymore because I couldn't stand the sight of her. She knew we were together when she slept with him; she'd seen us together that evening at the diner."

"Jesus, I may need to make a trip to Texas. I'm going to punch this Ryan guy in the face and then thank him for being such a fucking idiot."

For some reason, that made me smile, and I lifted my head to press a kiss on Auburn's sculpted lips. "Thank him for me too because if he hadn't cheated on me, I'd still be in Texas, and I never would have met you."

"So, what made you move here after graduation?"

"I was miserable the entire semester, and then on top of that, my nana died. When I found out she'd left me her apartment, I decided I needed a fresh start. Plus, my dad is my only family left, and he's here."

He lifted up on an elbow and stroked my face with the backs of his knuckles. "It must have been hard to trust in a man after that." I nodded. Auburn leaned forward, brushing my ear with his lips. "You gave me the two greatest gifts of all tonight. First, you said you love me."

"And the second one?"

"You gave me your trust, Gianna. You trusted me enough to do something so intimate with you. To take me inside your body like you did, with no protection."

I lifted onto my own elbow so that we were face to face though I could barely see him in the darkness. "Since I've met you, you've treated me better than I could have ever imagined. And I'm not talking about the clothes and stuff... the material things. When I'm with you, you make me feel like no other woman even exists."

His hand cradled my cheek. "They don't, Gianna. Even when you're not with me, you're all I see."

God, this man...

Chapter 21

I woke gradually, a groan rumbling past my lips as I pulled the covers back to find the most beautiful sight I'd ever seen: Gianna kneeling between my legs with my cock stuffed into her mouth.

"Gianna," I moaned, and she popped me free long enough to flash me a cheeky smile.

"You were expecting someone else?" She licked a long stripe up the underside of my erection before taking me back inside that warm, wet cavern.

"Never," I assured her. Grabbing her wild ponytail, I pushed her head down as I thrust roughly into her throat. She gagged, and I tugged her up until she could breathe before taking her throat again. She handled me perfectly that time. "There's only one woman I want choking on my cock when I wake up."

She hummed happily, and I gasped. "Fuck. That felt amazing. Do it again, little pet."

Gianna began humming a familiar tune—*is that the fucking alphabet song?*—as her mouth worked me over, the vibrations sliding up and down my dick as her tongue and lips worked some kind of voodoo magic on me.

By the time she got to Z, I was shooting off like a rocket ship. "Ah, that's it, baby girl," I growled, fucking her mouth hard and fast. "Don't waste a fucking drop."

She continued sucking and swallowing until the last twitch had subsided. Then she rose up on her knees and wiped her bottom lip with her thumb. "Good morning, Auburn."

I laughed. "It certainly is a good morning, gorgeous." Grabbing her waist, I pulled her until she was sprawled across my torso. "How are you feeling today?" We'd covered a lot last night. Her tumor. Our declarations of love. Her story about that prick she'd been with. I wanted to make sure she was okay.

"In love," she said, biting that swollen bottom lip.

"What a coincidence. That's exactly how I'm feeling." I rolled until she was on her back with me hovering halfway over her, my hand stroking up and down her side.

She giggled. "That tickles."

Widening my eyes in mock-surprise, I increased the pressure of my fingers against her ribcage. "What? This?"

Gianna was laughing and squirming, her hands swatting ineffectively at mine. "Stop it, Auburn!" Her perfectly round tits bounced with her movements, and my mouth was instantly drawn to them. When I closed my lips around one pink nipple and sucked, her laughter gave way to a moan as her hands found the way to my mussed hair. "Fuck!"

"Okay," I said in agreement, rolling fully onto her and parting her thighs with my knee.

"No, Auburn. We can't."

"Of course we can. I know exactly what to do. My penis goes in your vagina, and then we fuck," I teased.

"Thanks for the sex ed lesson," she quipped. "I mean, I think our guests are up. We don't want to be rude."

Sighing, I pushed off of her and flopped onto my back. "You're right. Dammit." My hand reached for her phone, and I scanned the white disc on her arm like I did every morning we woke up together. "Eighty. Not bad, but we need to get some food in you." Then I grumbled, "Though I'd like to get something else in you."

Gianna pushed off the bed, standing in all her naked glory beside me, hands on slender hips. "Later, Bouvier."

"You can count on it, Moschella," I shot back, rising and scooping her up into my arms. "The food delivery will arrive in thirty minutes, and it's more efficient if we shower together."

Twenty-seven minutes later, we exited my bedroom, Gianna rolling her eyes at my smug grin. I'd talked her into a quickie against the wall of the shower. I could be very persuasive that way.

Though I'd always had a hearty sexual appetite, I had never craved a woman like I craved Gianna. I was fucking insatiable when it came to her.

Before we got to the living area, she tugged my hand to stop me. "Auburn?" She was chewing her bottom lip nervously.

"What is it, sweetheart?"

"You can say no if you want to, but I had an idea." She paused and blinked up at me before continuing. "Since Charli and Beau's first anniversary is today, I thought it might be nice if they could have dinner out together. Alone." Her voice was hesitant, and her eyes were wary.

The corners of my lips crooked up. "And you want us to babysit?"

"Um, yeah. But we don't have to if—"

"I think it's a great idea, baby." Her eyes widened in surprise.

"You really don't mind?"

"Of course not. They're family, and it's their anniversary. I'll even arrange the dinner for them at a great restaurant I know. I dropped a kiss on the tip of her pretty nose. "You have the best heart, Gianna."

I turned and walked down the hall, and my woman slapped me on the butt as she followed me. "And you have the best ass, Auburn."

We found our guests in the kitchen, Charli with the baby on her hip as Beau poured some apple juice into a blue sippy cup.

"Hey!" Charli chirped. "I hope you don't mind, but we're stealing some of your apple juice."

Looping an arm around her neck, I kissed the top of her head. "Happy anniversary, hon, and stop being silly. My home is your home. Plus, do I look like I drink apple juice? I bought it for this little guy." I pecked the little boy on his head, and he grinned with his tiny teeth.

"Obbie!" he said, pointing at me.

"That's right. That's Auburn," Charli said, beaming at her smart little boy. "And who is that?" She pointed at Gianna, and the baby bounced on her hip.

"Geeee!" he said, holding his arms out for Gianna, who took him from his mother.

"Good boy," my girlfriend said, snuggling the little boy against her.

"I'm feeling a little left out," Beau said, handing the cup to L.J.

"Aww, I'm sorry," I cooed, grabbing his head and kissing the top of it. "Is little Beau being a good boy today?"

"Fuck off," he muttered, shrugging away, but he was grinning.

"Beau Atwood! Watch your mouth. You're going to feel really bad when your son blurts out *eff off*."

"Eff!" L.J. squealed, making us all laugh. Except for Charli. Her gaze narrowed on her husband. Beau was the most badass man I knew, but he withered under his tiny blonde wife's glare. The man was well and truly wrapped around her pinky finger.

"Sorry, Peach," he said, pulling her to him and kissing her lips softly.

I'd never understood that kind of affection, especially after witnessing my parents' lukewarm relationship all my life. But now that I was in love myself, I got it. And watching Gianna interact with my cousin's baby...

well, I was having some very uncharacteristic *family-oriented* thoughts right then.

My phone rang, and I answered it. "Auburn Bouvier."

"Good morning, Mister Bouvier," the concierge in my building said. "We have a food delivery for you."

"It's fine, Robert. Send them up."

"Will do, sir."

"The food is here," I announced after hanging up. "Beau, if you'll grab the high chair from the closet off the kitchen, I'll get the door."

"You have a high chair?" Charli asked in confusion.

"Yeah, I bought one when Axel and Blaire visited last year. Little Danica was only about nine months old then and needed a place to sit. I also got booster seats for the triplets because they were almost three."

Beau chuckled. "And because those little toots need to be strapped down at all times to avoid mass destruction."

"They're just... active," Charli said kindly, and Beau snorted. "That was very sweet and thoughtful of you, Auburn."

"I thought that if I made it easier for my family to be here, you all might visit more often."

"You're always welcome to come visit us in Texas, but you're going to have to learn to say *y'all* instead of *you all*," she informed me with a grin.

Chuckling, I headed for the door when I heard a knock. "I'll work on it."

Once I had all the food laid out on the dining table, Gianna cut her eyes at me. "Mister Overboard," she muttered. I surveyed the piles of food. Ham, scrambled eggs, fried eggs, bacon, sausage patties, sausage links, pancakes, waffles, crepes, biscuits, gravy and a variety of fruit. It looked fine to me.

"What?" I asked innocently. "I wanted to make sure to get stuff everyone would like."

"Mission accomplished. Thank you, Auburn," Charli said with a sweet smile, already cutting up a banana for the baby.

"Mama!" L.J. scolded, holding his chubby little hands out and making grabby motions.

"Hold on, you crazy baby. I'm going as fast as I can," she told him, sliding some of the fruit onto his plate. He promptly crammed three pieces of banana into his mouth, making him look like a human chipmunk. *So fucking adorable.*

Beau handed his wife a small plate holding microscopic pieces of sausage that he'd cut up for his son. "Here's some meat for him, Peach. And yes, I tasted it to make sure it's not spicy."

"Thanks, honey," she said, leaning over and kissing his cheek. The look they shared had my toes curling in my shoes. They were so in tune with each other.

"Mama!" the baby called again, breaking their moment. Charli scooted a few pieces of meat onto his plate, and he quickly gobbled them down.

"It takes a team of highly skilled slaves to feed our son," Beau informed us. "The boy inhales anything you put in front of him." My cousin cut up some scrambled egg and passed the pieces to his wife, who was feeding L.J. tiny pieces of biscuit. Neither of them had taken a bite of their own meals yet.

Now was as good a time as any to bring this up. "Gianna and I were thinking that, since it's your anniversary, you might like to have dinner alone tonight. We'd like to babysit for you."

The couple looked at each other incredulously before turning their gazes back to us. "I'm an excellent babysitter," Gianna threw in. "That's what I did for extra money in college. I'm even CPR certified for adults and infants."

A smile grew across Charli's face. "What do you think, Beau?"

He grinned. "I think it would be nice to pretend to be adults for one night. We could actually eat and not have to worry about feeding the little monster."

Hearing the word 'monster,' L.J. growled, "Rawr!" and we all cracked up.

"His cousin Carrie taught him that. That's Axel and Blaire's oldest daughter," she explained to Gianna. "She loves coming over to help out with him, which is a blessing when I'm trying to get stuff done around the house."

"How old is Carrie now?" I asked.

"She's ten and the smartest kid I know," Beau said proudly.

"She really is," I agreed. "She's a little doll."

"Can you recommend a restaurant?" Charli asked. "Something not too fancy because I didn't bring a dress."

"Hmmm. Any of mine would be too long on you," Gianna said thoughtfully. She was at least five inches taller than Charli. "Ooh, wait! I have an idea." She rose and dug through her purse, coming back with the Bouvier vouchers in hand. Plopping them down in front of the other woman, she grinned happily. "We can go shopping later."

"Oh, no. I couldn't accept those," she said, shaking her head. "You've already gone to so much trouble to have us here, and now you're babysitting for us tonight."

I waved my hand dismissively. "Don't worry about it, Char. I give those out to my employees so they can share with their friends and families."

"Yeah, my dad gave them to me, but Auburn had already sent me an entire wardrobe, so I don't need them." Gianna glanced at me. "I couldn't tell Dad that I already had clothes because... well, he doesn't know we're dating yet."

"Ooh, sneaky," Charli said, wiggling her eyebrows. "Beau and I were kinda sneaky at first too."

"Do you think your dad would have a problem with you two dating?" Beau asked, taking a sip of his orange juice.

"I'm not sure. The age gap thing might bother him, but he's also Auburn's personal assistant, so it's complicated."

"We're gonna have to tell him sooner or later, because I'm not letting you go, pet," I told Gianna, squeezing her thigh beneath the table.

"Hmm, guess I'm stuck with you then," she said with a playful smirk.

"You don't seem like an accountant, Gianna," Charli said. "You're really fun. Our accountant is old and stodgy."

My girl shrugged. "I love numbers. But I know what you mean. Most of the people in my accounting classes were rather anal."

The baby piped up with, "Ay-null," and I couldn't hold back my laughter.

"He's just like his daddy," Charli quipped, and poor Beau snorted juice up his nose and went into a coughing fit.

"Can we stop talking about this at the table?" he growled, making the rest of us laugh even harder.

"Speaking of accounting, after we go shopping, I have to study for a couple hours. I'm preparing for the CPA exam."

Charli scrunched up her nose. "I've heard that's brutal. Are you taking a prep class? A friend of mine from college used the Becker review course, and she passed on her first try."

"Yes, that's the best one out there, but it's pricey, so I've just made my own schedule. I mapped out a plan of what I need to study every day to be prepared when the test rolls around." She lifted one shoulder and let it fall. "It will be fine if I stick to my schedule."

Why the hell doesn't she just tell me if she needs something?

Beau's eyes met mine across the table, and he smirked. He knew exactly what I was thinking.

"Cruz is waiting downstairs to drive you," I told the girls after the breakfast dishes were cleared.

"Who is Cruz?" Beau asked, a scowl on his face.

"He's my driver. He's also trained for security, so the girls will be safe with him," I assured my cousin, and he nodded. The man was the most overprotective person I knew when it came to his wife.

"I love you," I told Gianna, kissing the side of her neck. The first time I'd told her that last night, I had been terrified, but this morning, it seemed like the most natural thing in the world to say, even in front of my family.

"Love you back," she said, wrapping her arms around me.

Charli and Beau kissed goodbye, and then she handed the baby off to him. When the women were gone, Beau said he was going to try and get L.J. to sleep. I strolled to my office and sank into my big leather chair, spinning it to face Central Park outside my window.

Picking up my phone, I dialed the flagship Bouvier store.

"Bouvier. This is Elena. How may I help you?"

"Hello, Elena. This is Auburn Bouvier."

There was a long silence, and then, "Are you shitting me?"

I cackled. "No, I'm not shitting you."

"Oh my God. I'm so sorry, sir. You caught me by surprise. What can I help you with today?" I could practically feel her blushing through the phone.

"Two lovely ladies are on their way to the store right now, a tall brunette and a short blonde. These two are very important to me, and I'd like them treated as such."

"Of course, Mister Bouvier. They will be given the full VIP treatment. May I have their names so we can greet them personally when they arrive?"

"The brunette is Gianna Moschella, and the blonde is Charli Atwood. I need you to do me one more favor."

"Anything, sir."

"Mrs. Atwood is looking for a dress and accessories. She's got four-hundred in vouchers, but I think we both know that's not going to cover many of our dresses, much less shoes and jewelry. So I'd like you to cut the tags off of anything she tries on so she doesn't see the prices. Under no circumstance is she to be charged a single penny. Understood?"

"Of course, Mister Bouvier. I'll handle that personally."

"Thank you, Elena. And anything that Miss Moschella shows an interest in, please make a note of it for me, and I'll come get it this week."

"Certainly. Is there a budget for Miss Moschella?"

"Absolutely none. Whatever she wants."

After hanging up, I called Tavern on the Green and made a reservation for Charli and Beau, giving the staff my credit card information to pay for the meal.

Setting the phone on my desk, I swiveled around and almost had a heart attack when I found Beau sitting in the chair across from me.

"Jesus, you're stealthy," I said, hand on my chest.

"I was a SEAL, remember? Stealthy is my middle name." He worked his jaw side to side before speaking again. "I can pay to take my wife out to dinner."

Nodding, I said, "I know you can, but you're my guests, and I'd like to treat you." I leaned forward with my forearms on my desk, clasping my hands in front of me. "You and Blaire have always been my favorite family members besides my dad. I pretty much tolerate my mother, and I hardly ever hear from my brother."

"How is Monty?"

"He's still a cop in Florida. He was recently promoted to detective."

"Hey, that's good. He was always really smart."

"Yeah, he got the brains of the operation, and I got the looks," I told him with a grin. "He's still not speaking to Mother and Dad, but I can't really say I blame him."

"Me neither. That was really shitty of them to kick him out when he was seventeen just because he got a girl pregnant. Because let's be real; we were all fucking in high school, and it could have happened to any of us."

"Things got really nasty really quickly. Dad was disappointed but didn't say much. Mother, on the other hand, got ugly about it. It was her idea to kick him out."

Beau winced. "Your mom isn't exactly the easiest person in the world to get along with, but your dad should have stood up for his kid."

"Tell me something I don't know," I said with a humorless laugh. My phone pinged with an incoming text, and I checked it. "Speak of the devil... she wants me to come over for dinner tomorrow night."

"Sounds like a blast. Thank God we'll be gone by then." Beau slapped his knees and stood. "I'll get out of your hair so you can deal with Chloe." He turned to leave. "And I'm sure you have a CPA course to purchase," he said over his shoulder.

"Am I that predictable?"

"Yep," he said with a smirk as he turned around to face me again, "because I'd do the exact same for Charli if it was something she really needed. She still gives me shit sometimes when I get too overprotective."

"Exactly," I said, pointing at him. "Why the hell do they like to bust our balls when we do something for them?"

"Because they can, cousin. Because they can."

I could still hear his laughter as he disappeared down the hall.

Chapter 22

"That was so much fun!" Charli squealed as Cruz dropped us off at Auburn's apartment building. She was carrying her dress bag, and I was holding the shiny red and black bag holding her shoes and jewelry. "The champagne was to die for, and everyone was so nice to us."

I rolled my eyes as we approached the elevator. "I have a feeling a *certain someone* called ahead of time. Did you notice how they greeted us by name as soon as we entered?"

Her pretty blonde head whipped toward me. "They did, didn't they?" Then she grinned. "He is so crazy about you, girl. His attitude reminds me of Beau. It's a lot to deal with at first, but you get used to it. That kind of devotion."

"How do you get used to it? It's overwhelming as hell."

We stepped inside when the doors opened, and I inserted the key Auburn had given me to reach his penthouse suite. Charli's lips twisted to the side in thought. "When you realize it's coming from a place of love and not a place of control. When you figure out that all he really wants is for you to be safe and happy. *That's* how you learn to accept it."

I nodded. "That makes sense."

"Now, that doesn't mean you can't still be strong, but you have to pick your battles. If it makes him happy to do something for you, sometimes you've just gotta let him do it."

"Auburn says that's what he likes about me. That I stand up to him."

"Yeah, Beau lets me boss him around all the time." She cut her eyes to me. "Except in the bedroom. I like him to be in charge there." Her face blushed the cutest shade of pink.

"Same," I agreed, "and I haven't been disappointed yet."

"Oh, but this one time, I did take his shirt off and used the sleeves to tie his arms behind his back so he couldn't touch me." She giggled as I gaped at her. "And then I did a strip tease and a raunchy little burlesque number in my bra and panties."

"Charli!" I said, unable to control my laughter. "What did he say?"

"Girl, he was spitting mad. Until I stood on his chair and wiggled my girly goodies in his face."

"That's one way to tame the beast."

"Or rile him up even further. He ripped the shirt to shreds like the damn Hulk, and..." Her eyes took on a faraway, dreamy look. "Let's just say it was a *very* good night."

"Damn, that sounds hot."

"You girls talking about me?" Auburn asked when the elevator doors opened to reveal him waiting in the foyer for us.

"No, we're talking about this hot construction worker we saw down the street."

"What!!!?"

"Yep," Charli threw in. "I think he may be in love with Gia. He called her 'hot mama' and everything." Auburn's eyes shifted back and forth between us.

"I think I should go talk to him. Plumber's cracks are so sexy," I sighed.

His tongue made a circle inside his cheek. "You're fucking with me, right?"

Charli burst into giggles, and I lifted onto my toes to kiss his lips. "Maybe a little bit."

He swatted me on the ass as we walked into the apartment. "You're gonna pay for that later."

"Ooh, retribution," Charli chirped. Auburn shut the door, and Char laid her dress over the couch before wrapping her arms around his waist. "Thank you so much, Auburn. We had so much fun, and they treated us like queens. They even fed us lunch."

He returned her sweet hug. "Excellent. And you found something you liked?"

"Yes! I got a red one that's just gorgeous."

"Is it the one with the beaded bodice? Because I was actually picturing that one for you."

"That's the one. I tried on about fifteen different ones, but that one was the best. That dressing room was bigger than my first apartment," she said with a giggle. "They put us in there and brought in dress after dress." Charli frowned a little. "The only problem was that I didn't know how much anything cost. There weren't any price tags on anything."

"Oh, hmm. I'll have to look into that," he said evasively. "The baby just woke up a minute ago. Beau is in your room changing him."

She did an excited wiggle. "I'll go show him my new stuff." Taking her bags, she scooted off toward their room.

"You still need to study?" Auburn asked, picking up my hand and kissing the back of it.

"Yes, I really do. You don't think Charli and Beau will think I'm being rude, do you?"

"Of course not. I set you up in my office because it's quiet. Your laptop and backpack are already in there."

"Thanks, babe," I told him. "I'm going to change into comfy clothes, and I'll get started."

Thirty minutes later, I was lounged across Auburn's huge chair with my legs hanging over one arm and a book propped on my thighs. Reaching for a highlighter, I marked a passage I wanted to come back to when I sensed someone else in the room.

I looked up to find Auburn leaned against the doorframe watching me. "Hey, I know you're studying, but I thought you might need sustenance." He set a small plate of fruit and a teacup on the desk. "I added honey to your tea just how you like it."

This man gave me all the warm fuzzies inside. "Thank you, babe. That was really sweet of you."

He nodded and stuffed his hands in his front pockets while rocking back on his heels. He appeared to be... uncomfortable.

"And I thought you might need this too." He pulled a piece of paper from one pocket and placed it in front of me.

"What's that?" I asked in confusion, attempting to comprehend the few words on the paper.

"Your login information for the Becker review course." He pressed his lips together and stared at me with wary eyes before speaking quietly. "Don't be mad at me, okay? I know six-thousand dollars seems like a lot, and it is, but it's something you *need*, Gianna. For your career. And that kind of money doesn't... I don't mean to sound arrogant, but six-thousand doesn't even put a dent in my finances."

I glanced down at the words on the sheet and then back up to Auburn as Charli's words rang through my head. *When you realize it's coming from a place of love...*

He looked so damn sincere, and the love was literally shining like blue beacons from his eyes. I stood and walked around the desk as his eyes followed me the entire way.

"Are you going to kick me in the nuts?"

I almost laughed at that. Instead, I wrapped my arms around his neck and pulled his face to mine. "No, I'm going to do this." And I pressed my lips to his, my tongue searching for entrance. With a small groan, he opened for me and dropped his hands to my butt, lifting until my legs curled around his waist. With all the passion I was feeling in my heart, I kissed the hell out of my man.

"Thank you," I murmured against his lips.

He pulled back, his face the picture of incredulity. "You're not mad at me?"

"Did you purchase that course because you love me?" He bit his bottom lip and nodded. "Then no, I'm not mad."

His beautiful grin stretched across his entire face. "You're being awfully reasonable about this."

My eyes widened in mock surprise. "I know! Maybe I need to see a doctor about that."

"Speaking of that, since you're in such an accepting mood right now, I, um, I talked to Betty and got the name of a neurologist here in New York. She's the best in the city, and one of the best in the world."

I nodded. "Okay."

His deep chuckle vibrated through my chest, "My, my. Aren't we agreeable today?"

"My doctor in Dallas told me he would help me find a new neuro here. Thank you for taking care of that for me. Just get me her info, and I'll pass it along to Doctor Tejada so he can send my files."

Auburn took a couple steps forward and planted my butt on the edge of his massive cherry wood desk. "If you didn't have to study, I would fuck the shit out of you on this desk right now. You look so damn sexy."

I glanced down at my clothing. Since my bags had arrived on Auburn's plane, I'd dug out my most comfortable clothes, a pair of soft, faded black leggings and an old sweatshirt that hung off one shoulder. And to top off my ratty appearance, my hair was wadded up on top of my head, and I was wearing the black-rimmed glasses I needed when I was going to be reading for long periods of time.

Raising a skeptical eyebrow, I asked, "You think I look sexy like this?"

"Mmm. Extremely. You look like a naughty accountant."

A giggle rose up in my throat. "I am a naughty accountant."

"I'm aware," he said, dropping kisses down my neck and across my bare shoulder. "You're going to wear this for me really soon, and I'm going to eat up every single inch of you."

Moisture pooled between my legs. "Is it the goofy glasses that have you all hot and bothered?"

He lifted his head and pulled a pencil from my bun, wiggling it in front of my face. "Actually, I think this was what set me off."

I patted the rat's nest on top of my head. "Shit. I've been looking for that."

He bobbed his eyebrows at me. "Ma'am, are you hiding any other office supplies anywhere on your person? Because I'd be happy to do a thorough search and locate them for you."

"So are we playing cops and robbers?"

"Unless you want me to be a construction worker since you find them so sexy."

"Stop it," I said with a laugh. "I really need to get back to studying. I want to check out the course schedule for Becker so I can make a new game plan."

"Okay, baby," he said amenably, backing away a couple steps. "Oh, one more thing. My mother invited me to dinner tomorrow night."

Disappointment spread through my limbs, which was crazy. I was an independent person and didn't need to be stuck up my boyfriend's butt all the time.

"That's fine. I can call Lehra and see if she wants to grab something with me. I haven't seen much of her lately. I think she may be dating someone, but she's been very evasive about it."

Auburn's face pinched into a scowl. "That's not what I meant. I want you to go with me."

"Oh. Are you sure your mom wants me there?"

"I don't give a shit. *I* want you there. I'll tell her I'm not coming without you, so she'll have to get over it."

"Is Magdalena still calling you?"

He shook his head. "I spoke with her once to let her know we wouldn't be getting back together, but... let's just say she was unaccepting of that idea. She kept calling and texting, so I blocked her number."

"Such a good boy," I purred, rubbing my hand up and down the stubble on his jaw.

Auburn looked down at the bulge tenting his jeans. "You're not helping my resolve to let you study, missy."

"Hey, I can't be held responsible for what that thing does. He's a rogue."

He closed his eyes and sighed. "Go study, Gianna, before you find yourself bent over that desk."

Maybe I could take a short break...

Before I could voice that, Auburn laid a soft kiss at the corner of my mouth with a whispered promise. "Later."

And then he was gone, leaving me wanting more.

"Hoo boy," I said, rounding the desk and flopping back onto the chair. "That man is something else."

Chapter 23

My nose drew me into my kitchen on Sunday afternoon. Something smelled fucking awesome. Like butter and sugar. Fruit and *home*. Not the home I'd grown up in, but someone's home for sure.

"What in the world is that delectable aroma?"

Gianna looked at me over her shoulder. She had a dab of flour on her nose and one on her cheek, which only made her more adorable. "I made a pie to take to your mother's. Do you think apple is okay?"

"Everyone loves apple pie," I told her, wrapping my arms around her from behind. "Holy hell!" I exclaimed when I saw the masterpiece she'd just pulled from the oven. "You made this?"

"From scratch," she assured me. "Does it look okay?"

"Gianna, it's absolutely beautiful." The crust criss-crossed across the top, and there was a cute little apple-shaped piece of pastry set right in the middle. "I can't believe you baked this."

"I just want to make a good impression on your parents," she fretted.

"I'm certainly impressed as hell."

"Does the apple look okay? I had to cut it out by hand because I don't have my little cookie cutter here."

"It's perfect, sweetheart. You're perfect." I turned her toward me and swiped the flour from her face. "Well, except for this."

"Oh, my God. I'm such a mess. Thank goodness I didn't get dressed before I cooked." She stepped back and looked down at my navy dress pants and light-blue button-down, which both had a fine dusting of flour. "Shit! I got you all messy." Her hands swiped in panic at my front before I grasped her wrists to stop her.

"Go easy on the family jewels, pet. I'd like to use them later." She giggled and apologized again as I dampened a cloth and carefully got rid of the remaining dust. "See? It's just a little flour. It comes right off."

"Can you help me pick something to wear?"

"Hmm, let's go see what you have here." I took her hand and led her to my closet, where I had cleared a large spot for her to keep some clothes here. My fingers moved over the line of fabrics before stopping and pulling out a garment. "How about this emerald shift dress? It will look pretty with your eyes."

"My black shoes are at my apartment. Can we stop by and get them?"

I bent to search the shoe rack beneath her clothes. "Or you can wear the taupe ones."

"You're the expert. Just let me freshen up, and I'll be ready to go. Can we stop and get some vanilla bean ice cream for the pie once we get close to your parents' house?"

"Of course. Can't have apple pie without ice cream."

Thirty-five minutes later, we were in my midnight-blue Bugatti Divo. "Did you get a new car?" Gianna asked.

Reaching over, I clasped our fingers together. "No. Why?"

A frown creased her forehead. "I thought the other car was a Jaguar."

"It was."

"And then you have the Bentley that Cruz drives you in."

"Yes."

With a shake of her head, she asked, "How many cars do you have?"

"A few. I'm a mood driver. I like to have choices."

Her lips quirked up on one side. "I've never heard of a mood driver before."

Bringing our hands to my lips, I kissed each of her knuckles. "I'm an original, baby."

"I can't argue with that. Are you a mood lover too?"

My eyes shifted to hers, and she appeared to be completely serious. "If you're talking about having choices of which position I want to fuck *you* in, then yes. I like a broad selection. If you're talking about different women, my answer is fuck no." When I stopped at a red light, I grasped her jaw firmly and kissed her hard on the lips. "That's something you never have to worry about with me, pet. I'm fully yours."

"Okay," she said, her smile sweet and laced with relief.

"It's normal to have insecurities after what happened with your ex. Anytime you need reassurances, all you have to do is tell me. I'll be happy to remind you. Multiple times a day, if necessary."

She leaned her head over onto my shoulder as the light turned green. "How are you so perfect?"

I let out an overly dramatic sigh. "I don't know, Gianna. That's a question I ask myself every single day."

Her laughter filled the car. "I loved getting to know Charli and Beau this weekend. Charli is a hoot."

"Yep, I really like her. And that little L.J. is a cutie pie." I pressed my lips against the top of her head, inhaling her fresh scent. "You were so good with him last night."

"You were too. The way you laid on the floor and let him crawl all over you like you were his own personal jungle gym."

My hand curled up and stroked her cheek. "He liked roughhousing with me, but when he got sleepy, he headed straight to your lap."

"I'm the best snuggler," she informed me.

There was a moment of silence, and then I asked, "Do you want to have kids, Gianna?"

She nodded against my shoulder. "I do." There was another long pause before she spoke again. "Do you?"

I moistened my lips with my tongue. "I've never thought about it much before. It wasn't something I'd ever planned for. But now... now I think I would very much like to have children. With you."

I heard her sharp intake of breath, and then she looked up at me with warmth and softness in her eyes. "Okay."

God, I want to kiss the shit out of her right now.

Seeing a grocery store up ahead, I turned on my blinker and pulled into the small parking lot. I put the car in park and swiveled in my seat to face her. My lips covered hers for a long kiss, our tongues rubbing sensually together. "I want everything with you," I said against her lips.

"Me too."

I gave her one last peck. "Okay, now that that's settled, I'm going to run in and get some ice cream. We're almost to my parents' house."

Five minutes later, we were on the road again, and shortly after that, I pulled into the driveway and stopped at the security gate.

"Mister Bouvier," the guard said with a friendly smile. "It's so nice to see you again. It's been a while."

Yeah, because I hate coming here.

The car wound up the curvy driveway until the house came into view, and Gianna's mouth dropped open. "This is where your parents live?"

The red brick building with large white columns could only be described as a mansion. "It's just a house, Gianna."

"A really fucking big one," she muttered, making me smile.

I parked in front and went around to help Gianna from the car. She carried the pie while I picked up the bag containing the ice cream, and we took the three wide, brick steps to the door.

"I'm so nervous," she whispered as I rang the doorbell.

"You'll be fine," I assured her, leaning down to give her a soothing kiss. The door opened just then, and I turned to find my mother standing there, her lips pinched together so tightly, they were turning white.

"Hello, Mother."

"Auburn, I'm so glad you came." Her eyes shifted to the woman beside me. "And you brought Gina. How nice."

"I told you I was, and her name is Gianna. It's not that difficult, Mother."

"Of course," she said, her smile obviously forced. "Gi-ah-nah," she said slowly, as if I'd asked her to pronounce a particularly long foreign word.

My girl, of course, responded with sweet dignity. "Thank you so much for having me, Mrs. Bouvier. I brought a pie."

"Gianna made it herself from scratch," I said proudly.

"Hmm, how very domesticated of you," my mother said, and I gritted my teeth. We'd been here less than a minute, and she was already starting with this passive-aggressive bullshit. I shot her a warning glare, and she straightened her shoulders and took the pie. "That was very thoughtful of you. Thank you."

"We brought ice cream too. It will need to go in the freezer."

"Certainly. I'll show Gianna the kitchen. Your father wanted to speak with you in his study, son."

My brow crinkled as I looked down at Gianna with concern. I really didn't want to leave her alone with my mother. "I'll be fine," she mouthed, taking the bag from me.

My Bouvier dress shoes slapped quietly on the diamond-patterned wood floor as I headed back to my dad's study, a little confused as to why he was there instead of on the couch watching football like he always was on Sundays.

I gave a light knock and then pushed the door open, but my dad wasn't inside.

Magdalena was.

Fuck.

"What the hell are you doing here?"

She crossed her arms, pushing her large breasts up until they almost spilled out the top of her fitted pink dress. "You've been ignoring me," she said with a pout. If she thought the tit lifting and lip pursing was going to impress me, she was sorely mistaken.

"Yes, I have," I confirmed. "I told you not to contact me again, but you persisted, so I blocked you."

"You... you blocked me?" she spluttered. "But how am I supposed to get in touch with you?"

She was really starting to piss me off, and anger boiled hot and heavy in my chest.

"You're not. That's the point of breaking up. You don't contact me, and I don't contact you."

"But we always get back together after one of our little spats." Her bottom lip rolled out like a petulant brat.

"Not this time," I said coldly. "I'm not sure how I can make this any clearer, Magdalena. We. Are. Done."

Large crocodile tears dripped down her face, as if on cue. "It's because of *her*, isn't it? That girl you were with at the benefit. Gina or whatever."

"I am with *Gianna* now, but that has nothing to do with this. We broke up before she came into the picture. This was *my* decision after you caused ten-thousand dollars worth of damage to my apartment with your little fit."

Magdalena let out a loud sob and threw her arms around me. "What about me? What am I supposed to do now?"

I tried to soften my tone a bit though I didn't return her embrace. "I don't know, Mag. It's no longer my problem what you do."

"Why are you being so mean to me?" she cried against my chest.

Christ.

I pushed her back by the shoulders to put some space between us, and she took the opportunity to grab my face and try to kiss me. Her lips were about an inch from mine when I roughly yanked my head back, spinning away from her.

"Jesus, Magda—" I froze when I saw Gianna and my mother standing just inside the doorway. Mother was smiling, which pissed me off, but Gianna's face looked stricken, which simultaneously cracked my heart.

Gianna recovered quickly, squaring her shoulders and lifting her chin before striding confidently to me, placing one possessive hand on my chest and the other on my ass. "Hi, babe," she purred.

Even though I was angrier than I even had been in my life—because my mother had clearly set this up—I couldn't help but smile at my girl's bravado. "Hello, precious."

She turned her face up to mine, and I gladly accepted her kiss, drawing it out longer than I normally would in front of other people. But my gorgeous woman needed what I'd promised her in the car on the way over here. Reassurance that I was completely hers.

After breaking the kiss, a tiny smile of satisfaction curved her lips upward.

"I'm sorry about *that*," I said, keeping my eyes on her while bobbing my head in Magdalena's direction. "I have no idea what she's doing here."

"Mom invited me," Mag snapped, and I turned to find my mother grasping her hand. *Mom? She's never called Chloe 'Mom' before.*

"That's right. We simply can't have a *family* dinner without Magdalena." Her smug smile made me want to strangle her with my bare hands.

"Well, I hope you enjoy your *family* dinner," I said haughtily, taking Gianna's hand and leading her past the stunned pair. "Tell Dad I'll call him this week for lunch and golf."

"Wh-where are you going?" Mother asked. "You just got here."

"I'm taking Gianna out for dinner," I said without breaking stride, leaving their stuttering responses in the dust.

"We're leaving?" Gianna asked quietly.

"Yes, I don't appreciate being ambushed," I said curtly. As we approached the front door, I changed course and headed to the kitchen instead. "We're taking this with us," I said, picking up the pie from the countertop. We exited through the kitchen door and took the flagstone sidewalk around to the front of the house, neither of us speaking a word.

After settling Gianna and the pie in the passenger's side, I walked around the car, taking a deep, calming breath before sliding into the Bugatti. I could feel Gianna's eyes on the side of my face, and I finally bucked up enough courage to turn and face her.

"I'm so sorry about that, Gianna. You have to believe me. I had no idea she was going to be here, or we never would have come."

"I believe you," she said, softly touching my cheek.

"You do?" I asked incredulously, and she nodded. "Fuck, I love you."

"I love you too. Now, where are you taking me for dinner?"

I barked out a laugh. "Wherever you want, pet."

Her teeth sunk into her bottom lip. "I did see a crab house on the way over here."

My brow furrowed in thought. "That little red building? Krab King or something?"

"Yes. We don't have to go there though. We're all dressed up, and it did seem a little dumpy." I knew exactly where she was talking about, and she was correct. It was very dumpy.

"No, it's fine. I think it's about fifteen minutes away." I put the car in drive and headed down the driveway.

"Then I'll just have to keep myself occupied while you drive," my lady said, sliding her hand over to cup my crotch.

"Christ, woman," I groaned, hardening beneath her small hand.

As I approached the gate, the guard motioned for me to roll down the window, which I did. "Is there a problem, Mister Bouvier?"

"No, no problem. We've decided we're not staying for dinner."

His eyes fell on Gianna's hand on my dick, and his eyebrows shot to the heavens. "I don't blame you," he muttered, his lips twitching as he met my eyes once again. "Have a good evening, sir."

"Thank you, James," I replied. "I plan to."

As we drove off, Gianna squeezed my cock. "I think someone once told me that orgasms are good for stress." Her hand slipped up and down my shaft, and I clenched the steering wheel with both hands.

Cutting my eyes toward her, I said, "If you make me come in my pants, we're not going to be able to go inside the restaurant."

"Hmmm," she hummed. "Then I guess I'll have to do a good job of swallowing." I almost choked on my own spit when she kicked off her shoes and kneeled sideways in the seat.

"Gianna," I warned, "sit down and put your seatbelt on."

She reached lower to cradle my balls as her sweet lips brushed my ear. "Daddy doesn't want to fuck his baby girl's mouth?"

And I was fucking *done*. With my dick twitching mightily, I unbuckled my belt and reached for the button on my pants. When I was completely unfastened, she bent at the waist, freeing me from my briefs and raising her round ass enticingly. My right hand automatically went there, giving her a hard swat as I thanked God for darkly tinted windows.

"Get that pretty mouth on me right now, baby girl," I growled. She teased me with long licks up and down my shaft before sliding her tongue slowly around and around the head.

She glanced up at me, giving me a playful smirk. "Daddy's cum tastes so good on my tongue. I can't wait to taste it in my throat."

"Goddamn," I groaned, elongating the last syllable when she took me deeply into that hot little mouth. "Fuck, my sweet pet. That's perfect."

Her head bobbed up and down my length as her fist stroked and twisted around my root. Then she started humming but not the alphabet song this time. It seemed familiar, though I couldn't quite place it because I was too distracted by the wet noises she was making around my erection.

Gianna's hair formed a curtain around her face, and I gathered it in one fist so I could get the full visual effect. "Beautiful, pet. You're so beautiful with your mouth full of your daddy's dick." She hummed louder, and the vibrations of her lips around me had my balls tightening up against my body.

I was white-knuckling the steering wheel with my left hand, holding her hair with my right, and fucking her mouth with sharp upward thrusts of my hips. My eyes flitted from the road to her face between my legs in rapid succession. How I hadn't already driven us into a ditch, I'll never know.

"That's it, baby. You're making me come." With a loud, moaned "ohhhhh," I let go and released my seed down her tight throat. "Fucking take it all," I grunted as she struggled to swallow me.

When I was completely drained, she lifted her head and licked her lips, flashing me a mischievous smile like she hadn't just rocked my fucking world to the core.

Then it hit me. "Were you just humming 'U Can't Touch This?'"

Pressing her lips together to keep from smiling, she nodded.

I released her hair, smoothing it behind one ear. "Gianna Moschella, you are something else," I panted.

"I know," she said with a wink, tucking my cock back inside my underwear before refastening my pants. "Feel better?"

"Much," I breathed, returning both hands to the wheel. "I think the restaurant was right up here on the left." My eyes searched and finally located the red cinder block building as Gianna fixed her smudged makeup in the mirror. When I'd parked, I bent my head and stared at the building. The paint was chipping off in places and the roof looked like it had been installed by a toddler.

Sensing my trepidation, Gianna patted my arm. "Come on, Fancy Pants. It will be fine." I cut her a look, but she was already getting out of the car.

"Fuck," I muttered, exiting the vehicle and rounding the front to meet her. Her heel caught in a crack in the asphalt and she stumbled until I wrapped an arm around her waist to steady her.

"Sorry," she giggled. "I'm a little klutzy sometimes."

We made our way across the beat up parking lot and I paused in front of the glass front doors. "Gianna, are you sure about this? There are iron bars on the windows."

She pecked me on the cheek. "Everything doesn't have to be a five-star restaurant. Live a little, Bouvier."

"That's what I'm trying to do, but you're insistent on getting us killed," I muttered as I pulled open the door. My nose was instantly hit with the smell of savory crab and spices, and I hoped we got to eat something before we were murdered because it actually smelled fucking amazing.

Every head in the place turned when we walked it. In our dressy clothes, we stuck out like a couple of sore thumbs. Gianna didn't even seem to notice, striding confidently up to the formica counter and staring at the overhead menu.

A table of six construction workers gawked openly at her ass, which I could hardly blame them for. This green dress looked amazing on her. Nevertheless, I placed my hand possessively on her butt and resisted the urge to yell, "Mine!"

Gianna popped a hand on her hip and turned to the workers. "This is our first time here. What's good?"

They were all openly drooling, but one of them pointed a stubby finger at the board and said, "The number two is good if you just want crab legs. If you want mussels or shrimp, go with the number three or four."

"Thanks," she said, flashing a brilliant smile, and they all smiled back as a unit with goofy-ass, smitten grins. "Hello, Florence. I'll have the number two," she told the short lady behind the counter.

"What seasonin' you want on that, honey?" She pointed to a laminated sheet on the glass case housing mounds of crab legs on ice.

"Hmm. I do love garlic butter, but the lemon pepper sounds good too. No. Wait. Spicy Cajun seasoning."

"You can get the Krab King special, which is all three of them mixed together."

"Oh, yes ma'am," Gianna exclaimed happily. "I'll have that."

"I'll have the same," I told her, amused by my woman's enthusiasm. "And two Cokes, please."

Florence plopped two chilled cans of soda on the counter. No ice or glasses. Just the cans. "That'll be fifty-six dollars."

Pulling my wallet out of my back pocket, I handed over my card. "For everything?"

"Yessir," the young lady assured me, taking my card and running it. I was shocked, to say the least. Every restaurant I'd ever been to charged at least ninety dollars a pound for crab legs. But then again, I was probably paying less for the actual food and more for the aesthetics. And drinking glasses.

I signed the credit card slip, and the woman gave me a warm smile when she noticed my generous tip. "I got two pounds, both with the special," she called over her shoulder, and a mocha-skinned kid who looked no more than fifteen came in from the back, opened the case, and extracted four huge clusters of snow crab legs. "That'll be right out," Florence informed us. "Bibs, buckets, and crab crackers are right there on that table."

Gianna led us to the table, put two crab cracking devices in a large metal bucket, and handed it to me. "Go get us a table, and I'll pick out our bibs."

"I'm not wearing a bib," I hissed, and she patted me indulgently on the arm.

"Of course you are. It's part of the experience. Plus, we don't want to ruin our nice clothes."

"For fuck's sake," I mumbled, spotting a table in the back and heading that way. I noticed that everyone in the place was indeed wearing a plastic bib with the Krab King logo and a variety of crab-related sayings, including *I'm just here to get crabs* and *You're crackin' me up.*

My gorgeous girl strolled to our table, grinning like the cat that ate the canary. She stood behind me, wrapping a bib around my neck, and I started to protest. "Gianna…"

She stopped me with a flicker of her tongue against my earlobe, followed by a soft, "Please, baby?" I shut my damn mouth because I would do anything for this woman, even wear a stupid-ass bib.

Glancing down, I bit my inner cheek when I read it. "Too cute to be crabby?" I asked, and she giggled.

"Wait till you see mine." She tied it around her neck and popped it out with a flourish, letting it drape down over her breasts. It read, *My boyfriend gave me crabs.* I buried my face in one hand, my shoulders shaking with laughter.

"You're totally insane," I finally managed to say.

"That's why you love me," she shot back.

"Completely," I confirmed, popping the top on my ice-cold Coke and taking a swig.

A few minutes later, Florence approached holding a large dented pan piled high with crab legs, corn, and potatoes. "Here ya go. Can I get you anything else?"

"No, thank you, Florence," Gianna said with a sweet smile. "This looks delicious."

As she walked off, I stared down at the food. "We don't get plates?"

In answer, Gianna tore a handful of brown paper towels from the dispenser and laid them out in front of her. "No plates. We're about to go medieval on these crab legs." She held up her fist, and I bumped it with my own before grabbing my own wad of paper towels.

I reached for a crab leg and separated it at the knuckle, pleased when the meat slid easily from the shell, which told me it was cooked perfectly. Gianna did the same and dragged the pink meat through the inch-thick pool of butter and seasoning at the bottom of the pan. I followed her lead, and we took our first bites together.

The flavor exploded against my tongue, and I literally moaned. "Holy fuck, that's good."

"Mmhmm," she agreed, hungrily breaking the next knuckle and extracting the meat. We ate in silence for a few minutes, intent only on getting our next bite. I'd been apprehensive about the mixture of seasonings, but they blended together flawlessly and enhanced the sweetness of the crab.

"I don't think I've seen you folks in here before. Y'all enjoying your meal?" a tall, thin Black man with a smattering of gray in his hair asked us. He was spraying and wiping down the table beside us.

I swallowed the bite in my mouth before speaking. "Best damn crab legs I've ever had in my life," I told him honestly, and his weathered face beamed.

"Are you from down south?" Gianna asked him, obviously hearing a similar accent to her own.

"Baton Rouge, Louisiana," he said proudly, "but I been living up here for about thirty years."

She licked some butter from her finger and grinned. "Well, we're kinda neighbors then. I'm originally from Texas." She patted the table in invitation, and the man sat beside us. It was amazing to me how she could make friends with everyone she met.

"I'm Ezra Johnson, head table wiper, chief trash hauler, and owner of Krab King."

Gianna's eyes widened, and she clapped her hands. "I can't believe we're meeting the crab king himself. Your food is fantastic. I'm Gianna, by the way."

"Auburn," I said with a nod. "I would shake your hand, but…" I wiggled my fingers, which were coated in butter and spices.

The old man chuckled. "I understand."

"I do have a question."

"Shoot."

My finger prodded a white oval on the tray, which I had uncovered while eating. "What is this? An egg?"

"Yep. That there's a chicken egg, but when I can get 'em, I sometimes use quail eggs. I drop 'em into the boiling water with the seafood so they can soak up the seasonings while they cook. Just swirl it around in the butter, and your mouth will love you for it."

My eyes met Gianna's, and she nodded. We each picked up our egg, swirled it as directed, and took a simultaneous bite. "Ohhh, I think I just died," she moaned.

"Me too," I agreed, dabbing the egg in the heavenly sauce and taking another bite. "Hey, Ezra, can we get some of these to go? They would be great for breakfast."

"Of course you can. Same seasoning?" I nodded, my mouth too full of the last bite of egg to speak. "They're a dollar each."

"Mmm, give us a dozen then," I said after swallowing.

Ezra rose and walked to the counter to place our order before returning to his table cleaning. "That your Bugatti out there, Auburn?" he asked, peering out the window.

"Yes, sir."

"Sweet ride. That midnight blue color is beautiful."

"I have a 1977 Corvette in the same color."

"Do you now? I've got a white 1953 'Vette my daddy and I worked on when I was a teenager. Still looks as good as the day it rolled off the showroom floor. Though it wasn't new when he got it. We had to do a lot of fixing to get it back into shape."

"Does it have the original Bel Air wheel covers?" I asked.

He looked surprised at my knowledge of the vintage car but shook his head. "Naw, I wish. Not many of those still around."

Gianna and I finished up our food before cleaning our hands with the wet-wipes provided on the table. Then I removed my bib and cleaned it off.

"What are you doing?" she asked, looking at me like I was crazy.

"I think I want to keep this," I told her. "To remember today."

Her answering smile warmed me from the inside out. "I'll keep mine too," she said, reaching for the bowl of wipes. "Maybe..." She shook her head.

"What?"

She bit her bottom lip shyly and shrugged. "I was thinking that maybe we could start a memory box. You know, of things we do together. Then when we're old and gray, we can look back and remember."

I picked up her hand and kissed the back of it as my heart thumped every beat for her. "I love you so fucking much, Gianna."

"I love you, Mister Bouvier."

In that moment, I realized that one day—soon—I wanted her to be *Mrs. Bouvier*.

We stood, and I went to the front to pay for and collect our eggs. Then I took her hand and walked swiftly from the restaurant after calling out a goodbye to our new friend Ezra.

"Slow down, Auburn. I'm wearing heels, remember?"

I hooked the to-go bag over my arm and literally swept my girl off her feet, carrying her the rest of the way to the car.

She was laughing her sweet, high laugh. "What's the rush?" she asked after we were both in the car.

"I'm ready to get you home. I have plans for that pie."

Chapter 24

"How does that feel, sweetheart?"

"It feels like you have me tied to your bed," I replied flatly.

He chuckled from his position on top of me with his legs straddling my waist. "I mean are the restraints too tight?"

I tugged at the soft cuffs he'd put around my wrists and chained to his headboard. "No, they're fine, but do I really have to be blindfolded? I like to watch you," I complained.

Soft lips caressed my own. "Yes, pet," he said, his warm breath washing over me. "I want everything I do to this luscious body to be a surprise."

My forehead creased. "That sounds ominous. Should I be worried?"

Another kiss forced my fears down until they were almost non-existent. The feel of his tongue thrusting roughly into my mouth turned my mind in other directions. "You shouldn't be worried because you trust me, don't you?"

"I do," I admitted.

"That's my good girl." His body slid down to my hips, allowing me to feel his erection against my panties. His tongue circled one nipple and then the other before his weight was suddenly gone. "I'll be right back. Don't go anywhere."

"I'm glaring at you beneath this mask right now, Bouvier. And where the hell are you going? You better not leave this room."

A finger stroked down my cheek, and my head instinctively turned in that direction, sucking the tip into my mouth. I heard his sharp intake of breath and smiled as he pulled his hand away. "Watch yourself, you little tease."

"What's good for the goose is good for the gander," I retorted, earning me a nipple pinch that had my back arching off the bed.

"I'll be right back, pet. I promise."

"What if you fall, and I'm stuck here, chained to the bed, unable to help you?"

I could hear the laughter in his voice. "I'll be careful."

"That's what everyone says just before they fall and can't get up. Maybe I'll get you one of those life alert necklaces to wear."

"If that's a crack about my age, I'm going to teach you a very valuable lesson."

"Bring it, old man."

Strong hands separated my thighs, and a second later, I felt a sharp slap against my pussy. "Oh!" I cried out in shock... and a surprising amount of arousal. "Do that again, Daddy."

But he was gone. I could sense it by the thinning of the air around me. "You better hurry back," I called. "Stubborn ass man. What the hell is he thinking, leaving me chained to the damn bed?"

I was still mumbling insults under my breath when the bed dipped beside me a few minutes later. "What did you just say?" a deep voice asked.

Showing all my teeth, I grinned winningly. "I said I missed you, Auburn."

"Uh-huh. That's what I thought."

"I wish I could see you."

His tongue slid across my bare shoulder, and I shivered. "Being blindfolded is all about anticipation, pet. You never know what I'm going to do next. Where I'm going to touch you. Kiss you. Bite you."

I tried to let go and just feel, but he was right; the anticipation was heady and heightened my sense of touch exponentially. Lips on my neck, sucking and biting, while gentle fingers traced lightly down my ribcage. One nipple in his hot mouth while the other was being thumbed to a hard peak. The dichotomous sensations were overwhelming until all I could feel was *need*.

"God, Auburn. It feels like there are two different people touching me at once."

"Maybe there are."

My spine stiffened for a second at the thought, and then I laughed. "Whatever. There's no way you'd let anyone else touch me."

Auburn lifted my gold satin blindfold, his bright blue eyes peering down at me as he smiled.

"You know me so well, pet," he said gently. His hand trailed from my shoulder down to my knee and then back up again. "When you're in my bed, this body is mine to do with as I please. No one else's. And I'll touch and tease it until you're begging."

"Begging for what?"

"More. Less. You won't even know what you want, but you'll trust that I'm going to give you exactly what you need."

"What if I beg now?"

Pulling the blindfold back down, he kissed me on the lips. "Hush, or I'll gag you too."

"Then you couldn't hear me beg."

I heard his long, exasperated sigh. "Will you ever just do as you're told?"

"Probably not. Where would the fun be in that?"

Even though I couldn't see him, I knew he was smiling.

Auburn was moving around, and I was trying to figure out what he was doing when something warm covered my right nipple. A second later, a freezing cold sensation puckered my other one, and I cried out.

"What is that?"

"Pie and ice cream," he said before closing his mouth over my right breast, his tongue lapping up the sticky sugar and cinnamon. When he moved to the left, his mouth instantly warmed my icy nipple, which was apparently coated with the vanilla ice cream we'd picked up on the way home. "Mmm, so fucking good. This is how I'm eating pie from now on."

He did it again and again, alternating the hot and cold from one side to the other until my panties were absolutely soaked with arousal.

He kissed his way down my stomach, and with his hands on my calves, he rolled me back until my knees were touching my chest. A warm tongue licked from my butt cheek to the back of my knee as a single fingernail scratched in the opposite direction on the other leg. He repeated the erotic action, and my body felt like it was on fire.

Then a sharp bite on my ass accompanied two fingers rubbing the crotch of my panties. The simultaneous pleasure and pain had me writhing for more.

"That's it, baby. I love to see you squirm for me."

"Please, Auburn."

"Please what, baby girl?"

"More. Touch me more."

When he moved my panties to the side, I almost cried in relief. But he didn't touch me where I expected. The tip of his finger circled my back hole. "Has anyone ever fucked you here, Gianna?"

"No. Well, yes. But…"

"Which is it, sweetheart? Yes or no?"

"I tried once but didn't like it, so we stopped."

"Were you properly prepared before you tried?"

"I-I don't know."

He cursed under his breath. "That means no." Kissing the inside of my thigh, he asked, "Do you trust me enough to touch you there?"

"Yes," I panted. *Just please fucking touch me anywhere.*

I heard the snick of a plastic cap, and a few seconds later, something cold touched my asshole. I flinched involuntarily. "Is-is that your—"

"I don't fuck a woman's ass unless she's ready for me, Gianna. It's just my finger." Auburn scooted up the bed and pressed his lips to mine as he rubbed some of the lube around my hole. Just as he pushed the tip of his finger inside, his tongue flickered against my mouth, and when my lips parted on a moan, he kissed me deeper. He kept his finger movements shallow and gentle as I relaxed against him.

"Good girl, Gianna," he murmured, pushing his finger in a little farther. "I'm not going to take you here tonight. You're not ready for that yet, but I am going to put an anal plug in to help stretch you out."

I'd heard of those, but I'd never had one stuck up my butt before. "Will it hurt?"

"It's a small one. You'll feel a little sting when it first pops all the way in, but other than that, no. It won't hurt." As he moved back between my legs, he smoothly slid my panties down and off my legs. A few seconds later, something touched my back door, and I tensed.

"Shh, relax for me, baby girl." His lips kissed a line from my hip to my pubic bone, and his hot breath coated me as he inserted the very tip of the toy inside me. "You okay?"

"Yes, it doesn't hurt at all. It feels... kinda good."

"How about this?" he asked, swiping his tongue through my sex.

"Mmm, that feels *really* good." His tongue flickered against my clit as he worked the tapered plug in and out of me, occasionally adding more cool lube. His mouth on me took away all my reservations as I chased my impending orgasm. "I'm so close, Auburn. Please make me come."

"Take a deep breath, pet, and then blow it out slowly."

I did, and as I exhaled, he sucked my clit into his mouth at the same time he pushed the butt plug home. I came. Hard. Like, *really* fucking hard.

I cried his name, the sound raspy as he widened my legs and ate my pussy with gusto. My wrists strained against the cuffs, the chain rattling against the headboard as my body writhed uncontrollably against the sheets.

"Fuck," he grunted, lifting up onto his knees and raising my hips with a tight grasp. "I need to be inside you, Gianna."

"Yes," I groaned. "Fuck me hard, baby."

Auburn gave me exactly what I asked for, entering me with a rough thrust. "Christ, that's tight."

The extra bulk of the plug in my ass made my pussy an almost impossibly snug fit for his thick girth. "I feel. So. Full," I panted as my inner walls rippled around him with the aftershocks of my orgasm.

He began to move with long, deep thrusts, his fingers digging so hard into my flesh, I was sure I'd have bruises tomorrow.

"Just wait until it's my cock inside that tight little ass of yours," he growled, lifting my hips a little more and finding that sweet spot with his crown as he moved one thumb to stroke my clit. "I'm about to blow just thinking about it, pet. Fucking your ass. Watching my dick stretch you out while you come all over me."

The visual of him fucking me from behind with his deep grunts filling the room had me right on the edge again. I'd never come this quickly twice in a row, but the fullness between my legs combined with his filthy talk had me *right there*.

"Auburn... please," I begged, and his hips picked up the pace, slapping against my ass and putting pressure on the toy in my backside. The banging of the headboard against the wall only added to the alluring symphony of sex noises, and I let myself fall.

"Fuuuck!" I screamed at the same time he held himself deep and filled me.

"Goddamn, Gianna," he groaned as he continued to pulse inside of me. He leaned forward and removed my blindfold, his hazy blue eyes shining down at me. "You are so amazing."

My eyelids closed, and a sated smile arced my lips. "You are too, but can you please untie me now?"

He reached over me and unsnapped the cuffs before gathering me in his arms. My face went automatically to the side of his neck, and I kissed him there as my arms wrapped around his back. We simply held each other for a while before he finally pulled out of me.

Helping me from the bed, Auburn scooped me up bride-style and carried me to the bathroom. He set me down on the edge of his gigantic tub, kneeling between my legs and gently removing the plug.

"Let me start you some bathwater," Auburn said, stretching to the side, and turning the knobs. He carried the plug to the sink and did a clean up before coming back, checking the water, and adding some lavender bath salts.

My mind and body were still in a bit of a post-sex haze, and he bent to look me in the eye. "Are you okay, sweet pet?"

I shook my head sadly, and a look of alarm crossed his face. "Did I hurt you? Why didn't you tell me, Gianna?"

"You didn't hurt me. I just didn't get any pie," I said with a pout. A grin spread across his handsome face, and he kissed me softly.

"Get your pretty little ass in the tub, and I'll go get you some. You want ice cream?" I lifted a *what do you think* eyebrow at him, and he winked. "Gotcha. Double scoop, it is."

A few minutes later, he handed me a bowl of warm apple pie topped with cold ice cream and climbed into the bathtub behind me. I gobbled it down, even sharing a few bites with Auburn before setting the bowl aside and twisting my face to look up at him.

"I don't think I've ever been happier than I am right now."

"Great sex, a couples' bath, and homemade pie with ice cream? I'm not sure we could ever top that."

He kissed me then, and we shared the taste of butter, sugar, and sweet cream on our tongues as I fell even more deeply in love with Auburn Bouvier.

Chapter 25

I STOOD LOOKING AT the woman sleeping in my bed, feeling like the luckiest bastard in the world. Gianna was curled up on her side, her dark hair fanned out on the pillow behind her, and one tanned, bare shoulder peeked out from the sheet I'd covered her with. As always, one of her long legs had escaped the confines of the bedding and rested on top.

Never in my life had I memorized a woman's sleeping habits, but I knew Gianna's by heart. The way she couldn't sleep with both legs under the covers. The way she preferred resting on her left side. Even the lavender vanilla linen spray she liked to spritz on her pillow.

After quickly checking her blood sugar, I kissed her sweet cheek as softly as I could, but she stirred anyway. "Auburn," she mumbled, and my heart swelled to twice its normal size when she smiled sleepily and blinked her eyes open. "G'morning, baby." Her soft hand stroked through the scruff on my jaw, and I tilted into her touch.

Sitting beside her on the edge of the bed, I brushed a stray piece of hair from her face. "Good morning, my beautiful pet. Did you sleep well?"

"Mmhmm. So good." She stretched, offering me a tempting view of her breast when the sheet slipped down.

Unable to help myself, I traced one finger around the supple curve before dragging the cover down the rest of the way. "Jesus, woman. I wish I could stay here all day and look at you."

Her responding smirk was so sexy, it had me hardening in my pants. "I wish you could stay here all day and do *other things*." Gianna slinked her hand inside my unbuttoned shirt, her fingers bumping over the ridges of my abdomen. "But you have an empire to run."

The feel and sight of her almost had me saying *screw the empire*.

"You're right," I sighed. "Go back to sleep, sweet girl. I didn't mean to wake you."

"It's okay. I'll make you breakfast while you finish getting ready for work."

"You don't have to—"

But in one fluid motion, she sat up, rose onto her knees, and slung a leg over mine so that she was straddling me. "I want to."

"Far be it from me to argue with a very naked Gianna," I told her, running my hands up and down her breathtakingly beautiful body. "I would sign over my life savings to you right now."

"Very tempting offer, but I think I'd rather have a kiss."

And this is why I loved her. Though I was teasing, she didn't even bat an eye at the prospect of receiving that kind of money. All she wanted was my affection. Magdalena would have already been writing down her account number and shoving it into my hand.

Holding Gianna's exquisite face in my hands, I kissed her, my tongue sliding in and out of her warm mouth until all I craved was her. I twisted our bodies until she was flat on her back and propped her feet on the edge of the mattress. Then I kneeled on the floor and ate her. Fucking devoured her.

By the time she'd come twice, my styled hair was a wreck from her eager hands. I lifted my wet face and pressed a kiss to her mound. "Thank you, sweetheart. You make an excellent breakfast."

She threw back her pretty head and laughed, the sound raspy from her repeated calling of my name while I was between her legs. "That's not what I meant, but I'm not complaining."

I stood, holding out my hands to help pull Gianna to her feet before reaching for my black terry cloth bathrobe on the chair near my bed. She slid her arms into it, and I tied it snugly at the waist, making a note to purchase her a robe of her own to keep at my place.

When she went into the kitchen, I returned to the bathroom and restored my hair to order. I decided against shaving because I wanted the taste and scent of her on my face for the remainder of the day… until I could taste her again.

After getting fully dressed, I wandered out to the kitchen and found Cruz eating pie at the counter as Gianna laughed at something he said. I managed to quell my annoyance by reminding myself that she was in *my* kitchen, wearing *my* bathrobe, after *my* face had been between her legs for twenty minutes.

It was hard to blame Cruz for being drawn to my sweet, funny woman. Everyone was. So I straightened my tie and entered the kitchen.

"Good morning, Cruz. I see you're enjoying the pie Gianna made."

"Oh, yes sir. It's the best," he said around a mouthful before taking a sip of his coffee.

"Hello, sweetheart," I said, pulling her to me and kissing her hard—just because I was a possessive sonofabitch.

Her tiny smirk told me she knew exactly what I was doing. "Sit down, and I'll bring your breakfast to you. Do you want juice now and a coffee to go?"

"Yes please, Mommy."

Cruz snorted coffee up his nose, and I pounded him on the back when he began coughing. Poor guy wasn't accustomed to seeing me be playful, I guess.

Gianna placed a plate and a glass of cherry-pomegranate juice in front of me. "Sorry they're just canned biscuits, but I didn't have time to make any from scratch if you're going to get to work on time."

I peered at my plate. "I thought we were eating the eggs we got yesterday."

"We are. I mashed them up, fried some bacon, and mixed it all together. Then I drizzled the buttery sauce on top, and voila! You have a breakfast sandwich."

I picked up one of the biscuits on my plate, took a huge bite, and almost melted into a puddle on the floor. "Sweet Jesus, that's good," I told her, and she beamed at my praise. Inhaling the rest of it in a single bite, I picked up the second one. "Did you try one of these?" I asked Cruz.

"No, I opted for pie, but the way you sucked that thing down in two bites, I'm a little jealous."

Gianna turned and grabbed a biscuit from the pan on the stove and began fixing another of the wicked little sandwiches. "I'll wrap you up one to go, Cruz. You can have it as a mid-morning snack."

"Thanks, Mommy," he retorted, and I punched him in the arm.

"Stop it. She's my mommy, not yours."

Gianna rolled her eyes and smacked us both in the head with a dish towel before setting a foil-wrapped bundle in front of my driver. "You two stop teasing me. I'm Italian, and I like feeding people."

"Ooh, can you make puttanesca?" Cruz asked, his eyes lighting up.

"Of course I can," Gianna scoffed.

My driver turned puppy dog eyes on me and whined, "Please, Daddy. If Mommy makes puttanesca, can I pretty please eat dinner with you?"

I gave him the side eye. "Call me Daddy one more time, and you're fired."

"What about me?" Gianna bit her lip and lifted a bold eyebrow at me. "Can I call you Daddy?"

Cruz coughed and stood, grabbing his sandwich. "I'm just gonna wait in the living room. I think Mom and Dad need some special grown-up alone time."

Downing my juice, I rose and prowled toward my gorgeous woman, who was leaning against the counter with a coy smile curling the edges of her pink lips. My hands found the edge of the granite, and I leaned into her.

"Do you realize, Gianna, that you just called me Daddy and gave me a very inopportune erection in front of my driver?" She pressed her twitching lips together. "What do you think I should do about that?"

She looked down contritely. "I don't know, Daddy." Her eyes turned upward, looking at me through long, dark lashes. "Maybe you should eat my pussy again. That would really teach me a lesson."

I busted out laughing and kissed her on the forehead. "I love your crazy ass. I might just spank it later... if you're lucky."

"I look forward to your punishment, sir," she purred.

"Dammit, would you stop it?" Pushing my hard cock against her stomach, I told her, "This thing is never going to go down, and need I remind you that I have to work with your father?"

"Well, that's going to be awkward." She pressed her soft lips against mine. "I hope you have a good day today."

"You too, baby. What are your plans?"

"Studying and then going through a few of Nana's things that were left in the apartment." She tilted her head and ran her fingers down my gray tie. "Are you free for lunch today?"

My mind mentally sifted through my calendar. "No, I have a meeting with a store owner who's in town from L.A. Then I have a phone meeting with a Japanese supplier this evening at seven because of the time difference. We can order something in, but I'll be late getting home."

"No, it's okay. I'll just stay at my place tonight."

My forehead furrowed. I didn't like that idea at all. "I want you to stay with me. How will I deliver your spanking if you're not with me?"

Her lips twisted to the side as she lifted her shoulders and let them fall. "I just don't want to overstay my welcome. You're going to get tired of me."

"Not going to fucking happen," I growled, sliding my hands down to her ass and holding her against me. "You can move in if you want to."

She giggled, but I wasn't even joking a little bit. "Call me when you get done, and we'll decide then. You sound like you have a long day."

"Which will only be longer if I know I don't get to see you tonight. I'll have Cruz get a key for my apartment made, and he'll drop it off at your place. That way, you can come and go whenever you want."

"Really? You trust me with a key to your place? What if I steal all your shit?"

I kissed her palm and placed it on my chest. "Well, you've already stolen my heart, so..."

"Okay, Bouvier. It's time for you to go. You're getting entirely too cheesy." She pivoted her body and picked up my favorite insulated cup. "Here. I already made your coffee."

Taking the coffee, I wrapped a napkin around my remaining sandwich and gave Gianna a quick peck. I was really running late now. "Thanks for breakfast, pet." My eyes swept up and down her body, and I winked. "Both of them."

Chapter 26

I WAS WHISTLING WHEN I got off the elevator on the fiftieth floor, and Tony looked up at me in surprise. "Good Morning, Mister Bouvier. Is everything all right?"

"Of course, Tony. Why wouldn't it be?"

"You seem awfully chipper today. Plus, you're running a few minutes late, and, well, I think you forgot to shave, sir."

Rubbing my fingers over my jaw, I shrugged. "I'm trying a new look." Striking a pose worthy of a catalog underwear model, I turned my face in profile. "What do you think?"

Tony chuckled, and I was pretty sure that was the first time I'd ever heard the man laugh. He was always so serious; but maybe that was because *I* was always so serious.

"I think it looks nice, Mister Bouvier. I've heard the ladies like a little facial hair."

I wanted to tell him that there was only one woman I wanted to impress, but that woman happened to be his daughter, so I kept my trap shut. "Is that why you always keep a goatee?" I asked with a grin as I sat on the corner of his desk. "To impress the lucky ladies of New York?"

"You know," he said, stroking his own facial hair, "I do what I can, Mister Bouvier."

This was the most normal and casual conversation I'd ever had with my PA, and to be honest, I think that made me kind of a jerk. Why had I never just talked to Tony like a human being instead of an employee?

"Tony, how long have you worked here?"

"Oh, let's see... eleven years for your father, and then the past six for you."

Crossing my arms over my chest, I nodded. "That's a long time. I'd like for you to call me Auburn, if you'd be comfortable with that."

His eyebrows hit the roof. "O-okay, Mister... Auburn. Sorry, that's going to take some getting used to."

I smiled at him. "It's all right. Take your time."

He swallowed and looked down at his calendar. "You remember that you have that lunch meeting with Mister Evans from Los Angeles today, right?"

Guess it's back to business. "I do. And the overseas phone call this evening."

"Right. I made your lunch reservation at San Carlo Osteria since you said you wanted to try somewhere different this time. It's in SoHo."

"Excellent. I've heard good things about it. If it's good, maybe I'll..." *Take Gianna for dinner one night,* I almost said, but amended it at the last second. "...try it for dinner some time."

"Sure, just let me know, and I'll arrange it for you."

"Thank you, Tony. And I just wanted to let you know that you do a tremendous job as my PA, and I'm very grateful to have you on my team. I know I don't say it enough, but I do appreciate you."

His mouth was hanging open so wide, I was afraid he was going to swallow a fly, but he quickly recovered. "Thank you for saying that, M-Auburn." I had a feeling I was going to be called Mauburn quite a lot until Tony got used to calling me by my first name. "So, one more thing," he said, changing the subject, "you have an awards dinner in three weeks. Should I go ahead and secure a date for you?"

I almost yelled, "No!" but reined myself in. I didn't want anyone except Gianna on my arm. Pretending to think about his question, I scratched the side of my face. "You know what, Tony? I might see if Gianna would like to go with me again. She did such an amazing job at the gala last month."

"Gi-Gianna? *My* Gianna?" he stuttered.

Actually, she's mine.

"Yes, of course. I didn't have to worry about a thing at the hospital charity. I found her to be bright and engaging, and I'm pretty sure she could have an intelligent conversation with that wall over there," I told him, tilting my head, and Tony chuckled.

"You got that right. She's never been shy."

"You've raised a wonderful daughter, Tony. Everyone was quite charmed by her." *Including me.* "She and Darian Knight seemed to hit it off well, and Darian is around thirty years older than Gianna. She even talked with grumpy old Grayson McCutchens, and that man is eighty if he's a day."

"Well, age is just a number. What really matters is the connection between people," Tony said wisely, and I had to fight a grin.

"You know, Tony. I couldn't agree more." I stood and headed toward my office. "I think I'll give Gianna a call right now and see if she's free in three weeks."

"Don't you need her number?" my PA asked, and I froze with my hand on the doorknob.

Fuck. Turning around, I faked a smile. "Yes, of course. Please send her contact information to my phone."

Once inside with the door firmly closed behind me, I sank into my chair and ran both hands through my hair. I'd almost screwed up royally. I hated this sneaking around shit, especially now that Gianna and I were in love with each other.

Picking up my phone, I noticed that Tony had forwarded Gianna's number to me. The number I already had. The duplicity ate at me, and

I clicked on her name to place the call, my heart picking up the pace when she answered.

"Hello, handsome. You miss me already?"

"Completely," I responded, "but I called because I need to talk to you about something."

"Okay, shoot."

"I was just talking to Tony, and he reminded me I have an awards banquet to go to in three weeks. He offered to find me a date." I heard only silence, so I continued. "I suggested that I ask you to accompany me to the event because you did such a stellar job at the last one we attended together."

"At least while I was vertical," she added, making me chuckle.

"Yes, that. Though I have enjoyed certain horizontal moments with you in private since then." A smile crossed my face when she giggled at my innuendo. "But sweetheart, all I wanted to do was blurt out the truth. That I only wanted *you* to go with me because we're in love. I absolutely hate hiding our relationship; we're not doing anything wrong."

She released a soft sigh. "I know we're not, Auburn, and you're right. We need to tell my Dad about us." A sense of relief washed over me. "Will you let me talk to him first?"

My finger slid back and forth over my jaw as I thought about that. "It's really important to me that we tell him together, Gianna. If he gets upset I want to be there for you. I also want him to see how serious I am and be able to ask me any questions he may have."

"I understand. I would just like to have dinner with him and feel him out a little. Maybe let him know that you asked me to go with you to the awards thing, and see what he says."

"Okay, baby. If that's what you want to do."

"Hmm, since you're busy for dinner, maybe I'll surprise him at his apartment tonight and see if he wants to order Chinese or something. Oh, and do you care if I study here this morning? Your apartment is so much quieter than mine."

"You know I don't mind, sweetheart. Just let me know when you plan to go to your place, and I'll have Cruz drive you."

"I'll probably leave here around one."

"Fine. Now that that's settled," I said, lowering my voice, "what are you wearing right now?"

"I'm still wearing your robe, and oh God, am I looking sexy!"

A groan escaped me as I thought about how Gianna looked before I left this morning. Even though my robe completely swallowed her, she was as alluring as ever. "I think you're joking, but I find you extremely sexy when you're wearing my clothes, pet."

"Do you now?"

"Mmhmm, I do."

"I'll have to remember that," she said, her voice soft and sultry.

A knock sounded at my door, and I was startled out of my little fantasy world. "Come in, Tony," I called automatically, then mentally kicked myself. I should have hung up the phone first.

He entered just as his brat of a daughter purred, "Would this be a bad time to tell you that I really enjoyed the oral this morning?"

Doing my best to smile at my PA, I replied with a simple, "Yes," into the phone.

"And that I would like to get on my knees and return the favor really soon?"

"Uh-huh. I would like that very much." I dabbed discreetly at the sweat beading on my forehead.

Tony sat in the chair across from my desk to wait for me to complete my call, as he always did when I was on the phone.

"Do you think it would be a good idea for me to wear that plug for a little while today, Daddy?"

Nearly choking on my own spit, I cleared my throat. "Yes, Gianna. I think that would be fine."

Tony smiled at the mention of his daughter's name, though I was pretty sure his expression would be completely different if he knew the things she was saying to me right then.

"I'll be thinking of you the whole time I'm wearing it."

Sweet Jesus! Cue the raging boner.

"I appreciate you agreeing to do that, Gianna, but I need to go now. *Tony* is in my office to go over some things with me."

"Okay, sir. I'm just going to go take a shower now." She didn't say it, but *naked* was implied with that statement, and my cock throbbed heavily in my suit pants.

"I'll have Devereaux contact you about clothing. Bye now." And I hung up before she could further taunt me.

"That was my daughter?" Tony asked, metaphorically splashing cold water over my errant thoughts.

"Yes, she's agreed to go with me to the awards."

"Good," he answered with a smile. "I'm glad you've found someone you feel comfortable with to accompany you to these events."

Comfortable is not exactly the word I'm thinking of right now.

"So what can I help you with?"

My PA slid two folders across the desk. "The red folder is the info on Mister Evans's L.A. location, and the blue contains my research and notes on Mister Izumi for your call this evening."

Flipping through the red folder, I made a couple notations in the margin before turning to the other one and doing the same. I rapped a knuckle against the folders and met Tony's eye. "This is excellent, Tony. Thank you for taking the time to be so thorough."

He seemed taken aback, but pleased, by my praise. Had I really been such a dick that he was surprised when I gave him an *attaboy*?

"I'm just doing my job, um, Auburn." He stood. "I'll be at my desk, if you need me."

As he left, I made a conscientious decision to be a better boss from now on. Not just toward my PA, but to all of my staff. I had an excellent team, and they deserved to know they were appreciated. Smiling to myself, I realized that Gianna had rubbed off on me.

Leaning against the back of the elevator, I grinned down at my phone when I read through my and Gianna's text exchange from earlier.

Auburn: You're going to pay for that, baby girl.

Gianna: Sorry.

Auburn: Are you really?

Gianna: Nope. It was fun listening to you squirm.

Auburn: You'll be the one squirming later.

Gianna: I'm squirming already just thinking about what you're going to do to me.

When the elevator doors opened, I pocketed my phone and walked out the front door to see Cruz waiting beside my Bentley.

"Ready to go, sir? Tony already forwarded me the address to the restaurant."

"Yes, and after you drop me off, I need you to get a key to my apartment made for Gianna. She's still at my place, so if you could pick her up and take her home, that would be great."

"Excuse me?" The loud, familiar screech from behind me had me shaking my head as I turned around. Magdalena was standing there, hands on hips and blue eyes blazing with fury. "Did I just hear you say you're giving *that woman* a key to your apartment?"

"Keep your voice down, Magdalena. And not that it's any of your business, but yes."

"Don't you tell me to keep my voice down. I'm fucking pissed! You never gave me a key to your apartment."

Glancing around, I noticed that people were starting to stare, and one woman pulled out her phone to start filming. *Fuck.* I needed to nip this shit in the bud before the paparazzi showed up. There's nothing they loved more than a dramatic scene.

I huffed out a harsh breath and hissed, "Get in the car, Mag. I'm not talking about this out here."

Cruz opened the door, his eyes holding mine as my ex stuck her nose in the air and climbed into the back seat. Giving him a nod that told him exactly what I wanted him to do, I followed her. Her look was triumphant when I settled into the seat beside her.

"What the fuck are you doing here?"

"I needed to talk to you, and since you so rudely walked out on me last night…"

"You thought you would ambush me in front of my office and make a scene so I would talk to you, right?"

Her overstuffed lips curled into a smug smile. "It worked."

Cruz got into the driver's seat, and Magdalena reached for the privacy button. "No," I said sharply. "That stays down."

She pulled her hand back and glared at me. "Fine."

"If this is about us getting back together, it's not going to happen. You can't strongarm me into having feelings for you."

"That's not what I want anymore."

Okay, we're finally on the same page.

"Then what do you want? What's so goddamn important, you had to cause a scene?"

"Money," she stated matter-of-factly.

"What about money?"

"You owe me."

A humorless laugh burst through my lips as I crossed my arms over my chest. "This oughta be good. Please. *Do* tell me what I owe you for." I glanced to the front seat, and my driver gave me an imperceptible nod.

"We were together for five years. That's longer than some marriages, so I want a 'divorce' settlement." She did little quote marks with her fingers around the D-word.

"You want a divorce settlement, when we weren't even married?"

"We were *practically* married," she retorted.

"Oh, really? You just said I never even gave you a key to my apartment, so in what realm of crazy do you think that constitutes practically married?" Her lips thinned, and two lines appeared between her fake eyebrows. "Let me just lay this out for you, okay? Yes, we were together for five years, but we were broken up for around half that time. Ours was a relationship of convenience. Nothing more. In those five years, did I ever once tell you I loved you?"

She lifted her chin in defiance. "No. You never said the actual words, but I know you did."

"I'm sorry you were under that impression, but no, I didn't. I tolerated you, Magdalena, mostly to keep my mother off my ass. And this entitled fucking attitude is exactly why I could never fall in love with you."

Her face contorted with anger. "God, you're a fucking asshole. Do you realize you never even let me spend the night? You just fucked me and then had Cruz drive me home."

I shrugged. She wasn't wrong. "Maybe I am an asshole, but I never heard you complaining while I was fucking you."

"Why don't we talk about that for a minute. Does your new girlfriend know what a depraved sonofabitch you are? Does she know you like to fuck with your hand around a woman's neck?"

I could feel my face flushing bright red. "One time, Magdalena. I did that one time, and when you said you didn't like it, I stopped."

"But you didn't stop when you were with other women while we were on our little breaks, did you? Yes, I've talked to some of them. They also told me you like spanking." She pursed her lips and lifted her eyebrows at me, her expression judgemental as hell.

"What I do in my private time is none of your fucking business," I growled.

"It's about to become everyone's business," she said sharply. "I want five million dollars, or I'm talking to the press."

Other than in a sexual nature, I'd never wanted to wrap my hands around a woman's neck, but in that moment, I easily could have choked the hell out of Magdalena. And it would have had absolutely nothing to do with asserting dominance or heightening sexual pleasure.

"What, precisely, do you think you're going to tell the press?" I asked, my voice as tight as a drum.

A self-righteous smile slithered across her face. "I'll tell them exactly how you act in the bedroom. All your dirty talk and alpha-male bullshit."

I laughed in her fucking face. Like a full-on, deep, belly laugh. When my eyes shifted to the front of the car, I caught a glimpse of Cruz's amusement as well. Wiping mirthful tears from the corners of my eyes, I turned my attention back to the bitch beside me and nodded.

"Okay, Magdalena. You win."

Her eyes almost popped out of her greedy little head. "Y-you'll give me the money?"

Leaning forward until my nose was an inch from hers, I relieved her of that notion. "Let me make this crystal fucking clear. You'll never get one thin dime from me. *Nothing*. So you go ahead and talk to the press. I can promise you, all that will do is have women lining up at my door. Women who don't fuck like a dead fish."

Her mouth popped open, and her face turned as red as a ruby. "But..." She seemed to run out of words then.

"Cruz, you can let Magdalena out here. I think she has some phone calls to make." He nodded, and the car rolled to a stop.

My ex found her voice, though panic had infused it now. "What's your sweet little girlfriend going to think when she finds out?"

"That's none of your concern. All you need to worry about is the lawsuit I'm going to slap on your ass for attempting to blackmail me. I'll get to that in between fighting off the hordes of women you'll inadvertently be sending my way."

Cruz opened the door, and her eyes bounced between him and me like she was attempting to figure out her next move. Good. I had her flustered. "You're going to regret this, Auburn Bouvier."

"To the contrary, sweetheart," I sneered, "I can't think of anything I'll enjoy more. Besides fucking my fiery little Gianna."

She let out a strangled scream and whipped her head around as she climbed out of the vehicle.

"Have a nice day, Magdalena," Cruz said with ultra-politeness, and I flashed him a grin.

As soon as the door was closed, my smile faded, and I picked up my phone and dialed a number.

"Samuel White," the voice answered.

"Samuel, this is Auburn Bouvier."

"Yes, Mister Bouvier. How can I help you?"

"You know that file you have on Magdalena Lewis?"

"Yes, sir."

"I need it. Now."

Chapter 27

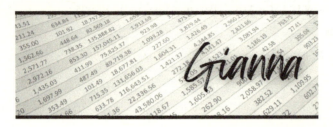

"Thank you for the ride, Cruz, but I really could have taken a cab."

He slid the car smoothly to the curb in front of my building. "You know how he is, Gia. Hang on, and I'll walk you in."

My eyes rolled until I could practically see my own brains. "There's literally a doorman *right there*."

Paying me no mind, Cruz got out and opened the door for me. I'd insisted on sitting in the front with him, and he finally relented when I told him he had to call me *Miss Daisy* if I sat in the back.

Cruz walked me inside and handed me a key. "Mister Bouvier said to give this to you. It's for his apartment."

"Thanks, Cruz."

"And you'll call me if you need a ride somewhere?"

"Yes, sir," I said, giving him a snappy salute. "Don't you ever get time off, Cruz? Or do you just drive around at Auburn's whims?"

He chuckled. "I definitely get time off. In fact, I'm going to my niece's dance recital tonight. Mister B is going to take an Uber after his meeting tonight."

"Awww, how old is your niece?"

"She's five and a complete doll."

My heart warmed at the obvious adoration on Cruz's face. "Okay, you have fun and enjoy your night off. I want to see pictures."

Once I got to my apartment, I went straight to work. I'd discovered several boxes of Nana's belongings in the hall closet, and I needed to sort through them.

Two hours later, I collapsed onto the couch amid the piles I'd made. My eyes fell on the stack of crocheted doilies on the coffee table, and I giggled to myself. "Who in the world actually needs forty-two doilies, Nana?" I asked the room.

I'd chosen a few to keep as mementos, but I would donate the rest to a local thrift shop. Maybe Lehra would know of one since I was pretty sure Auburn would have no clue. I shot off a text to my friend, and she responded a minute later with the names of several shops that accepted donations.

Tapping on an icon, I browsed the NYC gossip app I'd admittedly become a little bit addicted to. At least twice a week, there was something on there about Auburn, usually a picture of him entering or exiting a restaurant or a short article about a cause he'd donated to.

I'd learned my man was pretty damned philanthropic, though he never really talked about it. He was especially supportive of local law enforcement, maybe because his brother was a cop.

He'd told me a little bit about Monty, and I knew it bothered him that they didn't have a close relationship. He also mentioned a sister once, but when I asked about her, he clammed up.

I had saved several pictures of Auburn from this site, my favorite one being a shot of him exiting his building in one of his perfectly fitted suits, his thumb on his chin as he looked off to the side. He looked positively yummy, and I had to admit that the picture ranked high in my spank bank collection.

After reading the comments that enamored females left on the site, I was pretty sure I wasn't the only woman getting off to the image. It was pretty amusing reading some of their posts. One woman said she would "literally let that man crack my spine in half."

Don't blame ya one bit, sister. And he's quite capable of it.

My heart picked up a notch when I saw a new video on the site and immediately recognized Auburn standing outside his office. Then my heart stopped when I watched him usher Magdalena into the back of his vehicle.

What the actual fuck? My finger hit the volume button on the side of my phone, but I couldn't hear what they were saying. The video was taken from too far away, and the only sound was the background noise of the city. I watched it again, taking note of the nod he gave to Cruz before climbing into the back with *her*.

What was that about?

This must be an old video. It *had* to be. I scrolled down to the caption, which was dated today.

BOUVIER STILL PLAYING THE FIELD - *Auburn Bouvier was spotted getting into his vehicle with his old flame, Magdalena Lewis, a little before noon today. Are they rekindling? Only time will tell.*

Tossing my phone on the couch beside me, I stared at it like it was a bomb. My mind was reeling with possibilities and insecurities. I finally picked it up and decided to be proactive.

Gianna: How was your lunch today?

Auburn: Great. Evans will be carrying Bouvier's new line in his Rodeo Drive store.

Gianna: That's good. So you enjoyed meeting with Mr. Evans?

Auburn: Yes, the restaurant was excellent. I had the Pescato del Giorno. I really want to take you there for dinner one night.

I set my phone down and flopped over onto the couch. He hadn't even mentioned Magdalena. Had he really gone to eat with this Evans guy, or had he turned down my lunch invitation so he could see his ex?

"I'm being ridiculous," I said out loud to drive the point home, though it didn't stop the nervous flutters in my belly. The scenario of a man going back to his ex was all too familiar, but I reminded myself that Auburn was no Ryan.

"He loves you, Gianna. The man freaking adores you." The stomach flutters slowed down and eventually stopped altogether as I closed my eyes and calmed myself with images of Auburn Bouvier. The way he touched my face. The way he would do any fucking thing in the world for me. The way he loved me beyond anything I could have ever imagined.

I was dozing peacefully when I was startled from sleep by my front door hitting the wall. I popped up to find a frantic Auburn in the doorway, his chest heaving with exertion. "Gianna, are you okay?" he panted, rushing to my side without even closing the door. He kneeled on the floor and grabbed my face between his hands. "Answer me. Are you sick?"

"No, Auburn. I'm not sick. Why would you think that?"

"You stopped returning my texts, so I called you, but you didn't answer. I thought... I thought something was wrong." His blue eyes searched my face, and the concern there was evident.

I blinked a few times, trying to clear my head. That's when it came back to me. *Auburn and Magdalena.* Surprisingly, the worry from earlier didn't seem nearly as acute. Maybe because this man was kneeling in front of me, acting like his world would end if something happened to me.

"I guess I just fell asleep," I mumbled.

"Thank God," he breathed, kissing my forehead over and over. "I was so worried, baby."

"How did you get in here?"

His lips tipped up on one side in a guilty smile. "I own the building now, remember? I got Hanson to give me the maintenance key to your apartment." His hand stroked down the side of my face. "I want you to know that I value your privacy, and I never would have used the key unless I truly thought you were in danger. I promise."

Unsure what to even say to that, I nodded. "So you were really worried about me?"

"I was," he said, standing to close the door before taking a seat beside me on the couch and rubbing my back. "You're awfully quiet. Is everything okay?"

"Just a long day, I guess."

"Tell me about it. I had to deal with fucking Magdalena today."

I turned to look at him. "Really?"

He covered his face with his hands and groaned. "Yes. She confronted me in front of my building and started making a scene. I didn't know what else to do, so I made her get in the car before the press showed up."

Relief edged away any niggling uncertainties. *He told me about seeing her almost as soon as he got here. Surely he wouldn't have done that if he was hiding something.*

"What did she want?"

He uncovered his face and tipped his head against the back of the couch. "You're not going to fucking believe this. The bitch is trying to blackmail me."

"To get you back? Wow. She seems very... devoted to you."

Auburn scoffed out a disgusted noise. "She's devoted to my money. She wants five million dollars."

"*Five million dollars?*" My mind was freaking blown.

"Yep."

"Or what?"

"Or she's going to go to the press and tell them I'm some kind of pervert."

"You are some kind of pervert," I said, cracking a smile for the first time in hours.

"True," he said with a lopsided grin. "But that's my private life she's threatening to splash all over the gossip rags. She said she would tell them all about my dominant, alpha-male side."

Holy shit! "Wh-what did you tell her?"

"I told her to fucking bring it, and I'd slap her with a lawsuit for trying to blackmail me."

I leaned back against the couch beside him. "Does she realize that saying those things would only make you more desirable to women?"

"I told her that too. I have everything on video."

Looking at him in confusion, I asked, "How did you manage that?"

"I've learned that when you have money, some people try to bring you down. When I bought the Bentley, I had a tiny camera installed. I rarely use it, but it never hurts to have a full recording in case something comes up. Like this. I gave Cruz a signal before I got in the car, and he activated the camera."

That was the nod I saw. Unable to hold back another second, I admitted, "I already knew you met with Magdalena today." At his confused look, I pulled up the app on my phone and showed him the video and caption.

"What the hell is this bullshit?" he grinded out.

"It's a gossip app."

He turned his head slowly and looked at me, his mouth agape. "You don't seem like the type to indulge in gossip, Gianna."

Shame crept up and colored my cheeks as I tried to explain. "I look at it for the pictures. I guess it's kind of the opposite of reading *Playboy* for the articles." His lips twitched at that. "They have you on there a few times a week, and I save the pictures on my phone."

He blinked and shook his head. "They have *me* on there?"

"It's usually just still photos of you leaving your office or going into a restaurant or something."

"Why in the world would anyone in their right mind want to see pictures of me leaving a restaurant?"

"Because you're rich and incredibly handsome. Everything you do is interesting."

"That's ridiculous. And why do you need pictures from some website when you can see me anytime you want?"

I gnawed on the inside of my cheek. "The pictures are for when we're not together. So I can have... you know... *inspiration*?" The last word came out as barely a whisper as I averted my eyes in embarrassment. I couldn't believe I'd just admitted that out loud.

Auburn tapped his bottom lip with his long finger as a knowing grin slipped across his perfect mouth. "So, you're saying these pictures are spank bankable?"

I closed my eyes and nodded. "Yes, are you happy now? And can we please change the subject?"

"Yes, I'm very happy, and no, we can't change the subject." He pulled me across his lap so that my knees were on each side of his hips. "I need to hear more about you touching yourself to pictures of me."

"Fine," I snapped, resting my hands on the back of the couch and leaning into him. "I like to look at hot pictures of you while I diddle my biscuit. Okay?"

His shoulders shook with laughter. "Diddle your biscuit?"

"Stop laughing at me," I told him with a frown.

Holding my ass with both hands, he stood, and I wrapped my legs around him. "Grab your phone," he instructed me, and I reached down for it before he walked us back to my bedroom.

"What are we doing?"

"I'm giving you what you need?"

I lifted one eyebrow. "Do we really have time for that? You have a meeting at your office in a couple of hours."

"I'll always make time for that, but that's not what I'm talking about." At my questioning look, he explained. "I would prefer it if you didn't look at the gossip sites anymore, so I'm giving you spank bank material."

He set me on my feet beside my bed and told me to open up the camera on my phone as he shrugged out of his jacket.

"Ohh, I see where this is going," I said, biting my bottom lip with excitement.

Tossing his jacket aside, he said, "Tell me how you want me."

"Um, on my bed."

"Best offer I've had all day," he said, sitting and leaning back against my headboard.

I kneeled beside him. "Can I undress you?"

He stared at me flatly. "Is that a serious question?"

Giggling, I untied his tie before unbuttoning his shirt all the way down. I arranged the tie so that it draped down his hard chest and nodded happily at the results. "Okay that's hot," I observed, crawling off the bed and framing him on the screen. "No, hold on," I said, turning on the lamp and extinguishing the overhead light.

Auburn rested one arm behind his head, his bicep straining the seams of his tailored shirt. I started snapping pictures, walking around the bed for different angles, and his eyes followed my every step. "Shit, that's sexy," I said when his teeth sunk into his bottom lip.

"Thank you ma'am. What should I do with this hand?"

"Uh, maybe touch your face or your chest or something."

He lifted his hand to his jaw, his fingers rubbing against his hot-as-hell scruff. "Oh yeah, baby. Work it for Mama," I called out, and his responding grin was the sexiest thing I'd ever seen. Then his face turned serious as he moved his hand down his chest. With parted lips, he dropped his eyelids a bit, giving me a look I could feel right between my legs.

When his hand reached his eight-pack abs, I had to force myself not to toss the camera and crawl on top of him.

"I like seeing you touch yourself," I said softly.

"Oh really?" he asked, unfastening his belt.

I could barely breathe, much less speak, so I nodded and kept shooting. After unbuttoning his pants, he slowly slid his hand down into his underwear and closed his eyes. "I'm thinking about how you tasted this morning," he said softly.

"You are?" I panted.

"Mmmm, that's why I didn't shave today. So I could have the sweet scent of your cunt on my face all day long."

Good lord, this is some next-level shit right here.

"I'm switching to video so I can hear your voice," I told him, stepping up onto the bed so that I was shooting from above him. And let me tell you... Auburn Bouvier didn't disappoint.

"Gianna," he groaned, his hand moving inside his trousers now. "The taste of your pussy makes my cock so fucking hard. I want to pull you on top of me so you can ride my face while I tongue fuck you, and then I'll suck on your swollen clit until you come over and over on my mouth."

"And then what?" I asked, my voice barely audible. My panties were completely soaked.

"Then I'll turn you over and spank that sweet ass of yours before I slowly slide my dick inside you. I'll start out really slow so you can feel every inch of my fat cock stretching you, baby girl." He tipped his head back, his face the picture of pure ecstasy. "Mmmm. And when I can't take it anymore, Daddy will fuck you. Hard. Deep. Rough. You want it rough, pet? You want Daddy to own that pussy like no one ever has?"

"Yes, I want that."

His eyes were back on me now. "And only after I've made you come so many times and so hard that you can't even hold yourself up anymore, I'll come. Deep inside you, filling you up with my hot seed. So that every time you take down your pretty little panties the next day, you can smell me inside you."

He sat up then, a self-satisfied smirk on his face as he ran his hands up and down my legs. "So, what do you think, pet. Is that enough spank bank material to get you off?"

"Yeah," I croaked, turning off the video as my legs trembled. "That oughta do it."

Chapter 28

"I can't believe you just left me hanging like that," I said.

Auburn grinned and swatted me on the butt. We were back in my living room, and he was fully dressed in his power suit again. "I told you, Gianna. I want you dripping all night for me, anticipating the moment I get home. Then, I promise I will fuck you quite thoroughly."

"Are you headed back to the office now?"

"No, Cruz is driving me home, and then he has the rest of the night off. I need to forward a document from my home computer to my office, and then I'll drive myself back. What about you? Are you still going to try and meet up with your dad?"

"Yes, I'll take an Uber or a cab over to his apartment since it's so far from mine."

Auburn frowned. "Tony doesn't live too far from my place. Why don't you ride back to my house with me, and you can just take one of my cars?"

Crossing my arms over my chest, I informed him, "I'm not driving the Bugatti or the Jaguar. I would be a nervous wreck. Do you have, like, an old Chevy or something?"

"No, Gianna," he said dryly. "I don't have an old Chevy."

"What's the cheapest car you own? I'll drive that."

"Let's see." He tapped his bottom lip in thought. "I have a Cadillac SUV I drive when I need to haul stuff."

"Is it new?"

"It's about three years old, so no."

Sighing heavily, I agreed. "That'll do."

Bending to pick up the stack of doilies I was planning to donate, Auburn hummed in the back of his throat. "These are beautiful. Did your Nana make these?" He was sifting through them one by one, occasionally holding one up to the light.

"Yes. She had a shitload of them. I kept a few, but those are the ones I'm donating."

His face turned to me, his eyes flashing with interest. "You're giving these away? Can I take a few of them?"

I giggled, trying to picture Auburn's modern apartment with doilies all over the place. "Of course, but I don't really think they go with your decor."

He held up a multi-colored one, rubbing his fingers over the dainty lace. "They're not for me. I want to give them to Devereaux. He told me he's 'feeling lace' for next season, and these colors are astounding."

"I don't think I understand. You want him to make clothes out of Nana's doilies?"

Chuckling, he shook his head. "No, Dev gets inspiration from the strangest places. One time, I brought him a turquoise pen as a souvenir from a trip I took, and he adored the color so much, he made an entire women's line with that shade featured. I just think he would really like these."

"Please. Take as many as you want. That's less I have to haul to the thrift shop."

"This one," he said in awe as he inspected a pale ivory doily. "It's so delicate."

I nodded. "That was one of my favorites too. There were four of them, and I kept two."

"Hmmm, okay. I'll take these two. And this one with the purple." He sifted through them again and selected five more, carefully folding them in half. "You ready to go?" he asked, tucking his new treasures beneath his arm.

"Baby, I was born ready," I quipped, picking up my purse and taking his proffered hand.

A little over an hour later, I pulled into my father's parking garage. I had never driven here before, but I knew he had two designated parking places since he lived in a two-bedroom apartment.

"Let's see... 4G... 4G." I spotted his two spots, but both of them were taken, one by Dad's black Audi and the other by a red Toyota Corolla. "He's gonna be pissed that some stranger's parking in his space," I mumbled to myself as I drove a little farther down to find a visitor's space.

Exiting the elevator on the fourth floor, I found my father's apartment. Just as I raised my hand to knock, the door rattled. I opened my mouth to call out so I didn't give him a heart attack when he opened the door and found me on the other side, but I quickly clamped it shut when I heard my dad's voice like I had never heard it before.

"That's it, baby. Squeeze my cock tighter," he growled.

The door shook even harder as another voice cried, "Yes, Tony. Deeper."

"I'll give you fucking deeper."

My legs carried me backward until my back hit the opposite wall. I covered my eyes with my hands to block out the sight of that shaking door, but I could still hear them, so I rapidly moved my hands to my ears and clamped my eyelids shut.

Ohmygod, ohmygod... my dad is *having sex* against his door.

And that wasn't even the worst of it.

The thing that really threw me was... *I recognized the other person's voice.*

I was tipsy. Very tipsy. About half a bottle into a very fine wine, I realized the silver lining. At least I hadn't walked in on the *situation* and witnessed it firsthand. By the time I finished the bottle, I thought the whole thing was kinda fucking hilarious.

Tossing the empty bottle into the trash, I wandered back to Auburn's bedroom and entered his closet, pulling one of his button-down shirts from a hanger.

I had returned to Auburn's apartment after *the incident* and ordered takeout, eating it while I attempted to pickle my brain with a lovely Bordeaux I found in his wine rack.

After taking a quick shower to freshen up, I slipped into a pair of cheeky, green lace panties and Auburn's white shirt, leaving all the buttons open except for two at the bottom. I checked my reflection in the mirror and smiled, remembering that he'd told me he thinks I'm sexy wearing his clothes.

"I'm gonna blow your fucking mind, big boy," I said to my reflection as I applied a deep red lipstick.

As soon as I re-entered the living room, I heard a knock at the door. Creeping toward it, I called out, "Who is it?"

"Can you let me in?" Instantly recognizing Auburn's voice, I stuck my fingers in my hair and scruffed it up a bit to add some volume before smacking my red lips together and swinging the door open.

"Well, hello—" My words ceased as I took in the sight of my man leaning with one arm against the doorframe. "What in the world are you wearing?"

He looked down at his clothing, and then his eyes rose to mine, playfulness shining through his blue irises. "What I always wear to the construction site, ma'am."

Auburn freaking Bouvier was dressed in a denim work shirt with the sleeves rolled up, faded, holey jeans, and dusty work boots. The outfit was completed by a tool belt, a hard hat, and some dirt streaked across his forehead.

So he wanted to play, huh? I could fucking play.

"I'm so glad you're here," I gushed.

"Well, my foreman said you specifically requested me."

"Mmm, yes. I've been watching you at the work site, and you seemed like the most... *capable* man for the job."

He took a step into the room, and his musky cologne enveloped me. "Ma'am, I'm quite skilled at all construction tasks, but my specialty is plumbing. I understand you have a pipe that needs drilling?"

A tiny giggle escaped my lips before I schooled my features. "Oh, yes sir, I certainly do." I stroked a flirty finger down his chest and looked up at him with innocent eyes. "Do you think you could help me?"

Auburn's eyes slid smoothly around the room. "That depends. Is your husband home?"

Ahh, we're playing naughty-housewife-gets-drilled-by-the-dirty-construction-worker, huh?

Putting on my best pout, I crossed my arms beneath my breasts, boosting them and drawing his eyes there. "No, he left me home alone. Again."

"Am I to understand that your husband has been neglecting your pipes for a while?"

I nodded sadly. "Yes, that's why I called you."

"Hmm, it's a damn good thing you did. A woman's pipes should be properly flushed at least twice a day. Why don't you show me to the master bathroom? We'll start there."

Sinking my teeth into my bottom lip, I looked at him through my lashes. "But I don't even know your name, sir?"

"You can call me Daddy. And what's your name?"

Giving him my sweetest smile, I said, "My name is Baby Girl."

A low growl rumbled through his chest, and his nostrils flared. "Is that so?"

"Uh-huh. Come on back here, and I'll let you get to work, Daddy." I led him to the bathroom, feeling his eyes on my backside, so I put a little extra sway in my hips.

Auburn removed his hard hat and swiped a hand through his hair before kneeling beside the double sink and opening the cabinet door. "I can get out of your way," I said, starting to step away, but his hand closed firmly around my bare ankle.

"No. Stay right there. I might require your assistance."

I chewed on the tip of my index finger. "But Daddy, I don't know anything about plumbing."

His lips turned up into a wicked smile. "It's okay, Baby Girl. Just do *exactly* as I tell you." As he peered beneath the sink, his hand took a tempting trek up and down the back of my calf before crossing the border to my thigh. "I don't see anything abnormal under the sink," he said, pivoting toward me. "I should probably check this area though."

He watched me as his hand drifted slowly up the inside of my thigh. My legs shook in anticipation until he reached the apex and swiped his fingers across my soaked panties. Pressing his lips together, he shook his head. "Just as I thought. There's been a flood in this region."

I widened my eyes dramatically. "A flood? What can I do about that?"

"I'll let you know after I've completed my investigation." He lifted the hem of the shirt I was wearing and groaned when he saw my lace panties. "Yes, I'll need to do a *very* thorough investigation here." His rough tongue slowly licked a wide stripe from the inside of my knee up to my pussy.

"Y-you investigate with your mouth?"

He glared at me as he hooked his fingers into my panties at the hips and dragged them down my legs. "Don't question my methods, woman. I'm the expert here," he growled. "Now, lean back against the counter and spread your legs."

I eagerly complied and was rewarded with his tongue flickering against my clit. "Yes, Daddy," I panted as he inserted one long finger inside me, gathering some moisture before moving back an inch and circling my back hole.

"This right here needs to be taken care of immediately," he said. "I'm going to have to plug this hole." Reaching for his tool belt, he pulled out a small tube with a long, tapered nozzle and a pink butt plug. A larger plug than the one he'd put inside me yesterday. He glanced up at me and winked. "Tools of the trade."

"That seems like an awfully large plug for such a tiny hole," I said nervously, and he flashed me a naughty smile.

"Yet it's completely necessary. I'm going to drill the fuck out of this tight hole later, so I need to prepare it."

My nerves ratcheted up a notch but so did my arousal. "I think I would like that," I said breathlessly.

"Yeah?" he asked, and I nodded. Auburn uncapped the tube with his teeth and squirted a generous amount of lube on the end of the plug. "Put one foot up on the counter for me, baby."

I did, and he inserted the thin nozzle into my ass, squeezing to release the lube inside me. His mouth went immediately to my pussy as he began fucking my ass slowly with the toy, using just the tip at first. His lips closed around my clit, and he suckled me as he pushed the plug all the way in.

It stung, but only for a second, and I cried out. Auburn's mouth gave me all the attention I needed, kissing and licking my sex until I forgot all about the foreign feeling in my ass. I was focused only on the pleasure he was delivering.

"Mmm," he hummed against me. "Such a good fucking girl."

Pressing one hand against the countertop behind me, I buried the other one in his thick, dark hair, grinding my pussy against his face. His tongue was everywhere. Inside me, flicking my clit, licking up my wetness.

"D-daddy... I'm coming."

He snarled against me, his mouth working overtime as he focused on my hot little button. When his teeth scraped against me, I threw back my head and screamed my release to the ceiling. Auburn didn't slow down until the last tremble left my legs. Then he went slow and easy, savoring my taste on his tongue as he lapped at me.

"You were right," I panted, smoothing my hand through his hair. "You are the expert."

The cocky grin on his wet lips made my heart flip in my chest. He was so damned handsome, it was almost hard to breathe in his presence. As he stood, he grasped the back of my knee and lifted my other foot onto the counter so that I was spread wide for him. I leaned back with both hands to support me, thrusting my chest forward.

He diverted his attention there, separating my shirt so my breasts were exposed. "Such perfect tits, Baby Girl. Maybe I'll fuck them later. After I'm done with your pussy and your sweet little ass."

I moaned when his mouth closed over one nipple, sucking and biting it before moving on to the other one. Once they were both hard and pointed, he licked his way up my chest until his mouth was on that sensitive spot just below my ear. His deep voice vibrated through skin and muscle and went straight to my bones.

"I've been noticing you watching me, Baby Girl. I watch you too. Wondering what it would be like to fuck you. Wondering if your cunt would swallow me up, or if it's so tight, I would have to force my thick cock into you."

I swallowed audibly as he roughly pushed two fingers into me and groaned. His arm muscles bunched beneath the denim as he began to finger fuck me while his mouth suctioned onto the side of my neck.

"Please, Daddy," I purred. "See if your big cock will fit inside me."

"Fuck," he grunted, pulling his fingers out of me and sucking on them. "You taste like the dream I had last night."

My hand smoothed over his chest as he began to unbutton his shirt. "What was your dream about?"

"I was dreaming that I was eating the most delicious pink pussy, and when I looked up, all I saw were your green eyes looking down at me."

"You dreamed about me?"

He shrugged out of his shirt, revealing the most spectacular body I'd ever seen on a man. "I did. And then I fucked my hand and came all over my stomach."

"Here?" I asked, leaning forward to lick each ridge of his abdomen.

"Yes," he croaked as his tool belt hit the floor. A moment later, his jeans were unfastened, and his giant dick was in his hand. "Get it wet for me."

Running my fingertip around his thick crown, I looked up at him. "But it's already wet, Daddy. Is all that for me? Are you dripping for your baby girl?"

"Now," he grunted like an angry bear, gripping the back of my hair and pulling me down to him. I sucked him as deeply as I could from that position, loving the taste of his desire on my tongue.

His ab muscles tightened as he swelled inside my mouth, and he suddenly jerked me away, his lips crashing roughly against mine. Our tongues twisted and explored, each of us tasting ourselves on the other's lips.

"Hold on tight to me, baby. I may have to be rough with you to get it all to fit."

Wrapping my arms around his neck, I whispered into his ear. "I can take it."

"Christ," he growled as he lined up and slammed into me, his thickness stretching my walls to their absolute limit. "Fuck yes, baby. Take all your daddy's cock in this silky little cunt."

One of his hands was still tangled in my hair, and the other was gripping my hip like a vice to hold me how he wanted me. He pulled back and drilled into me again.

"Harder," I encouraged, and the man turned into an animal, absolutely railing me with his pistoning hips. All I could do was hang on for dear life.

Auburn was hitting all the right places, and I could feel an orgasm building at the base of my spine. Slowly it began to work its way up my back, and my legs trembled with anticipation. Untwisting his hand from my hair, he slid it between us and thumbed my clit, pushing me off the slim cliff I'd been teetering on.

"That's it. Come for me, Baby Girl." His teeth bit into my neck, marking me. "You're fucking mine now."

"Yours," I agreed willingly as I clutched onto him, my fingernails biting into his shoulders as my toes curled against the cool marble. Slowing his thrusts, he stroked my hip softly as I came down.

"You know," I breathed against his neck, "maintenance at my apartment really needs to up their game. This hardly ever happens when they come to fix a pipe."

Auburn jerked his head back. "What do you mean *hardly ever—*" His scowl faded when he saw my teasing grin.

"You like provoking me, don't you?" He pulled out and slid me off the counter, his hands gripping my waist when my knees wobbled. "Turn around, and I'll give you something to smile about."

When I turned and put my hands on the flat surface, Auburn reached around and ripped my shirt open, the two buttons pinging against the floor.

"You realize that was your shirt you just ruined, right?" I asked over my shoulder as he slid the garment off of my arms.

"You realize I don't give a shit, right?" he shot back. "I need you naked so I can worship every inch of your skin."

"Well, when you put it that way…"

He bent me over until my chest was pressed against the coolness of the black marble and spanked my ass. "That smart mouth is gonna get you in trouble, Baby Girl." He swatted me on the other side, and then soothed both cheeks with his hands. When he twisted the plug in my butt, I squirmed. "How does this feel?"

"Good. Really full, but good."

He twisted it again and pulled it out slowly, tossing it into the sink. Leaning over, he pressed his chest against my back and kissed my cheek. "Can I fuck your ass now, Gianna?" he whispered, using my real name for the first time since he'd gotten home.

"Yes, just... go slow, okay?"

"I will, baby. We've got all the time in the world."

He dug out another of the skinny tubes of anal lubricant and inserted it gently into me, squeezing to release the cool gel inside me. Then, taking his length in his hand, he lined himself up with my back entrance, meeting my eyes in the mirror.

"I love you," he mouthed, his words taking my nervousness down about forty notches.

"I love you too."

Auburn pressed forward, the head of his cock pushing through my snug ring, and I winced. He was much bigger than the plug. My hands tightened into fists, and I breathed deeply through my nose and exhaled slowly through my mouth.

"That's the worst part, sweetheart. Are you okay?" he asked, his voice thick with concern.

His eyes never left mine, and I felt myself start to relax. "I'm okay," I assured him.

Sliding his hand between my legs, he gently stroked my clit with two fingers, and arousal fluttered through my sex. "Yes, do that," I said, nodding my head. "That feels good."

Continuing his attention on my sensitive little button, he took another inch of my ass and groaned. "Jesus, Gianna. You're so fucking tight around me." He began to move his hips back and forth, stretching me with shallow strokes until my hands unfisted against the smooth countertop. "Tell me how you're feeling, pet."

The fullness in my bottom was unlike anything I'd ever experienced, and with his expert fingers between my legs, I was actually starting to enjoy it. "It feels intimate," I told him, and he smiled gently at me.

"It is, baby. For me too. Am I hurting you?"

He had used so much lube that, despite the extreme tightness, he slid smoothly in and out of me. "You're not hurting me. I want more of you inside me."

"Mmmm, you're being such a good fucking girl for me," he moaned, sinking deeper into me.

He knew exactly what those words did to me, and a shiver skimmed slowly down my spine. When he pinched my clit repeatedly with tiny pulses, I began to feel the telltale rise of pleasure that Auburn could always pull from me. I shoved my hips back, my tight hole swallowing the rest of his length as I grinded against him, and he bit out a harsh curse.

One of his hands slid up my back and grasped my hair, pulling until I was standing with my back against his chest. Bending his knees, he continued fucking up into me as he growled into my ear. "My cock has been in all of your holes now, Baby Girl. That means I fucking own you. Your pussy. Your ass. Your mouth." Twisting my head around, he covered my mouth with his own, sucking aggressively on my tongue before ending the kiss with a loud suck.

"I never want anyone else," I panted, overwhelmed by the power of his possession. "You own me."

"No other man will ever touch you again." He punctuated that with a hard, deep thrust. "No one fucking touches what's mine."

I nodded because my throat was completely clogged with arousal and emotion, and a look of possessive satisfaction crawled across his face, raising his sexy factor tenfold. *Like he needs any help with that.* Releasing my hair, he slid that hand around until it was encircling my throat. And then he spanked my pussy. Hard.

"Oh God," I groaned.

"You like that?" he asked, biting the side of my neck and sucking. "You like when I spank this pretty cunt while my cock fucks you up the ass?"

"Y-yes, Daddy," I squeaked out. He slapped me again, and I tightened around the thick intrusion in my backside.

"Goddammit, woman. I'm going to need you to come for me. I can't hold back much longer. Your ass is too tight and too sweet." The pace of his hips picked up, as did the pressure he was putting around my neck and the frequency of his other hand spanking between my legs. His blue eyes held me spellbound in the mirror. "Be Daddy's good little girl, Gianna."

And that did it for me. My entire body lit up, shaking with the intensity of my orgasm, and I cried out his name repeatedly as he completely seized control of my body. Before I even came to my senses, he pushed me forward until my chest was once again pressed against the vanity, and he lifted my leg so the inside of my knee was resting on the countertop.

Then he really let me have it. His hips were nailing me to the marble, eyes downcast to the spot where we were joined. "So fucking beautiful," he muttered through clenched teeth. Every muscle in his jaw was taut, and I stared at my breathtaking man as he lost all control, his thrusts becoming wild and erratic.

When he threw his head back and roared out his climax, I almost came again. Auburn continued pumping into me as his cock jerked repeatedly inside me, his warm release coating the inner walls of my ass.

He finally collapsed forward, his chest covering my back. "Jesus fucking Christ, Gianna. I've never come that hard." His lips turned tender, kissing from my shoulder up to my ear.

His voice was barely audible when he whispered, "I was wrong before, pet. *You* own *me.*"

Chapter 29

"Auburn, I have your mother on the phone. She says it's important."

Shit! Today was Friday, and I'd been avoiding her calls all week since I'd walked out of my parents' house on Sunday. Poor Tony had been fielding the calls and dealing with her increasing wrath.

"It's okay, Tony. Put her through."

The relief was evident in his voice. "Right away."

When I heard the line buzz, I picked it up. "Chloe," I said curtly.

"Well, finally you decide to take your mother's call," she sniped.

"What can I help you with?"

"First of all, you can apologize for rudely leaving before dinner on Sunday."

Yeah. Not gonna happen. "No. Next?"

I could practically hear her blood boiling through the phone. "*Next*," she sneered, "I have a message for you from Magdalena since you refuse to take her calls as well."

"Fantastic," I said flatly.

"Why do you have to be so rude?" When I didn't answer, she continued. "Your future wife said she talked to you on Monday and made you a proposition."

"Number one, she's not my future anything. She's a past mistake. And yes, I talked to her and rejected her… *proposition*."

"Well, she says to tell you she'll give you another chance to accept. You have until Monday night."

Shaking my head, I exhaled a long breath. "You can tell your little lapdog that I still won't be accepting her offer, but I want you to give her a specific message from me. You might want to write this down because I want you to tell her word for word." I paused for a moment. "You tell Magdalena Lewis that she better think long and hard before crossing me. She will not like the consequences at all."

"Oh don't be so dramatic, Auburn."

"Did she tell you what this proposition consisted of?"

"No, but I'm assuming she offered to forgive you and take you back."

I laughed, the sound harsh and humorless. "Okay, Chloe. If that's what you want to think."

"Why are you calling me Chloe? I am your mother."

"Then act like it," I retorted before hanging up.

After taking a moment to compose myself, I shook my head. I'd hoped Magdalena had been bluffing, but apparently not. Picking up my cell phone, I dialed a number.

"Owens, Kavanaugh, and Underwood Law Firm. This is Michelle. How may I direct your call?"

"Hello, Michelle. This is Auburn Bouvier. I need to speak with Edward Owens, please."

"Mister Bouvier, I'm afraid Mister Owens is out of the office right now. May I connect you to one of our associates?"

My brow wrinkled. "No, it's okay. I'll just call him on his cell phone."

"I'm so sorry, sir, but... well, actually Mister Owens is in the hospital."

Alarm bells rang inside my head. Ed was an old friend from college. "Is he okay?"

"He will be. He has kidney stones, so he's in no shape to speak to anyone right now."

"Ooh," I said with a wince. "Tell him better him than me."

Michelle laughed. "When he's feeling better, I will pass that on. Is there a legal matter you needed to discuss? Because his associate, Miss Ramirez, is handling all of his clients at this time."

I stroked my bottom lip with my finger. "It is a bit urgent."

"I can assure you that Miss Ramirez is highly qualified. She works directly under Mister Owens, and she is as sharp as they come. I can get you in with her at one today."

Trying not to let my disappointment seep through my voice, I replied, "That will be fine. I'll see you then."

At fifteen till one, I entered the law office, my navy shoes tapping softly against the wide-plank wood floor. I'd never actually been here before. Ed and I usually chose to talk business over a meal, or we handled simpler matters by phone.

This must be where the firm is spending the astronomical hourly rate they charge, I thought, my eyes roaming over the Venetian yellow walls and recessed lighting. Directly in front of me was a dark gray wall with *Owens, Kavanaugh, & Underwood* boldly printed across it. I stopped at the gold, brushed-metal reception desk and spoke to a pretty, young woman with light brown hair and blue eyes.

"I have a one o'clock appointment. I'm Auburn Bouvier."

Her eyes raked up and down my fitted navy suit, and when they returned to mine, she flashed a flirtatious smile. "Yes, I know." I gave her a quick nod, not returning the smile. I wasn't here to make friends. "I'm Michelle. We spoke on the phone. Come right this way, and I'll take you to Miss Ramirez's office."

I followed, keeping my eyes firmly on the back of her head rather than the extra swing she was putting in her walk for my benefit. A couple of months ago, my eyes would have been glued to her backside, and she probably would have been in my bed before the night was through, especially with the brazen *available* vibes she was giving off. But Michelle didn't hold my interest in the slightest.

She chit-chatted as we walked down the corridor and turned right, glancing back and batting her eyelashes occasionally. I replied with one-word answers, my vibe blatantly screaming *unavailable*. Because that's exactly what I was. Completely unavailable to every woman except one.

Michelle stopped beside a door and knocked before opening it and sticking her head inside. "Your one o'clock is here." She opened the door fully, and I stepped inside as her hand *accidentally* brushed against mine. I leveled her with a no-nonsense look, and she quickly backed away and closed the door behind her.

Taking a couple steps into the room, I had my hand extended in front of me for a handshake when my eyes fell on the woman behind the desk. My hand dropped to my side as I gawked.

"Kasserole?"

The Latina woman grinned and shook her head. "I see you haven't forgotten that stupid nickname." She rounded the desk. "When I saw your name on my schedule, I just knew it had to be you. No one else has a name as pretentious as *Auburn Bouvier*."

"Except for my brother," I shot back, and her smile faltered a bit.

"True," she said as I wrapped my arms around her for a warm hug.

"How are you, Kassie?"

The woman returned my embrace and then smoothed her hands up and down my lapel. "Excellent. And look at you! All grown up. Not that you haven't been grown up since you were twelve."

"Kinda had to be with my mother," I said dryly, and Kassie's lips tightened around the corners.

"How are your parents, by the way?"

"Dad is retired but stays busy avoiding my mother."

"Can't say I blame him," she said with an eye roll before taking my hand. "Come on and sit down." She led me to a seating area and sat beside me on a dark-gray, leather couch.

An awkward silence surrounded us until I finally spoke. "Kassie, I didn't get to talk to you much after... everything went down."

Her lips crooked up in a wry smile. "You can say it, Auburn. After your brother knocked me up."

"Yeah, after that. I wanted to apologize for how my parents acted. Mostly my mother, but my dad really should have shut her down. She was a real bitch to you."

"You have nothing to apologize for. You were always so kind to me and made me feel welcome. Unlike..." Her words trailed off, and she looked away before returning her eyes to mine. "And the way you took in Monty after your mother kicked him out... that was a wonderful thing for you to do."

"He's my brother," I replied simply.

Kassie's eyes dropped to her lap, where her thumbs twiddled rapidly. "How is he?"

I sighed. "I don't hear from him much. After you disappeared, he finished out his last year of high school and then took off to Florida. He's a police detective now."

She smiled at her thumbs and nodded. "That's good. Do you think it's because of what happened with... Evelyn?"

I tried not to visibly jolt at the mention of my sister's name. No one spoke it anymore.

"Probably. When you and Evelyn..." the name actually felt foreign on my tongue... "disappeared within weeks of each other, it really threw him for a loop. He skipped his graduation and left without a word." I stopped her fiddling with a gentle hand. "Can you tell me what happened? Where you went?"

She chewed on her bottom lip before speaking. "After I miscarried, my parents wanted to get me away from all the toxicity. I think they only allowed me to still see Monty because they were anticipating we would get married. Then after..." Her voice broke a little, and my heart clenched in sympathy. "After I lost the baby, they moved us to Pennsylvania. Took away my phone so I couldn't contact him. I borrowed a friend's phone a few weeks later, but Monty's number was no longer in service."

"He would have married you anyway," I told her, and her head jerked up.

She swallowed, and her pretty brown eyes filled with tears before she changed the subject. "Have you heard anything about your sister?"

Shaking my head sadly, I said, "No. Just the same information. She went on that trip to Cancún with her friends during spring break of her first year of college. Everyone decided to go to bed at about two in the morning, and the last her friends saw of her, she was headed to her room."

"I kept up with the case on the news for about a year, and then one day, they just stopped talking about it."

Running my hand through my hair, I nodded. "They moved it to the cold case files, though the FBI kept in contact with us for years. They're not sure if she was brought back to the U.S., but about a week after she went missing, a gas station clerk outside of Jacksonville, Florida swore that she recognized her. Said a woman came in very late one night, used the restroom, and left. She thinks she was with a man, but she couldn't recall what he looked like. She was too busy trying to figure out why the woman looked familiar."

Kassie covered her mouth with her hand. "Oh my God. That's... wow. I never heard about that on the news."

"They kept it out of the media. The clerk went home and went to bed the next morning, so it wasn't until she watched the news that night that she realized the woman she saw looked a lot like Evie. She called the local police, and they contacted the FBI, but there really wasn't much to go on."

"Did they have security cameras?"

I shook my head sadly. "No, it was a small Mom and Pop store, and the trail kind of died out after that."

"That sucks. Just enough to get your hopes up, but not enough to really go on."

"Yeah, I think that's why Monty decided to move to Florida. To be closer to the last place where she may or may not have been seen."

"They were always so close," she said thoughtfully. Evie and Monty had only been a year apart in age, but my brother was so tall, people often mistook them for twins. "I'm thirty-two, so she would have been thirty-three now, right?"

I nodded. "Yes, five years younger than me."

"I'm so sorry, Auburn. The not knowing has to be horrible."

"That's the worst part." Though I hardly ever spoke about my sister, that didn't stop me from thinking about her every day for the past fifteen years. Wondering if she's alive or…

Kassie's hand closed over my forearm. I'd forgotten how touchy-feely she was, something I'd had to get used to back in the day. My family wasn't what you would call *affectionate*.

"Now that we have all that out of the way, how can I help you today?"

Leaning back against the couch, I blew out a long breath. "I'm being blackmailed."

Her dark brows shot up. "Wow. Okay. Is this related to business?"

Shaking my head, I said, "No. This is entirely personal. It's my ex, Magdalena Lewis."

"What are the terms of the blackmail?"

"If I don't give her five million dollars, she's threatened to talk to the press about… things." Her smile was placid as she waited for me to continue. "Sexual things."

Kassie didn't even bat an eye. "Any of these things illegal?"

"What? No. Nothing like that. I just prefer things a… certain way." I could feel my ears turning red.

"Can you be more specific? I know this is very personal stuff, but anything you say to me is confidential."

I scrubbed my hands over my face. "If you're handling this, you're going to find out anyway, I guess. I have to be in control in the bedroom, and well, I can get a little rough."

"Have you ever left marks, bruises, cuts, or burns on her?"

My eyebrows practically hit the ceiling at her matter-of-fact tone. "No, nothing like that. She wasn't into anything other than vanilla sex, so that was pretty much our routine. Early in our relationship, I asked if I could spank her or tie her up, but she said no. I didn't pressure her or ask again." Resting my elbows on my knees, I pressed the heels of my hands into my eye sockets and groaned, "I can't believe I'm talking about this with Kasserole."

She laughed and patted my arm. "Just pretend you're talking to Edward."

I rolled my eyes toward her. "You smell a lot better than Edward."

She grinned. "I appreciate that. If you've never hurt Miss Lewis during your sexual activities, then what's the problem?"

"She said she's talked to other women. Women I was with when we broke up. They were a bit more amenable to my preferences. She's threatening to blab all of that information, plus tell the things I wanted to do to her." I clenched my eyes shut. "I don't want the entire world knowing how I like to fuck. My dad. Shit, my girlfriend's father."

"You're dating someone else now?"

I couldn't hold back the smile that broke across my face. "Yes. Her name is Gianna, and we met a little over six weeks ago. After Magdalena and I broke up," I specified.

"And you would prefer that Gianna not find out this private information about you either?"

"She's already aware." *And she loves me anyway.* "I've told her about the blackmail attempt as well."

"I see." Kassie crossed her arms over her chest. "Here's what I can do. To decrease the number of people involved, I can go directly to the prosecutor and avoid talking to the police entirely. That lessens the chance of something getting leaked to the press. Perhaps if Magdalena knows you've gotten the district attorney involved, she may back off. Blackmail is a very serious crime, especially with the amount of money we're talking about here. Anything over a million dollars, and she can be imprisoned for up to twenty-five years."

"Whoa. Okay." I let those thoughts gel for a moment before speaking again. "I don't necessarily want to see her go to prison; I just want her to back the fuck off and leave me alone."

"And as of right now, you haven't paid her any money?"

"No, and I'm not going to. I've cut off all contact with her, but she confronted me in front of my building four days ago. I pretty much told her to fuck off when she threatened me and asked for money. But today, she sent a message through my mother that I have until Monday night to reconsider."

Kassie's eyes bugged out of her head. "Your mother is involved in this scheme?" She shook her head. "She's really a piece of work, isn't she?" Her lips clamped shut, and she shook her head. "Sorry. I know that's your mother."

"Don't hold back on my account. I want nothing else to do with the woman. She's pressured me for years to be with Magdalena, but last Sunday, she really crossed the line. She embarrassed Gianna, and that's one thing I won't stand for."

My old friend's face softened. "You really care about Gianna, don't you?"

"I love her. She's the main reason I don't want this information leaked to the press. I never want her to be embarrassed of being with me."

"I'm glad for you, Auburn. You deserve all the happiness in the world." Her eyebrows pinched together. "So your mother knows you're being blackmailed?"

I shook my head. "She just passed on the message that Magdalena has given me until Monday to accept her 'proposition,' but I don't think she knows that proposition is actually blackmail."

Kassie rose and crossed to her desk, scratching some notes on a legal pad. "I'll send a cease and desist letter to Miss Lewis today. Sometimes hearing from a lawyer is enough to get the person to stop what they're doing."

"Do you need the video to show to the D.A.?"

Kassie's head whipped around. "You have video?"

"Yes. The conversation took place in the back of my car, and I had my driver turn on the camera."

Her grin turned absolutely wicked. "Excellent. New York is a one-party consent state, which means that you can record a conversation as long as one of the parties—that would be you—consents. There are some restrictions about whether or not it can be used in a trial, but we're not worried about that right now. If she knows you have proof of her committing a crime, then perhaps she'll back off. If she's smart."

My mouth twisted to the side. "She's not exactly the sharpest knife in the drawer, if you know what I'm saying. But maybe it will work." I stood, pulling the small chip from my pocket and handing it over to my brilliant new attorney.

"Great. I'll watch this after you're gone and make sure to add details in the cease and desist letter."

Rubbing the back of my neck with one hand, I said, "There's one more thing. I have, ah, certain information about Magdalena that she would not want made public."

Kassie's lips pressed into a thin line. "If it's revenge porn, forget it. Releasing nudes or sex videos of an ex is a crime."

"No, no. It's nothing like that," I said, shaking my head. "Magdalena and I were on and off for about five years. Last time we were together, I suspected that she was cheating on me, so I had a private investigator follow her."

"And he found something?" I nodded, and Kassie pressed her hands against her desk, leaning toward me. "Auburn, if you threaten to release this information, you're also guilty of blackmail."

I shook my head. "She doesn't even know I have this information, and I wasn't planning to tell her or threaten her at all. If she struck first, I was going to have a third party leak it to the press."

Her eyes rose to the ceiling as she thought about it. "While it's not exactly wise, I can't think of any reason that would be illegal. People release stuff to the press every day about celebrities or high-profile individuals." She leveled her gaze back on my face. "As your legal counsel, I'm saying be cautious. As an old friend—and not as your attorney in any capacity—I say be cautious but nail her ass to the wall."

A bark of laughter burst from my mouth. "Whatever happened to sweet little Kasserole?"

Kassie pursed her lips. "She's gone. I'm one of the top litigators in this firm, and I didn't get here by playing nice."

I stuck out my hand and she grasped it with a firm shake. "Thank you for everything. I'm very glad to have you on my team, Kassie."

"Glad to be here."

A thought popped into my head. "I noticed you're still going by Ramirez. You've never married?"

Her face hardened. "I was married a few years ago, but it's a long-ass story for another time. I have a son who is three and the reason I work so hard. I just want to give him the life I never had growing up."

Kassie had grown up poor, which was one of the reasons my snobbish mother didn't approve of her. But she was smart, kind, and driven, which was why I liked her so much.

"That's wonderful, Kassie. It's important to have something that motivates you. I didn't have that for a very long time. Sure, I wanted to impress my father, but now I have someone in my life that makes me want to be a better man for completely different reasons."

"Gianna?" I nodded. "She sounds like a very special lady."

My grin took up my entire face. "She is."

"Good for you, Auburn." She licked her lips nervously. "Could I ask you a huge favor?"

"Anything."

"I know you said you don't talk to Monty much, but I would appreciate it if you didn't mention that you saw me. Everything that happened between us is water under the bridge, and I'm sure he'd appreciate it if you didn't dredge up any old memories."

I wasn't so sure about that, but I agreed.

Hugging her again, I kissed her on the forehead. "It was good to see you again, Kasserole."

"You too, Auburn."

Chapter 30

I woke up alone on Tuesday and rolled out of Auburn's bed. After using the restroom, brushing my teeth, and slipping into one of his T-shirts, I went in search of my boyfriend. I found him in his office, glued to his computer.

"Anything?" I asked from the doorway, and he looked up and motioned me to come in.

Walking around the desk, I settled onto his lap. "Good morning, baby," he said, kissing my temple. "No. Nothing yet."

Last night, Monday, had been Magdalena's deadline, and I could feel Auburn's tension ramping up as the day turned into evening. The only way I'd gotten him to calm down was with a very long, very slow blow job. When I'd finally given in to his begging and let him come, he collapsed onto the bed and fell directly asleep.

But today? I could feel the stress pouring out of him once again this morning. "Do I need to give you more head?" I asked, nuzzling my face against his neck and kissing him there.

He smiled down at me. "No, baby. I'm fine. In fact, I probably owe you a jaw massage for last night." Cupping my face, he tenderly caressed me with his fingers and thumb.

"Would you like for me to skip lunch with my dad and stay home with you?"

"Of course not," he said indignantly. "I don't need to be babysat."

"Okay, if you're sure."

"I am," he said, patting my bottom. "I'm going to the office for a little bit anyway."

"On July Fourth?"

"Yes, I have a phone meeting with a supplier in Italy. In fact, go get ready, and I'll drop you off at the restaurant on my way."

"Hi, Dad," I said, kissing his cheek when I found him inside the restaurant. "This place smells amazing."

He led me toward the counter to order. "It's the best barbecue place I've found in the city. The owners are actually from Texas. I thought we should have barbecue since that's always what we had on the Fourth when you were a kid."

"I actually remember that. You cooking on that smoker in the backyard," I said with a smile before turning toward the big overhead menu. "What's good here?"

"Brisket and ribs," Dad replied immediately. "Oh, and they have hot water cornbread like your mom used to make. I'll order us a basket to share."

"Sounds good."

Once we were seated and a worker brought our food to us, I decided to broach the subject of Auburn. "Your boss asked me to go to some awards ceremony with him in a couple weeks."

Dad stuffed a piece of brisket in his mouth and nodded as he chewed. "He told me. I don't want you to ever feel like you have to go just because he's my boss."

I shook my head. "No, I wanted to go. You were right last time. I did meet a lot of people, and it was actually fun." *While I was conscious anyway.*

He breathed out a sigh of relief. "Okay, good. I know Auburn can be a difficult man to say no to."

That's for damn sure. "How has work been going?" I asked before taking a bite of the tender brisket.

"It's going great. Auburn has been quite pleasant to be around lately. He doesn't seem wound nearly as tight as he used to be."

Taking a sip of my Dr Pepper, I nodded. "I found him to be very easy to be around at the hospital function we went to. He was attentive, charming, and even a little bit funny."

Dad paused his chewing. "Charming, huh?" I nodded, trying to appear casual, even though my heart was beating rapidly. He laid down his fork and leaned toward me with his arms folded on the table. "Look, Gianna. I know Auburn is handsome and all that, but I want you to be careful around him."

"What do you mean?" I asked, a juicy rib halfway to my mouth.

"I just don't want you falling for him. He's not right for you."

My heart almost fell out of my chest. "What makes you say that?"

"He's a bit of a playboy, honey. He'll never settle down with one woman. Magdalena has been the closest for him. He's dated her for five years, and I've never once heard him talk about a future or marriage with her. He's just not the type. A lot of women fall willingly into Auburn Bouvier's bed because he's rich and good-looking," Dad smiled and patted my hand, "but I know you're too smart for that."

Um, no I'm not. I suddenly felt sick to my stomach. The man I love is the one man my dad will never accept. *What the hell am I supposed to do with that?*

Thinking the matter was resolved, my father turned the conversation back to the food. I managed to force down a couple more bites before announcing that I was full and would take the rest to go.

"That was so much fun, sweetheart. Thank you for having lunch with me." Dad put his arm around me in the back of the cab, and I leaned my head over on his shoulder. Would he ever forgive me for loving Auburn? Would he entirely cut me out of his life? Surely not. He loves me.

Maybe we hadn't always been close because of distance, but Dad had never made me feel less than important. He never missed a single important event in my life, even though it must have been a struggle for him to fly back and forth while also working full time and taking care of Grandpa and Nana.

"What are you smiling about?" my dad asked, squeezing my shoulder.

I looked up at him. "I was thinking about that play you flew all the way to Texas to watch when I was in third grade."

"Oh, honeybunch. That was my favorite one ever. You were a superstar."

"I was a giraffe," I said flatly. "And the paper mache neck cracked halfway through my solo and fell on Colby Simmons."

"And you just kept dancing and singing with the biggest smile on your face."

"Yeah, I did, and now that I think about it, I'm feeling a little cold-hearted. Colby had a concussion."

Dad's laugh shook his entire body. "You are the least cold-hearted person I know, Gianna. You were always a sweet kid, and you've grown into a warm and kind young lady. I'm so glad you live close to me now." Tears filled his eyes, and my heart broke a little. "It was the hardest decision of my life to move to New York when your mom and I divorced. Grandpa was becoming so ill with Alzheimer's, and Nana couldn't handle him on her own. I knew you would be okay because your mother was an amazing person, but I still feel guilty about it every single day."

A tear slipped down my cheek, and I wrapped my arms around my father. "Don't feel guilty, Dad. Even though we lived apart, you were not even close to an absentee father. You called me several nights a week before bed, and you came to visit as often as you could. And don't think I didn't know about the extra money you sent to Mom every month on top of the regular child support."

His face turned pink. "I told her not to tell you about that. I just wanted to make sure you had everything you needed."

"She didn't tell me. I would check the mail every day when I got home from school, and I saw the checks when I tore into the envelopes from you because you always sent me a letter." Dad kissed me on the top of the head. "I still have all of your letters."

A grin broadened across his face. "Really? You kept them?"

I nodded. "I have a memory box filled with your letters and ticket stubs from movies we went to together. And that little stuffed zebra you bought me at the Fort Worth Zoo. Of course, he's a little ratty because I slept with him until I was thirteen."

The mention of the memory box reminded me of the one Auburn and I had started together, and guilt seeped in around the outside of my heart. Because I was lying to my father by not telling him about my relationship with Auburn.

Before I could open my mouth and blurt it out, Dad's phone dinged, and he pulled it from his pocket to check the message. "Shit!" he exclaimed, a frown creasing his brow. "Driver," he called out, "can you please make the next right. I have to go to my office."

The man grumbled something under his breath but maneuvered into the other lane.

"What's wrong, Dad?"

He turned his worried gaze on me. "Auburn arranged for the kids from a local children's home to go to the park this evening for a picnic and to watch the fireworks." My heart flip-flopped at that. He hadn't even told me.

"So what's the problem?"

"Four of the kids need handicap accessible transportation, and the driver of that van just texted me. He has food poisoning, so I need to find another accessible vehicle ASAP."

I smiled and rested my hand on his arm. "It's okay. You'll get it handled. And I can just walk home from there since it's only a few blocks away."

He nodded as the cab took a right. "Just up here on the right."

When the driver stopped, Dad paid him and then helped me from the car before giving me a quick hug. "I'll call you tomorrow, honey." As soon as he was inside, I walked home and put my leftovers in the refrigerator. Then I sank onto the couch and ran my hands through my hair.

"What the hell am I going to do?" I asked the empty room. "Tell me what to do, Nana. Mom. Anyone?" No one seemed to have any advice from the other side, so I decided to straighten up around the house since I hadn't been here in days.

While I was wiping down the bathroom counter, I noticed I had dripped barbecue sauce on the front of my yellow blouse. *Thanks, boobs.*

Stripping off my shirt and shorts, I sifted through the clothes in my closet, smiling when I found a cute little red and white polka-dotted sundress. I slipped it on with white sandals and decided to take a walk.

I waved to Anderson and Hanson, and I'd barely made it out the front door when my phone notified me that I had a new email. Leaning against the wall, I checked it, my heart pounding when I saw it was from the accounting firm I'd interviewed at weeks ago.

Dear Miss Moschella,

We regret to inform you...

That's as far as I read before tears welled in my eyes. My thumb blindly found my contacts and tapped on Auburn's name.

"Well, hello there, beautiful."

"Hi."

I heard the squeak of leather, as if he had suddenly sat up straight in his chair. "Gianna, what's wrong?"

"I-I'm sorry. I'm being silly. I'll let you go."

"You're not being silly if you're upset about something. Tell me now," he said in that commanding voice of his.

A small sound hiccupped from my throat. "I didn't get the job."

"Aw, honey. I'm sorry. You want me to kick someone's ass?"

That made me laugh a little. "No, but I appreciate it."

"How about a hug?"

"That sounds pretty good right now."

"Okay, baby girl. Come up to my office, and—"

I cut him off. "I can't, Auburn. My dad is there."

"Oh. Yeah, right. Um, what are you wearing?"

"Seriously? You want to have phone sex right now?" I hissed.

His deep chuckle tumbled through the phone. "No, funny girl. I'm going to tell security what you're wearing so they'll let you in since the building is closed to visitors today. Go to the second floor, take a left off the elevator and then take the last left. I'll meet you there."

"Okay, I'm wearing a red polka-dot dress."

We hung up, and I walked the few blocks to the Bouvier building and pushed through the front doors.

"Good afternoon, Miss Gianna," the guard said, nodding politely at me as I passed, and I returned his greeting.

Once I got to the second floor, I followed Auburn's directions until I got to the last hallway on the left. There were only two doors down here, but I didn't see Auburn.

Maybe he's not down here yet. Or maybe he wanted me to knock on one of the doors.

I turned to one door, but before I could raise my hand, an arm snaked around my waist, and a large hand covered my mouth to muffle my scream.

Chapter 31

"Shhh, it's me," I whispered against Gianna's ear as I backed us into the room and kicked the door shut.

"Are you trying to give me a heart attack?" she asked when I uncovered her mouth and turned her around.

"No, I was trying to be sneaky," I informed her, wrapping my hand around the side of her neck as her pulse thrummed rapidly against my thumb. "Sorry I scared you." I bent to softly kiss her lips, and her sweet body molded perfectly to mine.

Banding my arms around her waist, I lifted her as our kiss deepened. I turned and sat her on the table in the middle of the room as I reluctantly pulled my lips from hers.

She rested her head against my shoulder and sighed. "Thank you. I needed that." Her hands toyed with the back of my hair. "Sorry I bothered you. I just freaked out a little because I really need a freaking job, and I haven't heard back from any of the other places about an interview."

"Don't you dare apologize," I told her. "You know you can work here, right? In my accounting department?"

She lifted her head. "That's really sweet, but I want to get a job on my own."

"I know you're a very independent woman, and that's one of the things I love most about you. The offer still stands though." I kissed the tip of her adorable nose. "How did lunch with your dad go?"

"It was fine," she said and then hesitated. "He did tell me you're having a picnic dinner for a bunch of kids before the fireworks."

"Oh, um, yeah. I thought it would be a nice treat for them."

"Can we go?"

I blinked a couple times and pursed my lips. "Actually, I already have plans for us for the fireworks show."

"Maybe we could at least go for the picnic?" When she batted those pretty green eyes at me, I could deny her nothing.

I brushed my knuckles down her cheek. "We can do that if you want."

She bit her bottom lip and nodded. "I think it would be fun."

"Whatever you want, baby. Are you going to wear this dress?" My eyes raked up and down her body.

"Is something wrong with it?" she asked, smoothing down the flirty little skirt.

"Not a thing. It looks cute on you. Very festive." Starting at her knees, I trailed my hands slowly up her thighs. "And short."

"Why are you looking at me like that?"

A wicked grin curved across my lips. "I think you know exactly why I'm looking at you like this. You remember my solution for stress relief, don't you?"

Her pink tongue slid across her bottom lip, and she parted her thighs. "I believe I do recall you mentioning something about that," she said coyly as I sank to my knees.

Twenty minutes later, my girl had a huge grin on her face as I opened the door to find Tora exiting the room across from us. *Shit.*

"Well hello there, you two," he sang.

Gianna froze in place beside me, her eyes as wide as saucers.

"And that's the thread room, Miss Moschella," I said, quickly dropping her hand. "We can take our fabrics in there and find the perfect matching or contrasting thread for any outfit."

"I do love visiting the thread room," Tora said with a barely concealed smirk on his face.

My girl swallowed and nodded, forcing a smile onto her flushed face. "It's fascinating. Thank you for showing me that, Mister Bouvier, but I really need to run now." And she scurried off toward the elevator like her butt was on fire.

"Tora," I said, taking a step toward him.

"You don't need to say a word, Mister Sir." He pretended to zip and lock his lips before tossing the 'key' dramatically over his shoulder. Then he ironically opened his mouth and said, "Oopsie. You seem to have gotten a little *thread* on your shirt." He pulled what was obviously one of Gianna's long, dark hairs from my shoulder and let it fall to the floor. "I'll see you tomorrow, boss," he called as he strode off down the hall.

Stuffing my hands into my pants pockets, I leaned my shoulders back against the wall and closed my eyes. *Christ. I'm tired of keeping secrets.*

Just before dusk, Gianna and I entered the park, me carrying a large cooler, and Gianna toting a blanket and her purse. The director of the children's home spotted me and scurried over, looking a bit flustered.

"Mister Bouvier! We didn't expect to see you here."

I smiled and set the cooler down before shaking her hand. "Hello, Mrs. Jenkins. This is my friend Gianna Moschella. She thought it might be fun for us to come and eat with the kids."

The director turned her warm smile on Gianna, and they shook. "We're so glad to have you both. Just set up your blanket wherever you can find a free spot. I'll grab you a bag of food. You always send way too much, sir, so there's plenty." She turned her gaze to the cooler. "Oh. Unless you brought your own food."

"No, we'll have whatever the kids are having," Gianna assured her. "We brought popsicles for them, if that's all right."

Mrs. Jenkins clapped her hands beneath her chin. "Oh, that is perfectly fine. They'll be so excited!" She scurried off and returned with two bags of food as soon as we got the blanket spread out in the grass. "Here you go, and there's a bottle of water in each bag." She was called away, and Gianna and I settled onto the blanket.

"I haven't had McDonald's in forever," I commented, pulling a small burger and fries from the bag. Sinking my teeth into the cheeseburger, I moaned a sound of approval. "I forgot how much I love Mickey D's."

Gianna pulled out her own food and giggled. "I never thought I would see Auburn Bouvier eating fast food."

I stuck my tongue out at her and took another bite. A little boy approached, pushing a small wheelchair with a young girl in it. They both had sandy blond hair and big blue eyes. He locked her wheels and stepped up beside her, reaching for her hand, which he clasped in his.

"Hi," he said, making direct eye contact with me. "What's your name?"

"I'm Auburn," I said, sticking out my hand. The kid shook it, impressing me with his firm grasp for such a little guy.

"I'm Jaxon, and this is my sister, Jane. We're five, and yes, we're twins, before you ask."

I suppressed a snicker. This kid had balls. "This is my friend, Gianna. We're not twins," I said, and the boy giggled. The little girl ducked her head shyly and gave us each a tiny wave.

"She doesn't talk much," Jaxon informed us.

"I have a friend named Jackson," I told the boy.

"Hm, is it spelled with an *x* or with a *ck*? Because mine is spelled with *x*."

"His is with the old school *ck* because he's an old man." I widened my eyes and whispered, "He's in his fifties."

Jaxon laughed before narrowing his eyes on me. "What did you say your name was?"

"Auburn," I replied.

His little eyebrows scrunched together. "Hmm. Mrs. Jenkins said some guy named Auburn Booby-A bought us the food tonight. Is that you?"

I had to cover my lips to hide my laughter. "Yes, I'm Auburn Bouvier. Did you both get something to eat?"

The little girl nodded, a hint of a smile on her precious face, but she still didn't speak. Her brother did though. "We love McDonald's. We don't get it hardly ever though. Jane loves the french fries."

Gianna held up her container of fries. "I'm pretty full. You can have mine."

Jaxon put his hands on his knees and bent toward his sister. "You want extra fries, Janie?" he asked gently.

She happily bobbed her head up and down, and her smile lit up the entire park. Tears prickled the backs of my eyelids when she quietly said, "Thank you." Glancing at Gianna, I caught her swiping at her left eye.

Jaxon patiently held the container in front of Jane as she ate the golden fries one by one. "You can have mine too," I said when she was finished. The little boy asked his sister if she wanted more, but she shook her head no. "Why don't you eat them, buddy?"

He shrugged and showed off a snaggle-toothed grin before flopping down onto my lap and taking the food. It felt as natural as breathing to wrap one arm around his small body as he munched cheerfully.

Gianna rose up onto her knees in front of Jane and asked, "Can I hold you?" The child beamed at her and held out her thin arms.

"Janie can't walk," Jaxon informed me around a mouthful of fried potato. "Somebody hurt her leg when we were two. That's when we got taken from wherever we lived before. She needs an operation." I was stunned, and my blood absolutely boiled at the thought of someone hurting that little girl. "I don't remember none of that, but Mrs. Jenkins told me. She says she's blessed to have us, and we should always try to be a blessing to others."

Christ, this kid is killing me, I thought, making a mental note to donate a large sum of money to the children's home.

Jaxon's head whipped around when his sister spoke more than two words for the first time since we'd met her. "Your hair is pretty," she was saying to Gianna. "Can I braid it?"

"Of course. Can you sit up by yourself?"

"Yes." Gianna settled the girl in a seated position and then laid back on her elbows so the kid could reach her hair. "I'm really good at braiding. I do my own hair."

"Really? It looks so professional," my woman praised.

"I do the other girls too, and they give me extra peanut butter crackers as payment."

Okay, make that a VERY large donation. Just thinking about these kids not having enough to eat broke something inside of me.

I watched as Jane's tiny fingers nimbly separated and twisted Gianna's hair until it was in a perfect French braid down her back. At Gianna's direction, I dug a hair band from her purse and handed it to the little girl, who expertly wrapped it around the tail of the braid.

Gianna sat up and rubbed a hand over her hair. "Well, that feels just fabulous, Janie. How does it look?" She wiggled her head, making the braid snap back and forth between her shoulders.

"Fabulous," the child said with a giggle.

My beautiful woman swiveled around until she was facing Jane and took both of her hands. "Thank you so much. I love having a braid during hot weather. Hey, we brought popsicles for everyone. Would you like to help hand them out?"

"Yes!" the kid said, her eyes lighting up with excitement. "I like to help. Mrs. Jenkins lets me hand out apples after dinner sometimes."

A tiny hand tapped my face, and I glanced down at Jaxon who was looking up at me with sad, blue eyes. "Auburn, can I help too?"

Ruffling his hair, I said, "Of course you can, bud. You and Jane can be the, uh, the popsicle distribution coordinators." I stood and lifted Jane, who weighed next to nothing, into her wheelchair before opening the cooler.

Gianna and I stayed busy snipping the ends off of the frozen tubes and handing them to Jaxon and Jane, who seemed incredibly proud to have such an important job. My heart swelled with pride as the little girl's voice grew stronger and stronger each time she asked one of the other kids, "Red or blue?"

I actually enjoyed meeting all of the children as they came up to thank me and Gianna, and I was impressed as hell at their manners. Mrs. Jenkins and her staff were doing an outstanding job with these kids, despite obviously having limited funds.

By the time the cooler was empty, everyone was a sticky mess, but they were happy. Mrs. Jenkins and the other eight men and women who worked with her walked around with wet wipes, cleaning everyone's hands and faces.

The director approached me, and with a stern look, said, "Hands, Mister Bouvier."

I held out my hands, and she began to wipe them down thoroughly as I laughed. "Please, Mrs. Jenkins. Anyone who gives me a mini-bath in the park should call me Auburn."

She laughed, and I noticed how kind she looked when she smiled. Her hair was almost completely gray, and worry lines creased her forehead and around her brown eyes. "Okay, Auburn. I'm Caroline. We certainly appreciate you doing this for the kids every year. And it was a special treat for you to come out and visit with them in person."

"That was all this pretty lady's idea," I said, fondly wrapping an arm around my woman's shoulders as Caroline turned her cleaning expertise to Gianna's hands. "Is there anything else you need for the home?"

Caroline shrugged one shoulder and held up the now-empty container of wipes. "These. We go through them like crazy. When we run out, we use washcloths, but that adds to our laundry costs. Plus, the wipes are more sanitary. We try to buy the biodegradable ones because it's better for the environment."

I was surprised she even worried about that with all the other things she had on her plate, but it made me like her all the more. "I'll have a delivery made this week," I assured her.

Chapter 32

After walking around and saying goodbye to all the kids, Gianna and I left the park. She stumbled a little when she looked longingly over her shoulder, and I dropped the cooler and caught her around the waist. Grasping her chin softly, I turned her face to mine.

"Baby, do you want to stay here for the fireworks? We can if you want to."

She shook her head as tears threatened to drip over her lash line. "No, I want to leave before I cry and make an ass of myself."

I pressed my lips tenderly to hers. "Crying doesn't make you an ass; it makes you a wonderful person for caring so much." When we got to where my SUV was parked, I loaded the cooler as Gianna stuffed the blanket in the back.

Once inside the car, I stared out the front windshield for a long moment. "I want to take some groceries to the home. I'd planned to just have some delivered, but I think I'd like to go shopping myself." I turned to face my kind, sweet woman. "Would you like to go with me?"

She'd never looked more beautiful to me as she smiled through her tears. "I would love that." I reached for her hand as I drove us back toward my apartment. "Where are we watching the fireworks?" she asked.

"It's a surprise."

When I pulled into my parking garage, she nodded her head. "On your balcony? That sounds amazing."

I didn't correct her false impression, just helped her out of the car and carried the cooler up to my apartment. "They should be starting soon," I said, leading her back to the elevator.

"Wait. Where are we going?" she asked, jogging a little to keep up.

"I told you, it's a surprise." I pushed my card in the slot. Then I opened a small panel that only unlocked when the penthouse keycard was inserted and pressed a button. The car began to rise.

"I thought your apartment was the highest one," she mused.

Leaning over to kiss her confused lips, I said, "It is." A few seconds later, the doors opened, and I smiled. Everything looked perfect, just as I'd specified.

"We're on the roof," Gianna squealed, rushing from the elevator and spinning in a wide circle. "Oh my gosh! It's beautiful!"

Not even a percentage as beautiful as you, I thought, pocketing my key card. "I'll get us some wine." Strolling to the small bistro table, I kept my eyes on Gianna as she took in the twinkling lights crisscrossed above us. I poured us each a glass of red and returned to her just as she found the sunken tub in the middle of the space.

"A hot tub? Seriously?" she asked, kicking off her sandals and sitting on the edge with her feet in the water. "I wish I'd known, and I would have brought a swimsuit."

After placing the wine glasses and bottle on the ledge, I leaned over and hooked my finger beneath her spaghetti strap, sliding it down her arm. "We don't need suits up here," I promised her in a low voice, tracing lazy circles over her bared, salty skin with my tongue.

"Really?" Her eyes darted around, finding the surrounding high walls that turned our little haven into a square rooftop bowl.

I helped her to her feet and reached for the bottom hem of her dress. "Are you comfortable with this, sweetheart?" She nodded, and I swooped the dress up and over her head, an animalistic sound rising up in my chest at the first glimpse of her. I didn't think I would ever get tired of seeing Gianna naked. "These aren't the panties you were wearing this afternoon," I said, running a finger along the top of her white silk underwear.

She blinked innocently up at me. "That's because some man stole my other ones."

I narrowed my eyes at her as she began to tug my navy polo shirt from my jeans. "Some man?"

"Uh-huh. I met this strange guy in a thread closet, and he made an absolute feast out of me before bending me over and doing very naughty things to me. He was quite... virile."

"He sounds like a stud," I commented as she pulled my shirt off over my head and started on my pants.

"Best I've ever had," she whispered, leaning into me and allowing the tips of her breasts to brush against my bare chest. I practically busted out of my pants before she got them pulled down. "And then he *stole* my panties and stuffed them in his pocket."

"What a bastard," I said, stepping out of my jeans. "I'll bet he took them back to his office and sniffed them while he was on a phone call with a very important client."

"Yep, probably," Gianna said, slipping off her panties. "He seemed like a bit of a freak."

Snatching the silky material from her, I held it to my nose, my eyes locked on hers as I took a long inhale and groaned on the exhale. "And freakiness is a problem for you?"

Stepping into the bubbling water, she tossed me a wink over her shoulder. "I didn't say that."

Laughing, I tossed her panties onto the dress pooled on the ground before stepping in behind her. I adored our flirty banter; I'd never had that with another woman before, but Gianna bought out something inside me. Something fun and freeing.

I sat and pulled her down into my lap, and she snuggled her back against my chest. Reaching for the wine, I handed her a glass and took a long sip of my own, the dry fruitiness sparking against my taste buds.

"Ooh, look! They're starting," Gianna said, taking a drink from her stemless glass as the first fireworks whizzed into the sky. I stretched my arm out and flicked the switch to turn off the overhead fairy lights so that the only illumination was the soft-blue underwater lights and the multicolored flashes against the dark sky.

We watched in silence for a while, drinking our wine as the extravagant display lit up the night. Gianna turned her head and looked up at me. "Auburn, you went to so much trouble to make our first holiday together romantic. Did I spoil your plans by asking to eat in the park with the kids? Had you intended for us to have dinner up here?"

"No, baby," I told her, fibbing a little because I actually *had* planned to have a fancy meal up here on the roof. "It was the perfect idea, and I can't think of anywhere else I'd rather have been."

Her smile was content as she sank back against me. "Who would've ever thought Auburn Bouvier would consider eating McDonald's in the park as a perfect night?"

"I've always done the park thing for the children on the Fourth of July, and I thought I was helping, but I've never actually gone down there and met with the kids. Tonight gave me an entirely new perspective, you know?" She nodded, and I set down my wine before taking hers and doing the same. With gentle fingers on her chin, I tilted her face to mine, whispering against her lips, "*You* give me perspective I never knew I needed."

I kissed her then, trying to convey with my lips and tongue even a fraction of what I was feeling in that moment. This woman had become my world in only seven short weeks, and she'd changed me in all the right ways.

"Auburn, I need you," she said, shifting her legs until they were outside of mine.

"I need you too," I told her as she sat up straight and lifted. I positioned my cock at her entrance, and she immediately sank down onto me, wrapping me in her wet heat. My hands held her waist from behind, and her hands grasped my wrists for balance as she started to move.

Gianna's head was tilted back, her long braid skimming the water and her back arched as she rode me. I'd always loved being on top, fucking a willing woman into the mattress or pounding into her from behind while my hand fisted in her hair. But *this*? The way Gianna fucked me when she was on top was next level.

She completely lost herself in the act, sliding up and down my dick like it was the only thing she needed. She squeezed me tight on every upstroke and grinded hard against me on the down. As the fireworks display neared its finale, the lights became more dazzling and the booms closer together, and Gianna and I found our own crescendo.

Water began to slosh over the sides of the hot tub as our hips moved faster against each other, and I was deeper inside her than I had ever been. My teeth bit hard into my bottom lip as I tried to control my orgasm until she was ready.

"Now!" she called as her pussy tightened around me, and I breathed out a long moan and let myself release inside of her.

As the overhead booms and crackles faded away, I was left with only the sounds of our heavy breathing and the smells of smoke, chlorine, and sex filling the air.

I banded my arms around her middle and pulled her beautiful body back against mine, burying my face against her shoulder.

"I love you," she said softly, her lips pressing against my temple.

"I love you too," I told her. "More than you'll ever know."

I managed to slip out Wednesday morning without waking Gianna. Though I'd wanted to. I'd wanted to wake her up with gentle good morning kisses and sweet words. The woman had turned me into a complete sap, and I was a hundred percent good with that.

"Good morning, Tony," I said cheerfully on my way to my inner office.

"Good morning, Auburn. Your attorney, Miss Ramirez, has called already and asked that you return her call as soon as you get in. She said it's important."

My merry mood sank a little as a frisson of unease slipped up the back of my neck. When yesterday passed with no word from Magdalena, I'd gained a small sense of relief that maybe she'd come to her senses.

"I'll call her right now." Closing the door, my thumb hit Kassie's number before I even made it to my desk. "Hey, Kasserole. What's up?"

"Have you been on the NYC Gossip site this morning?" she asked brusquely.

"No. What is it?"

"Magdalena released a tell-all story." I felt my heart sink, and my thoughts went immediately to Gianna and how this would affect her once our relationship became public. "Now look, it's really not that bad," Kassie continued. "It's nothing that eighty percent of adults have never done. Hell, I've done most of it myself."

"Fuck," I grunted, falling into my chair. "I'll check it out. Thanks for letting me know."

"I'll call the prosecutor and let him know as well."

"Thanks, Kassie."

After hanging up, I downloaded the app, drumming my fingers against the desktop as it loaded. When it finally did, the very first headline caught my eye.

AUBURN BOUVIER IS "A KINKY BASTARD"

Fucking great! My eyes dropped to the first paragraph.

Magdalena Lewis, ex-girlfriend to the enigmatic Auburn Bouvier has come to NYC Gossip—the premiere site for all exciting happenings in the city—with exclusive information about the fashion icon.

"I just want everyone to know what kind of man he really is. I don't want any other woman to be subjected to the utter humiliation that I felt. Because Auburn Bouvier is a kinky bastard."

When asked for details, Miss Lewis was more than happy to comply. "One time, he put his hand around my throat while we were having intercourse." Our experienced reporter asked if he had hurt her, and Bouvier's ex reluctantly admitted that it had only happened for a second, and he stopped as soon as she said she didn't like it.

"Oh, and one time, he asked if he could spank me. Like I was some kind of naughty child or something. What kind of person does that?" The buxom blonde seemed quite disturbed and went on to tell us that she had been in contact with other sexual partners of Bouvier's and that he had pulled the same acts of "depravity" with them.

"Mister Bouvier can be quite compelling, and I feel for these poor women for falling under his spell," she told our reporter. "He is a very dominant person, but I'm an extremely strong woman and didn't take any of his crap."

I paused in my reading for a moment so that I could gag. Strong woman, my ass. Magdalena was compelled by nothing except money. My reluctant eyes returned to the screen.

When asked if she had anything else to add, Miss Lewis said that she wanted to make clear that she wasn't doing this out of revenge. She was merely doing it as a public service announcement to unsuspecting women out there.

"I personally like to be treated like a princess in the bedroom, not as a dirty, little [redacted]."

So, readers... what say you? Do you think Auburn Bouvier is as twisted as Miss Lewis considers him? Or is he simply a stud who likes to get a little kinky between the sheets? We'll leave that up to you to decide. Tell us your opinions in the comment section.

I set my phone on the desk and buried my head in my hands. This was a fucking nightmare. I always tried to stay in my lane, keeping my circle small and going about my business. I made appearances when absolutely necessary, but I kept my private life just that... private.

This wasn't good at all, but I could handle the blowback. What concerned me most was Gianna. Would she even want to be associated with me after this? My cell phone rang, and I picked it up, seeing that it was my cousin, Blaire Broxton, on the phone. Clearing my throat, I answered.

"Hello, Blaire."

"Oh. My. God. You fucking pervert."

I couldn't help but laugh at that. "I'm assuming you've read that bullshit online?"

"Hell yes, I have. Do you want me to come up there and kick that bitch's ass?"

I had no doubt she could do it since her brother had been a SEAL, and Beau always made sure Blaire could defend herself. "I'll send my plane for you," I told her, only half joking. "I would like to choke the life out of *Miss Lewis* myself, but that probably wouldn't be the best idea. I don't need to look any worse than I do right now."

"Worse? I didn't think you came across bad at all, Auburn. She's the one who looks like an idiot, while making you seem like a bedroom rockstar. Hold on a sec." I could hear her talking to someone else in the room. "What? No, Axel. You may not talk to Auburn for pointers. I can barely keep up with your kinky ass as it is." Then she was back on the line. "Swear to God, I don't know what I'm going to do with that man of mine."

Her husband called back, "I'm reading the article again. I'm sure we could come up with something," and I chuckled, feeling slightly better than I had a minute ago.

"Anyway, I just wanted to check on you and let you know we think that was a shitty thing for her to do. If even half of what Axel and I do in the privacy of our bedroom was to come out, we'd probably both be in jail. Or committed to a psychiatric hospital. Don't ever let anyone make you feel bad about your kinks."

My head bobbed up and down. Those were practically the same words I'd said to Gianna a few weeks ago.

"Thanks, Blaire. I appreciate it. I think I'll pass on the ass kicking though. Your hands are much too valuable to risk on someone like Magdalena."

"I'm so fucking mad, I would almost risk my career as a surgeon to take a crack at that woman." She paused, and her voice softened. "How is Gianna handling all of this?"

My anxiety ratcheted up a notch at the mention of her name. "I'm not sure how she's going to take it. I just read the article myself, and I'm a little scared to break the news to her."

"Well, we're here for you both. I can't wait to meet her. Beau and Charli said they really like her a lot."

"I do too," I assured her.

"Are you going to sue the heifer for… defamation or something?"

"It's not actually defamation because she didn't say anything that wasn't true," I admitted. "Though she did tell me last week she wanted a large sum of money if I didn't want her to talk to the press, so the D.A. is looking into blackmail charges against her."

"Holy shit! I hope they nail her ass to the wall. See how much *princess* treatment she gets in prison."

I chuckled at the thought of prissy-ass Magdalena in a prison jumpsuit. "Thanks for calling and giving me a pep talk, Blaire."

"No problemo. It's what cousins do. Call me if you need anything, okay?"

"I will. Give my love to the kids."

"Sure thing. Carrie still talks about you all the time. Danica is currently stuck on the word Da-Da, and the triplets are in a weiner phase, so all they talk about is their penises. It makes going to church pretty awkward."

A loud laugh rolled up from my belly. "This is why you're my favorite cousin. Don't tell Beau."

"I'll rub it in every chance I get."

My phone made a noise, and I checked the display. "Speak of the devil, there's your brother calling now. Thanks again, Blaire."

"All right, talk to you later."

I clicked over. "Hey, Beau."

"What the fuck is wrong with that chick?" he growled. "And is Gianna okay?"

My heart warmed at his concern for my girl. "I haven't talked to her. I just saw the article myself."

I listened to my cousin rant for a while about respecting people's privacy, and he finally asked, "What are you doing about this?"

"This is strictly between us, but I have video of Magdalena attempting to blackmail me for five million dollars. My lawyer has turned it over to the District Attorney."

"Good for you. New York is a one-party consent state, right?" Beau owned a security business, so he was well-versed in surveillance law.

"Yep. And I hired that investigator you recommended, so I have some dirt on *Miss Lewis* that will be made public in the next few days."

"You didn't threaten her with it, did you? Because then you—"

"I absolutely did not. This is pure retaliation, not blackmail on my part."

"Excellent, I'll keep my eye out for it." His chuckle was a little on the evil side. "I can't wait to see what Samuel came up with."

"Trust me. That woman will regret ever fucking with me."

After hanging up with Beau, I fielded twelve more calls from acquaintances calling to voice their support for me and their outrage at Magdalena's betrayal. By the time I was done, it was almost lunchtime.

"Tony," I said, exiting my office into the anteroom, "I'm going home for lunch."

"Of course," he said, a look of sympathy on his face. Guess he read the article too. *Fucking great.* "That gossip site called, and I told them 'no comment' since we haven't discussed a game plan yet."

"That's fine. Thank you."

"I'll draft a statement in case your lawyer decides you need to make one. You two can go over it together and make any necessary revisions."

"I'd really appreciate that, Tony," I said, smiling warmly at the man.

"You keep your chin up, Auburn. What two people do in the privacy of their own bedroom is their damn business." He looked almost as angry as I felt. "This will all blow over soon. You've never once been involved in any kind of scandal. I think the majority of folks will be on your side."

I nodded appreciatively, and Tony gave me a small smile. "You really don't have much going on this afternoon. Why don't you take the rest of the day off? I can handle things here."

Placing my hand on his shoulder, I squeezed. "Thank you so much. I think I'll take you up on that."

Chapter 33

As I stood outside my apartment door, my stomach was in knots. Resting my head against the door jamb, I sent up a silent plea that I didn't lose the one woman I'd ever loved. What if she wasn't even here? What if she'd seen the article, packed up her shit, and left because I'm not worth this kind of trouble in her life?

My knees almost buckled when I pushed open the door and saw Gianna sitting on the couch in a pair of holey jeans and a red babydoll tee. Her phone was in her hand, and she was laughing at something on the screen. After a moment, she looked up, her face registering surprise.

"Hey, baby. Why didn't you tell me you were coming home for lunch? I would have had something ready for you."

"I'm not hungry," I said, closing the door and taking the seat beside her on the couch.

She tilted her face up to mine for a quick kiss and then went back to her phone. Resting my elbows on my knees, I stared at the floor and almost smiled when she giggled. I loved hearing her so happy. All of a sudden, she let out a howl of laughter and slapped her hand against my shoulder.

"Oh God. You've got to read this."

My words came out in a pauseless stream. "Gianna, I have to tell you something. Magdalena talked to the press and now I'm afraid I'm going to lose you." I covered my face with my hands. She took a moment to process everything I'd blurted out, and then her soft hand rubbed up and down my back.

"Why would you lose me, baby?"

Uncovering my face, I turned to look at her, incredulity painting my expression. "Because I'm *a kinky bastard*," I bitterly quoted from the article.

"Yeah, so? I'm a kinky bitch. We're perfect together." Her fingers tracked up and down my cheek, and I couldn't help but lean into her sweet touch. "Are you really upset about this?"

I nodded, the words almost choking me. "Yes, but mostly on your behalf. Do you really want our relationship to go public and have people think... *things* about you?"

Making herself at home across my lap, she focused those gorgeous green eyes fiercely on my blue ones. "I don't give a fuck what anyone thinks. I'm not from here, remember?"

"Yeah, but..."

"But nothing. We are consenting adults who have an active, healthy sex life. Does it piss me off that Magdalena betrayed you like that? Yes. I think she's a petty bitch. But again, I don't care what anyone else thinks."

"Have you even read the article? And I use that term loosely."

"Of course. I was just reading the comments when you came in."

"And laughing?" I asked, outraged.

She pressed a pacifying kiss to my lips. "Yes, I was laughing. They're hilarious." Her head tilted to the side. "Did you actually think people were going to judge you for getting a little freaky in the bedroom?"

I shrugged, unsure what to say to that. Gianna picked up her phone and held it in front of us. "It's not as bad as you think. There are over eight thousand comments so far, and I've only read three that were even mildly critical of you."

"Really?"

"Yes, really. Just read through some of these."

[Tommy ton ton]: What a prude! I wouldn't fuck her with Charlie Sheen's dick.

I snorted out a laugh and then pointed at a picture on the screen. "What the hell is that?"

"That's a close-up of a woman's neck. Read the caption."

[Gloria hole]: Mister Bouvier, I await my hand necklace, Sir.

There were more. A lot more. Not one of them was judgemental of me and my... proclivities.

[Mary S.]: I would let that man spank me to kingdom COME. Pun intended.

[Chels-E]: Meeeeee too, sister!

[Anna in NY]: A princess? Really? This Magdalena chick sounds like an immature bitch.

[BlaireBear]: Sounds like a typical Tuesday at my house.

[Tootie]: My grandma is freakier than Miss Lewis.

[CMK]: I've slept with AB and would do it again. In a freaking heartbeat. The man is a god in bed.

[JimmyJames]: *crosses Mag Lewis from my fuck list* I like women who actually move during sex.

[My Other Brother Darryl]: I'm with ya, bro. She probably thinks oral is "gross."

[Daddy Shark]: Who wants to fuck a block of ice?

[Michelle 128]: If this is depraved, she would be shocked at what goes on in my bedroom.

[HawkMan]: Fuck her. Do your thing, Bouvier. There are plenty of women out there who like it rough.

[Christi with an i]: DM me, HawkMan.

[Angelina not Jolie]: I've been a naughty girl, Mr B. I'm bent over my desk. Waiting for my spanking.

[Duck Duck Goose]: Not really my thing, but no judgment here, AB. You do you.

[Vera Kay]: That man just oozes BDE.

[The Real Cole]: Pretty shitty of this woman to do this. Who would want to date her now?

[Sara 4TT]: Auburn Bouvier is the hottest man on the planet. If he called me right now, I would open the front door, the back door, AND the penthouse for business.

I couldn't help but laugh with Gianna as we scrolled through page after page of comments. She didn't even flinch at the woman who said she'd slept with me. "Look," she said, "someone is even making T-shirts that read *Auburn's DLS.*"

"What's DLS?"

"Dirty little slut," she said with a grin. "I'm thinking of getting one." Laying her phone down, she rested her head on my shoulder. "Are you feeling better about everything now?"

I felt like the weight of the world had been lifted from my shoulders. "I am. Thank you, baby girl. I was stressing out so hard about how this would affect you."

"The only way it will affect me is that I'll now have thousands of jealous women eyeballing me and trying to take my place."

"Never gonna happen," I said, pressing my lips to her forehead.

"I'm getting hungry. Do you want a grilled ham and cheese sandwich, or do you have to get back to work?"

"That sounds good. And I have the rest of the day off." An idea sparked in my head. "Maybe we could go shopping for the children's home after we eat."

"Sounds good," she said, pushing off my lap and heading for the kitchen.

"Let me know when it's done. I have a phone call to make."

Closing the door to my office, I called Tony to check in and make sure everything was okay.

"Everything is fine," he said with amusement in his voice. "You've received no less than fourteen flower arrangements from what I'm assuming are various interested women. I didn't read the cards."

I laughed. "Are you serious?"

"As a heart attack. Oh, and there was another package. It wasn't marked personal, so I opened it."

"What was in it?"

"Panties. And they appear to be, um, used. Would you like me to put them on your desk?"

"God, no. Send them down to the incinerator and then disinfect the office," I instructed.

As soon as I hung up with Tony, I dialed Samuel's number.

"Samuel White Investigations," he answered.

"Hi, Samuel," I said, keeping my voice low. "Is everything ready to go?"

"Yes, Mister Bouvier. I was just waiting for the go-ahead from you."

"You've got it. Begin Phase One tomorrow."

"Yes, sir," he said and disconnected.

When I turned around, Gianna was standing in the door of my office, her eyebrows raised. *Fuck, fuck, fuck.*

"What is Phase One?"

Pasting on a fake smile, I crossed to her. "Nothing you need to worry about, sweetheart. Why don't—"

"Does it have to do with getting revenge on Magdalena?"

Sighing, I closed my eyes and nodded. Would she think I was a horrible person for what I was about to have Samuel do? "Yes, it does."

To my utter shock, her lips curled up into a wicked smile. "Awesome. Come eat your sandwich and tell me all about it."

Chapter 34

"Do you think we got enough?" Auburn asked worriedly as we pulled up to the back door of the large four-story home.

I peered at him around the 96-pack of mac and cheese that was sitting on my lap. "Auburn, we couldn't fit a gummy worm in this vehicle without it exploding, so yes. I think we got enough."

His head whipped around to face me. "Do you think we should have gotten gummy worms? Kids like those, don't they?"

Doing my best not to roll my eyes at the sweet man beside me, I said, "Honey, we got plenty of snacks, healthy foods, kid foods, fresh produce, fruits, meat, pasta, and drinks. Not to mention diapers, wipes, and formula for the babies. We practically cleaned out Costco."

He still looked unconvinced, but nodded and got out of the car. Fifteen minutes later, with the help of Caroline Jenkins and her staff, we had the vehicle completely unloaded and were taking a tour of the facility.

Several of the kids recognized us from last night and stopped to chat as we walked around the play area outside. The playground equipment was old but the yard was well-kept and free of weeds. The inside of the house was clean, though the flooring and walls were worn, which I guess was to be expected when you had over forty children living in one house.

As we walked down one of the corridors on the first floor, we saw little Jane rolling toward us. Her eyes widened, and she turned her chair sharply around and wheeled away. I couldn't help but be disappointed. Maybe she didn't recognize us.

Less than a minute later, she returned with Jaxon right behind her. "See, Jax? I told you they were here," she said, pointing proudly at me and Auburn. She was grinning broadly, and her brother was hopping from foot to foot in excitement.

"Auburn, Gianna! You're here!" he squealed. I squatted to hug each of them, and then Auburn did the same. My heart did some really weird stuff in my chest when Jane laid her little blonde head on his shoulder. "You want to see our room?" Jaxon asked, already heading back down the wide hallway.

"We normally don't let boys and girls room together, but these two are so young, and Jaxon will barely let his twin out of his sight," Caroline informed us. Her mouth turned down into a sad frown as she whispered, "I don't even want to think about what will happen if someone adopts one of them and not the other."

My breathing seized in my chest. I didn't want to think about that either. We reached the room at the end of the hall and entered the tiny space. It barely fit two small beds and a dresser. Colorful drawings dotted the walls, and I bent to inspect them.

"I drew that one today in art class," Jane said shyly, pointing out a picture of two dark-haired stick figures. "It's you and Auburn."

"I could tell!" I exclaimed. "It looks just like us."

The little girl smiled. "And you're holding popsicles, see? You can have it if you want." Then her bottom lip trembled as her eyes went to her lap. "But you don't have to."

"Oh, I would *love* to have that picture," I gushed.

Auburn reached over and unstuck it from the wall and studied it before leveling his gaze on Jane. "Are you sure you don't want to put this in a museum or something?"

The child's high-pitched giggle filled the room. "You're silly, Auburn. It's not *that* good."

"Well, I think it's beautiful." Looking up at me, he said, "Gianna, don't you think this would look good on our refrigerator?"

It wasn't lost on me that he'd said *our* refrigerator, even though we didn't actually live together. I did spend every night at his apartment now, mostly going to mine only to pick up mail or additional clothes.

"For sure. That way Auburn can look at it every five minutes when he goes to the fridge," I teased, making the kids laugh and earning me a good-natured eye roll from my boyfriend.

"Mrs. Jenkins, I need to... you know... go to *the bathroom*," Jane said, whispering the last two words as her face pinkened.

"Okay, sweetie," the lady said, maneuvering around us to grasp the handles of the little girl's wheelchair. "We'll be back in a sec," she told us.

Auburn stared after them for a moment before turning to Jaxon. "Where is the bathroom?"

"The girls' bathroom is across the hall, and the boys' is at the other end. Mrs. Jenkins gave us this room because it's closer to the potty for Janie."

"And how many kids share the bathrooms?"

Jaxon shrugged and sat on his tiny bed with a dark blue blanket draped neatly across it. "All the kids on this floor. Soooo, like seven girls and five boys, I think."

Auburn nodded and stuffed his hands into his pockets, his solemn gaze on the floor as his shoulders rose and fell with his breaths. He stayed silent as I sat on the edge of Jane's bed—which was covered with a sunny yellow blanket—and chatted with Jaxon until Mrs. Jenkins returned with Jane.

My boyfriend lifted his chin. "Caroline, can I speak to you in your office for a moment?"

"Oh, uh. Of course. Kids, would you like to finish showing Gianna around?"

"Just the first floor," Jane specified when Auburn and Caroline left, "b'cuz I can't go up the stairs."

"First floor is where all the coolest stuff is though, right?" I asked, and she nodded. The twins showed me everything downstairs, including the kitchen—which I'd already seen—the board game room, and the art room.

"Mrs. Jenkins is teaching me to play the piano," Jane said, wheeling herself up to the old upright in the corner as Jaxon moved the bench out of her way. "All I know is scales right now. You wanna hear?"

"I would love to," I said, standing beside her as her small fingers made their way up and down the keys, playing several scales.

"That's really good, Jane," I said, squatting to her level. "Would you like to learn a chord?" She nodded enthusiastically, and I showed her a simple C chord. She had to stretch her fingers to hit the three keys, but when she did, her brother gasped at the rich sound.

"That was so pretty, Janie," he said. "You're like Bozart!"

I stood and ruffled his hair. "I think you mean Mozart, kiddo."

His button nose wrinkled as he laughed. "Yeah, him too."

Jane hit the notes again as Caroline and Auburn entered the room. "I learned a chord, Mrs. Jenkins! Gianna taught me."

"I heard. You sounded wonderful," the older lady said, and Jane's smile beamed around the room. Caroline patted the top of the piano. "This old thing may not look like much, but my husband was a piano tuner before he retired, so he keeps it sounding nice. He's our resident handyman and groundskeeper too." Her phone rang, and she excused herself to take the call.

Jaxon tugged on Auburn's shirtsleeve, and he bent to pick the kid up. "Can you and Gianna come visit us again?" Jaxon asked, his big blue eyes focused on Auburn's.

My big, dominant man seemed to melt where he stood. "We would love to," he said, shifting his gaze to mine, and I nodded. "If Mrs. Jenkins tells me you've been really good this week, we may even bring ice cream to everyone this weekend."

Jane pointed accusingly at her brother. "That means you gotta eat all your vegetables, Jaxon Andrew," she said sternly. "Even the green beans." I had to cover my mouth to hide my smile.

He thought about it for a split second and pushed out a sigh worthy of a teenage girl. "Okaaaaay. If I don't die from eating green beans, I'll see you this weekend," he grumbled dramatically.

"Just give me two more months, Alice. I'm trying to find someone," we heard from the hallway. "Yes, I promise."

Caroline re-entered the small room, looking weary.

"Everything okay?" Auburn asked her.

A tight smile etched across her lips. "Yes, fine. Just staffing problems."

"Anything we can do to help?"

"That was my sister Alice. She's the CPA for the home, but she's turning seventy, and she's ready to retire. So no. I don't think you can help." Caroline set her hands on her hips. "Not unless you know a good accountant."

Chapter 35

THURSDAY, JULY 6TH
SCANDAL SURROUNDS MAGDALENA LEWIS AND DEMOCRATIC CONGRESSMAN

Photos have recently surfaced of socialite Magdalena Lewis and the very married—but for how long?—State Congressman Bennett Jameson. The two were seen entering Room 1451 of The Hotel LeBlanc, and NYC Gossip has the exclusive photos! (See below.)

As you can see, they entered the hotel room looking pristine, but when they exited a half hour later, they both looked a bit worse for wear. Miss Lewis's hair is visibly mussed, and her blouse is mis-buttoned, while the Congressman is carrying his tie and has scratches that look suspiciously like fingernail marks on the left side of his neck. (See zoomed-in photo.)

We at NYC Gossip won't speculate on what happened inside that hotel room. We'll leave it up to our valued readers to draw their own conclusions.

It's worth noting that the time stamp on the photos shows they were taken in April of this year, while the Congressman's wife was very pregnant with their second child.

Let us hear your thoughts in the comment section.

FRIDAY, JULY 7TH

THE MAGDALENA PLOT THICKENS

Yesterday, we dropped the bombshell of socialite Magdalena Lewis's alleged affair with Democratic Congressman Bennett Jameson. Well, things just got a lot more interesting.

If you follow NY State politics, you know that Jameson's arch-rival is Republican Congressman Rowan Stewart. In May of this year, none other than Magdalena Lewis was photographed wearing a hotel bathrobe as she kissed Congressman Stewart as he left Room 1451 on the fourteenth floor of The Hotel LeBlanc.

If you didn't read yesterday's story, would you like to guess which room Miss Lewis was seen leaving with Congressman Jameson not even three weeks prior to this event? If you guessed Room 1451, then you would be correct.

Is this merely a coincidence, or should we now refer to this room as The Magdalena Lewis Adultery Suite?

Oh, and that's not all, dear readers. The following set of photographs provided by an anonymous source show Miss Lewis arriving at the home of Congressman Stewart a week after the hotel pics were taken. And, pray tell, where was Mrs. Stewart at the time? She was seen being dropped off by her driver at Sloan Kettering for her chemotherapy treatments. We wish Mrs. Stewart a full recovery from her ongoing battle with breast cancer.

And the cancer that she's married to.

We would like to assure our readers that NYC Gossip will be at the state house when Congress reconvenes next week. The fireworks between Jameson and Stewart are sure to rival those from the Fourth of July.

SATURDAY, JULY 8TH
IS MAGDALENA LEWIS THE MOST HATED WOMAN IN NYC?

If she wasn't already, considering her hotel room trysts with mortal enemies Bennett Jameson and Rowan Stewart, she may very well hold that title after you watch this exclusive video.

We would like to warn viewers that the following footage is extremely disturbing, so please watch with caution. For those who would prefer not to view it, we will do our best to describe what occurred.

On May twelfth, Magdalena Lewis was filmed entering Central Park. She sat on a park bench, took out her phone, and placed a phone call. A few seconds later, a small dog entered the frame. As a squirrel ran past and up a tree, the Yorkshire terrier mix became visibly excited and let out two short barks.

Miss Lewis can be clearly heard yelling at the pup to shut up. When he barked at the squirrel again, Lewis took off her shoe—a red Louboutin Lipstrass Queen—and threw it at the little dog, striking him in the face and knocking him unconscious.

Amir Maroun, the owner of the one-year-old puppy, spoke to NYC Gossip about the incident. "It was the most callous thing I'd ever seen. She threw her fancy shoe really hard at Scooter, picked it up like nothing had happened, and walked off. She didn't even stop to check on him."

Mister Maroun became visibly upset and had to take a moment to collect himself before continuing. "Scooter is a rescue dog, and he's always well-behaved. He does like to bark at the squirrels in the park, but he's never hurt another animal or human. He's a very gentle little guy. And that... woman just attacked him."

When asked how Scooter was doing now, Mister Maroun informed the NYC Gossip reporter that, after thousands of dollars in veterinarian bills and almost two months of recovery time, his best friend was healing nicely. "But he refuses to go outside at all. My dog is completely traumatized, and I'll never forgive that woman for that."

If you would like to donate to Scooter's gofundme account, click the link below.

And tell us in the comments what you think about Magdalena Lewis's actions. The folks at NYC Gossip completely understand now why Auburn Bouvier dumped his long-time girlfriend. He's a staunch animal rights *supporter, donating thousands of dollars a year to various shelters and other animal-related causes. Mister Bouvier was unavailable for comment.*

Chapter 36

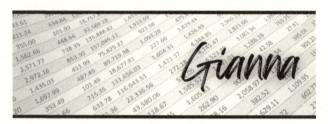

My mind wouldn't slow down. It was a little before noon on Monday, and I had so many thoughts swirling like tumbleweeds on a windy day. Job options—of which there weren't many, to be honest. My relationship with Auburn. My father and everything he had going on. The kids at the orphanage—specifically Jane and Jaxon, who were never far from the front of my thoughts.

My eyes lit on the drawing of me and Auburn on the refrigerator, and all of my ideas seemed to congeal. To hyper-focus. Like the little stick figures were telling me what I needed to do.

Picking up my phone, I dialed Auburn's cell phone. As soon as he answered, I blurted out, "I think I want to work at the children's home. As their accountant. I know it probably won't pay much, but I own my apartment outright, and I can live on ramen noodles if I need to. I feel like... like I can't stop thinking about those kids, and I just want to do my part to help. Especially the twins. It's only been a few days since I've seen them, but I kinda miss those two."

When I paused to take a breath, he replied, "Okay."

"Okay?"

"Yeah. Okay. I think it's a great idea. And you will not be living on ramen. Because *I* refuse to live on ramen, and we eat most of our meals together."

"True, but I don't want to be a mooch. I can make us some great meals on a budget. I got really good at that when—"

"Gianna." His deep, commanding voice halted my blabbering. "Breathe, baby." I did. "I have some ideas that I've been thinking about. I voiced some of them to Caroline on Saturday, but I wanted to really think hard about the specifics before I brought them up to you."

I put my hand over my chest, rubbing at the tightness that had my skin feeling like a thousand taut violin strings were embedded there. "What ideas?"

"Why don't you come to my office for lunch? I'd rather talk about it face to face."

"Umm, what about my father? Tony? Your PA? Remember him?"

His low chuckle tickled my eardrum. "Yes, I remember him. He and Tora are across town picking up some samples and doing some other errands. They'll be gone for a few hours. And anyway, we're telling Tony about us soon. I'm tired of all this secretive shit. I want my woman to be able to come to my office for lunch like we're a normal couple."

Blowing out a breath, I nodded at the phone, even though he couldn't see me. "You're right. We need to tell him. I can be there in about thirty or forty minutes for lunch."

"Twenty minutes. I'll send Cruz for you."

He laughed again when I called him a bossy butt before hanging up.

I was surprised when Cruz turned a block sooner than usual. "I'm taking you around back," he explained, pulling up to an industrial-looking metal door. "For privacy reasons."

"Ah, good idea." Otherwise, how would I explain to Lehra that I was going to the top floor when my dad wasn't even there? I was pretty sure she was getting suspicious that I was seeing *someone* because I'd been unavailable to go to dinner with her the last two times she'd called. She'd even casually commented that I must have a secret boyfriend or something, but I'd laughed and changed the subject.

Auburn was right. All this secret-keeping was exhausting.

Cruz pulled a matte black card from the console and handed it to me. "This will get you in the back door, and it also works for the elevator to the top floor. Once you're inside the building, go straight down the hallway and you'll end up at the back of the lobby, right beside the elevators."

"Thanks, Cruz." I gave him a warm smile before exiting, and he kept the car in park until I was inside. He really was a sweetheart.

When I reached the fiftieth floor and the elevator doors opened, the air stalled in my lungs. Auburn was leaning with his butt against my dad's desk, his long legs stretched out in front of him and his arms crossed over his chest. He looked fucking delicious in his charcoal gray suit and lavender shirt.

Strolling forward until I was directly in front of him, I wrapped my hand around his matching gray tie and tugged him toward me, kissing him on the lips. "You're looking mighty fine today, Mister Bouvier."

His hands went to my hips, and his eyes crinkled at the corners when he smiled. "As are you, Miss Moschella. I love this on you." I was wearing a red button-down shirt dress with a thin black belt and cute black sandals with just enough heel to make my legs look a mile long. "If they hadn't just delivered our lunch, I would be exploring what's beneath it."

Smoothing down his tie, I brought my mouth to his ear. "I think you're already pretty familiar with what's under this dress."

"Mmm, intimately," he said, reaching around to cop a feel of my ass. "Come on. The food is in my office." I left my purse on Dad's desk, and Auburn led me inside his office and removed his tie and jacket, tossing them across a chair before seating us on the couch. I kicked off my shoes and pulled my feet up on the couch, crossing my legs as Auburn rolled up his sleeves to expose those yummy, muscular forearms.

"I got us muffulettas from the place down the street. They're the best I've ever had outside of New Orleans." He handed me a ginormous sandwich, and I wrapped a napkin around the bottom to prevent dripping. Because... yeah... it's *me*.

Sinking my teeth into it, I practically had a mouth-gasm. The salami and ham were savory, and the melted cheese raised the sandwich to an absolutely decadent level, the olive mixture on top adding a subtle tang. And don't even get me started on the crunchy-on-the-outside, pillowy-on-the-inside bread. "Mmm, that is good," I concurred.

"The ranch kettle chips are homemade."

I dipped a finger into the white powdery seasoning at the bottom of the container and sucked it off. "Oooh, ranch dust."

Auburn laughed. "I've never heard it put like that."

After eating a couple of the crispy fried chips, I asked, "So, what did you want to talk to me about?"

He stared at his uneaten sandwich for a moment before setting it down and wiping his hands. "First of all, the reason I wanted to get your input on all this is because I think—I *hope*—what I'm about to tell you will impact your life too. Your finances... I mean *our*..." His intense blue gaze gripped me as I attempted to decipher his words. "Sorry, I'm bumbling around a bit here. What I'm trying to say is that I see a future with you, Gianna, and I need to know if you see that too. I'm not talking about months or years. I'm talking... forever."

The impervious Auburn Bouvier was laying himself bare to me, and my throat was so clogged with emotion, I had to take a drink of my iced tea before I could speak.

"*Forever* with you sounds pretty perfect."

His beautiful lips turned up into a nervous smile. "Yeah?"

"Of course. I love you, and I know you love me."

I hadn't noticed his shoulders tensing until they relaxed. "I do. I just wanted to make sure we were both headed in the same direction." He picked up his sandwich and took his first bite, as if he'd been unable to eat before he knew my response. "Okay, here's the deal. I want to do more for the kids' home. A lot more than just bringing food."

My head bobbed up and down. "I did notice that, while everything was clean, the floors and walls were fairly worn. I think if we painted, that would help a lot. I don't know much about flooring, but—"

Auburn cut me off with a shake of his head. "I'm thinking beyond simple repairs, and that's why I wanted to talk to you. I think it's important for a couple to share and talk about major purchases." He took a deep breath and huffed it out. "I want to buy an entirely new house for the children's home."

I choked on a bite of sandwich, and he patted me on the back until I recovered. "Do you have any idea how much space you would need for that many kids and how much that would cost?"

His grin was a little smug. "Actually, I do. Will you take a look at this for me and let me know what you think?" He slid a folder with the name and logo of a real estate company on it toward me.

"Auburn, I don't know anything about real estate." I said, staring at the gold letters emblazoned on dark green.

"But you know numbers, Gianna. You know the law regarding 501c3 donations. And you could counsel me on the tax ramifications and the financing options, right?" I nodded dumbly, picking up the folder with wary fingers. "There's no one I trust more with something this important," he said softly.

A warm, tingly feeling began in my fingers, slipped up my arms, and slammed right into my heart. I opened the folder and gasped. "Good God, Auburn. This is... this is a mansion." The photos were on top, and they were stunning. My fingers paged through each sheet until I reached the financial information, and a sharp breath pushed from my lungs. "This number can't be right?" I uttered, a question ringing through the words.

Auburn leaned over my shoulder to look at the way-too-low figure. "No, that's correct." He smiled when my inquiring eyes met his. "I have a friend who lost both parents this year, and he's the executor for their estate. He has six siblings, and his parents liked to entertain a lot, so there are fourteen bedrooms, not including the master."

"But the price is so low. Are they crazy?"

He shook his head, looking amused. "No, but they're all grown, filthy rich, and very philanthropic. Two of the brothers have cystic fibrosis, so they're unable to father children, and between the two of them, they have five adopted kids. The entire family is very supportive of any organization that takes care of children."

"That is wonderful and sad at the same time, but mostly wonderful," I said, feeling tears puddle behind my eyelids. "This is still an astronomical amount of money, but about a third of what I would expect a house like this to cost." Not wanting to pry too much, I let my eyes flit to his. "Are you... I mean, can you..."

"Yes, Gianna. I can afford it," he said, reading my mind.

"I didn't want to be a nosy butt. I mean, I know you're wealthy. You have your own plane and an apartment that's worth the GDP of most small countries."

"You can ask me anything you want about my finances. I want you to." He lifted my chin until our eyes were linked. "Very soon, I hope they will be *our* finances, so you have every right to delve as deeply as you want."

My heart stuttered behind my breastbone. He'd just confirmed what I'd suspected he was working up to earlier. "I don't want your money, Auburn."

"I know you don't, baby, but I don't want one of those marriages where everything is impersonal, and both parties have their own bank accounts. I want to share everything with you. I want your name on everything, right beside mine, like a real partner."

He'd said it. The M-word. *Ohmigod!* And the way he explained it—especially him opening up about the kind of, *gulp,* marriage he wanted—made my heart rate pick up about twenty notches. I wanted nothing more than to marry this man, but I couldn't deny that the money situation was a tad overwhelming.

"Can we talk about something else for a minute?" I asked, and concern etched two lines across his forehead. I smoothed them away with my thumb. "Not that I'm having second thoughts about us. Not at all. I love you, Auburn Bouvier, more than anything, and I always will. And I absolutely love what you said about us being partners. But the idea of going from a... hundredaire to a millionaire... it's just..."

"Billionaire," he corrected, and I flopped back against the couch.

"You're not helping," I groaned, fanning my face with my hand.

Auburn leaned back, mirroring my pose, and linked our fingers together. "You fell in love with a billionaire, Gianna, and other than me giving away everything I own, that's not going to change. But I'll do that if it's the only way I can keep you."

"Of course I don't want you to do that," I said, rolling my head toward his until our faces were only inches apart.

"I'm still the same man I was five minutes ago. This changes nothing in our relationship. Money is just a *thing*, Gianna. A thing that means we can pretty much help whoever the fuck we want."

"Like Jaxon and Jane?"

He smiled, his face softening. "Yeah. Like them. Did you notice that there's an elevator in the new house? So Jane and the other kids in wheelchairs aren't confined to the first floor. Oh, and the backyard is huge. Not like that little postage stamp they have now."

He'd really thought about this a lot, and that gave me a warm feeling deep in my belly.

"You move fast, Bouvier."

His chuckle reverberated through his shoulder and against mine. "So I've been told. Can we get back to the house? There are some other things I want to talk about with you."

Chapter 37

We ate in silence as I went through the information with a fine-toothed comb, my brain whirring and processing the numbers. After chewing and swallowing my last bite of food, I handed the folder back to Auburn.

"So, what do you think?"

"I think the house is outstanding, and the price is even better. Financially, you'll do better with option one that's presented in the paperwork, if you can liquidate that kind of cash. You'll avoid a shit ton of finance charges."

He nodded and licked some ranch dust off his finger. "I can do that."

"The only concern I have is maintenance costs. It won't be cheap to keep a house like this in its current condition without money, and from what I understand, the children's home isn't exactly flush with cash. Elevator maintenance alone would probably bankrupt them within a few years."

He leaned over and pressed his salty lips to mine. "Excellent observation, my brilliant girl. That brings me to my next task. A fundraiser."

I lifted my eyebrows, intrigued. "I'm listening."

"I know lots of rich people, and I attend all of their fundraisers. Everything from Save the Whales to urban redevelopment projects. All I have to do is call in some favors, and they'll show up with their wallets wagging."

My shoulders hunched up with excitement. "I really love that idea. How can I help?"

Auburn placed his arm around me and pulled me tight against him. "Actually, I want you to organize the fundraiser."

I gave him my best deadpan stare. "First of all, you shouldn't be drinking at work, Auburn. I don't care if you are the boss."

He laughed and kissed my temple. "I'm stone cold sober, baby girl, and I have complete faith that you can do this."

"But how? I have absolutely no idea how to organize a fundraiser for gazillionaires."

"There probably won't be many gazillionaires there. Maybe one." I fixed him with a glare that would have withered a weaker man. "Okay, I'm kidding. You don't have to do this alone. You can call and ask me any questions at any time if you're unsure about something. And you'll still have time to study because once you find florists and caterers, they will take over most of the workload on those fronts. Plus, whichever venue you choose will have an event manager that will guide you through everything."

"Are you forgetting that I just moved here? I don't know anything about venues or florists or caterers."

"No, but you know who does?"

"If you say your mother, I'll stab you with a tiny shrimp fork."

"God no!" he said with a laugh. "I wouldn't do that to you. I was thinking of Tony."

"My dad?"

"Since, as far as I know, he is your father, then yes."

"Your smartassiness is not helping," I retorted.

He pressed his lips together to hide his obvious amusement. "Sorry. But Tony would be a wonderful source of information for you. The man has notebooks going back over fifteen years. He can get you started, but I want you to take the reins on this."

"Why me?"

Auburn kissed me tenderly on the lips. "Because no one cares like you do, Gianna. You know these kids, and I know you'll put them first. I don't want to hand it off to some random event planner who will do their job but *only* do their job. I want someone who will put their heart into it."

"When you put it like that..."

"Plus, the pay is outstanding."

"I am not taking a nickel. That would defeat the point of fundraising," I shrieked with heated outrage.

Picking me up, he carried me across the room and set me on top of his desk. "I wasn't talking about monetary payment, baby girl." His hands climbed up my thighs, inching my dress up as he lowered to his knees.

"I'm listening," I said breathlessly.

"My plan is to pay you with orgasms. To bury my face between your legs and eat every inch of you. And then I'll fuck you until you forget who you are."

"That sounds like quite a benefit package," I said as he slipped my panties down my legs and tossed them to the floor. "It's the most competitive offer I've gotten so far."

"Better be the only fucking offer you've gotten," he mumbled as his tongue slid along the seam of my pussy.

"I—ohhh." I'd been about to spout off a smartass reply, but I was distracted by his tongue flicking rapidly against my clit. "Mmmm, that's good," I moaned, laying back on the desktop. True to his word, Auburn ate every inch of me, his mouth like a damn machine. A talented, pleasure-giving machine. As his tongue worked between my thighs, his hand slipped up and removed my skinny belt before popping open my buttons one by one.

"Fuck, you're beautiful," he said against my wet flesh as his fingers roamed across my stomach and up to my chest. Deftly unhooking my front-closure bra, his hand closed around my breast, and he pinched my nipple as his tongue quickened against my clit. Say what you will about Auburn Bouvier, but the man could sexually multitask like a boss.

Building me up as only he could, Auburn managed to slide his other hand between my legs and ease two fingers into me while maintaining his relentless pace on my little bundle of nerves. When he sucked it into his mouth, I arched against him, my fingers burying themselves in his hair to hold him close.

Not that he was trying to get away. By the hungry grunts coming from him, my man was enjoying himself as much as I was. The sensual sounds he was making, along with his tongue and hands *every-fucking-where,* finally pushed me over the edge, and I came. Hard.

"Auburn. Aub—oh god!" I lost my words then. All that existed was him and the unyielding pleasure he was delivering to every inch of my body.

Before I even came back to my senses, his cock was inside me, fucking me so powerfully, he had to hold onto my hips to keep me from sliding off the other side of the desk. My feet had somehow ended up beside his ears, and he turned his head and nipped at my ankle.

"You're so fucking sexy when you come, baby girl. I could watch it all day long and never get tired of the way you moan my name."

My fingers attempted to grasp onto anything in order to deal with the railing I was getting as Auburn's hips slapped against my ass, but there was nothing there but the smooth wood of the desk. I finally gripped his forearms and held on tight.

Those sharp blue eyes locked onto mine and didn't capitulate for even a second, holding me spellbound as he went impossibly harder. There was lust there. So much lust. But there was also a huge helping of love and adoration. No matter how filthily Auburn was taking me, he never made me feel less than the most important person in his world.

He was still wearing his shirt and pants, while I was completely exposed to him, but that only made the scene more erotic. When he leaned forward and changed the angle, the head of his cock struck something inside me that made me cry out with the intensity.

"Auburn. Please..." I begged.

"Please what, baby?"

"P-please *everything*," I stammered, aware that I wasn't making any sense.

"I'll always give you everything, Gianna," he murmured, and I was sure he wasn't just talking about sex anymore. Auburn leaned into me, practically bending me in half so he could kiss me, his tongue strong and demanding as he bucked into me with the full force of his back and ass. "Everything," he reiterated as he pushed one of my legs wide and bent to my breast.

After running his velvety tongue around the nipple, he sucked me into his mouth, his eyes closing as if he were in complete ecstasy. I damn sure was… completely consumed by everything Auburn Bouvier. I wrapped my fingers into his hair, tugging and urging him to move to my other, very jealous, breast.

His eyelids lifted as he switched to the other side, and once again, I was pulled into his orbit, as if I were his own personal moon. The base of his thick erection was giving my clit exactly the friction it needed, and the world began to crumble around me. I was convinced that the desk—no, the entire *building*—was going to cease to exist, and we were going to fall into nothingness together.

One of Auburn's hands slid up to encircle my neck, his thumb resting on one side of my throat, and his long fingers curling against my nape. His other hand slid beneath my bottom, lifting me a couple inches higher as he took and gave and took some more.

When he uttered a harsh "now" and sunk his teeth into my breast, his tongue fluttering ruthlessly against my nipple, the bottom dropped out, and the walls of my vagina enclosed like a vice around him. He jerked inside of me, words spilling from his lips—assuredly something dirty—but I didn't hear a word.

All I could hear was elation inside my head because this felt *so* good, and I loved him *so* much.

What made it even better was that I knew he loved me just as much.

Chapter 38

Tora and I exited the elevator on the top floor of the Bouvier building, both of us laughing hysterically.

"What the hell was that guy thinking?" I asked, wiping a tear from the corner of my eye.

"I have no idea, but he needed to put a shirt on." Tora visibly shuddered.

"Right? And I can't believe how light traffic was for a Monday. That took at least an hour off our trip."

Tora's laughter ceased, his eyes focused on my desk. As my eyes tracked in that direction, he suddenly moved, leaning casually against it and blocking my view.

"You know what?" he asked, his voice higher than usual. "I think we may have left a bolt of fabric in the SUV. We should probably go look for it."

"No, we definitely got everything unloaded. I double checked."

"I distinctly remember pushing that crimson lace under the seat. We should go make sure we didn't forget it".

My eyes rolled, and I shifted to the right. So did he. I frowned, and he smiled brightly. A little too brightly. "Tora, why are you being weird?"

He waved a dismissive hand. "Oh, you know me. I'm always weird."

"Tora," I growled, my voice tight with warning. "Move."

In response, he did a full body wiggle that normally would have made me laugh, but not today. I feinted left, and he moved in that direction just before I stepped to the right, my eyes falling on... a purse?

Why was he trying to hide a purse from...

My lungs ceased their intended function as I recognized the bag, a custom-made Bouvier original that I'd given Gianna for her birthday two years ago. There wasn't another like it in the world because I'd had Devereaux design it with a red strap, her favorite color, rather than the black strap that came on the original purse.

But... but... where is Gia? My eyes skimmed the room to make sure I hadn't missed her. That's when I heard laughter from the inner office. Two voices that I recognized instantly.

One because he was my boss.

And the other because she was my daughter.

Pieces began clicking into place. Auburn wanting to escort Gianna to his next function. Gianna's suit that he gifted to her. Auburn's sudden change in attitude the past—how long?—it had to be weeks ago that he'd shifted from total asshole to someone I was actually beginning to like.

Not any-fucking-more.

I felt Tora's hand scrabbling for my elbow as I stormed toward the inner office door, but I brushed him away. No. This couldn't be. I absolutely wouldn't believe it until I saw it with my own two eyes.

Eyes that felt the sting of anger and betrayal as soon as I swung the door open. There were so many things to look at. Wrong things. *Abominable* things. Red lipstick on a face that should not be wearing lipstick. A thin belt being fastened around a slim waist. Two heads of mussed hair. A pair of—oh god!—*panties* on the floor.

But the most damning evidence by far was the look of guilt on their faces as they noticed me. My beautiful, sweet daughter's face, and that treacherous asshole's stupid mug.

"What the *fuck* is going on here?" I roared, barely recognizing my own voice.

"Tony, calm down," came a voice from behind me.

"Don't fucking tell me to calm down, Tora. Are you... are you even seeing what I'm seeing?" I gestured with a wide wave of my hand and turned to look incredulously at him. To my dismay, he didn't appear to be surprised. "Did you know about this?" I hissed, and he nodded and then shook his head.

"Not really for sure, but I suspected."

The anger that was simmering deep in my belly turned to a raging boil. I would deal with Tora later. For now... I turned and lunged, and Auburn fucking Bouvier had the nerve to step in front of my daughter—*my* daughter—with his arms outstretched, as if I would actually hurt my own child. He needed to worry about his own damn self because I was about to kill him.

"Tony, can you please calm down? We can talk about this like rational adults," the rat bastard had the gall to say to me.

Why isn't my fist in his face already? I wondered, and then I realized that Tora had his thin arms wrapped around my middle, holding me in place with all his might. I could have easily overpowered him, but the last thing I wanted to do was hurt Tora, so I stilled, keeping my fists raised in front of me and my eyes on Bouvier.

Come on, you prick. Just take a couple steps toward me, and you're going the fuck down.

The sweetest voice in the world spoke then. "Dad, please don't be mad." Gianna, the person I loved more than my own life, stepped out from behind Bouvier, pushing his hand away when he tried to stop her. He put his arm around her waist, and I envisioned ripping it from its socket with my bare hands. But she didn't flinch away; she leaned into him.

Like he was... a comfort to her. The sonofabitch had her fooled. Their body language made it clear they were damningly familiar with one another, and I tried to step forward again and pull my baby girl from that lech. Tora's arms tensed, and I rolled my eyes.

"Tora, would you please let go of me?" I asked with as much patience as I could muster.

"No. Not unless you promise you won't hurt anyone. You know I abhor violence," he said against my shoulder. "Please, Tony. Just let them talk, okay?"

Goddamn it.

"Fuck! Fine, I won't murder this prick… yet," I gritted out.

His arms loosened, and he patted my back. "Just remember she's your daughter, but she's a grown woman," he murmured under his breath. I wanted to tell him to shut up, but this wasn't his fault. It was Bouvier's fault for taking advantage of my daughter.

"Gianna, d-did he force himself on you?" The pain was evident in my voice.

Shock bloomed across her lovely face as Auburn had the audacity to growl at me.

"Dad, no. Of course not. Auburn loves me very much and would never hurt me." His arm pulled her closer into his side, and it was all I could do not to break my promise of non-violence.

My god, this devious bastard had her convinced he was in love with her. She was so young and innocent. Another thought struck me. *How innocent was she before he got his vile hands on her? Was she a…* I felt as though I was going to vomit.

"Did he…" I inhaled a deep breath and blinked rapidly a few times, "*defile* you?"

Bouvier's face turned thermonuclear red. *That's it. Get pissed off and come at me, asshole.*

His jaw looked like it was about to snap in two, and when he started to speak, Gianna stopped him with the mere lift of her hand.

"Dad, you're being ridiculous. It's not 1875," she snapped, propping her hands on her waist. Tora snorted and Auburn's stupid lips twitched as my daughter continued. "I am a grown woman, and I can make my own decisions about who I date."

Grown woman, indeed. All I could see was a little girl with pigtails, asking me to read her "just one more story. Please, Daddy?"

My voice turned pleading. "Sweetheart, he's way too old for you. He's taking advantage of you, and you don't even realize it because he's so much more experienced."

"Fifteen years," she said, tilting her chin up defiantly. "Are you telling me that fifteen years is too big of an age gap?"

"Yes!" I practically shouted. She was finally understanding. "That kind of a difference is ridiculously indecent."

My daughter's green eyes narrowed on my face like she was attempting to pierce my skull with her gaze. "What about nineteen years, Dad? Is that too much?"

The blood froze in my veins. Why did she choose that particular number? "I, uh..."

"Is it, Dad? Is nineteen years offensive to you?" She tapped her foot impatiently, crossing her arms over her chest. "For instance, if a person was fifty-four years old, and they wanted to be with someone who was—let's say, thirty-five? Would that be 'ridiculously indecent?'"

A tightness gripped my temples and threatened to make my head explode. I couldn't answer that. I simply couldn't because I was fifty-four, and...

A soft hand grasped mine and intertwined our fingers. I looked down at Tora, and he gifted me with his sweet, gentle smile. "Honey, I think the cat's out of the bag," he said quietly. I didn't want to pull my eyes from his face, the face that never failed to comfort me, but he nodded. "It's okay, Tony."

Reluctantly dragging my gaze from his, I turned my face slowly toward my daughter, afraid of what I might see there. Disappointment? Judgement? Revulsion? I knew that some people liked to call themselves open-minded until it was *their* brother. *Their* child.

Their... father.

The clutching pain in my temples disappeared into nothing when my eyes lit on Gianna's face. On her smile. Her big, huge, extremely happy, but slightly smug, smile. She rushed forward, grabbing Tora and I in a bone-crushing group hug, and I relaxed into the embrace, pressing my forehead against her shoulder.

"You're not mad or... something?" I murmured, and she pressed a kiss against my cheek.

"No, Dad. I'm not mad or something." She pulled back, tears streaking down her face, and I swiped my own moist eyes on my shoulder. "I just want you to be happy."

"I told you, Tony," Tora said. "And you want Gianna to be happy too, don't you?" he asked pointedly.

Oh, that's right. Auburn fucking Bouvier. My eyes met his over Gianna's shoulder, and his gaze flitted between me and Tora, his expression morphing from perplexed to understanding as his lips curved up on one side. He gave me a nod, and I didn't hate him quite as much just then.

Don't get me wrong. I still hated him, but I only wanted to stab him maybe ten times instead of twenty.

Pulling my eyes back to my daughter, I swiped away her tears with my thumb. "I do want you to be happy, sweetheart, but why didn't you just come to me and talk about," I waved my hand in the asshole's general direction, "that."

"I guess the same reason you didn't tell me about," she made the same waving gesture at Tora, "that."

My... *boyfriend*—I was still getting used to that—pressed his hand over his belly and snort-laughed, and it made me smile. He always made me smile with that goofy laugh of his.

"I wasn't sure how you would react. It took me almost a year to admit I had feelings for Tora. I was confused, but it also made sense. Why I'd never found a woman after your mom. I did love Nancy, but there was always something missing that I couldn't quite define. I guess since I was struggling to figure it out myself, I was afraid you would struggle to accept it. Accept me."

Her eyebrows drew together as her head tilted to the side. "Dad, conditional love isn't true love. Do you all of a sudden hate me because I'm in love with Auburn?"

My heart broke a little that she could ever think that.

Releasing Tora's hand, I wrapped both arms around my daughter and hugged her fiercely. She was so sweet and kind, and in that moment, I wasn't sure why I had been so scared to tell her. "No, honey. I could never hate you, not even a little bit. *Him* on the other hand," I said, tipping my head toward the traitor who'd seduced my little girl.

"Dad," she whined, "don't be like that."

As much as I hated to admit it, she was right. I'd dropped a bomb on her, and she'd accepted me immediately and unconditionally. Didn't she deserve the same respect? Didn't she deserve a father who wasn't a hypocrite?

Attempting not to wrinkle my face in disgust, I asked, "So, you're in... love with him?"

"I am, Dad." Her beautiful smile was filled with pure joy, and it lit something inside of me. That's what I've always wanted for my daughter... for her to find happiness and love. Could this be real?

I kissed her forehead and then took a few steps toward Auburn, stopping a couple feet away. Then a thought smashed into my mind, and I glared at him. "Is this why your entire attitude with me has changed? Because you were trying to impress your girlfriend's father?" I almost choked on the G-word.

His direct stare shifted from me to Gianna, and his face practically melted. "No. And it's not just with you, Tony." He held out his hand to her, and she took it, smiling up at him like he'd just caught the moon and given it to her. "Being around Gianna has changed everything about me. Watching how kind she is to other people. Seeing her interact the way she does."

They were doing moony eyes at each other, and I didn't know whether to gag or swoon. Bouvier continued. "She's transformed me. Made me want to be a better man. The kind of man who deserves someone so beautiful and sweet and perfect."

Okay, that was pretty good, though I was leaning a bit toward gagging.

"And you're... in love with my daughter?"

"Madly," he admitted with a rueful smile on his face.

I closed my eyes and shook my head. His demeanor had changed drastically in the past few months. Could he really be deserving of my Gianna? The way he was looking at her with such adoration told me... *maybe*. And some of the anger seeped from my bones, only to be replaced with a grudging acceptance.

"If you call me Dad, they'll never find your body."

His lips twitched, but he nodded.

"And you're not coming to Thanksgiving dinner."

"That's okay. You and Tora can come to our place," he said easily, and Gianna smiled up at his extremely handsome face.

I sighed and looked at my daughter. "Couldn't you have found someone less ugly?"

She pursed her lips and then grinned cheekily. "Nope. I love Auburn, warts and all."

His laughter broke down a bit more of my anger, and I didn't even want to punch him when he tenderly kissed her temple. He seemed lighter and freer, not such a stick-in-the-mud prick like he used to be. And he let Gianna be Gianna.

For that alone, I thought *maybe* I could accept him.

As long as I never had to witness my daughter's underwear on the floor of his office. *Ever again.*

Chapter 39

"Hello, gorgeous," I said from the doorway of my home office. Gianna was in her customary study position, legs draped over the arm of the desk chair and laptop resting on her belly. She had a pencil in her mouth, one behind her ear, and the eraser end of another peeking out from her messy bun.

She looked up and gave me a smile. *That* smile. *My* smile. Striding across the room, I managed to rip off my tie, shrug out of my jacket, and undo the top two buttons of my white shirt before reaching her. I pulled the pencil from her mouth and set her laptop on the desk before lifting her and sitting myself in the chair with Gianna on my lap.

"Sorry to interrupt your studying, but I needed to do this." My hand cradled the side of her face, and I kissed her, my tongue lapping into her mouth as I drank my fill of her sweetness. "I missed you today."

She nuzzled her mouth against the corner of my lips and hummed contentedly. "I missed you too. How was work?"

"Good. Your dad only stared at me like he wanted to kill me three times today, so I think we're making progress."

It had been three months since the big revelations that day in my office, and while things were a little awkward at first, Tony and I had maintained a cordial working relationship. I would say we had even grown semi-close because we could openly discuss our mutual favorite topic: Gianna. That all came to a screeching halt when she'd officially moved in with me five weeks ago.

Bumping our relationship from *serious* to *moving in together serious* had thrown the man for a loop, even though he had moved into Tora's apartment a couple weeks before that. Gianna and Tora had both pointed out his hypocrisy, and he'd toned it down a bit, but I could tell it bugged him. It was probably because he knew for a fact his daughter was sleeping with me every night now.

I hated to throw more at him than he was already dealing with, but I'd had *the talk* with him today. Yes. *That* talk. To my utter shock, when I was done with my nervously delivered speech, Tony smiled—a real one, not the creepy one that looked like he was contemplating my homicide—and shook my hand. He'd even patted me on the shoulder and called me "less of an asshole" before going back to work. I counted it as a win.

Maybe he hadn't been totally convinced that my intentions were noble until that moment. I guess I couldn't really blame him since my track record before meeting Gianna wasn't exactly stellar.

"I'll talk to him. Again," she said wearily.

"Don't worry about it," I told her, tilting her chin up so I could take in the full force of her beauty. "Have I told you how proud I am of you?"

Two little lines appeared between her brows. "What did I do?"

"The fundraiser. I can't get over it, Gianna. You put that together in less than three months, and it was absolutely spectacular."

She scrunched her shoulders happily. "It was pretty good, huh? And we raised over ten *million* dollars for the kids."

"That should keep them stocked with mac and cheese for at least a month," I quipped, and she laughed. The event had been a little more than a week ago, just before Halloween, so she'd decided on a masquerade ball. "I got a call from Marion Bonner today. He said it was the classiest and most elegant party he'd been to in a while, and he wanted the name of the event planner for something he's got coming up next year."

"Hmmm. Maybe I should look into being a party planner on the side."

"You almost worried yourself bald over this one. Plus, I don't think you need another job. You stay busy enough going to the children's home every morning to train with Alice on top of studying in the afternoons. And keeping me sexually satisfied is a full-time job in and of itself."

She giggled. "True, and I do love the benefits package associated with being your cheap little fuck toy."

"Hey, don't sell yourself short. You're not cheap."

Her eyes widened in mock outrage. "Are you calling me high maintenance, Bouvier?"

"Seriously? The woman who admitted she once lived an entire week on fish sticks and french fries wants to know if she's high maintenance?"

"They weren't the crappy generic fish sticks," she defended. "They were the Van de Kamp's ones."

"Ah! So the ultra fancy minced pollock?"

"Shut up, smartass," she said with a laugh. "Jaxon came to my office while Alice was at lunch earlier. He's excited about the new house, but he's worried about Jane since she'll be rooming with other girls, and he can't take care of her."

I swiped a hand over my face. "God, that kid is so fucking sweet and protective. Do I need to go have a talk with him?"

"No, I explained it to him. She will only be rooming with Mariah, who is also in a chair, as well as the nurse you hired to stay in the room with them."

I'd also hired a nurse for the two boys who were in wheelchairs. The bedrooms in the house were so large, four beds would easily fit into one, and each room would have its own bathroom, similar to dormitory living. Since an adult would now be staying in the room with the disabled kids, Caroline and I had decided that there should only be two children assigned to each of those rooms.

"Did that help?" I asked, and Gianna nodded.

"Yes, he was just worried because Jane often has to get up to go to the bathroom in the middle of the night, and it's his job to go get the floor mother since he can't lift her, but when I explained that there would be someone in the room with her that could handle it—and that she and Mariah would have their very own bathroom—he felt a lot better."

"I love that he has you there every day so he has someone he can talk to." She nodded and silently studied her fingernails. "What's wrong, baby girl?"

"Nothing," she said, her voice practically a whisper.

I lifted her chin with my finger and coupled my eyes with hers. "Tell me."

She blinked and looked somewhere in the vicinity of my chin. "I just wish…" She stalled and shook my hand away, pressing her face into the side of my neck like she always did when she needed to be comforted.

"If you don't tell me what you wish, I can't do anything about it, Gianna."

She burrowed further into me and started talking. "I wish Jaxon and Jane didn't have to stay there at all. When Caroline let us take them trick-or-treating, I didn't want to take them back. I know that makes me sound like a crazy kidnapper person, but… I wanted to bring them home with us and check their candy and help them make caramel apples and read them a bedtime story."

"You want us to be their parents," I stated as my heart double-timed in my chest.

Gianna nodded, and I felt her warm, wet tears soak the collar of my shirt. "I know it's way too soon to be talking about this. Kids and family and all that."

I lifted her face again, forcing her to look at me as I swallowed the emotion throbbing deep in my throat. "It's not too soon. I've been thinking about the same thing, but I didn't know if you were ready." Her eyes widened, and a tiny smile played across her lips as I continued. "Every weekend when we go to visit, I get more and more attached to those two. It's almost physically painful to leave."

"Yes! Exactly. To be honest, I never planned to be a parent this young, but I also never planned to meet and fall in love with the most amazing man ever. I think people are put in our paths at just the right time."

"Like you and a couple of adorable little rugrats were put in my path?" She nodded happily.

My lips found her bare shoulder. She always wore this old ratty sweatshirt when she studied, and while I teased her about it, I secretly loved it. It, along with her faded leggings, black glasses, and plethora of pencils sticking out everywhere, made her sexier than ever to me. I slid a hand down to cup her round ass as my lips traveled up her neck to find that spot that always made her squirm.

"I want to bend you over this desk and have my way with you, baby girl. Then, when you're all happy and satisfied, I want to take you out to dinner tonight."

She placed a hand on my chest. "Auburn, wait."

"No wait. Waiting is overrated," I muttered against her silky skin.

"I can't go to dinner with you tonight. I already have plans."

Lifting my head, I kissed the tip of her nose. "Tell Lehra you'll eat with her another time. I want you all to myself tonight." *So I can ask you a very important question.*

"I'm not going with Lehra."

"Oh. Tony didn't mention anything about—"

"Not Dad either. I'm having dinner with Ryan," she blurted, her green eyes wary.

It took me a minute to figure out who the hell Ryan was because I'd put her ex out of my mind a long time ago. He was a non-entity. Apparently, that was a mistake.

"Why are you having dinner with your ex?" I asked, hearing the coldness in my voice.

"He's in town and asked to see me."

"Tell him no."

"I already said yes."

So many emotions were threatening to make me lose my shit. Anger. Disappointment. And yes, fear. Fear that I was going to lose her.

"Then text him and tell him you've changed your mind. I don't want you seeing him."

Gianna closed her eyes, inhaled, exhaled, and then opened her eyes again. "I wasn't asking for permission, Auburn. I was telling you why I can't go to dinner with you tonight. We can go tomorrow."

But today is the five-month anniversary of the first day I saw you, I wanted to yell. *I wanted tonight to be special.*

I lifted her off my lap before standing and pacing away, one hand raking through my hair.

"You're mad," she said quietly, and I whirled around.

"Well, I'm damn sure not happy that the woman I love would rather go out with her ex than me," I snapped.

"It's not like that. This is his last night in town, and he said he wanted to discuss some things since we never really took time to hash it out."

"Have you seen him since he's been in New York?" The tips of my ears felt like someone was holding a blowtorch to them.

Walking quickly to me, she took both my hands. "Auburn, no. How could you even think that? I had no idea Ryan was even in New York until he called me out of the blue today. It's only one dinner." She lifted one of my hands, kissing my palm before rubbing her cheek against it.

Goddammit. One sweet touch from her could put a leash on my anger, and I calmed a little bit. The anxiety was still there though, so I cracked open my chest and let my worst fears spill out. "I don't want you to go, Gianna. I can't even tell you how much this scares me."

Her forehead creased, and she actually looked confused before realization dawned on her face. "You think I still have feelings for him, don't you?"

"Why else would you want to see someone you used to be in love with?" I asked, pulling my hand away and stuffing both of them into my pockets.

"*Thought* I was in love with," she corrected, her voice firm. "I had no clue what love really was until I met you, Auburn Bouvier. I had no idea what it meant to feel something so powerful that sometimes I find it hard to breathe around you. What I felt for Ryan doesn't even compare to that. My love for you is... it's potent and all-consuming. You said once that I'm all you see. That resonated with me because I feel the same about you. You're all I see, and no other man has ever compared, and no one ever will." Her voice softened at the end, and she cradled my face with both hands, her green eyes penetrating straight into my soul.

I could literally hear her heart in her sincere words, and I couldn't help it; I had to touch her. My hands reached for her waist and pulled her flush against me. "So, you're over him?"

She nodded. "I've been over him."

"Then can you please tell me why? Why you would want to see him again?"

Her eyelids closed. "I don't want to. I dread this more than anything, but I need to know why he cheated on me. I never want that to happen to me again, so I need to know what I did so I can fix it. Was it something I said or did?" A tear seeped from between her lashes, and my heart broke for her. She thought it was her fault. When she opened her eyes again, the tears fell freely. "It's not something I think about all the time, but when I do, it's like this horrible weight in my belly. I need to know why I wasn't good enough."

Jesus Christ. The most perfect woman I'd ever met was actually insecure because of someone else's actions.

My lips pressed softly against hers. "I'm sorry you feel like that, baby. I know I could tell you all day long that this wasn't your fault, but you don't need to hear it from me, do you?" She shook her head sadly, and I made up my mind, forcing the necessary but reluctant words from my lips. "Okay, I want you to go talk to Ryan."

She blinked a few times. "You do?"

"Yes, but with one stipulation. I'm going with you."

Chapter 40

I thought Auburn was joking when he said he was going with me to meet Ryan. He wasn't.

I balked at first, and then as he explained his plan to me, the dread I felt in my stomach fizzled away. He truly wanted to be there for me. Not because he didn't trust me, but because he wanted to be my emotional backbone.

Entering the restaurant, I smoothed down my black wrap dress and looked around the dining room. Ryan stood and waved, and... I felt nothing. No butterflies. No heart quickening. Just as I'd told Auburn. I had no feelings for Ryan whatsoever, besides resentment.

As I approached the table, his eyes drifted up and down my body, and I held myself a little straighter. "Hello, Ryan."

"Gianna. God, you look great." His gaze froze for a moment on my cleavage, which I had to admit looked amazing in this dress. The one Auburn had chosen for me because he said he wanted 'that dumb son of a bitch to see what he gave up.'

Ryan reached to hug me, but I side-stepped him and pulled out my chair, sitting down and glancing at the table behind Ryan's seat. Auburn was there, and I instantly felt a sense of relief. He smiled at me before mouthing "I love you."

"You too," I mouthed back as Ryan took his seat across from me.

He cleared his throat and then did it again. I'd forgotten how much that little habit used to annoy me. "So…"

"Soooo," I repeated, drawing the word out.

"New York City, huh?" I simply stared at him, smiling placidly. "It's really loud here."

"You get used to it."

He rested his forearms on the table and let his eyes wander around the restaurant before coming back to my face. "How long are you staying here?"

"I live here, Ryan."

He rolled his lips in and nodded. "Yeah, but you're planning to come back to Texas, right?"

"No, this is my home now."

His mouth twisted to the side. "I want you to come back to Texas. I miss you."

Movement from behind him caught my eye, and I glanced at Auburn. His back was ramrod straight, and his fists were clenched on the table. I gave him a subtle shake of my head before turning my attention to the man across from me.

"How are Emma and your son?" I asked pointedly, and Ryan seemed to deflate like a popped balloon.

He couldn't even meet my eye, his gaze fixed on his water glass as he cleared his throat again. "We're not together anymore. When the baby was born, it was, um, *obvious* that he wasn't my son." His brown eyes flickered to mine for a brief second, looking for something they didn't find before skittering away again.

Picking up my water glass, I took a long sip and set it back down. "I'm sorry about that, Ryan. I know how much it hurts to be cheated on."

His chin dropped to his chest, and he was silent for a long moment. "I'm so sorry, Gianna. I never—" He stopped when a middle-aged server appeared at our table.

"Good evening. My name is Isaiah. Have you decided what you want to drink?" he asked with a smile.

"A bottle of your best champagne," Ryan said, turning his gaze from the server to me. "We're celebrating tonight."

I smiled at Isaiah. "I'll have a bloody mary. Extra spicy and extra olives, please."

Ryan frowned a little at my slight, but I didn't give a fuck. I wasn't celebrating shit with him.

When the server departed, I opened my menu and scanned down the page. "You were saying?" I asked, not even deigning to look at him.

My ex cleared his throat again. "Right. Uh. Oh yeah. I was saying that I never should have left you, Gianna. And—"

Cutting him off, I calmly pointed out, "But you never actually left me. I left *you* after I found out you'd gotten another woman pregnant." I finally lifted my gaze from the menu to find Ryan's forehead creased in confusion.

"I just told you the baby isn't mine." *Good lord! Did he really think that was the correct thing to say here?*

"Then let me rephrase. I left you after I found out you'd been fucking around on me and stringing me along. You didn't even have the decency to tell me you were engaged and expecting a baby with someone else. I had to find out on Facebook." I lifted my eyebrows. "Better?"

I caught the subtle thumbs up from Auburn and had to fight a smile. I was really glad he was here. He strengthened me.

Ryan wiped the sweat beading on his upper lip with his napkin. "The point *is*, we can be together now. And I swear I'll never cheat on you again. I learned my lesson." He twisted the linen cloth between his fingers when I said nothing. "I never stopped loving you, Gianna. It wasn't about you at all. I guess I got lonely when you studied on the weekends, and I just started fucking around with Emma when I went home. But it didn't mean anything, and I was thinking of you the whole time I was with her."

A snort erupted from behind him, and it took a Herculean effort not to glance at Auburn, but I could imagine his expression in my head. Probably the exact same expression that was on my face. Disbelief mixed with disgust. Had Ryan really just said he was *thinking of me* while he was fucking his side piece?

Isaiah returned with our drinks, setting my bloody mary in front of me before turning to Ryan. "The champagne, sir. I brought two glasses. I wasn't sure..." Poor guy had no clue what was going on.

"Yes, we'll each take a glass," Ryan informed him, and I resisted the urge to remove the long toothpick holding the olives from my drink and stab him in the eye with it. *Barely.* I had forgotten how much I hated when he tried to make decisions for me, everything from what drink I should have to which apartment complex I should live in.

Isaiah expertly popped the top and poured, setting a long-stemmed crystal flute in front of each of us. "Are we ready to order?"

"Yes, we'll both have the venison," Ryan informed him, and my fingers toyed with the four-inch long toothpick in my drink. *Don't do it, Gianna. You're not cut out for prison.*

I didn't care for the taste of deer meat, and he knew that. Or he should have. Closing my menu, I handed it to the server. "I'll have the salmon with dill sauce. Thank you, Isaiah."

"So, um, one venison and one salmon?" he clarified, and I nodded politely. From the corner of my eye, I could see Auburn's shoulders shaking with laughter. He loved when my sass came out to play, and I loved *him* for supporting that side of my personality. For not trying to control me.

Except in the bedroom. I liked Auburn being dominant and bossy when we were fucking. My mind drifted to last Saturday night when he'd tied me to his bed. Again. The way he'd flipped and turned me so his velvet tongue wouldn't miss a single inch of my body. The way I'd squirmed when his mouth sucked on my...

I realized I was staring at Auburn, and by the way his hooded eyes were boring into me, I was pretty sure he knew precisely what I was thinking about. My suspicions were confirmed when his tongue slid over his bottom lip before his teeth sunk into the plumpness. Wetness flooded my panties.

God, he's so fucking hot. I just want to...

"Gianna? Yoohoo. Earth to Gianna."

Oh yeah. Ryan. Ugh. A metaphorical wet blanket cooled my body heat when I looked at my ex smiling at me with his stupid fantasy-interrupting smile.

"I was making a toast," he said, nodding at my untouched champagne glass.

I ignored it, picking up my tall bloody mary instead, taking a long sip and looking at him over the rim of the glass. Ryan's jaw tightened, but he recovered quickly, lifting his champagne in the air and apparently toasting with himself.

"To new beginnings."

New beginnings, my ass. I came for closure, you dickhead.

Ryan apparently didn't share that sentiment because what he did next almost made me swallow my teeth. Fumbling around in his pocket, he came out with... a ring. More specifically, an engagement ring.

I heard rumbling in the background, and vaguely thought, *I didn't know we were expecting thunderstorms tonight.* Until I realized the sound was coming from the table behind Ryan. *Auburn's table.* He was growling like a papa bear with a stolen cub.

Shooting him a look, I gave a subtle shake of my head—telling him to let *me* handle this—before turning back to the ring in my ex-boyfriend's fingers. I recognized that ring. Pink stone in the middle with a diamond on each side. I'd seen it on Emma's finger on Facebook.

This fucking idiot was proposing to me *with a ring he'd given someone else.*

"Sorry, I lost the box," he said with a little chuckle. "So, Gianna, I want you to marry me. What do you say?"

Placing my elbow on the table, I dipped my head and massaged little circles with my fingertips for about ten seconds. *Prison jumpsuits are not attractive, Gianna. Don't do it,* I reminded myself before raising my face to the moron across from me again.

"Is that the same ring you proposed to Emma with?" I asked, ice covering each syllable.

Ryan's bright smile faded a bit. "Oh, uh, yeah. She gave it back to me, and I didn't want it to go to waste. It's so pretty, and pink is your favorite color, right?"

Try again, nimrod. Just as I was about to voice something to that effect, a hand appeared on Ryan's shoulder. My eyes tracked up the suited arm, over the broad shoulder, and straight to the handsome face of Auburn Bouvier.

Oh. Shit.

A weird little laugh escaped my mouth—just a high pitched *hee hee* that sounded like a dog's squeaky toy—and my thoughts immediately shifted from *me* going to prison to the love of my life being locked up for homicide.

Auburn would probably look hot in a prison jumpsuit. How much would bail be? He has his own plane, so he'd definitely be considered a flight risk, right? I don't have the kind of money for that. Maybe Dad has access to Auburn's funds. No way we'll be able to adopt Jane and Jaxon if one of the parents is in prison for murder. Maybe if we tell the jury the story, they'll have mercy on him because this scenario is completely insane. Justifiable homicide or something. Are conjugal visits a real thing or just something you see in movies?

My jumbled internal ramblings were cut short when Auburn spoke. His voice didn't sound angry at all though. It was quiet, and was that... amusement?

"Son, you're doing it wrong."

Oh Jesus.

Ryan's face pinched with displeasure at being interrupted from the very important task of proposing to me with someone else's ring, and he tilted his head upward. His expression changed as soon as he saw who was standing above him, and he practically knocked his chair over in his haste to stand.

"Y-you're Auburn Bouvier," he said, his voice laced with awe.

"I am," my gorgeous man replied with a curt nod and a cold stare.

Ryan held out his hand for a shake but was rejected, and he let his arm hang awkwardly in mid-air for a few seconds before dropping it to his side. "I wrote a paper about you when I was in business school. I... wow. I can't believe I'm actually meeting you," he gushed. He seemed to remember that I was there and glanced at me before turning back to Auburn.

"Mister Bouvier, I'd love to get together and talk with you about your transformative marketing techniques." He pulled a business card from his pocket and handed it to my boyfriend, who didn't even glance at it; he simply tossed it on the table.

Ryan looked crestfallen, but continued valiantly. "Like I said, I would love the opportunity to speak with you some time, but, well..." He chuckled and tipped his head toward me. "I'm kinda in the middle of proposing here."

"I see that. And as I pointed out, you're doing an abysmal job of it."

Ryan's face turned chalk white, and he stammered nonsensical syllables before Auburn interrupted him.

"If you'd like, I can show you how it *should* be done."

Without waiting for a response, he walked right past the stunned man and twisted my chair to face him. His blue eyes were directly on mine even as he spoke to Ryan.

Holy crap. No he is not going to...

"What you should have done is get down on one knee." Auburn lowered himself in front of me, the hint of a smirk teasing his perfect lips.

Oh. My. God. Yes, he is going to.

"You want to show her that she's your queen and that you submit to and honor her above all others, including yourself." He took my hand and kissed the back of it. "And you don't tell her why she should be your wife. You tell her why *you* should be her husband."

I was completely shocked that my ass was still planted firmly in my chair. I felt as though I would melt and slink to the floor at any moment.

"Gianna," he began, his blue eyes cemented to my own, "since the very first day I saw you, I was intrigued by you. Then I got to know you, and that intrigue quickly turned into affection, and then love. I'm pretty sure I started falling for you the minute you opened that smart mouth and rightfully put me in my place."

I giggled at that.

"You are absolutely the most gorgeous woman I've ever met, but that's not what sealed the deal for me. It was your *inner* beauty." He tapped my chest. "What's in here. The way you make everyone you meet smile just by being yourself. Every single day, I strive to be even half the person you are, Gianna. Every day, I wake up wondering how I can be the man you deserve."

He reached up and swiped away the tears that were starting to drip down my cheeks. "I want to be your husband, baby girl. I want you to wake up every morning and go to sleep every night knowing that you are my priority. That you are loved and cherished by the man who is lucky enough to call himself your husband."

"You're making me ugly cry," I whispered through my happy little laugh, and tears welled in Auburn's eyes as well.

His gaze remained fixed on mine as his head turned slightly toward Ryan—who I had honestly forgotten was even there because Auburn's words had cocooned me. "Ryan? Are you still paying attention?"

"I, um, yes sir."

"Because this part is really important." Auburn pulled a Tiffany blue ring box out of his jacket pocket, and I was pretty sure my heart was about to fall out of my chest and right at his feet. "The most critical thing is to present your woman with a ring that you haven't used to propose to someone else."

I had to cover my mouth to keep from laughing hysterically as a wicked smirk crooked up the edges of Auburn's lips. He was literally hijacking Ryan's sad excuse for a proposal.

"The woman you want to marry deserves more. She deserves to know that you were thinking only of her when you chose it." His grin widened until tiny creases appeared at the corners of his eyes. "And that you asked the jeweler to surround the perfect diamond with rubies because you know without a doubt that *red* is her favorite color."

When he popped the box open, I had to press my hand over my chest to keep my heart in place. "Oh God," I uttered. The large central diamond set in a platinum band was flawless on its own, but the red stones turned it into a work of art. And the best part was that it was *me*. "It's perfect."

Auburn nodded in relief before taking a deep breath. "Gianna, will you allow me the honor of being your husband? Will you let me cherish and love you for the rest of my days?"

Before the last word had slipped past his full lips, I practically yelled, "Yes!" I heard laughter and cheers around us and realized that we apparently had an audience.

"Thank God," I heard him say under his breath as he pressed his lips to my finger and slipped the ring on it.

Then I tackled him. Launching myself from my chair, I bowled Auburn over onto his back and landed directly on top of him. We laughed amidst the catcalls and whistles surrounding us before our mouths crashed together. The kiss was way more passionate than would normally be considered respectable in a nice restaurant, but we didn't give a damn. We were getting married. *Married!*

"I love you, baby girl," he murmured against my lips.

"I love you too. Yes, yes, yes," I said, just so he would be a hundred percent positive of my response. His hand cupped the back of my head as he kissed me again.

When we finally broke apart, Auburn managed to get me to my feet without exposing any vital parts of my anatomy to the other diners before standing up himself.

As he wrapped a warm arm around my waist, I heard Ryan's voice call out, "Wait." We turned toward him, and his face was a mask of suspicion as his finger moved slowly back and forth between us. "Do you two know each other or something?"

Auburn's entire body shook with his laughter before he kissed my temple. "Yes, Ryan. The future Mrs. Bouvier and I know each other quite well. So, if you'll excuse us, I'd like to take my bride home and celebrate." His eyes sparkled down at me. "In bed."

And on that parting note, we walked out of the restaurant with our arms wrapped around each other, leaving Ryan standing there scratching his head in confusion and trying to figure out what the hell had just happened.

Chapter 41

"Are you sure you want to do this?" Gianna asked, her eyes filled with concern as we pulled up in front of Tony and Tora's building.

"Of course, baby. You were right about everyone videoing in the restaurant. News of our engagement will be plastered everywhere within the hour. It's best that we tell your dad in person before he sees it online."

"You know that's not what I mean. Are you sure you don't want to let me go talk to him by myself?"

Lifting her hand to my lips, I pressed a firm kiss there. "Not a chance. I'm going with you come hell or high water."

"I'm afraid my dad is going to bring hell down on you and then try to drown you in the high water," she muttered.

Inhaling a deep breath, I blew it out on a long sigh. "Actually Gianna, I've already talked to your dad about this. I made my intentions known to him earlier today."

"You did what?" she shrieked, and Cruz's eyes flickered to mine in the rearview mirror. He gave me a *Dude, you done fucked up* look.

"Sweetheart..."

"Don't you sweetheart me, Auburn Bouvier. That is the most archaic, misogynistic thing I've ever heard." I could scarcely see the green of her irises behind her narrowed lids. "I'm not a piece of property to be bartered."

"You know I don't think of you that way, Gianna. You're my equal partner one million percent. I just..." Pushing out another breath, I tried to think of the proper words to explain to her. "You've been the most important thing in Tony's life since you were born. I did *not* ask him for your hand in marriage, and I did *not* ask for his *permission* to marry you."

Her smooth forehead creased. "Then what did you talk about?"

"I simply told him that I respected him, and that I hoped he respected me as well. Then I told him exactly how I felt about you, how I planned to spend the rest of my life with you. I wanted him to know that I'm so fucking serious about this, Gianna. I've never been more serious about anything in my life."

The wrinkles smoothed out, and she touched my face with her fingertips. "You needed his acceptance."

Closing my eyes, I leaned into her touch. "Yes," I whispered before opening my eyes to see that her almond-shaped green ones had softened around the corners. "I want us to be a real family, and that includes Tony and Tora. I didn't mean it as any disrespect to you as a woman."

In the next instant, her lips were on mine, soft and soothing and gentle, both of her hands cradling my face.

"What did my dad say when you told him?"

"He said I was less of an asshole than he'd originally thought."

She laughed and pushed open the door, and we both stepped out.

Wrapping an arm around my waist, she tilted her head over against my chest as we walked. "You make it really hard to stay mad at you, Bouvier."

"Hmm, do you think you could hold on to just a teeny bit of that anger until we get home?"

"Angry fuck?"

"Yep," I replied, opening the building's door for her. She knew me so well.

"Gianna! This is a nice surprise," Tony said when he pushed open the door to his apartment. He offered me a slightly less enthusiastic greeting. "Auburn."

"Hi, Tony. I hope it's not too late to stop by."

"It's fine!" Tora chirped from the dark-red couch, and Tony ushered us inside.

There was a matching love seat perpendicular to the couch, and Gianna and I sat side by side as Tony lowered himself beside his boyfriend.

My new fiancée tugged at the hem of her dress, and I could practically feel the nerves rolling off of her. "Dad, Tora... we have some news."

Tora screamed, and I almost fell off the couch. "You're wearing an engagement ring!" He was on his feet in a second with Gianna's hand in his as he inspected the jewelry. "Wow, you could take an eye out with this thing," he said, turning her hand this way and that.

Tony's eyes were lasered on mine, his expression unreadable. "You move fast, Bouvier."

"So I've been told," I replied with a wry grin.

"Yes, we're engaged," Gianna confirmed. "The proposal will probably end up online very soon, and we wanted to make sure you two heard it directly from us."

"Very considerate of you," Tony replied flatly.

"Dad, don't be like that. I want you to be happy for us."

The tightness on his face melted marginally. "I am, honey. This just seems awfully fast. What's the rush?"

"Well, that's what we wanted to talk to you about."

"Oh. My. God. You're pregnant," Tora cried before pivoting back to sit beside Tony. He grabbed both of my future father-in-law's hands. "Babe, don't do anything stupid. Remember that prison orange is not in your color palette, and stripes are not our friends."

"I'm not pregnant," Gianna said with a giggle, and the two men breathed a sigh of relief. "But it does involve children."

All eyes were on her when she pulled up a picture of Jaxon and Jane on her phone and handed it over.

"Auburn and I have decided that we want to try and adopt these two kids. They're from the children's home that Auburn donates to, and before you can say it's too fast... Well, maybe it is really fast, but Jaxon and Jane need a home, and we have the means to provide that for them." She glanced at me, and we shared a smile. "We've fallen in love with them."

"Jaxon and Jane," Tony said quietly, studying the picture intently. Tora was doing the same as he leaned against his shoulder. "I'm gonna be a grandpa." His voice sounded almost reverent.

"Yes," Gianna said quietly, her voice apprehensive.

Then Tony grabbed Tora around the neck and smooched his cheek loudly. "We're gonna be grandpas!"

I could feel the tension seep from Gianna's bones as Tony's excitement became palpable. He was laughing, unable to peel his eyes from the photo.

"I'd like to say for the record," Tora said, lifting his index finger, "that I am entirely too young and gorgeous to have a grandpa moniker. I'll be Lolli, and Tony can be Pops."

Gianna giggled. "Lolli-Pops. That's adorable."

I thought it was a little cheesy, to be honest, but I was keeping my fucking mouth shut because Tony was finally looking up from the phone, and his smile was radiant.

"When can we meet them?"

Gianna and I glanced at each other. "Actually, we need to tell the kids first, and hopefully, they'll be open to being adopted by us," I told him.

"Of course they will," he said, glancing down at the picture again before standing and crossing to us. My fiancée stood to face her father, and I rose as well, placing my hand on the small of her back. "You two are going to be fan-fucking-tastic parents."

I felt like I was going through a bit of emotional whiplash, and then we were engulfed in a bone-crushing hug.

"Dad," Gianna said with a laugh, "I can hardly breathe."

"Sorry," he said, releasing his hold on us. "I just want to say that only a couple who is secure in their relationship would make the decision to take on a family while they're still newlyweds. I'm very proud of you, Gianna." He turned his watery eyes to me. "And you too, son."

"Thanks, Dad," I said, my voice sounding a bit husky.

"Don't press your luck," he said with a droll smirk.

"That went better than expected," Gianna said as we climbed into the back of the Bentley an hour later.

"I think the kids sold it for us."

My fiancée widened her eyes. "I know! I thought he would be freaked out by that, but he went from *This is happening too fast* to *Welcome to the family, son* in about five point two seconds."

"I was definitely expecting a lecture about how we shouldn't think about starting a family until our relationship is more solid."

"Me too, but what Dad said made sense. We *are* solid."

"As a rock, baby," I assured her, lifting her chin so I could kiss her.

"Auburn," she said against my lips.

"Mmhmm?" I trailed kisses from her mouth to her neck. She smelled so fucking good.

"I think we're going to have to save the angry fuck for another night. I'm too happy tonight."

Nipping lightly at her pulse point, I tugged her until she was straddling my lap. "Then how about I make love to my future wife all night long instead?"

She rocked her hips over me, and I groaned at the heat that was always present between us.

"I like the way you think, future husband."

"Maybe I'll start right now," I said, raising the dark partition and unbuckling my belt.

Chapter 42

"What if they don't want to be adopted by us?" I fretted, twisting my fingers in my lap.

"Gianna, there's no need to worry until after we talk to them," Auburn said, covering my hands with his own.

"I can't help it. I'm so nervous. Are you sure I look okay?" I stood, and my hands smoothed down my royal-blue dress, suddenly convinced I wore the wrong thing on this important occasion.

"Honey, you look as beautiful as always, and yes the dress is perfect."

I'd changed clothes no less than four times. I wasn't sure why I thought what I was wearing mattered. Maybe it just gave me something to think about instead of...

"Oh God, I hear them," I whisper-shouted in Auburn's face.

He swallowed hard. "Okay. It's going to be okay. Everything is fine."

But he didn't look like everything was fine. He looked like he was about to puke, which was precisely how I felt.

We were in Caroline's office at the children's home, and we could hear the kids coming down the hallway with the director.

"All right, you two. Are you ready to meet them?" Caroline's voice filtered through the wooden door.

"I don't know," Janie said. "What if..."

"What is it, sweet girl?"

"What if we don't want to be adopted? What if we want to stay here?"

I covered my mouth with my hand as tears welled in my eyes. "I'm going to be sick," I whispered, and Auburn stood, pulling my face into his neck. He didn't speak, probably because he was as lost for words as I was.

Clinging to him, I listened to the conversation taking place in the corridor.

"Jane, why wouldn't you want to be adopted? You would have a home of your very own," Caroline asked gently.

I heard sweet Jane sniffle, and I almost broke in two.

"What if our new parents won't let us see Auburn and Gianna anymore?"

I'd never moved so fast in my life. In a split second, I had the door open and was dropping to my knees in front of the kids.

"You can see us every day," I cried. "It's us. We want to be your Mommy and Daddy."

Then they were in my arms, and everyone was crying, including the enigmatic Auburn Bouvier, who had kneeled down beside me. Tears flowed all over the place as the four of us group-hugged for a very long time.

"You really want to be our parents?" Jaxon asked, finally lifting his head and looking between Auburn and me.

"Of course we do, honey. We love you and Janie," I said, wiping the wetness from his face with my fingers. "But only if you want us to."

"We do," he practically yelled, and Jane giggled and nodded.

"We decided if it was anybody else, we weren't going to go with them," she informed us, lifting her little chin defiantly.

"Yeah, we were gonna run away if they tried to make us," Jaxon said.

Auburn cleared his throat and swiped beneath both eyes with his knuckles. "How about we all go out for ice cream and seal the deal?"

The kids—*our kids*—cheered happily, and my fiancé pushed to his feet, kissing the tops of their heads before turning to Caroline. The poor woman was sobbing quietly into a tissue.

Auburn pulled her into a sweet hug. "Would you like to go with us to celebrate?" he asked kindly, and she nodded, a little hiccup squeaking up her throat.

Several hours later, we'd reluctantly taken Caroline and the kids back to the children's home after eating half the ice cream in New York City. I was so glad Auburn had invited the kindly director to go with us because Jaxon's curious little mind came up with at least a hundred questions about the adoption.

Of course Auburn and I had done our homework, even speaking to a family attorney who specialized in adoptions, but Caroline was a wealth of information. After all, she'd been doing this for decades.

"It feels anticlimactic to come home without the kids," I noted as we walked into our bedroom.

"Yeah, I feel like they're already ours and we should be able to keep them."

"Stupid damn law."

Auburn chuckled. "I'll tell you a little secret," he said in a low voice, pulling me to him. "I may have greased a few palms to get things moving a little faster."

"Ooh, that's hot, Mister Bouvier."

"You know what would be even hotter?" he whispered in my ear, his warm breath sending a shiver down my spine.

"What's that?"

"If my future wife would get her fine ass on the bed and let me fuck her." His fingers deftly unzipped my dress, and I stepped back as it pooled to the floor. "Fuck, you're beautiful," he breathed, his eyes stroking like a soft caress down my body.

I ran my index finger teasingly over the rose-colored lace covering my breasts and batted my eyelashes at him. "Does Daddy want me on my back or on my hands and knees?"

"Hands and knees," he growled, stripping off his sage-green dress shirt without even unbuttoning it. "And leave the heels on."

I finished undressing, leaving my black stilettos on as directed, and crawled onto the bed.

"Now that's a sight I could get used to." His large hands rubbed softly over my butt.

"You'd better get used to it. You're marrying me."

"Damn right I am," he said, kneeling on the floor behind me.

At the first brush of his tongue, I buried my face in the sheets and moaned. The man's mouth was a force of nature, pulling pleasure from me with every lick of his tongue and scrape of his teeth.

Combine that with the sexy noises of enjoyment he made, and I was coming in less than four minutes.

"Damn, you're good at that," I panted against the mattress.

Wet kisses trailed over the curve of my butt and all the way up my spine. "Because it's my favorite thing to do," he rasped when he reached my ear. "Besides this."

Lubricating the head of his cock with my juices, he rubbed himself up and down between my legs.

"Teasing me?" I asked cheekily and was rewarded with his erection slamming into me in one hard thrust. *Jesus Christ!*

"Does this feel like I'm fucking teasing, Gianna?" He swatted my ass before wrapping his hand around my throat and pulling my body up until he was pressed against my back. "Does this feel like I'm just fucking around?" Pulling out to the tip, he took me with another rough thrust.

Daddy Auburn had come out to play, and I loved it, despite knowing I was going to be walking with a limp tomorrow.

One of his arms banded around my hips, holding me firmly in place as he fucked me with brutal precision. His other hand remained around my neck, and I whimpered with an equal amount of pleasure and pain.

But it was the very best kind of pain. The kind that said I had turned my fiancé into a raging animal.

"No, Daddy," I purred, and he groaned, his hips working at a piston pace as his teeth sunk into my shoulder.

"Daddy's girl loves when I stretch out that sweet pussy doesn't she? Such a good fucking girl taking me so deep."

"Yes. Sir," I panted, reaching behind me with one hand to bury my fingers against his scalp. I twisted my hand, and he grunted, his hips moving impossibly faster.

"That's it, baby. Show me your fire."

Turning my head, I licked a striped across his cheek and nipped his earlobe as the sounds of our bodies slapping together resonated through the room.

"Make your good girl come," I purred. "Please, Daddy."

"God damn," he gritted out, sliding one hand between my legs. He knew my body so well now, and he pressed my clit with the perfect amount of pressure, circling those magical fingers until vectors of pleasure radiated out from my core. "Now, Gianna. Fucking come now."

His talented fingers... his thick cock... his strained, dirty words... they all combined to shove my body into a bone-shaking orgasm that had blissful tears streaming down my face.

The sensation of warmth as Auburn filled me only added fuel to the fire, and I was still trembling when he finally pulled out and carried me into the bathroom.

My sexy fiancé kissed me gently, whispering sweet words of love and affirmation, as the tub filled. I loved how he could go from raging beast to doting sweetheart in the span of five minutes.

"You're going to be an amazing mother, Gianna," he told me once we were settled down into the steamy water with my back leaning against his chest.

"I hope so." Even I could hear the apprehension in my voice.

Tilting my face up until we were eye to eye, he said firmly, "You will. You have the kindest, most loving heart of anyone I've ever known, and that's what those kids need. Your age doesn't matter; what's on the inside does."

I sighed, some of the tension plaguing my mind expelling with the air. "How do you always tap into my insecurities? Are you a mind reader or something."

He laughed and kissed my nose. "Nope. I just know you. Numbers don't matter when it comes to love. I thought we'd proven that."

"You're right."

"I know," he said smugly. "I never met Nancy, but from what I've heard from you and Tony, she was a beautiful soul."

"She absolutely was."

"You had two good role models as parents, something I didn't have. I mean, my dad was great, but I don't have a single memory of my mother hugging me as a child, so I'm the one you need to be worried about."

The thought of a little kid growing up with that cold woman made my blood boil. I'd met Paul Bouvier a few times over the past few weeks, and I'd found him warm and welcoming. He never even batted an eye at our age difference.

"Auburn Bouvier," I scolded, "you are going to be a super dad. I might even get you a cape." He chuckled as I continued. "When you open your heart to someone, they have a special piece of you. You are the most generous, giving person I've ever met, and I don't mean with your money. I mean with what's in here." I laid my hand over his heart and felt its strong, steady beat.

He nuzzled his nose into my hair and tightened his arms around me. "I didn't know how to open my heart until I met you."

We sat there in silence, basking in the pure love we felt for one another until the water turned cold.

Then Auburn dried me off with gentle strokes of a soft towel before taking me to bed and wrapping me in his arms.

"I love you, Gianna," he whispered into my hair.

"I love you, Auburn," I replied, closing my eyes and sinking into a sated, dreamless sleep.

Chapter 43

As I adjusted my bowtie, I caught a glimpse of Jaxon's reflection in the mirror. He was slumped in his chair, staring at his feet swinging back and forth, and his teeth were gnawing on his bottom lip, something he did when he was worried.

Turning, I addressed the room. "I need to speak with Jaxon alone, please." Tora, Beau, and Edward, my attorney and friend—who was now thankfully kidney-stone-free—headed for the door.

Tony gave my shoulder a reassuring squeeze, telling me he would go check on the bride, before he also retreated.

Kneeling in front of my sad-looking little boy, I laid a hand on his shoulder. "Hey, buddy. Anything you want to talk about?"

He lifted his little blond head, and the troubled expression in his blue eyes made my chest tighten.

"Are you really gonna be my dad? Like, for real?"

Smoothing away a tiny curl from his forehead, I said, "Of course. And Gianna's going to be your mom. If that's what you and Jane still want."

Oh God. Please don't change your mind. We were already so attached to these little ones, and it would crush us both if they decided they didn't want to go through with the adoption.

Jaxon nodded eagerly. "We do. We love living with you and Mom."

Gianna and I had gone through all the steps to become foster parents, and the twins had been living with us for the past four months.

"So what's the problem, Jaxon?"

The boy sighed, and his eyes focused on the red rose in my lapel. "Billy at my school said that we shouldn't be calling you Mom and Dad because the 'doption isn't done yet. His dad is a lawyer." His blue gaze met mine once again, and he looked scared, like he had done something wrong. My temper flared.

"Well, Billy is a..." *Pretentious little shit* came to mind, but I shifted to what Gianna called my *kid language*. "Billy is mistaken. You can call us whatever makes you comfortable. Just like we talked about, okay? If you want to call us Mom and Dad, you do that. If you want to call us Batman and Robin, that's okay too."

He giggled at that.

"The adoption will be final in about two months, and then you and Janie will *officially* be members of the Booby-A family." We grinned at each other, and I lowered my voice to a faux whisper. "But let me tell you a little secret. I don't care what the paperwork says. You're already my son, and Jane is already my daughter." Tapping my chest with two fingers, I pushed through the emotion building up in my gut. "In here."

He smiled and then began gnawing that lip again. "You said being the ring bearer is a really important job, right?"

"Very," I said, straightening his tiny bow tie.

"What if I mess up?" he whispered, his little chest heaving. "What if I drop the pillow or fall down or something?"

"You're nervous." His little blond eyebrows scrunched together, and he nodded. "What about if I walk down the aisle with you? Would that make you feel better?"

The relief on his face was obvious. "Yes," he breathed, "if that won't mess up the whole wedding. That lady said you would already be at the front, and I had to walk by myself like a big boy."

I waved a dismissive hand at him. "Pssssh. It's our family's wedding, and we can do whatever the heck we want. In fact, I'm a little nervous too, so I think I might feel better if we walked together."

"For real?"

Holding up my fist, I said, "For real." He bumped knuckles with me. "Anything else you want to talk about?"

"No, I think that's it. And I'll take real good care of Janie while you and Mom are on your hornymoon."

Giving myself a lot of credit for not snickering at that last word, I also didn't correct it because it was so perfectly apt.

"You let Lolli and Pops worry about that, and you just have fun."

His broad smile took up almost his entire face. "We always have fun at their house."

"I'm sure you do, and I don't even want to know what they let you eat for dinner," I said teasingly.

Jaxon's little face turned mischievous. "I'll never tell."

On the advice of the family therapist we saw every week, we started letting the twins stay with Tora and Tony, who had to go through all of the necessary background checks by Child Protective Services. Just for dinner at first, and then an occasional overnight stay. Going from living in an institutional setting to an actual home was a huge transition, and we didn't want to upset their routine.

We'd even offered to put off the "hornymoon," but Doctor Wise explained that, while the children needed stability, it was also important to build trust that Gianna and I would always come back for them. That's why we started out small with visits that only lasted two hours before working our way up to overnight stays to see how things went.

We needn't have worried. The grandparents spoiled the shit out of them, and they often begged to go stay at Pop's and Lolli's. The kids had spent an entire weekend there a few weeks ago, and when we'd called to check on them, we were dismissed after only a couple minutes because they were going to the zoo.

"If you miss us too much, I'll have my plane on standby, and we can be back the same day, okay?" I promised him, my voice serious. "And we'll call you every day to check on you."

Jaxon rolled his eyes. "I knooooooww. You tole us a million times already. And make sure not to call on Tuesday 'cuz we're going to Coney Island."

I'd given Tony and Tora the week off from work, and they had a full itinerary planned out, assuring us that the twins wouldn't even have time to miss us. I still worried though, which was why we were going to a private island with an airstrip so we could leave at a moment's notice.

"I'll remember that," I said.

He stood and took my hand. "You ready to go, Batman?"

I laughed. "Ready to go, Joker."

Chapter 44

"Would you stop wiggling, Janie?" I said gently.

My little girl could barely sit still as Linda, the hair stylist, pinned a small crown of flowers in her long, blonde hair. "I can't help it. I've never been a flower girl before, and I'm sooooo excited."

Squatting in front of her, I took her hands to settle her fidgeting. "You are absolutely the prettiest little flower girl I've even seen." She beamed happily. "Do you remember what we practiced last night?" I knew she did; I was just trying to keep her distracted long enough to get her hair finished.

"Uh-huh. Lolli is going to push my chair down the aisle so I can chunk the flowers everywhere."

Linda snickered before turning Jane's chair around to face her. "You did such a good job today, Miss Wiggle Worm. Would you like some lip gloss?"

"Can I have some, Mommy?" she asked, twisting her head around to look at me.

"Of course. It's a special occasion."

As the woman applied the light pink gloss, Charli stuck her head in the room and gave me a conspiratorial wink. "Gianna, could I please borrow Jane for a few minutes? I want her to look at these bows on the doors and see if they're centered."

"Bless you," I mouthed, and Charli flashed a cute smile that made her nose crinkle. She, Beau, and L.J. had arrived earlier this week, and she'd been invaluable at keeping the kids distracted while I took care of last minute wedding details.

"Will you be okay if I go help with the bows?" Jane asked, concern in her big, blue eyes.

"I'll be just fine, my sweet girl. You go and help Charli, and then maybe you can check on L.J. with her." Her eyes brightened a shade. She adored her new little cousin, and the feeling was a hundred percent mutual. The almost-two-year-old loved riding on Jane's lap. "No wheelies," I called, but Charli was already behind Jane with her head bent whispering to the kid. I was positive they were wheels-up before the door had shut behind them.

"I'm going to kidnap that Charli chick whenever I pop out a kid," Maribeth, my best friend from Texas, drawled. "She's been a dang rock star this week."

"She has a doctorate degree in early childhood development," I said with my eyes closed as Linda touched up my eyeshadow. "It's like she can sense a child's personality through osmosis or some shit, and then she adjusts her way of dealing with them on an individual basis."

"That's not how osmosis works," Maribeth informed me.

"Oh, excuse me for being an accountant and not a biologist, smarty britches," I retorted as Linda began spritzing my hair with a light dusting of hairspray. "Like I was saying, within minutes of meeting Jane, she knew she was a helper, so anytime Charli wants Janie to do something, she turns it into *oh, woe is me... can you pretty please help me with this?* The woman purposely lost her left shoe for fifteen minutes the other day to keep Jane occupied looking for it while I was on the phone with the caterer."

Maribeth and the Broxton family had also arrived in New York this week, and Auburn put everyone up at a hotel around the corner from our apartment since we didn't want complete chaos in our home with the twins there.

"Hmmm. I might look into cloning her," Maribeth said thoughtfully. She ran a research lab in Dallas, and if anyone could clone a human, it would be my brilliant friend.

Lehra busted through the door then, her face pink as she smoothed down her dark red dress. "What did I miss?"

"Charli kidnapped Jane so our beautiful bride could finish getting dressed," Maribeth reported. "Where did you run off to?"

"Oh, um, I just took some water and a plate of food to the, uh, security guard."

"You mean Cruz?" I asked, my voice a teasing lilt. Those two were always eyeballing each other, but neither of them had made a move.

"Yes," she said, her cheeks turning a bright red. "You know how dedicated he is. He would stand there and starve before he left his post. I was just being nice."

"That big hunk with arms for days? Yeah, I'd like to be *really* nice to him," Maribeth said with a lascivious eyebrow wiggle.

A laugh burst from my lips, but Lehra did *not* appear to be amused. Cruz Estrada was a very good-looking man. He was Latino, with dark hair and a muscular form reminiscent of his Marine and SWAT team days. His eyes were blue and popped against his tan skin, making most women take a second—and sometimes third—look when they passed him on the street.

"Okay," Linda said, "I'm all done with you for now. Let me know if you need a touch up before the ceremony."

"Thank you so much." I looked in the mirror and was so pleased with my reflection. She had done exactly what I'd asked. My hair was half up and half down, and my makeup was flawless. "Go grab some food in the next room, Linda. There's enough to feed half of New York City." She laughed on her way out the door.

"You look sooo gorgeous," Lehra said, stepping up behind me.

Maribeth, my maid of honor, wrapped a gentle arm around my shoulders. "I can't believe my best friend is getting married. To Auburn Bouvier!"

"I can't believe I called your fiancé Sexy Shrek the first time I met you," Lehra groaned, covering her face with her hand.

I giggled at the memory. "Yeah, but he wasn't my fiancé at the time. We hadn't even met."

"And he's totally nice now. Not that he wasn't nice before," she added hastily. "God, I keep sticking my foot in my mouth. Are you going to fire me as your bridesmaid?"

"Don't be silly," I said with a laugh. "I'm well aware that Auburn used to be a bit of a grouch."

"I mean, he was always polite, but he never smiled." She nudged me with an elbow. "And now he smiles. All. The. Time."

"Damn, girl," Maribeth chimed in, twirling one of her long, dark curls around her finger. "What are you putting on that man to make him happy like that?" I lifted one eyebrow at her, and she whined, "Staaaaahp it! I haven't gotten laid in so long, I think I've forgotten where all the parts go."

"Me too. Maybe Gianna can draw us a picture," Lehra said with a snort.

"Seriously though. Are you and that Cruz guy a thing?"

My other friend answered way too quickly, shaking her head vehemently. "No, of course not. Why would you say that?"

"He's hot as fuck and looks like he'd know what the hell he's doing between a woman's thighs. That damn mouth of his! Could you just imagine those lips on your—"

"I don't think he's looking for anything," Lehra interjected, the tips of her ears turning red. "I mean, not that I know that or that we've talked or anything, but I get that vibe from him. That *unavailable* vibe."

"Hmm. I'm not from here, remember? So I'm not looking for anything serious either, but I would love to let him blow the cobwebs off my panties."

Lehra's full lips tightened until you could barely see them. "Fine. If that's what you want to do."

My eyes bounced back and forth between them like I was watching a fast-paced tennis match. I could tell Lehra was getting annoyed, so I changed the subject. "I'm nervous about the honeymoon."

Both sets of eyes shifted immediately to me. "Oh, babe. I'm sure it will be fine," Maribeth said.

"Definitely. Married sex won't be any different than dating sex. In fact, I heard honeymoon sex is the best thing ever," my other friend crooned.

"Not the sex part. We've pretty much got that down to a science," I said wryly. "I'm worried about leaving Jane and Jaxon. Auburn and I have been going to an excellent family therapist since we started discussing adopting them, and now we go as a family and still sometimes as a couple without the twins. Doctor Wise assured us she would let us know if she advised putting off the honeymoon, but… I don't know."

"She thinks it's okay?"

My head bobbed up and down. "She thinks they've adjusted remarkably well, and they love Tora and my dad."

"Who doesn't?" Lehra said with a grin. "Hell, I want to go spend the week with them."

"I know, right? Auburn insisted on having his plane nearby so we could leave immediately if we needed to. The twins did have a little anxiety the first three weeks they were with us. Every time I would drop them off at kindergarten, Jaxon would find at least ten different ways to ask me if I was *really* going to pick them up after school. 'You remember what time school is out, right? Remember we get picked up on the side of the building. You have our school's address in your phone, don't you, Mom? What time are you picking us up?' It broke my heart."

"I can't even imagine," Maribeth said, whipping out a handkerchief from seemingly nowhere and dabbing at the corner of my left eye.

"Then, about four weeks in, Cruz and I got stuck in traffic, and I was freaking the fuck out. We were only about three minutes later than usual, but instead of being one of the first couple of cars in line, we were stuck way back."

"Oh shit. Were the kids freaking out too?"

My lip turned up into a smile. "Not in the least. I jumped out of the car—against school pick-up line regulations, by the way—and sprinted up to the covered area to find Jaxon and Jane waiting calmly with the other kids. I cried and apologized like crazy but Jaxon shrugged and said they weren't worried because they knew I would be there."

Snatching the hanky from my maid of honor, I blotted at my other eye before continuing. "I told Doctor Wise about it, and she said that it definitely showed progress. That the kids were slowly starting to feel a sense of permanence with me and Auburn. She also said that us getting married was a good thing because it taught Jaxon and Jane about commitment."

"Those poor babies," Maribeth said, grabbing her handkerchief back and wiping her own eyes. "Was the orphanage just horrible? Like kids mopping and scrubbing the floors?"

That made me belly laugh. "This isn't *Annie*," I told her. "No one spontaneously broke into songs about the sun or anything."

"But you do have your very own Daddy Warbucks," she shot back with a smirk, and my face pinkened. *Daddy Auburn is more like it.*

"Anyway, the entire family is excited about the adoption. Tora and Dad, of course, but also Auburn's dad."

"And his mom?"

I shook my head. "Auburn has gone no contact with her and refuses to let her meet the children. She's apparently *heartbroken*," I said with an eye roll. "But it's her own fault. Auburn found out his mother paid Magdalena's bail when she got arrested for blackmailing him."

"No freaking way," Lehra breathed her face scrunching up in distaste. "To be honest, I never liked Mrs. Bouvier. She was snooty as hell when she would come to the office to see her son, but I never expected she would do something like *that*."

"What does his dad have to say about it?" Maribeth asked.

"Paul was pissed. Moved out of their house but hasn't filed for divorce yet, and he won't tell Auburn why not. He's been very kind to me, and I'm happy to have him in the kids' lives as long as Chloe's not around. Auburn is disappointed that his brother Monty couldn't make it to the wedding, but he's in the middle of a huge case down in Florida. He thinks he may have a serial killer on his hands."

Both of my friends' eyes widened. "Holy shit. He's a cop, right?"

My fingers toyed with the sash on my white satin robe. "Yes, a detective. Auburn has really been trying to get closer with him, to mend fences. I think cutting Chloe from our lives has gone a long way in doing that. She was horrible to Monty."

"But the important question is: is Monty as hot as Auburn?" Maribeth asked, her eyes lighting up.

"You really are desperate, aren't you?" I asked, laughing and squeezing her hand. "They could practically pass for twins, though Monty is a little broader through the chest and shoulders."

"Mmmm, I do love me some wide shoulders and a chest I can curl up on." She sighed. "Like Cruz. Bet that man could bench press me. With one hand."

Lehra opened her mouth. Clamped it shut. Opened it again and then stared at her shoes. Bless her heart. I think she really had a thing for our sweet driver. Just as I was about to tell her to go for it, to flirt with Cruz and see if he reciprocated, a knock sounded at the door.

"I'll get it," she said, turning on her heel. "Hey, Tony," she said brightly when she cracked open the door. "Are you here to see the most gorgeous bride to ever exist?"

"I am." I could hear the smile in my dad's voice.

"We'll give you two some privacy," Maribeth said, giving me a hug. "Come on, Lehra. Let's go see if they have any of those little shrimp kebabs left."

My father entered the room as they left, and his breath hitched in his chest. "Gianna, you look beautiful."

A blush rose to my cheeks. "Thanks, Dad, but I'm still in my robe. Auburn hasn't brought me my dress yet."

He checked his watch. You still have about two hours. He'll be along soon. He was just having a chat with Jaxon."

Concern edged my voice. "Everything okay?"

"Of course. I think maybe he was having a little stage fright, but Auburn is handling it." Dad smiled fondly and reached for my hand. "He's such a good dad, Gianna. And he's going to be an amazing husband."

Pressing my fingertips into his palm, I returned his smile, trying not to tear up again. "Thank you."

"I know I gave you two a hard time at first, but when he proposed to you, it was like all my worries about him faded away. Auburn Bouvier isn't a man who does things on a whim, especially something as serious as marriage. I'm truly happy you found someone who loves and adores you as much as he does."

I threw my arms around him and sniffed away my tears. "I love you, Dad."

"Love you too, honey," he said, his voice hoarse as he hugged me before pulling back and producing a tissue from his pocket.

I blew my nose, and my mouth curved up into a chagrined smile. "I seem to be tearing up a lot today."

Dad pulled out another tissue and handed it over. "I'm afraid I'm about to make that worse. I have something for you. From your mom."

Pressing my lips together at the mention of my late mother, I simply nodded as he pulled a black velvet box from his pocket. "Last time I came to visit you in Texas, when Nancy was... sick... she asked me to give these to you on your wedding day."

My hand held the tissue against my mouth as Dad opened the box to reveal a pair of dainty ruby and diamond earrings. I'd seen these in photographs of her and my dad on a cruise they'd taken before I was born.

"Oh." It was all I could manage as my fingers reached to lift one of them from the pillowy material. "Oh..."

"Nancy was truly a beautiful and sweet soul, Gianna, and I loved her very much, even though things didn't work out between us."

Stemming the flow of tears with my tissue, I croaked out, "She was, and she loved you too. I never heard either of you make an unkind comment about the other, and..." I cleared the thickness from my throat. "And that really helped me as a kid. It's not easy when your parents divorce, but that obvious respect you had for each other made it so much more manageable."

Dad pulled yet another tissue from his pocket to wipe his own eyes, and I giggled. "Your pocket is like a clown car full of Kleenex. How many of those do you have in there?"

"Not enough to get me through this day, I'm afraid," he said with a gentle smile. "But I promise they're all happy tears. I'm so proud of you, and I know your mother would be too." Dad helped me fasten the earrings onto my earlobes. "I bought these for Nancy on our first anniversary."

"Red was her favorite color too," I said as we both pivoted toward the mirror and checked our reflection. "We're a damn good-looking family."

Dad's crooked smile warmed my heart. "We are. Too bad you're marrying a troll of a man."

My delicate earrings flashed in the sunlight from the window as my body shook with laughter. "Stop it, you nut. You know my almost-husband is hot."

He flashed me a good-natured eye roll. "Yeah, yeah. I guess he's okay. And your kids are super cute."

My face melted with happiness. "They really are."

Dad tilted his head to the side, his eyes thoughtful. "Have you noticed that Jane resembles your mom a bit?" He drifted a finger down my cheek. "You all have the same heart-shaped face, but Jane resembles Nancy with her blonde hair and light-colored eyes."

I bit my bottom lip and nodded. "I haven't noticed before, but now that you mention it... I wonder if that's why I was instantly drawn to the twins."

"Maybe, but it's probably because Jane is the sweetest little girl in the whole world, and Jaxon is so damn funny and full of sass. Just like you were when you were a kid." He turned me toward him and kissed my forehead tenderly, letting his lips rest there for a long moment.

I couldn't speak so I simply nodded. Dad kissed my head again before stepping back. "I'll give you a few minutes to yourself."

As he walked to the door in his black tuxedo, I finally found my voice. "I love you, Daddy."

He turned and smiled at me over his shoulder. "I love you too, sweetheart."

Chapter 45

Jaxon and I entered the three-bedroom hotel suite I'd reserved for my family, and my son was immediately swarmed by Max, Dex, and Rox, the Broxton triplets.

"Lessgo, Jax," Rox said, grabbing his hand and dragging him toward one of the doors off the living room. "We're playing airplanes in the Room of Doom." Blaire and Axel's four-year-old boys had dubbed him Jax and informed him that he was their quadruplet now.

My gaze went directly to Jane, who was sitting in her chair with a sad smile as she watched the boys tumble toward the...

"Room of Doom?" I asked Blaire, who had appeared beside me.

"Don't ask," she said dryly. "Any room they're in is the Room of Doom."

Her eyes followed mine to my daughter across the luxurious space. I'd gotten this suite in the wedding hotel for the Broxtons and Atwoods to have a place to entertain their kids before the wedding and during the reception, if need be.

"I need to talk to you about her," my cousin said quietly, and I nodded.

"Just give me a second first." I headed toward Janie in her chair, but before I could get there, my father squatted in front of her, said something, and then picked her up. I couldn't help but notice how her legs dangled limply as he carried her to a recliner in the corner.

Jane was all smiles by the time I approached, her fingers flipping through a pink and purple book my dad had just handed her. She was such a sweet and good-natured child, but my heart ached because I knew she wanted to run and play like the other kids.

"Auburn," Dad said jovially. "My little Janie-Bug was about to read this book to me and teach me all about fairies."

I squeezed his shoulder in thanks as I kneeled beside the chair. "I think Janie-Bug might actually be a fairy," I said, tickling her chin.

She giggled. "It's 'cuz of my reaf," she said, pointing at the flower wreath nestled in her blonde hair. "I saw one in a book once, and I always wanted one, so Lolli made it for me. He made my dress too."

I made a mental note to ask Tora to make my daughter a "*reaf*" of every color in the rainbow. "Well you look so beautiful. I've never seen a girl so pretty."

"Wait till you see Mommy," she said, her blue eyes widening. "She looks like a princess." My heart flip-flopped in my chest. After I talked with Blaire, seeing my bride was next on my agenda.

Kissing her pale forehead, I asked, "Will you be okay here with Grandpa while I talk to Blaire and then go see Mommy?"

"Uh-huh," she said, laying her tiny head on my dad's shoulder and turning to the first page of the book. My dad looked down at her like she was the greatest treasure in the world, and I couldn't help but wonder if he thought of my sister Evelyn when he held Jane.

Pushing away those thoughts, I stood and set off toward the kitchen as Blaire tilted her head in that direction. Once there, she leaned back against the counter and crossed her arms over her chest, and I was aware that I was now speaking with *Doctor Blaire Broxton* rather than *Cousin Blaire*.

"First of all, how is Gianna's tumor?"

Slipping my hands into my pockets, I nodded. "Good. Really good. She saw the neurologist here in New York again this month, and the tumor hasn't grown at all. She agreed with Gianna's previous doctors that no surgery is recommended."

Blaire smiled. "Excellent. You never want to go poking around in the brain unless it's absolutely necessary." Her smile faded away as our eyes met. "Now, let's get to Jane."

I sucked in a deep breath and blew it out. "Okay, what did you find out?"

"I looked at Jane's medical records and X-rays you sent, and I think I can help." Relief flooded my chest, and I started to thank her, but she held up one hand. "It's going to be a long road for that little girl, Auburn. The damage is only to the fibula and tibia of the right leg, but the muscles in the upper parts of both legs have atrophied due to lack of use."

"What does that mean in normal human terms?" I asked because I had no clue what she'd just said.

Blaire cracked a tiny smile. "It means she will need physical therapy for about a year to strengthen her muscles before I can do surgery." A frown creased her forehead beneath her red hair. "She should have been getting PT a couple times a week for the past almost four years, but I understand resources were limited at the home."

"Very, but I'll look into adding physical therapy services for the kids who are still there."

"You're a good man, Bouvier." She grinned wickedly before adding, "For an asshole."

On the pretense of wrapping her in a hug, I gave her noogie, and she swatted my hand away. "Stop it! I don't want to have to redo my damn hair. I already had to wash it again because Danica used it for a tissue earlier." Danica was her two-year-old daughter.

"Where is Dani anyway?"

"She and L.J. are napping. Charli and I talked and we thought we'd let them stay with the sitters during the service since they're so little." She smiled up at me with perfect, white teeth. "Thank you for doing that, by the way. We could have provided our own childcare."

My head shook side to side. "It's no problem. I asked around to find the best agency in New York and hired two of their most highly rated child care specialists. I also hired two teenage girls from the orphanage who Jaxon said were, and I quote, 'the most funnest.' I thought they could use some spending money. Gianna said I went overboard, but damn... you guys have a lot of kids."

Blaire grinned. "There's strength in numbers where my kids are concerned."

Turning serious, I took a deep breath before asking, "Did the medical records give you any indication what happened to Jane?"

She stared at me for a long moment. "Are you sure you want to know that?"

From the grimace on her face, I wasn't sure I did, but I jerked my chin once in a curt nod. "She's my daughter."

Blaire took a deep breath and exhaled it through pursed lips. "Jane suffered multiple breaks in both bones of her right lower leg." *Multiple breaks. Dear God.* I turned to the counter and braced both fists on top of it, letting my head hang between my shoulders. "Do you want me to go on?" my cousin asked gently.

"Yes," I croaked, trying to hold back my tears.

"The bones didn't set right, which tells me the poor baby went months without medical care."

"Jesus fucking Christ," I grunted. "How does someone just... fuck!" The thought of my little girl as a two-year-old suffering like that made me nauseous.

A soothing hand rubbed between my shoulder blades as I squinched my eyes shut. "I'll never understand that, Auburn. Some of the things I've seen in my job... It's the hardest fucking part."

"And Jaxon's records?"

"I noticed an area on his ulna." She indicated the spot with her index finger on my forearm. "There was evidence on the X-rays of an old injury there, but it was probably little more than a fracture because it's healed completely."

"So he doesn't need any surgery or anything?"

"Not at all. I know of an excellent pediatric physical therapist here in New York. She was going through her PT training at the same time I was doing my orthopedic surgical residency, so we worked together on some patients. Elaine is kind and wonderful with children, so I recommend Jane start working with her if you want to go forward after talking with her about it."

"But is Elaine the best?" I asked, turning my head toward her.

"If one of my children needed extensive PT, I would fly up here to use her." I nodded my consent, and Blaire patted me on the back. "I'll get it set up. You need a minute alone?"

"Yes, please," I said, and I heard her quietly leave as I dropped to my elbows and cradled my head in my hands.

Christ, my poor baby girl. How the fuck could anyone hurt a child like that? And not even get them medical attention? Just let the baby suffer in agony for months? If I could get my fucking hands on her parents, I swear to God...

"I can help."

Jerking my head up, I barely managed to refrain from screaming like a little girl, clamping my lips shut when I found Beau sitting on the counter right beside me.

"Shit, you scared the hell out of me," I said, swiping the tears from my cheeks with both palms. "Are all former SEALs as sneaky as you?"

He bobbed his head to the side once. "Pretty much, but I've managed to achieve a superior level of stealth."

"You get a merit badge for that?"

Beau almost smiled. "I can help you with what you were thinking about just now."

I eyed him warily. "You a mind reader or something?"

"No, but I know what I'd be thinking if someone hurt my child. Do you know who it was?"

Pressing my hands onto the gray marble countertop, I heaved out a breath. "The parents. They dropped both kids off at the orphanage with a note saying that they were high when they hurt Jane, but they *really didn't mean to*." That last part tasted bitter on my tongue. "And that they were too scared to take her to the hospital because they knew they would call the cops."

"Sick, cowardly fuckers," Beau growled.

We were both silent long enough for the cool marble to warm beneath my hands as my eyes traced the veins and flakes embedded in the surface. Then I turned my head to face my cousin. "What do you mean you can help?"

"My brothers and I can *take care* of the parents."

"Your brothers?" I asked in confusion.

"They're not my blood brothers. They're more than that," he said simply, and I instantly knew he was talking about his military brothers who now worked for him at his security firm, DFW Security Force.

"So, you mean..." I could picture what I wanted done in my mind, but I couldn't quite voice it out loud.

"Whatever vile, sadistic thoughts were just going through your mind, we can make it happen. I can promise you, neither of those assholes would ever be able to walk again." His gaze was steady on mine.

Blinking, I tried to clear my thoughts. Thoughts I really shouldn't be having, but... "Have you done this kind of thing before? I mean, after your military days?"

"Only once since opening my security business seven years ago, and I can assure you that mission was personal and completely necessary."

Am I really thinking about doing this? Could I go through with it? Would I tell Gianna? How would she react?

"Beau, I appreciate the offer, but I'm just not sure."

He nodded sagely. "It's okay. Take some time to think about it. If you want me to just do some fact finding and see if I can locate them, I can do that. See if they're even still in the city."

Running a hand through my hair, I shook my head. "I didn't even think about that. I guess I assumed they high-tailed it out of the state to avoid the law."

"Probably did, but what if, one day, they remember they have a couple of kids and come back looking for them?" My heart dropped into the pit of my stomach. "I know you'll make sure the adoption is airtight, but what if they show up to Jane's school or Jaxon's baseball practice?"

A cold chill worked its way down my spine, and that fear made my decision for me. "I'll email you what I know. See if you can find out where they are, and then we'll talk."

"Will do. I'll put Tank on it. He's a whiz at computer research."

"Thanks, Beau. I really appreciate this."

He hopped off the counter and punched me in the arm. *Ow! Fuck!*

"No need to thank me. Those kids are my family now, and I would go to fucking war for them."

As he walked from the kitchen, I couldn't help but think, *let's hope it doesn't come to that.*

Chapter 46

After leaving the family suite, I gathered Gianna's dress and shoes and knocked on the door of the bridal suite.

"Whatever you're selling, I don't want any," she called out.

A grin slipped across my face. "What about a wedding dress and a very eager groom?"

"Okay, I suppose I could use both of those."

I cracked open the door. "Are you sure you're okay with me seeing you before the wedding, babe?" We'd discussed this, and Gianna assured me that while she was traditional, she wasn't superstitious.

"Get in here now, Bouvier, before I have to walk down the aisle in my robe and slippers."

Pushing open the door, I froze as my heart thumped twice—hard—and then stopped for a concerning number of seconds. That's when I realized breathing might help. My lungs pushed out a breath and inhaled another before I was finally able to speak.

"Wow." *Okay, not the smoothest ode to my bride, but it was the best I could do in the moment.*

She was seated at the small dressing table swiping beneath her eye with a Q-Tip. If her reflection alone could render my body unable to perform its basic regulatory functions, I was completely unprepared when she turned around and stood.

I set down the boxes and draped the dress bag over a chair as neatly as I could without looking. After locking the door behind me, I simply stood there. Staring at her. At my Gianna. In a silky white robe and white fuzzy slippers, the belt of the robe cinching her slim waist and showing off her luscious curves.

Her dark hair was set in long, loose curls with half of it pulled up to show off her God-given, gorgeous face. It was smooth and tan, and a hint of peach highlighted her high cheekbones.

At the same time, her eyes swept up and down my tuxedoed form before resting on my face. "Wow, yourself. You look..."

"Like the luckiest man in the world?"

"I was going to say 'hot as hell in that tuxedo,' but yours sounds better."

A grin crooked up one side of my mouth. "You look hot as hell in that robe."

She struck a sexy pose and said, "Why, thank you, sir."

Though several of my internal organs were malfunctioning, my legs remembered how to work, and I prowled slowly across the soft gray carpet as my eyes fused with Gianna's.

I reached for her waist as my eyes covered every inch of her face. "You look stunning, pet. You're positively glowing."

She popped her eyebrows up and down before wrapping her arms around my neck. "Because I'm getting married today."

"Are you? Congratulations. I'll be sure to send a gift."

My blushing bride giggled at that. "You already did. Thank you for the spa treatments for me and the bridesmaids this afternoon. It was sweet of you to include Blaire and Charli too."

"I thought you could use some pampering, and Axel, Beau, and I managed to keep all the kids alive."

"Mmm, very impressive. I got a ninety minute Himalayan salt stone massage that was the best thing I'd ever felt." When I lifted an eyebrow, she grinned. "Okay, maybe not *the best*, but it was in the top five. Then I had a vichy shower scrub and a facial, which probably accounts for my glow."

"I know something else that would make you glow," I growled in a low voice, "but we don't have time for that right now." Cupping her face, I hovered my thumb over her pretty lips. "I want to kiss you so damn bad, but I don't want to mess up your lipstick."

"It's okay. It's smudge-proo—"

She didn't even get the last consonant out because my hungry lips were on hers, my tongue probing softly into the warm cavern of her mouth. My bride let out a contented hum as we kissed slowly, our arms wrapped around each other.

"I've never been happier in my life than I am right now," I murmured against her lips. "You're the love of my life, Gianna."

"And you're mine," she said, her green eyes glued to my blue ones. "I love you so much."

My smile took up my entire face as I traced a gentle line down her cheek. "Mrs. Bouvier."

She lifted one perfect eyebrow at me. "Not yet, and I won't be unless we get to this wedding. And for that, I neeeed…" She drew out that last word, and I filled in the blank.

"Your dress."

"Bingo."

"I have it. Are you ready to see it?"

"The results of the top secret Bouvier dress project? Yes, please."

I laughed and took her hand, leading her to the chair where I'd hastily laid the masterpiece. At least I hoped she would think it was a masterpiece. Nerves began to creep in, and I took a calming breath.

"I can't believe you trusted me enough to design your wedding gown without your input."

"I'd trust you with anything," she said softly, and I leaned down to press my lips briefly to hers.

"Stop making me love you even more."

"Nope," she said with a cheeky grin before stomping each foot impatiently. "Show me the dress now, Bouvier."

"Okay, bossy. Close your eyes."

She muttered, "So dramatic," but did as I asked.

I removed the dress from the bag and hung it on the tall, metal rack, adjusting the six-foot train and making sure everything looked perfect before turning to my gorgeous bride.

"Okay, you can open your eyes now."

Gianna hesitated for a second before lifting her lids. I held my breath as her eyes swept up and down the yards of candlelight-colored fabric.

The sheath dress was fitted all the way to the floor, and every square inch of the Mikado silk bodice and skirt was hand-beaded with Swarovski rhinestones. Mostly crystal and aurora borealis, but we'd scattered in a few red ones to give it some *Gianna personality*.

The full skirt overlay was made of the finest silk gazar and was open in the front to allow the straight, beaded skirt beneath to peek through. The off-the-shoulder neckline would show off her slim shoulders, and the two-inch sleeves were long enough to cover up her glucose monitor.

Though it wasn't revealing at all, it was the sexiest dress *Bouvier* had ever made. But maybe that was just me because all I'd done for the past six months was picture Gianna in this creation. *My creation*. I didn't usually do the designing; I left that to the professionals. But I designed this gem from the ground up, with expert advice on fabrics and potential flaws from Devereaux.

But the back... God, I was worried about the back. The nerves got the better of me, and I bit down on my knuckle to keep from asking her a hundred questions about her thoughts. She wasn't giving much away with her expression. She was a little slack-jawed, but I didn't know if that was a good thing or a bad one.

Her fingers brushed along the beading on the bodice and then down to the ballgown-style overskirt. When she finally turned to me, a brilliant smile broke over her face, and she leaped at me. Took me by surprise, but I caught her, and she wrapped her legs around my waist.

I've never been more relieved in my life than when she started peppering my face with kisses between words. "I... love... it... I... love... you... so... much... Perfect... Just perfect."

As she was kissing me, I laughed and spun us around in a circle, so filled with fucking joy, I could barely stand it. "You really like it?"

"Like it? I absolutely adore it. Auburn, it's the most exquisite dress I've ever seen in my life."

"Only appropriate since the most exquisite woman will be wearing it."

"You're amazing," she said, squeezing me around the neck before straightening her legs. "Put me down. I want to look at it again."

Her excitement was palpable as she stood with her hand at the base of her throat, staring at her custom wedding gown, so I decided to go for it.

"I need to show you the back. It's the most special part."

I twisted the dress around on the rack, and she stared for a few seconds before recognition hit her. She took a tentative step forward. "Is that... are those Nana's... doilies?"

This had been the tricky part. I knew the creamy lace doilies were special to her, and I wanted to incorporate them into the dress somehow. Dev and I had discussed it, and I'd finally decided to dip the dress low in the back and stretch the lace across the opening. Tiny rhinestones were dotted across the surface of the lace to make it congruous with the rest of the dress.

"Yes, is that okay?"

Gianna covered her mouth with her hand and nodded, and I whipped a handkerchief from my jacket pocket. Pulling it from me, she dabbed at her eyes, and I held her from behind as she let the fingers of her other hand drift over her grandmother's creations.

Finally, she let out a little laugh and waved the handkerchief in front of her face. "Thank goodness you and Dad came prepared today," she said. "And for waterproof mascara."

"And smudge-proof lipstick," I added, turning her head and giving her another kiss on the mouth. "Are you sure you're happy with the dress?"

Her smile was positively radiant. "It couldn't be more perfect if I'd designed it myself. The little blips of red, Nana's doilies, and all that beading!"

"I know you like sparkles," I said, releasing her and picking up a shoe box. "There's something else. Do you remember what you told me your favorite movie to watch with your dad was when you were a little girl?"

"Of course. *The Wizard of*—" Her eyes went round. "Oh my God. You didn't."

"I did," I confirmed, opening the box to reveal glittery ruby-red slippers. "I brought a more traditional pair that are dyed to match the dress, if you'd rather wear them."

But she was already shaking her head, her eyes lit up like a kid's on Christmas morning. "No. I want those."

"Okay then. Let's get you dressed. Devereaux is on standby in case you need any alterations, but since I know your body better than anyone else, I don't think that will be necessary."

My mouth went dry as a desert when she removed her robe, bra, and slippers, and I resisted the urge to pant like a dog. She stood in only a pair of tiny, white thong panties made of satin and lace—and *lord have mercy*—this woman had a body made for sin.

"Concentrate, Bouvier. There will be time for that later tonight," she scolded.

Shaking off my desire, I readied the dress and helped her step into it. "This overskirt is completely removable so we can take it off for the reception. That way you'll just be in the sheath part of the dress and can move about more comfortably."

As I fastened up the back, she said, "When you're done here, will you please go tell Cruz that we hired plenty of security, and he is a *guest* here. Lehra said he's standing beside the ballroom door like a guard dog."

"I told him already. You know how he is, but he did promise to have a seat before the ceremony started."

"And Ezra too. Make sure he's seated and not in the kitchen bossing his staff around."

Gianna and I had decided that we wanted Krab King to cater our reception dinner, and our buddy Ezra was over the moon about it. "I'll let him know. You remember how he kept trying to give us a discount on the catering?"

"Because you gave him those original wheels for his 'Vette. He thinks he owes you."

"Yeah, well, I opened the bill this morning, and it was two-thousand dollars too low."

"Dammit, Ezra," Gianna cursed.

Leaning down to help her into her shoes, I said, "I handled it. Paid the invoice online and added a five-thousand dollar tip."

"Good. That'll teach him to try and give Auburn Bouvier a discount."

I grinned and then said, "Oh, look at this." Pulling a piece of plastic from my pocket, I handed it to her as I buckled the straps around her ankles. She shook it out and immediately started laughing.

"This is the cutest thing I've ever seen! Did you do this?"

"No, Ezra decided to have custom bibs made for our wedding." The bibs had two crabs on the front, one in a tuxedo and the other wearing a bridal veil. Beneath them, it read, "Gettin' crabby with the Bouviers."

"I'll bet this is the first time this fancy hotel has had guests wearing bibs at a reception," Gianna said with a giggle.

"It's part of the experience," I said, parroting her words from the first time we ate at Ezra's restaurant. Standing, I walked around my bride, my hand going immediately to rub the tightness in my chest.

"Does it look okay?" she asked with apprehension.

I nodded, my lips pressed together because there were no words to adequately describe how beautiful she looked.

Gianna pivoted to look in the wide, full-length mirror, tucking her hand in my elbow. I couldn't take my eyes off her reflection. The skirt and train billowed out behind her, and the dress hugged her curves perfectly.

"I guess you do know my body better than anyone. It fits like a glove."

Turning her toward me, I took both of her hands in mine. "*We* fit together perfectly, Gianna. You, me, and our kids. We're going to be a real family now." Her smile was more dazzling than all the Swarovski rhinestones in existence. "Are you ready to marry me, baby girl?"

Gianna reached up and cupped my cheek tenderly.

"I am. Let's go make me... Mrs. Booby-A."

Epilogue

One Year Later

I stood staring down at my little girl. She looked even tinier in the hospital bed with tubes and machines hooked up to her.

As she slept peacefully, I sat on the edge of her bed and stroked her hair away from her face. Her skin was cool to the touch, but her soft puffs of air were warm against my wrist.

"And you're sure everything went okay?" I asked quietly, not looking away from Jane's pale, closed eyelids.

My cousin Blaire laid a comforting hand on my shoulder. "Everything went great. I was able to surgically repair all the damage, and she should be able to walk by the end of the year."

My mouth turned up into a cautious smile as I looked over at Gianna. My wife was sitting in a chair beside the bed with an uncharacteristically quiet Jaxon curled up on her lap. This was so hard on him, seeing his twin like this.

"You hear that, Jax? Your sister will be chasing you around before you know it," she said, her voice soft and soothing as she kissed the top of his head.

A tiny smile crossed his lips even as tears streamed down his face. "Why isn't she awake?" he asked, and Blaire crossed to him, squatting beside their chair and wiping his damp face.

"She's just resting. This was a big day for her. She should be waking up in a few minutes though."

"Okay," he said, leaning his head against Gianna's shoulder but keeping his eyes on his sister.

We were in a private recovery room in the Dallas hospital where Blaire was an orthopedic surgeon. There were only supposed to be two guests and absolutely no kids, but Blaire had arranged for Jaxon to be in here, with the promise that he would be very quiet and still.

When Jane stirred, the pace of my heartbeat picked up a notch. Her eyes fluttered and then opened slowly, as if she had ten pound weights attached to them. "Daddy," she whispered, her voice hoarse.

"Right here, honeybun. Daddy's right here." I kissed her forehead tenderly, and she smiled. Janie always smiled, even during the hardest, most intense physical therapy sessions, our little girl was a ray of sunshine. "How do you feel?"

"Thirsty," she said, and after a nod from Blaire, I held a cup and let Jane sip some cool water through the straw. "Where's Jaxon and Mommy?"

"Right here, baby," Gianna said, standing with Jaxon on her hip. After lowering the rail on the right side, she sat carefully on the edge of the bed, and they both gave Jane a kiss. Jaxon slipped off Gianna's lap and curled his arms around his sister. It seemed to comfort her, and Gianna gently reminded him to be careful of Jane's right leg.

Our daughter's eyes found Blaire. "Did my surgery go okay, Aunt Blaire?" Blaire was technically their cousin, but both kids called her Aunt.

"What do you think? They don't call me the Bone Master for nothing." She flexed her biceps and smiled down at my little girl when she giggled. "Yes, everything went perfect. You just keep doing your physical therapy, and you'll be walking by Christmas. Doctor Elaine said you're the best patient she's ever had."

"I like her," Jane said. "She smells like oranges." She yawned and closed her eyes for a second before opening them again. "Where's Carrie? And Uncle Axel?"

"They're in the waiting room. They can come visit when we get you in a regular room. In fact, I need to scoot you guys out of here so we can get Jane transported to the third floor. One of you can stay with her."

"Jaxon," Janie announced, and Blaire shook her head.

"One of the grown-ups," she said wryly.

"Okay... Daddy." My precious daughter was a Daddy's girl through and through, but Gianna didn't mind. Jaxon was a Momma's boy when he needed to be comforted.

I kissed the back of her small hand, avoiding the IV needle. "I'll stay with you, baby." Then I looked up at my wife, my voice turning stern. "Gianna, you need to eat something. You barely touched your sandwich at lunch."

She nodded in agreement. "I know. I was so nervous. I'll message our dads and let them know the surgery went well while I'm in the cafeteria."

Turning my attention to my son, I said, "I need you to be a big boy and go with your mom."

He puffed up his chest. "Okay, Dad." After giving his sister one more hug, he reached for his mother. She set him on the ground, and he grasped her hand. "Come on, Mom. I'll make sure you get enough to eat." That was my boy. Give him a task, especially something he could do to take care of someone else, and he was all over it.

I stood and wrapped my arms around my wife. She was as gorgeous as ever, even with the bags under her eyes from not sleeping a wink last night. "She's okay, pet," I whispered, kissing her temple, and she nodded and nuzzled against my neck.

"Moooom," Jaxon said, tugging on her hand until I released her. "Come on. You need food."

As she walked from the room, she looked over her shoulder at me, grinned, and mouthed, "You've created a monster."

Jane slept through the entire transport but woke up once we were in the private room on the third floor. "Can I see Carrie and Uncle Axel now?" she asked Blaire.

My cousin went to find her husband and daughter, and they quietly entered the room a few minutes later. Axel Broxton was huge, an NFL tight end who filled the room with his presence, but Jane wasn't intimidated by him at all. In fact, he and Carrie were two of her favorite people.

Carrie was twelve, had dark, curly hair and her dad's blue eyes, and was the sweetest preteen I'd ever met.

Axel sat on the edge of the hospital bed and gave Jane a kiss on the cheek. "Hey, little chickadee. Aunt Blaire said you did so good."

She shrugged. "I tried, but I think I fell asleep." We all laughed. "Hey, did you know Aunt Blaire's nickname is the Bone Master?"

"Of course I did. I'm the one who gave her that name."

"Jesus," Blaire said, burying her face in her hand. Luckily the double entendre went right over their daughter's head, and she sat on the other side of Janie, opening the small pink *Bouvier* purse I'd brought her.

"I made you this last night," Carrie said, pulling out a tiny beaded bracelet and slipping it on Jane's free arm. She pointed out the various beads. "This one is for health, the blue one is for courage and balance, and this one here is for strength."

My daughter's eyes brightened as she inspected each of the beads. "I love it, Carrie. I'll wear it every day when I go to therapy." She reached her arms up, and the girls shared a sweet hug.

Axel spoke up. "I brought you something too." He pulled his hand from behind his back and produced a Jane-sized, number eighty-seven,

Fort Worth Wranglers jersey. "This is my number when I play football. I got one for Jaxon as well."

"So we can be twinsies," she said with a giggle.

"Exactly," he said, booping her on the nose with his big index finger. The man was a beast on the football field, but he was a kind, gentle giant with little ones. He was always a fan favorite when the league players visited the children's hospitals.

"Daddy said we like the Giants, not the Wranglers."

"Is that so?" Axel said, leveling a look at me.

"Isn't it time for your nap, motor mouth?" I asked my daughter, and she playfully stuck out her tongue at me.

"But I like the Wranglers because you play for them, Uncle Ax."

"That's a good girl, Janie," he said, rubbing his giant hand through her hair. "You keep on cheering for me, and if your dad gives you any lip, you call me. I'll give him a knuckle sandwich."

Putting on the fakest smile I could manage, I waved my hands in the air and mock-cheered, "Goooo, Wranglers!"

"You're... si-silly... Daddy," Jane said, attempting to talk through her yawn.

"All right, let's keep it down to a dull roar and let my favorite patient rest," Blaire ordered. "I'm going to make rounds, but you have my number, Auburn. Call me if you need me."

I gave her a hug before she left and settled into a chair as Jane drifted off to sleep. The second my butt hit the cushion, my phone vibrated. My face creased into a frown as I extracted the device from the pocket of my jeans. *It better not be work*, I thought. I told them I wasn't to be disturbed so I could focus solely on my daughter.

The display read *Paul Bouvier*, and I answered with a quiet, "Dad, hold on a second." My eyes found Axel, and he was already waving a hand at me to let me know he and Carrie would stay while I took the call. I nodded my thanks and exited into the long, white corridor.

"Hey, sorry about that. Jane just fell asleep again. Did Gianna not call you? Blaire said the surgery went really well, and—"

My father cut off my rambling with one word, "Auburn..."

I could tell by the strain in his voice that something was wrong. Very wrong.

"What is it, Dad?"

He spoke without pausing for the next three minutes as I pressed one hand against the pale wall, hard enough to leave a handprint.

When his choked voice stopped, I nodded my head, even though he couldn't see me. "Okay, Dad. I'll handle it, and..." I forced the next words out. "I'm sorry."

After hanging up, I turned and leaned my shoulders against the wall behind me, dropping my chin to my chest. *Fuck! Not what I want to be dealing with right now.*

I was so lost in my thoughts, I didn't even notice Gianna and Jaxon's approach until she gripped my arm and hissed quietly, "What? Did something happen with Jane?"

Her body looked like it wanted to pull itself apart, half of it needing to hear what I had to say, and half of it ready to spring inside our child's hospital room.

Cupping her face with one hand, I met her eyes steadily. "No, sweetheart. Jane is fine; she's napping." Her tense posture relaxed marginally as I continued, "It's... it's something else. Can you please take Jaxon inside while I call my brother?"

Her forehead furrowed with reluctance, but she nodded and opened the door to the room, ushering our son inside. My finger hit a number on my phone, and before the first ring, Gianna was back at my side, wrapping her arms around my waist.

The phone rang once more, and I looped an arm around her shoulders as she quietly held me, giving me strength, even though she had no idea what was going on. "I love you," I whispered into her hair, and she squeezed me tighter.

"Auburn," my brother's voice boomed through the phone, "how did Janie-Bug's surgery go?"

I swallowed. "It was fine. Blaire said everything went really well, and hopefully, she'll be able to walk in a few months."

"Thank God. I've been so worried." My brother and I had been working on mending our relationship over the past year and a half. We talked at least once a week, and he always insisted on Facetiming with the kids. He freaking adored his niece and nephew. "How is Gianna holding up?"

"She's tired but doing okay. We're both glad this part is over. Look—"

"And Jaxon? Poor little fella. I know he's been worried sick."

Attempting to keep the impatience out of my voice, I answered, "He's okay. He got to see her in the recovery room for a couple minutes, so that helped. Listen, I really need to talk to you about something."

"Okay, bro. Shoot."

I inhaled a deep breath through my nose and blew it in a long gust from my mouth.

"Monty, something's happened. It's time to come home."

THE END... for now.

Wow! What a wild ride, right? You'll see more of Auburn and Gianna, as well as their adorable kiddos, in **Love Without Influence: Book Two of the Bouvier Family Saga**, available now on Amazon.

This is Monty Bouvier's story. Learn what happened to finally bring him back to New York. Will he and Kassie be able to get over their past hurts and finally be together?

You'll also find out why Chloe was so intent on Auburn marrying Magdalena. Oh, and what caused Paul Bouvier to remain under his bitchy wife's thumb for so many years?

All will be revealed in **Love Without Influence**, so check it out! Trust me – shit's about to get juicy!

HUGE NEWS!

If you liked **Love Without Numbers**, you'll be pleased to know it's now available on audiobook, exclusively on Audible and Amazon! Narrators JF Harding and Emma Wilder bring this one to life, and I hope you'll give it a listen. Get your fire extinguishers ready because if you thought Daddy Auburn was hot on paper, just wait till you can actually HEAR him call ~~Gianna~~ me a good girl.

Also by Jade

If you thought Auburn Bouvier had a dirty mouth, wait till you meet his brother, Monty. **Love Without Influence: Book 2 in the Bouvier Family Saga** is available now on Amazon.

Love Without Demands, Book 3 is coming this fall! Available for pre-order now!

IF YOU LOVED CHARLI and Beau in this book, you need to check out **The Fierce Protectors Series.** It features six super-hot, possessive, growly former Navy SEALs who live to love and protect their women. Beau and Charli's book is first, and their story is beautiful, funny, and emotional. It's available on Amazon.

Dauntless Protector- Beau and Charli's Story

Devoted Protector – Tank and Bristol's Story

Deadly Protector – Cam and Shiloh's Story

Young Protector – Cam and Shiloh's Prequel Novella

Disgruntled Protector – Woody and Taz's Story

Determined Protector – Bode and Landree's story

Damaged Protector – Hawk and Mallori's Story

Blaire and Axel also have their very own book that takes place before the Protectors Series starts. See how Blaire and Axel ended up together and follow their rocky road to their HEA in **Delay of Game**

I also wrote a spicy rom-com about a dirty-talking Cajun genie named Johnny. This man is so hot, you'll be sweating into your gumbo, so check out **I Dream of Johnny** and let him make all your reading wishes come true.

One of the easiest ways you can help indie authors is to leave them a review, so please take a few minutes to hop over to Amazon and let other readers know what you thought.

Make sure to follow me on Facebook, Instagram, and TikTok to keep up with news and my latest releases.

Acknowledgements

First of all, thank you so much to my **readers**. It means so much that you took a chance on an indie author, and I appreciate the time you took to read **Love Without Numbers.** I love when readers reach out to me while they're reading, so feel free to do so on my social media platforms that are listed on the "Also by Jade" page.

To the fabulous TL Swan: Thank you so much for your encouragement, advice, and humor. If it weren't for you, my stories would still be collecting virtual cobwebs on my computer.

To my beta readers: You chickies are amazing! Lizzie, you're my OG beta, and you always keep me in line by not letting me overuse "certain words." Lakshmi and Thorunn, my days would not be complete without seeing you two argue in the comments. I'll keep writing just for this reason. Also, thanks for the "inspirational" Instagram reels you send me.

AK Landow: You're my sister from another mister. My book signing roomie. My book bestie. You're an amazing author, and you inspire me every day with your brilliance. Thanks for hashing out every single detail that goes into publishing a book with me. (But seriously, do you REALLY like the L in this font, or should I switch to another one?)

Carolina Jax, and LA Ferro: Thank you all for being such wonderful and supportive friends. It's so awesome to have people who will tell you like it is while always having your back.

Chrisandra: You are the most amazing editor in the history of ever. Thank you for the REAL TALK and for your confidence in me and my writing. I'm also so happy to be your fave – but don't worry... I won't tell the others!

Chanel and Kalie of Good Girls PA services: Wow! I am so freaking lucky I've found you two. Thank you for handling business like boss bitches so that I can spend more time writing. Your support means everything to me.

To my ARC and Street Teams: I honestly couldn't do this without you! I love getting to know all of you in the groups, and I just want you to know that I think you're the most amazing, beautiful, fun, book-pimping people on Earth. So keep pimping! Mama's got hot pics to buy for her covers.

About the Author

Jade Dollston is a Texas author who loves reading, Doritos, and rum. She is married to her high school sweetheart, and they have one amazing daughter.

Her love of reading all things smutty has turned into a love of writing all things smutty. She enjoys a diverse selection of romance, and this is reflected in her writing style. Be prepared to laugh, cry, cringe, and fan your face, possibly all in a single chapter.

Jade is so excited to share her work with the world and hopes that you enjoy reading the words from her heart.